Around the po[...] were—shapes. Ca[...] so that at first she [...] but suddenly she knew what they were. They were women, very much like those bodies at the massacre site. Primitive, part animal, some scampering about with animal-like motions, others crouched down and eating or gnawing on something. They looked like the visions of Hell painted by the church in sermon after sermon. In fact, except for the eerie warm light the whole scene resembled a painting of Hell that hung in the temple at Anchor Logh.

Suddenly, from the cave behind the small waterfall, emerged a group of four of them carrying on their shoulders a body strapped to a cross-like structure made of wood. They walked through the waterfall and down a small path approaching Cass and the others. There was a neatly drilled hole in the rock at the base of the grisly amphitheater, and the structure and its occupant were hoisted into place so that the base of the cross was securely in the hole. It swayed a moment, but then settled and held firm. Cass gasped as she finally could recognize the figure on the cross.

It was Dar.

BOOKS BY JACK L. CHALKER

JACK L. CHALKER

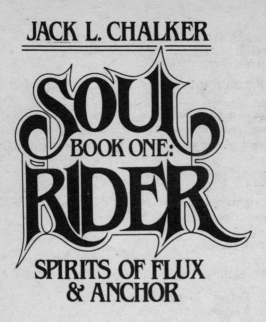

SOUL
BOOK ONE:
RIDER

SPIRITS OF FLUX & ANCHOR

A TOM DOHERTY ASSOCIATES BOOK

SOUL RIDER I: SPIRITS OF FLUX AND ANCHOR

This is a work of fiction. All the characters and events portrayed in this book are fictional, and any resemblance to real people or incidents is purely coincidental.

Copyright © 1984 by Jack L. Chalker

A TOR Book

Published by:

Tom Doherty Associates, Inc.
8-10 West 36th Street
New York, New York 10018

First TOR printing, March 1984

Second TOR printing, October 1984

ISBN: 27298-03

Can. Ed.: 812-53-276-7

Cover art by Dawn Wilson

Printed in the United States of America

For Mike Resnick
—*from one madman to another.*

1

ANCHOR

There was no need to tell anyone in Anchor Logh that the man in black was dangerous. Any stringer who rode the Flux was more than dangerous—he was someone to be feared for more reasons than one.

Cassie watched the man ride in on his huge white horse and felt a sudden chill at the very sight of him. She had a particular reason for that chill, being of The Age and with the Census Celebration barely three days away, although she didn't really believe she was in any danger. The quota this year was the lowest in her lifetime, thanks to an unusually abundant harvest and a high number of deaths among the Honored Elders, and her odds, like all those with her birth year, were barely one in a hundred. In fact, only four stringers had been invited to the Celebration this year and, it was said, only two had accepted, the rest preferring fatter pickings in other Anchors with more potential victims—and profits. That fact alone made the appearance of this one even more of a standout than it normally would have been.

He was a tall, lean, muscular man with coal-black hair and a handlebar moustache, and in normal circumstances and with a normal background he would have been considered a handsome man, even a desirable man, by those Cassie's age and older. But he was not a normal man with a normal background, and it was clear to any who looked upon him that this was so. There was just *something* about him, something you couldn't put your finger on, that radiated a fearsome chill to all he passed. His face was worn and aged well beyond his years, his skin seemed tough as leather, and his eyes, a weirdly washed-out blue, radiated contempt for World and its offerings. He was dressed in black denim, including black boots, gloves, and a wide-brimmed black hat that had one side of its wide brim tied up in stringer fashion, and a black leather jacket lined with weathered sheepskin that must have once been white.

Weathered. . . . That was a good word for him. His boots, his clothes, even his sawed-off shotgun with the fancy carved handle that hung from his silver-decorated belt in a special holster—they all were weathered almost beyond belief.

He rode slowly, imperiously, right past Cassie, but those cold, distant eyes took no notice whatsoever of the thin, slightly built girl nor of much of anyone or anything else, either. She shivered a bit, then turned and began walking back towards the communal farm where she had been born and raised.

The farm lay at the end of a winding, rutted dirt road, about a kilometer back from the main highway, and on either side of the girl stretched broad fields of grass dotted with grazing cows. She knew every rut in that road by heart, and every cow as well, but somehow, today, they seemed more distant and remote than anything ever had.

It was a bright, cloudless day, and the Holy Mother was in all Her divine glory in the sky, filling Anchor Logh with her brightness and slightly coloring the landscape with subtle and different shadings. It was a glorious sight, yet She was al-

ways there when the clouds parted, and Her visage
was so omnipresent, so taken for granted, not just
by Cassie but by all those on World, that the Holy
Mother was rarely paid attention to except when
one was praying—or sinning.

Today, though, the Holy Mother seemed particularly close and needed, and Cassie stopped and
looked up at Her reverently, seeking some comfort
and inspiration. The sparkling bands of gold,
orange, deep red and emerald green that gave the
slight color shifts to the land showed the beauty
and glory of Heaven and reminded all humankind
of the Paradise it had lost and could regain, in the
same way as night showed the emptiness of Hell,
the distant, tiny stars representing the lost souls
that might be consumed by darkness if not redeemed.

After a time she moved on, a lonely little figure
walking back to the only home she'd ever known.
Although the day was pretty, there was a chill in
the air, and she wore a heavy checked flannel shirt
and wool workpants.

Cassie had the kind of face that could be either
male or female, and this, along with her tendency
to keep her black, slightly curly hair clipped extremely short—as well as her slight build—often
got her mistaken for a boy, an error her low, husky
soprano did nothing to correct. She'd been the last
of four children, all girls, and her parents had
really wanted a boy. Particularly her father, a smith
who wanted very much to pass on the family trade
as his father had to him, and his father's father
before that. She had not been spared that knowledge, and was often reminded of that fact.

Perhaps because of this, or at least in trying to
please them, she'd always been a tomboy, getting
into fights and walking, talking, and now working
with the boys, herding, milking, and even breaking horses. Tel Anser, the hard old supervisor in

the corral, often held her up as an example to the boys he worked with, teasing them that she was far more of a man than any of them. That didn't win her any popularity contests, of course, but she didn't really mind. She was proud of the comment.

Still, she was a lonely girl. Partly because of the way she was, she never got asked to dances, never, in fact, had even been asked for, let alone been out on, a single date. Those few boys who *did* accept her did so as an equal and a friend—and that meant as just one of the boys. It was hard, sometimes, sitting around and listening to them compare notes on girls they were attracted to, driving home by their very indifference to her sex the fact that she would never be the object of such conversations, either by them or by others.

Still, the flip side of that never appealed to her much, either. Perhaps if she'd been pretty, or sexy, or at least cute, or had big breasts and a big ass she might have thought differently, but she didn't have those attributes and never would.

That meant, at least, never having to dress in those silly, fancy outfits and do all that highpitched giggling and gushing about that absolutely *dreamy* boy in the third row in school, or flirting, putting on phony perfumes and painting eyes, cheeks, lips— well, it just seemed so damned silly and *stupid* to her, if not downright dishonest. She never saw why girls had to go through all that stuff anyway, when boys scored extra points just by taking a bath.

She'd never gotten along with, nor much liked, her sisters, either. Of course, part of that was in being the youngest, and, therefore, the target for older siblings, but, later on, it was because she neither liked nor identified with them or their concerns and they knew it. Well, now she was riding and herding and milking while her oldest sister was pregnant with her second kid, the next was trying hard to have her first while working in the commune laundry, and the third was an apprentice bull cook who seemed content. Some wonderful ambition *that* was.

Ambition was very much on Cassie's mind right now, for she was The Age, graduated from general school, and on her way to either higher education or an assigned trade depending on how she did on the massive battery of tests she'd take after Census.

She'd always had an affinity with animals, particularly horses, who were prettier, stronger, and far more loyal and dependable than most people she'd met, and this had not gone unnoticed by those who were always referred to as "the powers that be." She was aiming for one of the two slots open for veterinarian's training. *Then* she'd show them! Then she'd show then *all!* Status, a true profession, rank that commanded respect, top pay, and a skill that was vitally needed.

Her father was working iron when she entered the smithy, and she stood and watched until the red-hot metal had been skillfully shaped and formed and dunked into the water. He spotted her then, standing there, and frowned. "Well, Cass? Parcel man have anything for us today?"

She looked suddenly disgusted with herself and shook her head. "I'm sorry, Pa. I—I guess I forgot to check."

"*What!* Didn't you go out to the highway like I told you to?"

"Yeah, I went, only . . ."

"Only *what?*"

"Well, soon as I got there a stringer rode by and I just sort of forgot anything else. I'm sorry, Pa."

Her father sighed. He was a huge, superbly muscled man with thick black hair and a full beard, looking every bit the smith he was, and he had a hell of a mean streak in him and the short temper to bring it out. He didn't usually let it get the better of him, though, unless he'd been drinking, and while she braced for at least a hard and foul tongue-lashing, it never came. Like everyone else in Anchor Logh, her father had once been The Age himself, facing his own Census. As rough as he was now, and he'd been even rougher back then, he knew what the sight of a stringer this close to Census would have done to *him* back then, and he was never the sort of man to hold anyone to a higher standard than that to which he held himself.

Instead he said, "Well, don't fret about it. The Holy Mother knows you got enough on your mind right now."

Feeling very relieved, she decided she should make amends anyway and so she responded, "Want me to go back out there now? I don't mind. I got nothing much to do."

"Naw, that's all right. I hav'ta go out there myself in an hour or two anyway, and if there's anything I guess it'll wait 'til then. You just get along now and enjoy yourself."

She thought for a moment, the crisis already far in the past in her mind, and decided to take advantage of her father's unusual good nature. "Maybe I could take Leanspot into the city, then? I got to return some books to the Temple library and pick up some others."

He thought it over. Under ordinary circumstances he'd have given a flat no, but she *was* The Age, and if she couldn't take care of herself and gain self-confidence now, she sure as hell better know it.

"Yeah, sure," he said at last. "Take all the time you want. But if you stay past nightfall, you'd best stay at the Temple overnight. With this crowd coming in and Census coming up you don't want to take no chances, you hear?"

She nodded soberly. "I promise."

In point of fact, people were very safe in the city unless they aided and abetted their own downfalls.

Citizens had full rights and protections and those were jealously guarded and enforced by the government and police. Minors—those under The Age—were even more zealously protected. Naturally, if someone went over to one of the Main Street dives and flashed a lot of money around, or solicited immoral favors and lived to regret it, there wasn't much to be done, but, on the whole, anyone could walk in any part of the city in safety even late at night.

Citizenship, however, came with being counted in the Census, which was always on a predetermined date. That left those like Cassie, who'd reached The Age well before Census, in the position of being neither minors nor citizens, and during that period they were vulnerable to those who saw profit in this loophole. There were tales of young men and women being abducted and held through Census and the registry. If not caught in the Paring Rite, which was a fate worse than death, and if they then did not register as citizens, the law regarded them not as people at all, and, therefore, recognized no rights in their case. They became, in fact, property, animals like horses or cows or pigs in so far as the government was concerned—the property of the abductor or whomever the abductor transferred them to. They were even registered, as animals, with the Veterinary Office. The law, even the church, would actually support the owner over the victim, and this condition would last for life.

It was explained by the church that such things were the Holy Mother's will, since She dictated the laws governing World, and meant that this life was forfeit to some terrible deed or lifestyle in the life immediately past that required a lifetime's punishment to expunge. There was no way to get out of it, then, since anyone who tried to escape or thwart this working out of punishment would be doomed to the same fate in every subsequent life until the evil done was cleansed. Cass had never, to her knowledge, seen such people, but she knew they existed, usually traded from Anchor to Anchor through the stringers so that there would be no family revenge.

She kissed her father and went back to the block where she lived. It was one of several dozen buildings, all four stories high, composed literally of large prefabricated cubes that locked together. Because of the design, though, the buildings were asymmetrical, each row of cubes set slightly in or out of the row and with four large ones at its base, five slightly smaller on top, the end two protruding, six still smaller atop that, then five of the same size on top. The size cubicle you got depended on your family size and ranking within the commune. Once they'd lived in the relatively palatial ground level, but now she climbed the stairs to the second story. A family of six needed more space than a family of four, and with two daughters married off it was only the high regard for her father that had moved the farm council to allow them to live even where they were now.

At this time of day there was no one home. Mom was on the other side of the farm, in the Administration Building, working her usual job in accounting, and Tam was in the bakery today, so it seemed unnaturally quiet and still. It was just a basic three-room apartment, the living room and two decent-sized bedrooms, but it was home. She found a long match and lit one living room lamp, then went back to the bedroom she and Tam shared and lit the lamp there. Throwing some of Tam's clothes out of the way, she rooted in the closet and came up with a basic change of clothing and a small toiletries bag which she packed quickly. While picking and choosing the toiletries she looked up at herself in the small mirror and stared into her own face for a moment.

Dark brown eyes stared back at her out of a young boy's face. For not the first time she reflected that she'd make a better boy than girl all around. Except, of course, she didn't care for girls much and she *did* like boys. She chuckled a bit to herself, remembering the several times at fairs elsewhere in the Riding she'd drawn the adolescent attentions of more than one girl who'd made that mistake. They'd often said she'd outgrow it, but that was obviously not going to happen now. She was stuck with the physique of permanent boyish adolescence, although she'd never grow more than her current 163 centimeter height nor reach 50 kilos no matter how much she exercised and how much she ate. Or worry about packing a bra, either.

She sighed and turned away and zipped up the travel bag, picked it up, and left the cube, putting out the lights on the way.

Only then did she remember the books she was supposed to be taking back to the library, and she returned for them. It was, she decided, just going to be one of those days.

2

RIDER

We are the spirits of Flux and Anchor and some call us demons. It is possible that we are such, for certainly we know not our natures or origins. Everything is born, yet we were not born. At least, I can remember no such experience, nor can any of my kind. It may be true, as some of us argue, that since no human clearly remembers his or her birth it might just be the same with us, yet that makes no sense to me. Humans are born, and humans die, yet we who are the Soul Riders do not die, and our number is constant and fixed to the number of Anchors on World.

Certainly it seems as if I have been thus forever, yet there must have been an origin at some time in the far past, or at least a coming to World, since it is clear that World has a no more infinite past than infinite future. It, too, was born, whether by creation of the Holy Mother as the church says or by more natural and predictable processes, and the time of its borning is written in the rocks of Anchor and the decay rate of Flux. It has been here, although not in this form always, no more than four or five billion years at best, and humans have been here a far shorter time than that—a few thousand years at best. And yet I can remember no time without humans.

If humans and World were both born, and will

both surely die, as will all things known to us in the universe, then why and how do we exist as we do?

The Holy Church says that we are demons left from the Great Rebellion, when angels in their pride rose up and slew angels and threatened to usurp the Holy Mother's domination of the universe in foolish and futile insurrection. It was then, or so it is written, that the Holy Mother acted, changing the angelic seditionists to foul and horrible monstrosities whose outer forms and very existence mirrored their most terrible inner selves and exiled them to Hell, sealing the seven gates to Hell against their coming again into this universe save by proxy.

The misguided, misused, and misshapen ones who followed the Seditionists in their terrible mutiny, and those who took no side in the fray, were changed to human form by the Holy Mother after Her inevitable victory, in that way to suffer pain and torture and purify themselves in life after life until they again be cleansed and worthy to reenter the kingdom of Heaven shown so tantalizingly close in the day sky. It is also written in the holy books that the gates of Hell will be reopened one day by the evil ones known as the Seven Who Wait, who roam World supervising the misery of human existence and take joy in inflicting it. When and if those gates are again reopened, Hell will pour once more into World, and humanity will be caught once again in the midst of battle between Heaven and Hell and will again be forced to make a terrible choice. Then will humanity have a second chance at Paradise, and depending on their souls' progress through the lives they lived, they will choose rightly or wrongly. Those who choose correctly this time around will be allowed back into Heaven, while the rest shall be permanently recast into foul Hell.

But if that's true, where does it leave us? Just as we are neither born nor die, what is our purpose and role in this scheme if it be true? We have been around a long time and have long memories, and know that

*holy books are often adjusted, and religions go through
social evolution the same as governments. And yet
there is some consistency and truth in all of it which
gives us pause.*

*The Seven Who Wait exist. The gates of Hell exist,
and there is certainly something foul and evil beyond
them. That something is so seductive to some humans,
but not to any of us. It is that sense of overwhelming
evil emanating from those terrible sealed gateways
that drives us ever onward on our missions. We fight
the Seven and their agents wherever and whenever
we can, and we seek them out for this battle. We
alone are feared by them, for we are the immortal
last line of defense.*

*And, still, while we do the work of the church it
continues to brand us demons, agents of the Seven,
Hell-spawns and half-creatures. They will not listen
to more rational pleas, nor change their view, for
they do not understand us and so fear us as much as
the Seven do. Nor is this fear without some justification, for this is a place of certainty in its beliefs,
a place where everything has an explanation and
where Heaven and Hell can be glimpsed. We are the
wild cards, the unexplainable in the midst of the
totally explained, and if we do not understand our
own selves then how can they be expected to do so?*

*It is certain that somebody, somewhere knows
the answer. Someone who knows why World has the
holy name that must not be spoken aloud, the cryptic
and unintelligible Forfirbasforten. The church says it
is an angelic name bestowed on World by the Holy
Mother and is not for humans to know or understand,
but someone does. Someone, or somehing, directs
our actions in unknown and unseen ways, so that
we go to a new host at just the right moment, and
live their lives with them unknown and unseen to
them until they have need of us against the Seven.
Perhaps it is the Nine Who Guard, but I have en-
countered some of them many times and they seem*

as mystified by our presence and natures as are we ourselves, although, at least, they understand that we are not enemies but allies in their unending battle and do not fear us.

Some say that humanity did not originate on World at all, but came here from some other, better place. That is, of course, consistent with both the evidence and scripture, but did we come with them? Or were we, perhaps, here before, the original inhabitants of this place caught in the middle of a great war we were powerless to do anything about? Some believe this, and see us as the ghosts and racial memories of such a race, yet this is not at all consistent with cosmology, for it would put us outside the Holy Mother's creation until wrenched into it, and that opens up a series of philosophical knots that can never be untied.

I think, perhaps, that we were once humans ourselves, and walked the face of World directly. It is possible that, for some reason, our souls were not placed into new bodies but remained suspended in the spirit world, bound to World but not of it. Why this should be so I do not know, but it was clearly not a random choice, as our numbers, as I said, are quite fixed.

I prefer to think of us as once-great warriors, the best of our human race, who were so valued that we were appointed the last line of defense against the forces of evil, supporting first the church and then the Nine Who Guard.

If what they say of birth and death are true, intellect survives memory, but memory dies as it gets in the way of true intellectual, or spiritual, growth. Thus we have no memories of our human lives, no sense of all those trillions of stimuli that flood in and confuse the mind even as it grows. Perhaps, I certainly hope, we were the ones who reached purification far ahead of the masses and were thus given our guardian duties with no need to be born and reborn again and again.

And yet I feel that I was once a soldier. Certainly I feel most comfortable when mated with one, and it certainly fits my own theory of origin, as well as our long and complex work.

I digress as I float, my random thoughts going out to any of my kind who may be in the area and less inclined to introspection. Very well, I will stop, for matters press, and I feel myself drawn from the Flux, where I have been these past seven lifetimes, back again at last to Anchor. Whoever or whatever guides our destinies has a new job for me, and I am anxious to begin.

I emerge from the energy flow and there bursts upon me the clean, crisp certainty of Anchor. Which Anchor it is I do not know, but it seems somehow familiar, and welcomes me as some long-lost relation. This is an odd sensation, worthy of further study on its own.

I drift above the hills and treetops, and below me burn the souls of Anchorfolk, the sheer density and clarity of their life matrices telling me that this is a large Anchor indeed. The specific features are beyond my present perceptive abilities, yet all around me screams not merely life but, most importantly, unambiguous life, its mathematical symmetry and distinct solidity oddly reassuring. I have been too long in the Flux.

I sense the capital ahead of me now, with a density of souls that I can scarcely handle, and in its center, a shining beacon, its Focal Point. It is truly odd, this particular Focal Point, for it seems to broadcast directly to me. It seems *right* somehow, in a way I cannot explain. It is almost as if it sends to me a half-completed equation, for which I am myself the other half, and which, if joined, will give the answer to it all. The answers are here. The threat is

*large and the time is short. That much I am certain
of.*

*Ah, but no, I am to be stopped short of the Focal
Point, the answer so close and yet so disturbingly out
of reach. I am directed not at the Focal Point, but at
a human soul who lives below, and even now I
descend for the mating. Down, down, to ground level,
and forward to the soul whose matrix will mate with
my own. The one is moving, yet I come upon it,
envelop it, mate with it and draw within those re-
cesses of its mind it does not even know exist. I
bind myself, and see, hear, and feel once more as
humans do. I ride a new soul.*

Cassie walked from the cubicle towards the
stables, her bag hanging from her shoulder, deep
in thought. Suddenly she stopped as a cold chill
came over her, and for a brief moment she felt
both dizziness and nausea. It passed quickly,
though, leaving her standing there a moment,
puzzled, and wondering if she should go at all
now. She must be coming down with something—
she was still a good ten days from her period. But,
no, she felt fine now.

Just nerves, she told herself, and continued walking towards the stables.

3

STRINGER

Matson wasn't his real name. No stringer ever allowed his or her real name to be known—that way led to potential blackmail, for anyone could then determine the stringer's relationship to others and have a hold on them. Stringers feared only that someone would have something on them, something that would eat into their absolute independence and freedom. They did not fear challenge, and particularly did not fear death, since it was better to die free than live with any strings at all, including compromises of their lifestyle. To have it any other way would be to be harnessed just as surely as they harnessed their characteristic mule trains, the long strings, or ropes, giving them their name and title.

Matson was a stringer in his mid-thirties, which meant he was a very good stringer indeed in an occupation that often saw you dead in the Flux while still in your teens or twenties. He'd been around a lot in his time, and he still enjoyed the constant challenges of the job.

He'd left his duggers and mules at the clear spot at the western gate. At the moment he was deadheading, and he hated like hell to do that—all expenses and no profits. This particular Anchor's census, though, should make up for it. He'd heard that only one other stringer was close enough to take advantage of the bargain, and that meant a good deal of business. Usually there were so many stringers you had trouble even filling your local Fluxland orders and paying back your I.O.U.s for the quarter, but here, even with a small census, he'd wind up with half the crop.

It did not trouble him to deal in human beings, just as he also dealt in gold, silver, various manufactured goods, and anything else that was in demand in one place and surplus in another. While he lived by a strict personal moral code, this was the way of World, a system he'd been brought up to accept and believe in and, since "right" and "wrong" are always defined by the culture of a place, this sort of traffic—for which there was good socioeconomic justification—was simply taken for granted.

It was a good two days' ride from the Anchor wall to the capital, and a pretty boring one at that. Farming Anchors were perhaps the least interesting of all, all the more so because these people considered themselves free and autonomous. Theirs was a happy little worldlet, and most would never leave nor want to.

They were as domesticated and spiritually dead as their cows, he thought sourly.

He amused himself by playing mental word games and by double and triple checking his mnemonic tricks that allowed him to keep all his orders, requests, I.O.U.s, and accounts in his head. Permanent records were dangerous to a stringer's freedom, too, even if you could keep decent account books in the Flux.

Still, it would be good spending a couple of days in a real city, one that was what it looked like and wouldn't change or dissolve on you because of a paranoid wizard's bad dreams, and to sleep in a nice, comfortable bed, drink some decent booze, and maybe fool around a little.

He reached the city before nightfall, and went immediately to Government House to register himself and then paid the usual brief courtesy call on the local temple, writing out his specific requirements for their perusal, while also dropping off a box of the local Sister General's cigars. It always paid to do a little homework before coming in to a new town.

Next he went over to Main Street—dull name for the entertainment district, the kind of name you'd expect a bunch of cow herders to come up with—and checked into a decent hotel. Capital districts were always nice if only because they alone had electricity, which included hot and cold running water and in-room baths. Since the hotel was taking care of his horse, he quickly stripped and ran the bath water, then slipped into the hot tub. It felt *really* good. He never realized just how many minor muscle aches and pains he lived with until they were taken away. About the only trouble was, they always made the damned bath tubs about a finger's length too short.

Still, he leaned back, lit a cigar, then reached over and picked up the small pile of papers he'd been given at his two prior stops. One set was a bunch of orders for various goods the Anchor needed, and these he would either try and fill or, if a better trip came along, he'd pass along to some other stringer going this way for the usual finder's fee. Also included was a smaller list of what was usually called "desired personnel," and those were more high-ticket items. He might find and arrange transport for the two needed gunnery instructors, although why they needed them for this place was beyond him, but he suspected that they were going to have to pay and pay big and actually hire by enticement the electrician with experience and the civil engineer, and they'd be damned lucky if they got either one at any price. Anchorfolk didn't like to travel in the Flux at all, and for good reason. Making it worth the while of this level of skill to travel would cost them before, during, and after. Still, he'd see what he could do.

He had only raw numbers on his own outgoing goods. They would have to check their census and see how many of the unlucky losers fit what he needed to fill other orders. He liked the numbers, though. A hundred and six to go out, fifty-six females and fifty males, split between two stringers. True, he'd have to make a good stab at filling the Anchor's orders, but he liked this kind of arrangement. No up-front outlay and the goods came on consignment.

After bathing, he unpacked a bit and rummaged through his pack to find civilized clothing. Although he'd be here three to five days, he did not even glance at the drawers and closets in the room. He never unpacked any more than he had to, the quicker to make a getaway if it were ever needed.

Dressed in the same manner as when he arrived, but with all clean clothes save hat and boots, he rearranged his belt, removed the shotgun holster and its deadly occupant and clipped on a knife in its scabbard and the bullwhip. He liked the bull-whip—it had such an intimidating effect on the locals, particularly the self-styled toughs.

Finally, he shaved, all except the moustache. It was still just coming in, but he'd been suffering lately from a series of runny noses and decided that a moustache was the best local cure for a constantly chapped upper lip. Finally satisfied, he left his room and went down to the street, looking first for a restaurant and a good meal. Before he was ten meters down the street, though, he stopped, seeing a black-clad figure riding in on a spotted horse. The second stringer had arrived.

"Arden!" he called out. "Good to see you!"

The horse stopped and the rider stared for a moment. "Matson? That you? Well, I'll be damned!"

She was several years younger than he, but still tough and long on experience. She was tall, lean, and lanky, but well proportioned, and if the strain of the job showed as much in her face as it did in his it made that face no less pretty, and while she hadn't bothered to put on a wig as yet to hide her shaven head, her oval face seemed complimented by its very baldness. She jumped down off the horse and walked over to him. "It's been a long time," she said softly.

He nodded. "Tuligmon, two years ago."

She grinned. "How sweet! You remembered!"

"How could I forget? You beat me out of some of the best damned merchandise I've seen since I started stringing."

She laughed. "Well, no contest this time, unless a couple of wild card stringers show up. Good stuff here and it's all ours, my dear."

"Well, since we're not competitors this time, what do you say to a night on the town? Um, such as it is, anyway."

"You're on! But let me check in and get cleaned up a little first."

"I'm not starving. I'll wait for you in the hotel bar."

He'd first met Arden years ago, when she was just out of her teens and he was a big, experienced stringer in his mid-twenties and anxious to show off to the younger generation. That was over in Anchor Mahri, a depressing factory land half a world from here. She'd been such a sexy, wide-eyed innocent, hanging on his every word and vamping him constantly, and he'd started regarding her less as a stringer than as just another barroom girl with not much future. She'd hung around with him while he'd made some of his calls and discussed orders and deals, and he hadn't thought much of it. She'd even moved into his hotel room.

Of course, one morning he awakened to find her gone, and thought little of it, until he made his rounds to firm up his deals and found that she had been there first. Not just to one, but to every damned account on his list—and with a better offer and a take it now or forget it style. She'd taken note of every single item of business he did and every offer under discussion and beaten him by just the exact deal that would make them switch. She'd given him one hell of a sour stomach and a worse wallop in the pocketbook, but he also admired her gutsy style. He was pretty sure afterward that, given a day alone with a recalcitrant prospect, she would wind up owning his business.

She also had a quick mind, a superbly trained body and the reflexes to make it work for her, and more talent with the Flux than anybody he'd ever met. She could hold her own in any fight, and he'd heard the stories of some of those as well.

She joined him in about half an hour, having washed up and changed into her city clothes. They were still stringer black, of course, but made out of some tight, clingy material that seemed to form-fit itself to her body and make her seem, while fully clothed, almost naked. At least it left very little to the imagination. She also wore her dress boots, with the heels so high it gave her the sexiest walk in the world.

"Well? Shall we go?" she prompted.

He nodded and signed the tab. "I guess steak would be the best in a place like this. At least farmers make good home-grown beer and booze."

They barely noticed the stares and nervous looks they got from those they passed. Stringers were used to such things, and both Matson and Arden were experienced enough that they no longer even got the slight charge from knowing they were feared by all the "decent" folk of Anchor and Flux. Like monarchs, they tended only to notice when such reactions were absent.

The food *was* good, and perfectly prepared, although the wine was lousy. While the beer and booze were good, this was clearly not grape country. They relaxed with shop talk, mostly telling tales of good and bad experiences and filling one another in on people and places the other hadn't been to, at least in a long time. Neither, of course, discussed future plans or routings—she would never give away anything by reflex, and she'd sure taught him long ago not to, either. So it surprised him, after dinner and after checking out a couple of inferior bar shows, when she said, "You know, I've been thinking of quitting for a while. Going to a Freehold and contribute while there's still time."

That stopped him. "Huh? *You?*"

"So what's wrong with me?"

He chuckled. "That would take too long to list, but it's all mental. No, I just can't see you taking off all that time and becoming a mama to a screaming kid, that's all. I think you'd go nuts."

"Most mothers do, I'm told. But, you know, I've been a lot of places and seen and done a lot of things. I'm very well off, so that's not a problem, and it's one thing I've never done."

"You've never cut off your left arm, either. But if that's the way you feel, why not just do it? You could have any man you want."

"Uh huh. And there's one I have in mind who, I think, will make half of the best new stringer in a century. I decided that fate would make the decision if I met him again in time, and it looks like I have."

He stared at her. "You're serious?"

"I'm serious. I made the decision the moment I

saw you, riding in here." She flashed him her patented evil grin. "I already arranged with the hotel to share your room."

He thought of the sheets of business documents there and felt a mild chill. She caught it and laughed. "Yes, I saw them. Want to see mine? The same stuff. We're not competing here, remember?"

He smiled and shrugged. "Okay, then. The shows here are pretty lousy anyway."

She smiled and patted his bottom. "Let's go put on our own, then. The next few days are exactly the right time for it."

Bending to fate, he followed her back to the hotel.

4

TEMPLE

"Where ya goin', Cass?"

She stopped and turned to see Dar and Lani. Dar was a big, strapping farmboy with a tan complexion set off by flaming red hair, while Lani was a pretty, tiny—shorter and lighter than Cassie by far—and extremely overendowed young woman. Cassie's father had once cruelly joked that Lani got not only her own attributes but the ones that were supposed to go Cass as well. Both had been in her class through school; Lani was a little more than a month older than Cass, Dar just a week younger than she.

Cassie would have liked Lani to have been as short in brains as she was endowed in beauty, just to provide some symmetry to life, but the truth was it was Dar who was rather slow—one teacher had used the term "vacuous"—while Lani was quite bright and in line for a scholarship to teacher's training or perhaps into agricultural research. It said something about the beauty that, while she could have had any boy not only in the commune but probably in the entire Census, she had chosen Dar, whose mind was nil but who was certainly pleasant and cheerful and, like so many large men, uncommonly gentle, but who was also, from all reports, rather well endowed himself.

Both were simply too nice to stay mad at, and Dar had been one of those boys who'd always been a friend.

"I'm going into the city," she told them. "I have some books to return and some more I need to take out. The exams are only a couple of weeks away."

They both nodded. Lani said, "I think it's a little too late for the books now. These tests aren't like the ones in school, remember. Relax, Cass. You're a natural for the vet's spot."

She smiled at the compliment. "I guess you're right, but I can't help worrying and studying anyway. It can't hurt, and maybe it'll help if I *do* get the slot. Anyway, it beats sitting around being bored."

"Yeah, you're right about that bored stuff," Dar agreed. "In fact, we were thinking of going into the city ourselves. Census Carnival opens tonight, remember."

Cass was surprised at herself for not remembering that. The fact was, she never thought of things that cost money, because communards didn't have it or need it. All was provided by the council, with bonuses for the best work being used for catalog purchases. That's why they went to the capital so seldom despite its closeness.

"You have money for that this early?"

"Sure," Dar responded, "and so do you. A hundred cubits of silver on account, for coming of The Age."

She had, quite frankly, forgotten all about that, although she had the slip for it in her overnight bag where she'd stuffed it after they gave it to her. It was redeemable almost everywhere if cash was available, and cash was readily available during Census Celebration. "I'd been thinking of putting that away for later," she told them.

"Aw, c'mon! That's not what that's for," he retorted. "Hell, you get staked after classification, plus expense money. *This* money's strictly for having a good time. What say we all go into town and go to the Carnival? Just relax and let loose for a while, have some fun." He looked suddenly uncertain and turned and looked at Lani, but she gave him a nod and a smile.

Cassie thought it over for a moment. "Well, okay. Maybe you're right. I knew I was going to have to stay over tonight anyway, since it's already so late. Go and get your things. I'll wait for you here."

The Census Celebration was part of the system dictated by the holy scriptures, and it was a curious blend of circus, government report, and public execution. Its root was in the absolute prohibition of any sort of birth control on the part of the individual—although the priestesses who were midwives had the authority and duty to terminate the life of any baby determined by a host of very strict standards to be defective—and the concurrent duty of all married couples to have as many children as they could. Large families had greater status in the community, preferential treatment, and huge allowances.

Unfortunately, an Anchor could support only a finite number of people. Each year a massive census was taken across the entire 680 square kilometers of Anchor Logh, a census of people, animals—everyone and everything that consumed things. This was then compared with the harvests, known reserves, and anticipated demands for the following year, and a total number of supportable people was determined, which was then compared against the total numbers of young men and women reaching age 18—The Age—between census periods. The difference, less the average birth-death differential for the past five censuses, was the number of surplus people, and that surplus had to be disposed of.

The church and holy books gave ample theological backing to this cruel rite, since the selection was done in the most random and fairest of ways by a great lottery on the last day of Census Celebration. The Holy Mother, of course, operated in such a circumstance, and those selected were actually selected by Her for reasons of atonement or whatever other reasons She might have that were inscrutable to humans. The Paring Rite, as it was called, was a most sacred and holy rite, performed by the Sister General herself on the front steps of the holy Temple. Those "pared" in the rite were forbidden citizenship and became Property of the People. As such, they were sold or bartered to the stringers as any other goods and removed from Anchor Logh. What the stringers did with them was the subject of wild speculation and terrible stories, most contradictory, but nobody really knew for sure since no one returned to tell the tale.

And so it was with some horror that, as the three rode towards the city, Cassie remarked, "I saw a stringer riding in today."

The light mood of the other two seemed to vanish at once. Dar shivered. "Them vultures! Demon bastards from the Flux!" Neither of the women was going to argue that the stringers were actually essential to the economy of World; that they alone kept commerce of all kinds going. And even if they had, for they actually knew this, it would not have changed their opinion in the slightest. Anyone who rode the Flux for a living simply couldn't be human and remain mentally and spiritually whole.

Cassie had seen the Flux once. They all had, on an overnight field trip in school. It was a terrible and frightening sight, a wall of nothingness surrounding World. Although they all knew World was round, since it had been made by the Holy Mother in the image of Heaven, it still looked like the edge of the earth.

There were a fair number of people in Anchor

Logh who had gone through the Flux in a stringer's train, of course. Many professional schools were located in other Anchors, and occasionally needed professionals were imported. The Sister General herself had come from an Anchor far away. But stringers controlled your mind in the Flux, and the images of the journey were either too muddied or too bizarre and fantastic to believe when others were told of those trips. Usually, after a time in Anchor, those who recalled and told of those trips found the experience hard to believe or accept as well.

Only the stringers knew for certain what, if anything, was out there in the Flux, and even if you had nerve enough to ask one—well, who could believe a stringer?

Spirits lightened again when they reached the city. Already there were huge crowds of people in from the outlying ridings and the streets of the city were festooned with multicolored lights and decorations and there was a festive air. They headed straight for the carnival grounds, oblivious of the time, and it was a fantastic sight indeed. This year the government had outdone itself in rides and sideshows and attractions, all powered by the electrical energy supplied by the sacred modules located well beneath the Temple. Although the crowd was large, it felt *good* to be with so many merry people in such close quarters.

Anticipating that all young people of The Age would be physically present as required by law, and knowing that each had their hundred cubit marker, the Central Bank had a booth set up to cash in the markers, and after standing in line for quite a while all three were, for the first time in their lives, cash solvent. They wasted no time in enjoying the money.

For the first time in a very long time Cassie felt good. For a few hours all the worries and tensions of the day and the time slipped away, as did much of the loneliness. It was easy, for a time, to even pretend that it was she and Dar there at the Carnival, with Lani the guest instead of herself.

It was quite late before they pooled their money and saw just how quickly it could vanish and knew that it was time to leave. Cassie came to the conclusion with extreme reluctance, as it also brought her back to reality. Dar and Lani planned to stay at the Youth Hostel, where lodging and basic meals were free to commune members. She recalled her books, and said, "I have to stay over at the Temple. I think it's too late to return these tonight. Want to stay over there, Lani?"

The pretty girl looked slightly embarrassed, and Dar sort of shuffled his feet. Finally Lani responded, "Uh, Dar can't stay there, Cass. You know that."

She started to reply, but then thought better of it as the social wall went up once again. Having been so mentally up that evening, her euphoria came crashing down with more than usual force. They were not a threesome. They had never been a threesome. They were two plus one, and guess who was the odd girl out?

"Oh, that's right. I don't know why I said that—forget it," she recovered as best she could. "You go on and have a good time. I'll see you tomorrow."

They seemed relieved now to break it off, and she wanted away from them at this moment, too, so it was after quick and perfunctory goodbyes that they went their separate ways.

Church and state were inexorably linked in Anchor Logh, as in most Anchors, yet they were quite separate institutions. As the Holy Mother was female, only women could enter the priesthood or hold any office in the church. To balance this, only men could hold office in the Anchor government or in riding or commune governments as well.

However, since the government acted in ways holy scripture dictated, and because legal disputes with the government were settled by special priestesses who decided things according to their interpretation of scripture, the fact was that women ran the Anchor. This, too, balanced out quite a lot, since priestesses took vows of not only poverty and obedience but absolute chastity as well, vows that, once taken, could not be withdrawn. Only virgins could enter the order, those with an intact hymen. When they did, they were no longer subject to the Paring Rite, but they became, forever, not citizens but the Property of the Church, and second thoughts and reconsiderations were strictly for the next life.

These thoughts went through her own mind as she walked to the Temple.

She had left Leanspot at the Youth Hostel stables and brought her luggage with her. Now she redeemed it from the check stand near the carnival entrance and started off towards the Temple. Off to one side of the route was the brightly lit gaiety of Main Street, but she had no intention of going there, or, in fact, anywhere near there. Particularly with stringers in town. She approached Temple Square and stopped a moment to look at the massive structure, an impressive block of some unknown reddish material from which rose nine great pyramidal spires, the central one reaching some one hundred meters into the air. The whole building was indirectly floodlit with multicolored lights, and the sight was nothing if not awe-inspiring.

The huge stage and platform had already been erected against the front steps of the magnificent building, in preparation for the Paring Rite that would come now in only three days. The sight only added to her sense of gloom and despair, and she went around to the side and mounted the long stone stairs to the Temple's great bronze doors as quickly as she could.

She saw an unusual number of priestesses about, not only in the scarlet robes and hood of the temple but in whites, blues, greens, and just about every other color as well, indicating local church and provincial staff had already arrived in great numbers for the holiest days of the year.

She had occasionally toyed with the idea of joining the priesthood herself, for it was a tempting opening to potential power, position, and prestige. She certainly would have no trouble with the celibacy part, but she'd always hesitated because it meant living in a woman's world, cut off from the outside for more than three years of intense religious education leading to ordination, then more years in advanced education in a secular school where her devotion would be tested. The novitiate period, it was said, was the toughest time, since you were already a priestess bound for life and yet you would be tempted by all the things you gave up.

Except, of course, what had she to give up? The shaving off of all her hair, head and body, as required of novices, would hardly detract anything from her already nonexistent sex appeal. She had never liked the loss of self-control brought on by hard drinking or light drugs, and she'd never much liked being around those who took them, so she could forgo the usual social life of a campus, and as for owning nothing and subsisting only on charity—well, she'd basically had that for her entire life anyway. . . .

Slowly she walked around the huge platform and up the one hundred steps to the Temple entrance. When she reached those great bronze doors, though, she did not enter immediately but instead turned back and stared again at the broad platform below, looking out at the massive, empty but well-lit square beyond. Empty now, but not three days from now.

It looked more sinister and frightening in the darkness. She felt an odd chill run through her, and an unreasoning churning in the pit of her stomach, and her already deep depression grew even more intense. She reached into her bag and took out one of the books she was returning and stared at the cover. *Introduction to Biochemistry*, it said.

Who am I trying to kid? her black mood asked. *I couldn't even understand the first two exercises in this thing.* She turned and pulled open the door and stepped into the Temple antechamber, but she did not turn and go downstairs to the small section with complimentary rooms for people with Temple business who were obliged to stay the night. Instead, she walked straight ahead to a second set of doors and entered the Inner Temple itself, not quite understanding why.

Although deserted at this hour, the altar flames burned brightly in the colors of the Holy Mother, casting a different colored glow on each of the huge statues of the Loyal Angels. To her eyes those Angels seemed to come alive, and they all looked down directly at her and smiled invitingly. She prostrated herself before the main altar, her innermost fears surfacing and driving her, although she neither understood nor realized this. Her black depression, fed by her frustration at what the books had told her she did not know or understand, and by the sight of that platform in Temple Square, had transformed and magnified her insecurities to the point where she could no longer bear them.

And so she had fled, quite naturally, to the Holy Mother, where all this was instantly transformed in her mind. Nobody else wanted her, but the Holy Mother did. She felt this with such a sense of conviction at revealed truth that she never doubted for a moment that the Holy Mother and Her blessed Angels were speaking straight to her. *Come to the mother church*, they seemed to whisper to her. *Come to the church and banish all insecurity, all fear, all uncertainty. Give us your soul, and we will guide your destiny perfectly.*

It was suddenly all so simple, so clear in her mind. A sisterhood of equals, bound together in piety and love. Reason fled and was replaced by emotional ecstasy. As if in a dream she got up, bowed again to the altar, then went to the sacristy door and then through it into the Temple complex itself. She had never been back there before, and she was thinking not at all, so she just walked in search of a priestess, any priestess, to tell her she was ready to commit her life, body and soul, to the church.

There was, however, no one in the back administrative area, for it was meditation time and very late now, and she continued to walk in her daze down darkened halls and up and down flights of stairs. In all that time she met no one, but time had lost its meaning to her and she did not seem to notice the futility of her search.

Finally there was a room down at the end of a hall that was brightly lit and she heard muffled voices coming from it. She walked towards it, but paused nervously in the darkness before going on, some measure of sanity and self-control returning as interaction with other human beings faced her. She had not wavered in her decision, but now she seemed to realize that she was where she had no business being, and she became afraid that the discovery of her presence here, in forbidden quarters, might be some sort of violation that would impede or exclude her from the sisterhood.

Cautiously and nervously she peered inside the doorway to see who was in there. The sight almost sent her into shock again, but a far different kind than the one that had churned her emotions only moments earlier.

The room was a large one, and three women sat within. The one in a plush, comfortable chair to the left of a projection console would have been instantly recognizable anywhere in Anchor Logh—but not quite like this.

Her angelic Highness, Sister General Diastephanos, sat in that chair in a state more of undress than anything else, puffing away on a big, fat cigar. Sharing the chair, and equally in a state of undress, was undoubtedly a Temple priestess, and she was essentially sitting on the Sister General's lap. There was no mistaking the placement of this unknown woman's arms and the reciprocated gentle gestures from the Sister General.

The third woman in the room was still in her priestly robes, the rich mottled silver of administrative services. She sat at the projector controls, occasionally looking over at several small blinking screens, and appeared totally oblivious to the grotesque scene going on just to her left.

Diastephanos sighed. "Enough, Daji. We have to get through this *sometime* tonight, you know, or we'll be working all the way up the Paring Rite." The other woman untangled herself and got to her feet, pouting a bit like a hurt little child, but she went obediently over to another chair, pulled it up, curled up in it and relaxed to watch. "Next," Her angelic Highness ordered curtly.

The projectionist touched a switch, and a photograph of a boy appeared on the screen, under which was an enormous amount of typed data that seemed to be an abbreviated life history. Cassie could hardly suppress a gasp. She *knew* that boy! She'd gone to school with him!

"Good looking bull," Daji remarked absently in a high-pitched voice that sounded vacuous but was also oddly accented. Her comment was ignored by the others.

"Okay socially, but the brains of a head of

cabbage," the projectionist noted matter-of-factly, looking down at the screen. "Barely literate, four-teen separate disciplinary incidents starting at age eight. A real brawler. He'd be a good soldier as long as he only had to take orders, not give them."

"Wall guard type, then?" the Sister General suggested.

"Hardly. Oh, sure, if he could be bent into shape, but it's doubtful that he'd be receptive to military discipline."

"Sounds tailor-made, then," the high priestess noted. "Didn't that stringer Matson put in an or-der for replacement field soldiers?"

The projectionist checked her data. "Um, yes. Up to ten for Persellus, if we had them. No sex preference as usual."

"What's it matter out in the Flux? What's the old bitch offering for them?"

"The usual. The goddess, you might remember, has a real gift for duplicating printed circuit boards even though she hasn't the slightest idea what they are or what they're used for. Fratina has been complaining about how she's had to cannibalize a backup unit to keep the water treatment system running, and I could use a couple of extra memory modules. Three like this one and we'll be set on that score."

Her angelic Highness thought for a moment. "Persellus would be close by. How many have we given Matson already?"

"Eleven so far, but they're mostly girls. You know the taste of some of our local customers."

The high priestess chuckled. "Do I ever! Well, we'll give him muscle-brain here and two others for the parts list you supply—draw it up and sup-ply the patterns for her. We've got a lot of leeway in assignments with only two stringers but we're in a weaker position. Arden wants a lot of beef, too, if I remember."

"Well, there's the two males and two females, perfect physical specimens, for Taladon. For experimental purposes, it says here."

"Gad! And we're almost completely through the list *now*. Looks like we're going to have to have a second run-through and give up some people we don't want to."

The projectionist touched the switch again and a new boy's face and record appeared. "Nope, forget him," she muttered.

"What? He some kind of genius?"

"No, he's a snot-nosed absolute bastard with an asshole where his brain should be, but he's also Minister Alhred's son."

The Sister General sighed. "*Another* political goodie! Holy Mother of Heaven! No *wonder* this takes so long!"

Cassie knew she should turn right now and chalk up her earlier feelings to the shortest religious conversion on record, but her shock and horror at all this was mixed with a horrid fascination as well. The sexual habits of the Sister General were but a momentary shock. As disillusioning as it was to one who had so recently decided to join the church, it was no more than was commonly rumored and whispered about all priestesses by half the population. No, what was the true and total shock was what those women were doing in that room. It was something quite obvious, yet it undercut the very foundation of Cassie's entire system of beliefs, and those of her whole society and culture. *They were fixing the Paring Rite!* They were exempting the privileged, and evaluating and choosing who would go and who would stay according to their own personal criteria.

She watched as two more boys were evaluated and quickly passed over because they had aptitudes for jobs that were needed in Anchor Logh. It was obvious by the comments, though, that all of these were the finalists in a long selection process that probably began as soon as the numbers had been turned in months ago. These, then, were the worst of the worst, those of The Age who, for political or personal reasons, were of least use to the Anchor. The fact that a Minister's son, the child of a high-ranking government official, had made it down this far indicated that such a relationship was handy but not a guarantee of safety. It was, rather, a political club to be held over a recalcitrant politician.

Sin, too, was a criteria, but not necessarily for the boy or girl under review. From the off-handed comments about the "orders" they had taken from Fluxlands, whatever they were, for various types, it was clear that being too smart, or asking too many questions about the system and the church, could be just as dangerous as having as much brains as a head of cabbage. Troublemaking parents could be punished by having their child chosen, too, the selection being a confirmation by the Holy Mother of their parental sins, while some were chosen simply because they fit a specific requirement of some other place in need. This was well across the fine line separating natural balance of population in the Anchors and divine punishment from real crime.

This was out-and-out slavery, the selling of human beings as property.

Reluctantly, Cassie decided she'd better get out of there, even though she'd love to just stay and see who was still to come up on that screen. Maybe—her? She shuddered at the thought and turned to go, then realized that she was totally and completely lost. How many corridors and stairways *were* there in this place, anyway? She moved as quietly as possible away from the door and towards the nearest stairwell anyway, remembering that she'd seen no one on the way and that, at least, she might have all night to figure it out. She reached the opening to the stairs, turned in—and ran smack into two of the largest, meanest-looking Temple Wardens she'd ever seen. Both women, even in the dim light, looked like they could pick her up with one finger each and chew her to bits for lunch—and enjoy every minute of it. Her heart sank, but she couldn't help wondering just how long they'd been there.

There was no use in even trying to make a break for it. Even if she managed the unlikely feat of getting away from these two, they knew this place inside out and she had no idea where she was. One of the wardens gave a smirk and gestured with her finger for Cassie to turn around and retrace her steps. She had no choice, really, and walked as directed back to the lighted room. She hesitated at the doorway and got a rude shove into the room that almost sent her sprawling on her face.

The three women inside all turned and stared at her. Finally the Sister General said, "Well, well, well. . . . The sewer rats are growing very large this year, I see."

"She was pretty blatant about it," one of the wardens noted. "Tripped every alarm on the main board. The only reason she got this far was she got lost real fast. Her trail's so tangled you can't even figure it out on a security chart and floor plan without getting lost yourself."

"How long was she outside the room here?"

"Ten, fifteen minutes. After the first minute, when she decided to stay and watch, we didn't feel there was any reason for interrupting Your Highness before we had to. Actually, we were just going to pick her up on her way out, if she could manage it—we were betting on that, see—but she stayed around here so long we figured you'd want to deal with her personally."

"Oh, yes, I do indeed," the Sister General purred. "Come here, child."

She was none too gently prodded towards the leader of the Temple. When she was standing right in front of the woman, the high priestess reached out and grabbed her arm, pushing back the sleeve and seeing there the slim bracelet that all wore until they were registered.

"It figures," the priestess muttered to herself. "We get two or three a year around this time. Huah, check her out on the board." She looked again at the bracelet and studied its tiny charm. "CXT-4799-622-584M," she read.

The projectionist nodded and punched the numbers into a keypad. The screen stayed blank. "Nope. Not on our Bad Girl list," Huah said, and keyed in some more commands. This time the screen flickered and Cassie's picture and data came up on it. They definitely updated their files constantly—it was her very recent graduation picture.

The women studied it for a moment. "Very high I.Q., but only average in school. A dreamer, butch beyond the usual age for such things," the projectionist noted. "Rather *be* one of the boys than be with one, but still classified heterosexual. Prefers horses to people."

"Kinky," Daji put in. It was ignored, as usual.

Cassie was forced to stand there silently as the details of her life and interests were read out, including many incidents and anecdotes she had long forgotten. It was obvious that these files were extremely elaborate and would have been impossible to keep and keep straight without the strange powered devices that worked only here in the city and with the constant cooperation of local priestesses, government officials, and spies that had to permeate the whole of Anchor Logh. It was here that their destinies were plotted, not in Heaven, that was clear—but they were plotted on the basis of very complete information.

"We had her down for psychological counseling," the projectionist concluded, "but she's really good with animals. Wanted a vet's slot but doesn't have the mental self-discipline for the boring and routine work required to get the degree. Currently we had her down as a good church prospect—she'd be an excellent midwife, for example—with the usual twist of giving her a choice between that and a menial job like stable hand."

"That's all I came in for—to apply for the novitiate," Cassie blurted out. "I didn't mean to do anything wrong!"

"Too bad," the Sister General commented without a trace of sorrow or pity in her voice. "Well, girl, you surely understand that that way is out now. Even if we could overlook your sacrilege to the Temple and what you saw in this room—nobody would ever believe you anyway, no matter how you blabbed—we can't overlook the fact that *you* would know. You'd be a latent rebel, never fully able to take church doctrine or discipline, uncontrollable by us or the government without extreme measures, and you're smart enough to figure ways around those. You could be the source for some major inconveniences at some point down the road, and we can't have that. When we identify a potential agent of such instability, we really have no choice."

"What could *I* do?" Cassie asked, half-pleading.

"Who knows? Perhaps nothing. Very likely nothing. But a society like ours works and survives because it is in a very delicate balance. It works primarily because its people *believe* it works, and believe that they live in a free democracy where jobs and promotions are based solely on merit and loyalty to the system, and that it's possible for the lowest—or a child of the lowest—to become the highest. It doesn't take much to upset that balance.

That is really why we do all of this, and why we do it this way. Left to itself, this land would get periodically out of balance, opening the way for radical ideas and resultant radical changes. The whole thing would collapse into anarchy, and the living would envy the dead. It's happened before, child, more than once, long ago and far away. No matter what you think of us, we take our responsibility very, very seriously and are totally bound to scripture. The church's sole mission is to preserve stability, to shore up the system and eliminate its weakest and most threatening spots, so that the Holy Mother's plan can continue. By your own actions you have made yourself a potential source of such instability, and you have learned the truth decades before you were ready to understand and handle it."

She was about to continue when a buzzer sounded on the projectionist's console. The controller reached over and picked up a small oblong-shaped object that was apparently some sort of communications device and talked in a low tone for more than two minutes. The rest of them waited, wondering what it was about.

Finally the projectionist was finished and she turned to the Sister General. "More headaches. That was Ranatan over at the Lazy Bull on Main Street. Seems that last year he got a new girl for the upstairs room from another dive in Anchor Thomb. Now the stringer Arden told him his chit's been called, and he's pulled an abduction to pay up."

The Sister General frowned. "Damn. Anybody we know?"

"Not on our list, if that's what you mean. I remembered her when we were checking slots. A real looker, Ranatan says, although she's got some brains. Wait a moment." She punched in a code and checked a screen.

"Anybody we can live without?" the Sister General asked hopefully.

"Yeah. Good I.Q. and solid aptitudes, but not in anything we aren't already overstocked in. I guess we can spare her, but Ranatan owes us one now, coming up with this so late. Says he forgot about it until his marker was called."

"I'll bet," the high priestess sneered.

"One problem, though. She has a steady boy-friend, and he woke up from the sapping Ranatan's boys gave him in a rotten and angry mood. He's raising holy hell with the local cops right now. Farmhand type. Not on our list but he could easily be our third soldier."

The Sister General nodded. "Arrange it. Since there'll be something of a cover-up necessary to pacify the police and families, better use the tunnel and bring 'em here. Keep 'em on ice until after Paring Rite, then just add her in with the crowd and make sure they leave at night. You know the routine."

The administrator nodded. "What about her and the boy?" By "her" it was clear that this meant Cassie.

"We'll keep 'em on ice until Paring Day. Use two of the cells below, ninth level. Somebody can work out cover stories for them staying in town. As for Ranatan's girl, put her in with this one until then. We'll have to check with the stringers and see who's heading in the right direction to make delivery."

"Check," responded the administrator crisply, and that was that.

5

RITE

The cell was not, strictly speaking, a jail, but it was clear from some of the graffiti on the walls that it had served as one many times. In point of fact, it was the kind of barren cubicle that novices used when living and studying at the Temple. Under other circumstances, Cassie thought ruefully, she might have been in a similar or identical cell in this very place as a priestess-in-training.

The box-like cell was roughly three meters wide and three deep, with old and rotting straw on the floor. The rear of the place contained two fixed wooden "beds" of sorts, one on each side; really nothing more than two rectangular boxes filled with more straw. In front of these were two small shelves mounted on each wall, empty now and probably for some time, although, hanging from a nail in one was a tiny oil lantern that provided some, but not much, illumination. Sitting on the floor near the door was a very old chamber pot that was cold, shallow, and rust-encrusted. The door itself was of solid wood with the hinges on the outside and a tiny window in the middle. The window was not barred, but it was barely large enough to get a hand through. The door, however, *was* barred, and with a very solid plank.

The wardens had stripped her completely before

shoving her in, and had warned her that should she cause any problems while there, they would be perfectly willing to bring down some manacles and a gag, too, if need be. She didn't intend to make any trouble, though—at least not right now. Even if she managed a miracle, where could she go and what could she do with both church and state against her? Anchor Logh was a big place, but the Sister General had been right about one thing—the people believed totally in the system because the alternatives were so horrible. She might make it back home for a couple of days, but once her number was picked in the Paring Rite even her own parents, sad and grieving as they might be, would turn her in.

She felt curiously ambivalent about her future. The fact was, the high priestess had been correct about her. She had seen too much, and she had lost her faith. The system was based on the scriptures, and now she had caught the church redhanded circumventing its own system. If the church could do *that*, it must follow the scriptures only when it was convenient for it to do so, and if the *church* didn't really buy those holy writings, how in hell could she?

She wondered again about the stringers who'd invoked such horror in her. It was obvious that *they* knew it was all a sham, for they participated and even profited by it. Perhaps that explained their callous attitude towards everything and everyone. They *knew* it was all phony, strictly business and cynically amoral. If you knew that right from the start, as they most certainly did, and you also knew that there wasn't a damned thing you could do about it, what sort of person might you become? The answer to that one made stringers at least understandable as people, although she still couldn't agree with or like anyone who assisted so eagerly in perpetuating the fraud for personal gain.

The church equated disorder with evil. The Seven Who Wait really personified that disorder, and, thus, were depicted as the ultimate evil. Did the Seven, in fact, exist, or were they a convenient invention of the church to scare people with, she wondered? Perhaps it was a grisly sort of joke on all of them, even the church. Perhaps this was not some testing ground but Hell itself, and they were in fact the fallen angels, suffering pain and anguish and being reborn again and again, forever, into eternal punishment, with Heaven so tantalizingly in sight and always totally out of reach, everyone living rigid and mostly unhappy lives because they were working towards ultimate salvation—an ultimate salvation that would be forever denied them. Now *that* made sense—and would be the ultimate joke. Perhaps this is the secret the stringers knew, that it was all for nothing and that nothing really counted.

She shivered, only partly from the damp chill of the cell. Well, if that *were* the way of World, then something, however minor, could and must be done about it. If the angels rebelled against the Holy Mother and created disorder, and if those angels now ran World, then it was time they got a little disorder of their own. It was not in stability that hope lay, but in rebellion. Somehow, some time, she swore to herself, I will help be the instrument of that.

Strong words from someone who knew that she was to be cast into the Flux, a prisoner and slave, in a matter of days, and who was now pacing a tiny cell, stark naked and alone.

How long she was there, alone with uncounted tiny vermin and her own sour thoughts, it was impossible to say, but occasionally the heavy bar that kept her door securely closed would move back and a warden, backed up by another, would enter, leave a bowl of foul-smelling gruel, a cup of water, and check the chamberpot. She'd also slept, off and on and fitfully, although she was never quite sure for how long. The small oil lamp continued to burn, and she was afraid to turn it off for fear it would remain that way.

Still, three "meals" into her imprisonment, the door opened again, but it was not for food. She just stood there, amazed, as two wardens tossed another naked figure into the cell. "Let your roommate there tell you the rules," one warden sneered, and the door was slammed shut and barred once more.

Cassie stared at the figure now picking herself up off the floor. "Lani? Oh, Holy Mother of World! Not *you, too!*"

The other got up, frowned, and stared at her. Finally something seemed to penetrate the shock. "Cass?"

Quickly Cassie helped her friend over to one of the beds. "Sit here, or lie back," she soothed. "There's mites and everything else in here but they'll get you no matter where you are so you might as well be as comfortable as you can."

It took some time for the small, attractive girl to get a grip on herself, but Cassie was patient, knowing that time was the one thing they had plenty of. Eventually Lani was able to talk about it, sort of, in small bits and pieces, and the story came out.

The truth was, there wasn't much to tell. After leaving Cassie at the fairgrounds, she and Dar had headed for the youth hostel. On their way they'd come close to the bright lights and raucous sounds of Main Street, and both had, more or less on impulse, gone over there. It was just curiosity, really—the area was always denied them in the past, and now that they were The Age it was open to them both. Open, yes, but dangerous. They had finally gone into a bar, just to see what one was like, and had been befriended by this nice young fellow working there. He'd been very easy to talk to, and *extremely* nice and friendly without being anything more than that, and eventually he offered to buy them one drink each just to celebrate their coming of age. It seemed so nice, so reasonable. . . .

Nor, in fact, was there much more to the story. She had more or less awakened in a room much like a hotel room, but she felt too dizzy and sleepy to see much or tell much about it. She was conscious only of being bound, somehow, and of several people coming in and out at various times, some giving her sweet-tasting things to drink that put her out once more, others just standing there and having some sort of conversation or other that she couldn't follow, although she seemed to think it was about her. Finally somebody came in with a novice's white robes and bundled her, still drugged, out a back door and down a series of back streets to some sort of tunnel, and through there to here. She was just coming down from the drugs, and just realizing her status.

"I've been abducted!" she suddenly said, sitting up straight. "Oh, Holy Mother protect me from my sins! Abducted!" She started to shake a little, and began sobbing quietly. Cassie felt sorry for her and let her cry it out, giving what comfort she could. Finally Lani seemed to realize Cassie's own situation. "You—you've been abducted, too!"

Cassie sighed. "Not quite, but I might as well have been." Quickly she outlined her own story, and why she was now there. "So, you see, I'm above board from their point of view. I'll be picked in the Paring Rite. You won't. You'll just—disappear."

Lani shook her head in shock and wonder. "What's to become of us after that, Cass? What can we *do*?" Another thought suddenly struck her. "Poor Dar! He must be worried sick!"

"Yeah, just like us," Cass told her. "He made such a fuss they copped him, too. He's probably somewhere in a hole like this one until Paring Rite, then they'll let him out just long enough to get picked. It's less messy that way."

Lani still could not quite accept it. "The church in league with stringers and kidnappers. . . . I'm sorry, Cass, it's just so—*hard* to accept, even now. And—why *me*?"

Cassie sighed. "You were handy. You were, sorry to say it, foolish enough to walk into a joint with your bracelet showing, and the bar owner owed a favor to some bar owner in an Anchor far away. I saw them operate, Lani. They put in orders for people—size, shape, physical stats, you name it—like they were ordering a horse or new plow."

"But what would anyone want with *me*? I mean, was it just because we were the first ones dumb enough or naive enough to walk in there, or what?"

Cass shook her head. She'd been pretty naïve herself, and maybe she still was, but she didn't recall *ever* being *that* naïve. "Uh, Lani, a bar doesn't exactly want you for your brains."

For a moment the other girl looked puzzled; then, slowly, the light dawned, and she seemed to wilt a bit. "Oh," she managed, sounding shocked. "Oh, oh, oh. . . ." She sighed. "What can we *do*?" she wailed.

Cassie shrugged. "What *can* we do? Oh, sure, if you could escape you might kick up a fuss, but nobody would believe the church was involved, so nobody would find me or Dar, and all it means is that they'd get some other girl in your place and your number would be picked like mine and Dar's will be. They don't like problems, Lani."

"I'd make a stink they *couldn't* sweep away," Lani retorted bitterly.

"If you managed anything, they'd just kill you. That's the kind of people they are, Lani. I've watched them in action. Look on the bright side. At least you're going to an Anchor, and you know why and for what. If you're very lucky, and if they don't mess with your mind or something—you're smart. You'll figure something out. You always have a chance at getting them back. Me—I don't know. I'm being sent into the Flux, whatever that means. If I get back I'll be the first I ever heard of to do it."

Lani just shook her head sadly and was silent for a moment. Finally she said, "You just don't *know*, Cass. My field is—was—biology. I read up on it a lot. Some of the drugs they have . . . I can even tell you right now the formula for the drug they probably used on me. And the ones they *will* use on me when I get—where I'm going. Somehow, when you read about them in cold, scientific language you never think of them being used on people, particularly anybody you know. Particularly not me. . . ." She seemed to lapse into a sort of impersonal world of horror.

"First they'll give me a series of doses of aphalamatin. It's used on the criminally insane, mostly. It burns out certain localized areas of the cerebral cortex, leaving you very nice and happy all the time and very, very compliant—you'll do just about *anything* to please, like a little kid, and you're dumb enough you can't even add without using your fingers. Then, after a tubal of course, they'll give me massive hormonal injections to get me super-endowed and horny all the time, and . . ."

"*For Heaven's sake, stop it!*" Cassie screamed, reaching down and shaking her. "You've got to *fight* them! Fight as long as you can, with whatever you have! Sure, maybe it's impossible, but, damn it, you fight anyway! Maybe, just maybe, we can do something, *anything* to get these bastards!"

Lani just sat there and didn't seem to hear. Cassie finally gave up in disgust and tried pacing around a bit. Maybe it was possible to be *too* smart, she thought. Anybody who ever figured the odds on anything radical and believed them probably would never try it. As for her, she couldn't name a dozen drugs and wasn't sure what half of *them* did, except stop a bleeding cut or cure a headache, but she wasn't about to give up, or count the odds. Her bitterness and hatred was far too strong and too deep for this, and while Lani's surrender to the inevitable frustrated and disgusted her, it only reinforced her own anger.

The fact was, she couldn't really blame the girl. Like herself, Lani had been brought up very secure in the system and was a solid true believer. Unlike her, Lani had not witnessed the total betrayal of that system firsthand. Lani was here because she was pretty; Cassie was here because she knew too much. It was a major difference. Secure in her knowledge that the system was rigged, a total sham, she had no qualms whatsoever about betraying it. Lani, on the other hand, faced her unpleasant future still shackled with the beliefs of her upbringing, beliefs shaken only by Cassie's admittedly biased account and by no real supporting evidence. Lani had only Cassie's word they were in the Temple.

Lani, then, had surrendered to the total fatalism that the church and scripture brought, and as the hours wore on she seemed to wrap herself more and more in the comfort of those beliefs.

"It is the will of the Holy Mother," Lani pronounced at last, and relaxed a bit. "It was my own past sins that led me to go to Main Street, and this is my payment. Well, I will do it. I will be the best damned stripper, dancer, whore, or whatever they will me to be. The Holy Mother's will be done!"

Cassie could do nothing but sigh and get more disgusted. This, of course, was the trouble, and why things worked so well for the people who ran it. They probably wouldn't have to use a single drug on Lani, or much of anything else.

That, in fact, discouraged Cass the most. A rebellion was impossible if only one rebel existed. Lani in fact showed just how formidable a task rebellion was, and why it was unheard of in Anchor Logh. What could a liberator do when the slaves of the system would fight like hell against the rebels for their right to remain slaves?

Still, perhaps unwittingly, the Sister General had offered some slight hope. There *had* been rebellion elsewhere, in other Anchors. The old bitch as much as admitted it. And, by their conversation, it was certain that there was more than nothingness in the Flux. There were, in fact, real places with real rulers and real names, although just what sort of place would be ruled by somebody who thought herself a goddess was hard to imagine.

Well, let the sheep be led to the slaughter if they wanted. She, Cassie, would have none of it. She would probably die or suffer terribly; even she was logical enough to realize this. But she'd die or suffer *fighting*, and if there was any chance, any chance at all, for something more she would have what revenge she could.

They came for her after what seemed like an eternity. At first she had welcomed Lani's company, but by now the poor girl was far gone into her own fantasy rationalization, practicing being sexy and alluring and seemingly looking forward to her fate with a near messianic fanaticism that Cass found bizarre in the extreme. Separation was now a relief.

Of course, Cassie and Dar had to be produced for the Paring Rite, for the same reason Lani had to stay hidden. They took Cass out of the cell and upstairs to a comfortable dressing area, where she found all her clothes neatly cleaned and pressed. She put them on and gave the wardens no trouble. If nothing else had, Lani had convinced her that whatever future she had was not in Anchor Logh, but out there, somewhere, in the terrible Flux. The system was simply too good for easy solutions. Revenge, and revolution, must come from without, for it would certainly never come from within. That she knew now with a certainty equalling the certainty that her name would be picked today in the Paring Rite. In a way, she was like Lani—she'd stopped bemoaning her fate and actually welcomed getting it over with.

Anything rather than go back to that damned, cursed cell with its other occupant.

They kept her in the ante-room while things started up outside. She could see their plan, and it was really pretty clever. No matter who was outside, or what family had attended, she was to be released just before the "lottery," out a side entrance. She'd be out there, free, but pinned in one location by the crowd and with no time at all to do much of anything before being called. It would look very convincing—and there was absolutely nothing she could do about it, damn them.

Outside, the great square was filled with people, overflowing down the side streets as far as the eye could see. Speakers had been set up all over town so that the sacred rite and its result would be known to all, and at exactly mid-day it all began with the grand processional.

It was still an impressive sight, even to one who knew that it was all just a different version of carnival showmanship. At the mid-hour the great gong sounded from the high steeple, not its usual six times but, for the only time in the year, thirteen times. As the gong started, the great bronze doors opened as if on their own, and the processional began from within.

First came the novices, all in bright white cloaks with hoods up, then the associates and professional orders, headed by their superiors—the Midwife General, the Judiciary General, the Educator General, and all the others, followed by their members. They fanned out, providing a riot of colors in their formal robes and vestments, on both sides of the platform. Now came the ranking priestesses of each parish, large or small, from the entire Anchor, followed by their associates and assistants, and, finally, the ranking members of the priestly guilds of the Temple itself. Below, in the square, directly in front of the platform, were roped-off rows of chairs, and now the processional filed down the steps on both sides of the platform and filed into those seats, novices in the back, Temple personnel in front, everybody else in between.

Finally the Sister General herself appeared, dressed in a robe of sparkling gold inlaid with gems that contained all the colors of all the orders below, carrying her gold septre of office and wearing a crown made up entirely of colorful flowers. She looked in every respect the absolute monarch she actually was, subject only to the orders of Her Perfect Highness, the Queen of Heaven, who was safely in her palace in Holy Anchor half a world away.

She walked to a small, flower-covered lectern that had been set up for her in the front and center position on the platform, and stood there while aides lit incense in small stands flanking the high priestess. The day was cloudy and damp, but nobody seemed to mind.

She raised her right arm and the entire crowd went down on one knee, or as far down as the packing would permit.

"Peace be unto you, and the blessings of the Holy Mother be with you always," she intoned, the small hidden mike carrying her blessing clearly throughout the city.

"And to you and the Holy Mother Church," came the mass response. Even Cassie found herself mouthing the required responses, although she viewed the whole procedure cynically. Even so, she couldn't help but wonder what the effect on this crowd would be if they'd seen the same majestic-looking Sister General the way *she* had.

There followed the long and complex sacramental service, through which the local priestesses of the various churches represented their parishioners, interspersing prayers and responses. As it was winding down, though, the chief of administration for the Temple and two wardens brought down the large wire mesh drum and placed it behind the Sister General, anchoring it firmly in pre-drilled slots in the platform base. At that time a warden inside came up to Cassie and said, "All right, you—down and out that door there." And, with that, she found herself pushed out the side and onto the street right in the midst of the throng. She looked around on the off-chance that somebody familiar would be there, someone who, at least, could carry news of what was going on for Dar and Lani as well, but she saw no one.

The Paring Rite itself began.

"Sisters and brothers, we are gathered here today for a most sacred and holy duty," the Sister General began. "The Holy Mother and Her Angels have directed the welfare of this Anchor for the past year and have determined it is in all ways in accord with the holy scriptures and divine will. People were born, people died, in accordance with the divine cycle of death and rebirth, so that we who once failed our great test could, by Her infinite mercies, regain the richness of Heaven.

"Those souls which are darker than others, and which must learn much more to reach this holy perfection, are revealed to us in the Paring. This is surely the most clear illustration of divine will and direct intervention in our affairs, for it is the Holy Mother who determines the size of the harvest, the death and birth rate, and so, by comparing the two, creates the miracle by which souls who need purification in the Flux that surrounds us are revealed to us. This year the number is fifty males and fifty-six females, out of a blessedly large generation, showing us indeed that Anchor Logh is among the most blessed of the communities of World.

"Now," she continued, "through Her divine intervention, the names of those souls will be made known to us. Do not judge anyone of a family of the chosen to be in any way blamed for that selection. To blame another is to substitute the will of humankind for the wisdom of the Holy Mother, and She will not hold blameless those who cast aspersions on any family member. Likewise, do not grieve for those who are chosen, for they are not lost, but rather found, and through their Paring and subsequent purification they, too, gain in the eternal quest for perfection. Do not judge them—let the Holy Mother alone do that, or you, yourself, may be judged wanting by Her in your next life, and may have been so judged in the past."

Nice of her, Cassie thought sourly. *Next thing you know she'll be saying that we're the lucky ones.* She wondered idly where Dar was. Probably stuck in a crowd just like her, and even less understanding of just what was happening to him and why.

"When each child becomes an adult, she or he was given a bracelet and charm by the local parish to which that person belonged," the Sister General went on. The explanation was hardly necessary, but it was required of the Rite. "Those people are here now. For most, this will be the day of their true coming of age. Those whom the Holy Mother does not choose will report, as soon as they can after returning to their homes, to their local parish church and receive a registry number, and then they shall go to the government house in their communities and register and receive the rights, privileges, responsibilities, and duties of full citizens."

She turned and looked back at the huge drum behind her. "Here are copies of the charms each wears. Seven times does the drum spin, and then the Holy Mother will tell us the names one by one."

The administrative chief and one of the wardens started the thing spinning the requisite number of times, then, finally, brought it to a stop. The hundreds of gold and silver colored amulets made quite a racket.

"We will now begin to read the divine will," the Sister General told them. With that she moved back, opened the small door in the drum, and without looking at anything save the crowd, now hushed and tense, she drew the first small tag. Cassie couldn't see much of the spectacle, but she *had* been wondering how they fixed it.

The first tag was handed to the administrative chief, who took it and then consulted a large bound volume—the birth register. "JRL-4662-622-125K," she announced. "Dileter of Kar Riding, come forward to the platform."

As easy as that, Cassie reflected. Who was *ever* going to check all those numbers against the charms drawn and find out that what the clerk was reading had actually been worked out in advance and had no relation to the charm whatsoever?

As each number was read out, there was a collective sigh, or moan, from the crowd, plus occasional shrieks, wails, and protests from those called or from their friends and family. Dar was the ninth called. Cassie was the fourteenth. They were taking no chances on giving them any freedom at all.

Resigned, she made her way, with difficulty, through the crowd, which only gave way when she told each obstruction in turn she'd been called. Then they were very solicitous and their pity just dripped from them, yet it was mixed with a strong sense of relief as well. *It's not me. It's not someone I know.* And, in the midst of it all, the acute observer could pick out a small fortune in betting slips changing hands with each and every pick of the Sister General. Cass hated them for their pity and for their hypocrisy as well. *I'm coming back, you bastards!* she swore silently. *I'm coming back to tear down this damned city and wipe those looks off your holier-than-thou faces.*

She reached the platform and was actually assisted up by two wardens as if she were some sort of honored guest. Talk about hypocrites! She was led over to where those called were assembling in neat rows. Most of them looked scared to death or still in shock, and one or two were trembling uncontrollably or sobbing softly to themselves. Occasionally someone would pass out in shock when a name was called, and there were several unconscious bodies around by the end of it.

Finally, it was over. The last number had been called, and the crowd knew it, and gave the hundred and six lost souls on the stage the final indignity.

They cheered. They clapped. They built their joy into a thunderous crescendo that echoed off all points of the square and throughout the city, sweeping over the sobbing and shaking friends and family of those on stage who would now be declared property, then dead, never to be seen or heard from again.

Out of a class of 3,941, 3,835 rejoiced, as did their friends and families. Although a hundred and six were now condemned, it was a small fraction of the total, and would soon be forgotten except for the parents, siblings, friends, and relatives of those now gone. Even that, in time, would fade, as it always did, the same as if those hundred and six had been felled by accident or injury.

It was not so surprising that three of the unlucky picks did not show up for the public honor; rather, it surprised Cassie that so few had run for it. They didn't have a prayer, though, as the Sister General pointed out as soon as the crowd let her get a word in.

"Know you all that the Holy Mother has chosen three and looked for them and they are not here," she announced. "Know that all those declared property of the state must surrender within one day of the first bell of Paring Rite. Know, too, that if those we will now designate are not turned over to the Temple here within that period they will be declared agents of evil and discord. *Any* who help them shall suffer the same fate as they. *Any* who do so much as give them a cup of water, or simply not report them at once and aid in their apprehension, shall be guilty of a mortal sin beyond any redemption in this life and punished by terrible torments in their next, and shall forfeit all rights, citizenship, and property and themselves become property of the state. Even one who hides this from us cannot hide from the Holy Mother, who shall wreak a terrible vengeance on those who help thwart Her divine will."

She read the names and numbers once again, and gave the benediction. The lottery drum was already removed to one side, and she turned and walked regally back up the steps to the Temple, and inside. Wardens flanked the miserable chosen, many of whom had to help their comrades merely stand, and they were then directed back into the Temple as well. Even Cassie found herself trembling slightly now that it was done, and more than a little scared. Knowing that it was fixed and that it was all a lie did nothing to change the fact that she had been declared property and banished, and was now going to the same unknown fate as those around her.

6

MULES

They were ushered into a lower level room that was large but spartan. In fact, it was often used as a small gym by the Temple priestesses, and the remains of some gym apparatus were still there, pushed against a far wall. The entire group was lined up in seven rows of fifteen each, without regard to much of anything. Wardens with nasty looking batons were posted all over the place, but the bulk of the personnel were priestesses in medical yellow. While the wardens kept them in line and menaced someone here and there who made a sound or flagged in position, the nurses measured out a clear-looking liquid into small cups and put them out on tables.

"All right—first row, walk to that table there and each take a cup," the chief warden instructed. "Then get back into line."

They did as they were instructed, some sniffing or looking dubiously at the unfamiliar substance. It smelled a lot like lemonade.

Cass stood in the third row and waited her turn with the rest. She looked, of course, for others she might know in the group, as some of the others did as well, and saw several familiar faces. Her riding seemed particularly wicked this time out.

Finally she got her drink and was back in line,

and after a while everyone had one. "Now, first row, drink all of the liquid and, when finished, turn the cup upside down," the warden instructed, "then sit on the floor where you are."

They did as instructed, although a couple of attempts to hold the stuff in their mouths brought sharp and painful blows from the batons and yelps of pain, and one was singled out, pinned down, and had a cup force-fed down his throat. The object lesson was well-taken; nobody in any of the subsequent rows failed to drink their cups dry.

Cassie had had more than a few qualms about downing the stuff after Lani's grisly catalog of horrible drugs, but the drink turned out to be some sort of tranquilizer. It produced an odd effect. She felt her body getting very sleepy, very distant, to the point where she was barely conscious that it was there at all, and her emotions seemed to be equally suppressed, yet her mind remained seemingly clear and sharp, and she was both conscious of and interested in the proceedings around her. In fact, it was an effective hypnotic, putting them all under yet retaining their undivided attention.

The head nurse went to each of them and checked to make certain that the drug had taken effect, then came back and stood in front of them. "You will give me your total attention and cooperation," she began, and instantly she had it. "The first row will get to its feet now." All of the first row moved as one.

"Take two steps forward, first row," she instructed, "then remove every piece of clothing you have on you and place it in a bundle in front of you." Again, they did as instructed, without regard to modesty or sex. The curious thing was, they felt wide awake and totally alert—they just did what they were told as if they had no control whatsoever over their body movements.

"Now you will all pick up your clothing and

hold it in front of you. That's right. Now, you will all turn to your right, so that you form a line, and walk slowly to the large box over there, drop your clothes in it, then go to the first table next to the box."

The procedure was repeated for each one. At the first table non-Temple doctors of both sexes gave each a fairly routine physical, then they were directed to the second, where their heads were shaved clean, first with some sort of powered razors, then with a creamy compound that removed any last vestiges of hair, right down into the pores and to the base of the roots. This was the first mark of those chosen in the Paring Rite. If, somehow, one or more got away, they would be forever marked by total and complete baldness.

The second mark was the most degrading, and was administered by a very strange chair-like machine. Each in turn was told to sit in the large contraption, their rears against a metal plate of some sort. An attendant punched a button, and, when they got up, there was an indelible long number tattooed in purple on their behinds. Similarly, they were told to put their right thumbs in a hole in a small device, and that gave a purplish stain that made the fingerprint really stand out. Boys, Cassie noted, also had the shave and cream treatment for facial hair of any sort.

Finally, they were given a series of injections, purposes unknown, then broken up into small groups and taken to smaller rooms where they were given a basic meal to eat—some sort of stew, not very good, but far better than the crap they'd given her in the cell—and then were taken to basic showers and rinsed from head to toe. This done, they were taken back to the gym, where all of the equipment had been cleared and the floor covered with huge, gray cushioned mats of the usual sort found in school gymnasiums, and the chief warden told them, "All right. You will remain here until it is time to leave. All exits will be guarded by wardens who would just love to make an example of somebody trying to leave. There is a basic bathroom through those small doors over there if you need to take a crap. Anybody still thinking of leaving before we let you should remember your stigmata and know that these will make you known to one and all. There is no place to run in Anchor Logh." And, with that, she departed.

The drug was wearing off rapidly now, and Cassie could feel the sting on her ass where the number had been tattooed, but a side effect of the stuff was that it made you terribly tired and sleepy. Most of them, herself included, just sank down on the mats and passed out.

It was an unpleasant sleep and an unpleasant awakening, although in a sense it was better because, once it was determined that what had happened was no nightmare, there was a sense on the part of most of the group to adapt to the situation as something new to be faced, with unpleasant future realities shunted to a back part of the mind.

Cassie awoke with a mild headache and a little dizziness that soon passed, and she looked around. Some of the others had apparently been awake for some time, while others were still in various stages of half-sleep, but there was some moving around, whispered talking, and once in a while somebody would stagger to the bathroom.

They were a strange sight, all these people with no clothes or hair and numbers on their asses, but since *everybody* was that way it soon seemed somewhat normal, sort of like a uniform binding them together. Cassie got up and, after a false start or two, started to walk around and see if she could find anybody she knew. A large boy sitting up against a wall called to her. "Hey! Cass! Is that you?"

She smiled, turned, and went over to him. Hairless, Dar looked more the country bumpkin than ever.

"I saw you come up when you were called," he told her. "I really wasn't expecting to see you here, though." His face darkened. "I kind of figured it'd be Lani."

She sat down beside him, paused, trying to collect her thoughts, then said, "Lani's not with our group, Dar, but she'll probably go out with us. I've seen her." Carefully, hesitantly, she told the story from the point at which they'd split up at the Carnival until she'd been shoved outside for the Paring Rite. She spared nothing, but was as gentle as she could be.

He took it well, although for a moment he just sat there, thinking hard. Finally he said, "Damn. And I always figured she was so much smarter'n me. That's just dumb foolishness." He paused a moment more, then added, "But, like you said, this is *all* just dumb foolishness, isn't it?"

She smiled wanly. "That's about it. I'm a little surprised at how you're taking it all, though. Don't you go along with her that it's the divine will?"

He snorted. "Divine will—hell! I already figured that any goddess that would do this mean thing to nice people like you and Lani wasn't much worth a damn. It ain't fair, that's all, and who wants a bunch of gods who ain't fair?"

She almost kissed and hugged him for that, but kept still. Eventually he told her of his own experiences, of getting the knockout drinks at the bar and waking up in the youth hostel, trying to see Lani, and being told she wasn't there. He'd become something of a wild man at that, realizing that she'd been abducted and blaming himself for it. He'd stormed back to the bar looking for the guy who'd done it and, when he couldn't find him, he'd started tearing the bar apart. In the end, the cops came and arrested *him* and had refused to listen to his protests about Lani. A cop *did* take his statement, when he'd calmed down enough to give one, and promised to check for the missing girl, but they'd left him locked up.

Finally a magistrate, who was, of course, a Temple priestess, had heard his case, but refused to even allow any testimony on Lani's disappearance. She told him there was no excuse for such misbehavior, that there were proper channels if he had a problem, and she sentenced him to remain in jail until Paring Rite, which he had.

"I kind of figured my number was up then, and Lani's too," he told her. "I mean, when that bitch of a judge wouldn't even *listen* about a kidnapping— hell, I smelled rotten meat. Then, when I was called so quickly, that just cinched it."

She nodded, feeling better than she had in a long time. It was good to be believed, and to find a kindred spirit in all this mess. They talked for a while, mostly on inconsequential things, and Dar remarked, "Hey—you know, it's funny."

"Huh? What's funny?"

"Well, here we are, all naked and all, with a bunch of guys and girls, and nobody's the least bit turned on, if you know what I mean. I mean, if you can't be bad *now*, when can you?"

She hadn't really noticed it before, but he was right. Dar was, in fact, as amply endowed in his area as Lani was in hers, yet she felt not the slightest urge or inclination there. At first she just put it down to the situation, or the public nature of the room, but now she realized that this wasn't explainable by that at all. In fact, even if some of the boys were restrained, others like Dar would not

be, and their sexual arousal would be impossible
to hide.

"It must be those shots they gave us," she decided.
"I guess one of them just, well, turned us all off."

Dar sighed. "Yeah. It ain't enough to make us
bald and dye us purple. They got to make us mules,
too." He looked at her. "Too bad, too. I got to
admit, Cass, I never much thought of you except as
one of the boys, but, like this, well, you're kind'a
cute. Ain't no mistaking you for a boy, anyway."

She grinned broadly, leaned over, and kissed
him gently on the cheek. "That's the nicest thing
any boy's ever said to me. I appreciate it, Dar. I
really do."

"Yeah, too bad. The mind's willin' but the motor
just won't start." They sat there a while longer,
and eventually several others recognized them and
came over and joined them. They were a mixed lot
from the riding, and also somewhat mixed in their
reactions to all this. Cass was surprised to find
how few were deep-down religious about it all. It's
easy to see someone else get picked for sin, but
pretty tough to get picked for it yourself when
others whom you *know* are far worse than you
were freed to live normal lives. Not that there
weren't a few wail-and-doom fanatics, but not
many.

Some friends, old and new, banded together with
them for at least a brief association. There were
Suzl and Nadya, two girls who crushed Cassie's
old belief—or hope—that the pretty and sexy ones
would be nothing without hairdos, makeup, and
careful dressing, and Canty and Ivon, one a short,
squat boy with a mischievous streak, the other
built like a bull. Ivon, the big, muscular one, was
pretty bright, but he had both a temper and an
attitude that showed a bull-like lack of fear—and
lack of self-control.

"Turned us into damned mules, that's what they

did," Ivon grumped. "Shaved, sexless, and branded. I suppose a halter's next."

The shots seemed to have affected them all more than they'd expected. "I was in the middle of my period yesterday," Suzl noted. "Now—nothing. I wonder what else those shots did? I wonder if it's permanent?" That last was the unspoken primary fear of all of them.

Cassie reassured them at least that there was evidence of civilization in the Flux, between the Anchors and having trade with them. What sort of civilization could exist there none of them could imagine, and Cassie decided it was better not to mention the place that wanted perfect specimens for experimental purposes. What they had now was bad enough.

They were fed at intervals, again in small groups, and there was some variety despite the basic lack of quality in the food. Two of the three missing ones also arrived during that period, both girls who said that they had been hustled away by parents or other relatives and had just bought a little more time. They had paid for that time, though, and dearly. Every hair on their bodies had been removed, and not by machine, either—even their eyebrows—and they had been tattooed by hand, without anesthetic, not merely with the number on their rump in the standard purple but all over in various colors. They had been tied down and anybody who was around was given a needle and told to write or draw something. From the looks of them there had been an awful lot of people around, and most had cruel or obscene minds.

The third missing one, they were told, would not be coming at all. She had gone someplace and found a large knife, then entered the Temple and began hacking and stabbing everyone she met, screaming that she was one of the Seven Who Wait, wreaking vengeance on the Holy Mother and

Her church. It'd taken seven wardens to subdue
her, and in the process they'd beaten her to death.
Talk was she'd taken several in church robes with
her to the next incarnation. They didn't know her
name, but she became something of an instant
hero to the group in the gym.

They were just beginning to get used to the routine and their new situation when the moment
they dreaded arrived. The doors opened and in
walked not Temple wardens but uniformed soldiers of the border guard, looking tough and nasty.
The group was formed up into its now standard
rows, and an officer of the guard stepped forward
with a list.

"When I call your name, you will step forward
and form a new set of ranks to my left," he instructed them. "Failure to move immediately or
not carry out *any and all* orders any member of the
Guard may give you without question will result
in you experiencing more pain than you have ever
felt in your lives. There will be no talking or whis-
pering or gesturing of any sort. I don't care if you
have to shit—do it in line. Now, listen and move
when I call your name."

Fifty-two names were called out, slightly more
boys than girls, which left Cassie's group with a
decided female numerical superiority. Whether by
chance or what, Dar, Ivon, Suzl, and Nadya all
remained with Cassie's group, although Canty and
several other friends were split.

Now the roll was called for the remaining people,
just to make sure that everybody was in fact in the
correct group, and both were formed up into regular rows, four across for the smaller group, with
one straggler in the odd-numbered other group.
They were then told to extend their arms and
stand that far away from the person next to them,
which they did. There was the sound of clanking

metal from the doorway, and everyone in both groups stiffened.

The guards were quite efficient. First worn-looking collars of some cheap metal were placed around their necks, then tough rope of some unnatural-looking but extremely tough white material was passed through rings on either side of the collar until they were all linked together. More of the rope was then passed through other collar loops right to left, so that they were linked and secured in a cross-hatched pattern. Some adjustments were made for height, but not a lot of attention was paid to niceties that might make things more reasonable or comfortable. Now waistbands of similar metal were brought out and more of the strange rope was used to have them affix the waistbands as the neckbands were.

There were some attempts to miss loops, of course, but the guards were sharp-eyed and dealt with anyone causing trouble by pointing and shooting small hand-held pistols of some sort at the offenders, who received bloody welts where they were hit and screamed in agony. Few examples needed to be made.

Finally, it was done, and the final indignity was performed by a guard who used his pistol to melt and seal all the endings, effectively welding them into this incredible position. The officer of the guard stepped forward once more.

"Stretch yourself out so that both of your ropes are tight," he instructed. "*Keep 'em tight*! No slack. Some people have short legs, some long. Be responsible for your own ropes—the one across and the one directly in front of you. So long as you keep those ropes as tight as you can, you won't get into any trouble. If anybody isn't doing their part, one of us will deal with that person. If anybody falls, you are not, repeat, not to stop, but to yell out for help. Those of you in the lead, you will match the pace of the sergeant of the guard. You will move when we tell you, stop *instantly* if commanded to do so. Now, let's practice."

Cassie was unprepared for the wrenching motion that twisted her around as they began, and there were many people stumbling and falling. The officer and sergeant yelled and screamed and cursed and made all sorts of comments, yet seemed to have almost infinite patience and self-assurance that, sooner or later, they would get it down pat. They did not. Finally, the officer sighed, and brought out a chest of leg manacles. These, however, were not strung together with rope but with rigid telescoping rods that could be adjusted, then locked into position.

Again they practiced, and this time the rods, running only front to back on both legs, acted like pistons. When those in front moved their left legs forward, those farther back had no choice but to do the same. For most it was a terribly unnatural gait, but after what seemed like hours of marching they managed some semblance of order. At least nobody was likely to fall down.

The rods could be twisted to telescope, revealing a ball joint that allowed them to sit, so long as they just about hugged their knees, and it was only after a number of perfect marches that they were allowed the luxury. By the end of the day they ached all over, yet they were never released and, in fact, were fed in line—some sort of tasteless meat cake, a small stale loaf of bread, and some fruit juice. That last was the most welcome, and they downed it eagerly.

It contained, of course, more of the previous day's hypnotic drug, as many, including Cassie, had suspected, but none of them cared. The thirst could not be denied, and at least the stuff made all the aches and pains seem to disappear.

After the drug had taken effect, the guard moved

rapidly, ordering them to their feet and affixing the rods in place once again. Again they marched, but this time corrective measures were easily implemented. To Cassie, as to them all, the most important thing in the world, the *only* thing that mattered, was keeping a perfect pace with the ropes taut.

And, with that, the large doors to the gym were opened, and both groups were marched out, down a corridor, and out through a delivery entrance into the back of Temple Square.

The chill was still in the air, and there was a light, misty rain. It had obviously rained far harder in the hour or two preceding their exit, for it was quite wet. Night had fallen, but police were posted at all intersections to block off the curious as the sad marchers passed. Once out of the city the roads were unpaved, and the rain had turned them into a sea of thick, gooey mud, although the type of dirt used and the stone mixture in it did not make it particularly slippery, only messy.

The sergeant of the guard knew his stuff, and kept the pace exactly right, also sensing what they could not—when they had to break—and halting them at regular intervals. Each time they were given cups of juice that contained drug boosters. Finally, near dawn, they were marched into a field guarded from view on all sides by thick trees and halted, fed, and given a different drink. Within minutes of finishing, all had lapsed into the deepest sleep they had ever known.

They slept through the day, but when they awakened near dark they were all so wracked with tremendous pains through their bodies that they almost fought to drink the hypnotic that would take that pain away, and the pattern repeated.

They continued to move only after dark, thus avoiding meeting very many curious onlookers or creating the kind of crowd that always seemed to materialize around accidents, and thanks to the drugs and the preset pace one time seemed to merge into another, until they had completely lost track of how long they had been marching. It was certain, though, that the distance was over a hundred kilometers from the capital to the west gate, and their pace was quite deliberate but slow. In a sense the entire period seemed like some sort of hazy nightmare in which there was only the clanking, the occasional chanting and commands of the guards, and the single set of purposes. *Keep the ropes taut. Keep the pace exactly. . . .*

The most curious thing, for those able to think about it at all, was that, after a while, they awoke with less and less pain and linked up and marched with perfect adjustment without being told.

And then, late one night, they reached the west gate, the high fortified wall stretching out into the darkness on both sides of them, its inner guard walkway illuminated by torches every few meters. The whole structure, including the gate structure itself, was made of solid stone. The wall was four meters thick, with a stone guard station every fifty meters around the entirety of the Anchor. The gate added another three meters on each side, and had a headquarters building on top. The inner gates were of solid steel, a third of a meter thick themselves, and it took an entire team of mules just to turn the mechanism to open or close them. Inside was a passage called, with good reason, the Deathway: a stone opening through the wall that had its own small openings from which guards could not only monitor anyone and anything inside but fire upon it as well.

Above, just inside the gates on both sides, hung a heavy steel portcullis held up on a winch. A single kick of a lever by any guard could cause both to drop, imprisoning anyone inside who managed to jam the gates. The gates themselves were on a clever mechanism that had the outer gates always open if the inner ones were closed and vice-versa. It was said that vats of boiling hot oil could be unleashed in the Deathway with the same ease as dropping the portcullis.

The officer and sergeant of the guard halted them, then rode forward to the gate itself. There they were met by other uniformed border guards and there was a long conversation. Then there were some shouts, men ran one way or another, then a single shouted signal, and, slowly, the massive closed gates began to open.

It was a dramatic event in and of itself, but as they opened more and more a figure was revealed framed between them. It was the stringer Matson, on his white horse, idly smoking a cigar.

As soon as there was clearance he eased his mount slowly forward, then approached the sad-looking column, stopping here and there but taking a ride completely around the group. He mumbled something to himself and then rode back over to the guards watching him.

"A pretty miserable-looking lot," he commented sourly. "You could have at least sized them to make it easier."

The officer shrugged. "Not my problem. After ten days with 'em on the trail seasoning them up for you on the juice, I ain't too particular about anything except gettin' rid of 'em. You don't like their condition, *you* take the next batch out from the city."

Matson snorted. "That *ain't* my responsibility," he responded sarcastically. "How well seasoned are they?"

"Meekest group in years," the officer told him. "Hardly any trouble at all. Today they were barely on the juice at all and they made the best time of the trip. You could take them ropes and rods off now and I bet they'd keep perfect distance and interval and even sit just right. Ain't but a handful complained about any aches or pains when they woke up today, either. Some of 'em got real good leg muscles, even the women, and they're all in better shape than they ever been in their lives. 'Cept in the head,'' he added.

Matson nodded, a sour expression on his face. "Okay, then, get those damned rods off and remove the strings. I can't take 'em through all at once, you know.''

"You got to sign for them first,'' the officer reminded him. An orderly who had been standing nearby brought up a clipboard with pen attached. Matson took it and looked over the forms carefully. They matched the ones he was carrying in his head.

"All present, if you want to count 'em,'' the officer assured him.

"I already *have* counted them, and checked their general condition,'' the stringer replied curtly. He scribbled a signature on the sheet. "All right—let's get 'em over to my side.''

It was a strange experience to have the leggings and ropes removed. It had been such a seemingly endless time with them that their removal seemed almost an unnatural, out-of-balance thing to the exiles. The drug used, which was occasionally used for religious indoctrinations and retreats by the church and by guards in basic training, was quite a powerful conditioner. Highly repetitive actions performed over a sustained period were reinforced a hundredfold or more each time, and they had been almost continuously under for more than ten days. The officer was not exaggerating—freed of all linkages, they all still stood as if bound, and guards had to actually restrain the rear part of the party to keep it from following the first group through the gates and in the Deathway.

Matson went with the first group so he could

effectively reassemble them on the other side. The inner gate slowly closed, and, as it did, the outer gate opened to reveal a large, brightly lit tent city crowded with strange and misshapen creatures. This area, technically referred to as the Anchor apron, was as close as most from the Flux were ever allowed into Anchor. Beyond the apron, barely visible in the darkness and reflecting none of the light from wall or apron, was the Flux itself.

7

FLUX

It really wasn't until they had been fed, bedded down, and slept for some time that their senses started to return to them. Cassie awoke with a strangely disoriented feeling, not quite understanding where she was or what had happened. Opening her eyes and looking around only helped slightly, for the sights of the tent city and its milling throngs of very strange human beings and very scruffy animals did little to orient her or the others. It was only when she looked up and saw the Flux before her, then turned and saw the great wall and gate behind, that she understood exactly what was going on.

It took a moment more to realize that the leggings, rods, and even the ropes were now gone, although the collar and waistband remained, the latter hanging rather loosely on her hips. Her muscles ached, but not with the terrible pain of the first—what, days?—out. They had just been used to their maximum, pressed to their limits, and were letting her know it.

All of these discomforts were minor compared to seeing the Flux—and from outside the gates. It was a terrifying sight, even more than it had been when she'd stood on top of that wall back there as a young schoolchild and stared at it.

There was no difference, really, between the apron and the Anchor itself. The wall had been built well in from the Flux boundary for a number of reasons, some practical and some superstition. There was grass here, and well-worn paths, and it felt quite normal. Still, the Flux lay just beyond.

It rose upwards as far as the eye could see, blocking off the sky and everything else from view. It looked like a great, infinite wall of opaque glass, a light reddish tan in color, and it *shimmered* something like an early morning fog in the fields. Inside there seemed to be tiny little flashes of energy, so small they would not even be noticed in isolation but so numerous that they could not be ignored. The overall effect was of a smooth wall or container holding a mass of fog-shrouded, moving sequined material.

There were a number of grumbles and groans as the group slowly awoke to the new day and the same realizations that Cassie had felt. They had very little time to socialize, though, for Matson, looking sharp in his black outfit, hat, boots, and with his shotgun, knife, and whip on his belt, strode over to them from a nearby tent.

"All right—everybody up on their feet!" he ordered. "We're going to have a little orientation talk and then you'll get food and drink but with no drugs to help you along. That part's over. And don't give me any trouble or any shit or I'll skip food and water in your case for starters, and once we're in the Flux you'll wish you'd never been born."

There was no problem now. They were too scared to do much more than obey. Scared—and curious.

"All right. Now, my name's Matson and I own you. Yeah, I know that sounds funny, but it's literally and legally true. You stopped being people when your numbers got drawn. Now, that means that there's no place to run, no appeals, no protection. I'm the law, the absolute authority and if I don't like you I can do anything I want with you and I don't even have to have much of a reason. If I wake up in a bad mood and decide that the first two of you I see will have their arms chopped off because I feel like it, that's the way it'll be. You remember that. And you remember, too, that anybody who gives me lip can have his or her tongue cut out with a gesture from me and I won't even lose any sleep over it. Do you understand?"

There were a few mumbled assents. The rest had progressed in one short moment from being scared to being terrified.

Matson looked slightly peeved. "When I talk to you as a group I expect to be answered by the group. Now, let's try that again. Do you understand me?"

"Yes," came an almost uniform response.

"When you talk to me you call me 'sir' always. Now, what was that again?"

"Yes, SIR!" they responded.

"Louder! Sometimes it's hard to hear in the Flux, so shout everything, you understand?"

"YES, SIR!" they screamed at him.

He nodded. "That's better. All right. Let's start with the apron here. Those people that you see are Flux people. They usually live in the Flux, except when they have business here, although some of them are permanent residents of the aprons, dealing in goods and services for stringers like me. Just in case you never heard the term before, they are called duggers. Duggers are one kind of group that lives in the Flux. Forget that bullshit they sold you in school and church—the Flux is full of life, and death, and is anything but empty. In fact, a lot of stuff that keeps the Anchors going comes from Fluxlands. Anchors trade for the stuff, and what they trade is often information or services, but is also people. You, to be exact, in this case."

He paused to let that sink in.

"Now, you may wonder why the hell the Flux needs people. Part of the reason is that it's a pretty hard, violent place compared to Anchors. They have a very high death rate. The odds are that your own lives will be short, but don't let that upset you too much. There are still a lot of folks out there who live to ripe old ages, and some who live so long they seem almost immortal. Children are born in the Flux, too, but the infant mortality rate is very high, and the odds are against somebody growing to adulthood there. Again, that doesn't mean everybody. I was born in the Flux, and I've lived more than twice as long as any of you."

Again he paused, looking at their faces to see how they were taking it.

"Okay, then. Right now you're imagining some wild, savage kind of Anchor or something. Well, forget it. In fact, if you want to stay alive, forget every single bit of science or logic that you were ever taught. All that applies only to Anchors. In fact, that is the real difference between Anchor and Flux.

"In Anchors, everything's following a clearly defined set of natural laws. You drop a stone, it falls at a specific rate to the ground thanks to gravity. That's a good example. In the Flux, there are no natural laws. None. There *are* standard conditions—what we call 'default conditions,' but those exist only where not modified. You will not go floating into the air. You will be able to breathe it, and the temperature is rather warm although usually extremely dry. But these are all defaults, not fixed conditions. They are subject to change. You can take *nothing* for granted in the Flux. Nothing.

"Now—what changes these conditions? Well, the fact is, the Flux is as you see it over there. That's the default, too. A big nothing. What looks like fog, though, isn't fog at all—it's energy. The Flux *does* obey one natural law—energy can neither be created nor destroyed, but it *can* be changed. When you put a match to oil in a lamp you let out the energy in the oil. When you were in the city, though, you saw electric lights and powered gadgets. That power came from turning some matter, some solid stuff, into energy. You can do that in the Flux, too—but there you can also do it backwards!"

That caught some of them off balance. Those who had been able to follow things so far tried to figure out his last comment and fit it in, the others just stood there trying to look like they understood it all.

"What that means," he went on, "is that energy, what you see back there, can be changed into matter. Solid things. If you're good enough, or smart enough, you can do almost anything there. Those who can totally control it are like gods. In fact, some of 'em think they *are* gods and act like it, too. We call 'em wizards—master magicians. They really *do* have the power of gods in the Flux, and they run things. They're the ones who created the Fluxlands, the independent places in the Flux, and they run them like gods as well. Watch out for them.

"As for the rest, there are those who have varying degrees of skill in manipulating the Flux. Some of 'em are what we call false wizards. They, say, turn you into a bird. *You* think you're a bird, and everybody else thinks you're a bird, and when you jump into the air off the cliff you and everybody else thinks you're flying. But you're still you, and you can't fly, so you crash and die. Watch out for the false wizards. In their own way they're more dangerous than the real ones."

He looked them over, then allowed a half-smile to come over his face. He knew they didn't understand much of it, and probably the ones that did didn't believe a word of it, but that was okay. This lecture would come in handy when they saw the reality of Fluxlands.

"Now, within the next day we'll be going into the Flux itself," he told them. "You'll be on my strings, but relatively free and loose. It might be possible for somebody to escape." He turned back towards his tent. "Jomo! Kolada! Front and center!"

From the direction of the tents came two creatures that probably were human once. One of them, Jomo, must have weighed a hundred and fifty kilos or more, but that was not what struck anyone who looked at him. His face was a mottled, misshapen mass with the standard features barely recognizable in it. His hands were massive, clawlike things that seemed useless for grasping much, and his shoeless feet were enormous caricatures of what feet should be. He looked, in fact, very much like Cassie's vision of a troll from the old children's stories. He wore only a skirt-like rag fastened by a crude belt.

Kolada was even worse. It was hard to tell if the creature was male or female. It was tall and humanoid, but its entire body was covered by tremendously thick brown hair including the face, from which gaped an animal-like mouth with two fangs rising up from the lower jaw and a pair of blood-red eyes that seemed to shine with an inhuman fury. Its arms were so long that they just about reached the ground, terminating in two huge paw-like hands.

"These two duggers are my chief driver and my point guard," Matson told them. "To answer your question even though you haven't asked, both are, or were, human just like you. Both, at different times, escaped from stringer trains into the Flux. Anybody who does that and either has no natural power over it or doesn't run into somebody who

lives there will be dead quickly, for there's no food
and water you don't make yourself in the void, nor
any way at all to get your bearings to know where
you are, where you've been, and where you're going.
Only stringers and wizards know their position in
the Flux, and we make certain that nobody else
ever finds out how we do it. No dugger can do it,
and they try all the time.

"Now, if you're wondering what happened, both
of them *did* run into others, but they ran into
different sorts. Jomo has a little of the real Flux
power, you see, but no control. We've all got our
little fears and insanities in the back of our minds.
Well, see what Jomo's do to him. He doesn't
always look like this. Sometimes he looks worse,
occasionally better. Kolada, on the other hand,
ran into somebody with real power in the Flux,
somebody who was very, very dangerous. In a story
far too long to go into here, that person changed a
nice, normal Anchor woman into the creature you
see here. And, because it was a wizard, she's absolutely stuck like this unless somebody even more
powerful changes her, for she has no Flux powers
at all.

"Most of the people on the apron, the duggers,
have similar stories. They're all quite mad and
they've all been changed in one way or another by
wizards or their own minds. But they're the rare
lucky ones. They survived in the Flux, and, after a
while, they signed on with stringers like me and
have about as much security and stability as it's
possible to have in there—and some independence.
In the Flux, most people more or less belong to
other people, because whoever has the most power
over the Flux can control everybody below them.
Duggers belong to no one except themselves. These
people work for me and they get paid for it. Now,
if anybody wants to take a risk on surviving long
enough to become a dugger, now you've seen what

duggers are like, you just escape. That's it. Get some food over there at the big tent and come back here to eat."

They went in orderly silence. The earlier lecture hadn't had much effect, but the duggers had, and as they entered the apron camp and saw that Matson's "employees" were among the least exotic variations around, the effect was greatly enhanced. The whole place was a terrible, crawling creep show. Most had little appetite when they returned to their grassy spot.

The small group reformed for the first time since back in the gym, but they were a sober lot.

"Did you see that one that looked like a squirmy, squishy thing?" Nadya asked, shivering a bit.

"And how about the one with the wavy things coming out of its head?" Ivon added.

"I think I've seen more than I want to right now," Cassie put in. "I don't need to catalog it. It's tough enough to eat now, and I was *starving* ten minutes ago."

They nodded agreement, but most managed to get something down nonetheless. At least the food was palatable—some sort of warm meat and vegetable pies and a very sweet cake, with some sort of wine that was not at all sweet but a good thirst-quencher. Ultimately, though, the conversation returned to their own fates, past and future. They talked about their long drugged march, and compared aches, pains, and bruises, as well as leg muscles which were pretty outstanding, even on the girls. Finally, it was Nadya who noticed. "Hey— what happened to the other group?"

They all looked around. Sure enough, there was no sign of the first group, the one that was to go with the other stringer. Jomo, who was looking to the mules grazing nearby, heard, turned, and in a gruff, barely human voice, said, "They go before you wake up with Missy Arden. They well into Flux now."

Rather than be startled by the dugger's attention, they all turned and looked towards the imposing Flux itself. The void, Matson had called it. The void between the Fluxlands. After a while they snapped out of it and attention turned to the future, although it was mixed with a little caution. Jomo had accomplished his main purpose of letting them know that they were being overheard.

"What do you think is going to happen to us?" Dar asked at last. "I mean, once we go—in there?"

Cassie sighed. "I don't know, but it doesn't sound very promising, does it?"

"Do you buy this magic business?" Ivon put in. "Sounds like those crazy old stories to me."

"I think he's telling the truth. Some of it, anyway," Suzl opined. "If what he was saying was true about the Flux energies, then it's very possible to have magic and a whole little set of mini-godhoods. The only thing I can't figure out is why some people have the power and others, probably most, do not. It seems to be something you're born with, anyway, if the story of Jomo is right, not something you learn or get from your parents, although practice probably makes you better and better."

Nadya looked worried. "They have made a lot of changes in us, you know, so I can see how that might be taken further. I wonder, though, if they can change your mind like they can change your looks?"

"They can do it with drugs and conditioning in Anchor," Cassie pointed out, "so why not in Flux as well? What's really odd, though, is that the changes seem to be so real, so permanent. I mean, if it was just in Flux, then these people would change back to their old selves here in Anchor, right? They didn't. That means to me that we've got some real trouble in there. Anything they did to us in Anchor can be changed around in Flux, but anything done to you in Flux is *permanent*."

Nadya looked at the Flux. "A world of magicians, madmen—and slaves. It's horrible."

Cassie thought of the Sister General, the machines, the Paring Rite, and Lani's catalog of terrible drugs, and could only wonder just how different it was from Anchor Logh after all. In a way, it just might be a more direct, more honest and open version of the world from which they had come.

It took quite some time to form the stringer train, and it was an impressive affair. There were twenty mules, all loaded down with things in large packs, as well as two horse-drawn wagons driven by duggers. Between the mules and the wagons Matson placed his human cargo, four abreast in familiar pattern, and linked together with common thin rope of the sort used on farms for clotheslines. He had expertly reformed and sized them so that the shortest were in front and would thus set the pace. The lines were then tied off to the last pair of mules ahead of them. None of the lines were intended to keep anyone captive, it was pointed out to them, but merely to give some logical distribution to the train and set a logical pace. It was also their lifeline, Matson added, for it was very, very easy to get lost in the Flux, and with a train this size, even with a dozen or more duggers managing it, it would not be possible to keep an eye on all parts of it at once.

All the duggers were mounted on horses except the impressive Jomo, who preferred being on foot, the better to get wherever he needed in the mule train. They noticed that Matson and all the duggers had small bugles or some similar instrument on their saddles or in their belts. These, it turned out, were the means of communication along the train, and each stringer had his own private codes so that none could easily trick him with false signals.

After the train had been completely assembled,

Matson rode slowly all the way down it from front to back on one side, then back up to the front on the other, stopping occasionally, shouting orders to adjust or fix this or that, positioning and repositioning people and things. This went on for some time until he was completely satisfied and then rode quickly up to the front and stopped. He unclipped his bugle from his saddle, raised it to his lips, and, turning back, blew a series of sharp notes of differing length and pitch, repeating the same pattern three times. The duggers on the wagons to the rear returned a slightly different signal twice, and they saw the hairy creature called Kolada suddenly ride forward and vanish into the Flux at full gallop. They waited then another minute or two, then Matson gave one last, long blast on his horn which was returned by all of the other duggers. The train began to move forward, towards the Flux.

Dar and Ivon were both big men, so they were well back in the group, but Nadya, Cassie, and Suzl had maneuvered themselves to be near one another, being only slightly different in height, and Matson had allowed it. They began to walk towards that huge, shimmering wall.

"Here we go," Cassie muttered under her breath. First Matson vanished into the stuff, followed by Jomo and his mules. As the great Flux region came ever closer, they all felt themselves stiffen, felt an urge to break and run, but duggers on both sides kept shouting and growling curses at them and they slowed and staggered a bit but went on. The first rows went in and essentially vanished from view, then it was Cassie's row and they were through before they even realized it.

They entered an eerie world such as none of them had ever known before.

There are a few times in everyone's life when they feel totally and completely helpless, at the mercy of fate. The bull that suddenly appears out of nowhere and charges when it's fifty meters to the nearest fence. The time when you're patching the roof and grab frantically for something to break the fall, only nothing's there. Cassie and the others felt that way now, which is why even the roughest and most boisterous of them were meek and quiet through this experience. They were caught in the web of deceit in Anchor Logh and now they were tethered and bound together by the stringer's spidery lines.

The effect of suddenly entering the Flux was too much for some who had endured so much. Somebody screamed, somebody else started sobbing hysterically, as they were pulled, helplessly, by the mules away from the Anchor that was all the reality they'd ever known, away from all that was safe and sane and real, into the terrible, shimmering void.

There was a sensation of dry heat, like being in an oven that had not yet quite warmed up to intolerable temperatures. The raw Flux was around them all now, producing an odd, slightly tingling sensation that was more eerie-feeling than uncomfortable.

There was also a terrible absence of sensation. It was dead quiet in a way that simply could not exist in Anchor, the only sounds those of the train itself, and even those beyond the immediate people in front and back seemed curiously damped or muffled. The air, too, was perfectly still and had none of the odors that were always present in normal air. No scent of grass, or the very subtle fragrances of things you never even knew were there until they were gone. The effect was to heighten the sense of smell of everyone in the group, but the only source for that was the now very pungent body odor that was already hard to take even back on the apron.

Nor had Matson been exaggerating when he warned them that they would have no sense of direction in the Flux. Every direction looked exactly like every other direction, and there were no landmarks, no markers of any sort. Even the ground was more sensed than seen; it felt slightly soft and spongy, and visually, they and the train walked as spirits through empty air on a surface that was totally invisible and indistinguishable from the air around them. It was extremely disorienting, and only the solidity of something underfoot, seen or not, allowed them to keep their balance. It was still better, they found, if you didn't look down.

The duggers on either side of the train dropped back in alternation, checking on the marching lines. They seemed somehow different now, far less deformed if no less mad, and they seemed to radiate an air of comfortable confidence. This was their element, and they were comfortable with it.

Some of them still slobbered and drooled and made bizarre, often animal-like sounds, but they never seemed to look the same way twice. For a while Cassie thought they might be different people. She soon made a sort of game of it, something to occupy her mind in the midst of the terrible nothingness, watching the one nearest her on her side as best she could. The dugger seemed almost hunchbacked one time, then ramrod straight the next. The creature went from fat to thin, almost but not quite while you were looking at it. One time she was sure she saw a beard on the dugger, yet the next time it went by it seemed clean-shaven and even had rather formidable breasts. The clothes, too, so tattered and filthy on the apron, seemed to undergo changes in color, design, and newness. It was both frightening and confusing. The horse, though, seemed solidly real.

Matson was unchanged through it all, but in constant motion, riding up and down, back and forth, making certain that all was going well. He was all business and he had no patience with anyone or anything that was out of step. Once in a while, of course, somebody in the group would become disoriented and slip, and there would be a yell from those around, a blast from the nearest dugger's bugle, and this would bring everything to a stop as the blast was echoed by all—and bring Matson at full and angry gallop. Maybe nobody else knew where they were, but he did, and he had a schedule he wanted to keep.

It was strange, though, that gallop, and those of the dugger horses. The horse was making no sound as its hooves struck invisible ground, although you could hear the great beast breathing hard and the sounds of saddle and rider.

Suddenly, in the row in front of her, one girl stepped in some mule droppings, slipped, and fell. There was the yell, the bugles, the very efficient stop, and here came Matson. He stopped and looked down at the fallen girl in disgust.

"We can't keep having this," he said, mostly to himself. "You! Get up—*now!*"

The girl gaped at him, then broke down and started sobbing, but she simply couldn't bring herself to her feet. Matson spat, gave a disgusted sigh, and made a casual gesture in her direction with his hand.

Energy flew from that hand in a pencil-thin line, striking the girl in the head, and she screamed in terrible agony. Just as quickly as it had appeared, the beam was gone, and the victim almost collapsed in relief. Matson waited a moment, then asked, casually, "Want me to do it again?"

"No! Please! I—"

Another, very brief jolt was sent. "Please *what?*"

"P—Please, sir!"

He nodded. "Now get up and resume your place

in line. You just had your warning. Next time it gets tough."

"That son of a bitch," some boy in the back muttered loudly. "One day I'll kill the bastard for that."

The stringer's head shot up, and his eyes seemed to glisten. "Well, well, well. . . . The gallant tough guy standing up for the little lady. How chivalrous. Trouble with chivalry, boy, is that then you got to make good on it." He rode back several rows and looked directly at the offending boy, although it was impossible to see how he could have identified the speaker. "I don't want to break you, son, because my customers are buying that spirit of yours, but I think I'll put a mark on you so I can remember you."

Cassie found it hard to turn around and see properly without twisting the line, but she managed, as did most of them forward of the incident. She remembered the face of the boy Matson was confronting—he'd been the strong one with the "brain of a cabbage" they were talking about as some sort of soldier.

Matson seemed to concentrate a moment, then he fixed his eyes intently on the outspoken boy. Energy flashed and coalesced around him, but only for a few seconds, and then vanished. The watching duggers chuckled, and those among the exiles who didn't scream either gasped or gaped.

The boy was in every way the same as he'd been from the shoulders down, but above that point he now had the perfectly proportioned head of a mule. The mule-mouth opened to say something, but only a mule's bray came out. His hands went up and felt along his neck and head, and you could feel the horror in his body movements.

"What I can do I can also undo, punk," Matson told him. "You give me no more trouble and I *might* be able to remember what your head used to look like and give it back to you. Any time you make threats in the Flux to *anybody* you be sure you can back 'em up all the way. There's worse things than being dead." He moved forward on his horse and looked again at the girl whose fall had precipitated it all. "Now, little lady, if you can't hack the pace, I can always use another pack mule. That's how I got most of the ones I'm using now anyway. Time is money, and I don't have much use for somebody who can't make the grade." With that he raised his bugle, gave his command notes, and the train started forward once more through the void.

"It's *impossible*!" somebody muttered, and it was what the others were thinking. "It can't be real! It just *can't* be!"

"It's magic, that's what it is," a girl said worriedly. "He's an evil wizard back in his own foul home."

Matson was all the way forward again before he allowed himself a self-satisfied grin. The challenge had come very early this time, and he was glad of it. The earlier you acted, and the earlier you used your little bag of parlor tricks, the less trouble you had later on. That mule-head alone would hold them for a while. Like most stringers he was a false wizard, a weaver of totally convincing illusions, but they were good enough for kids like this. He liked to imagine what it would be like to be a *real* wizard, but he always had doubts. He liked to think that he'd still be a stringer, but you never could tell what that kind of power would do to any human.

8

CULT

After a while, the monotony of the void replaced any sense of fear or awe in their minds over the Flux. Their fear was still real, of course, and focused partly on their unknown fates and partly on their fear of Matson's frightening powers.

Every few hours they would break from their slow but steady pace and get something to eat. One of the wagons in the rear had a sort of mini-kitchen in it, and while the meals were not very tasty nor varied they were nutritious and filling, and everyone, Matson included, ate the same thing. The other wagon contained an enormous quantity of hay in small bales which were apportioned out to the mules by the ever-doting Jomo. It was clear that part of Matson's mania for a schedule once they started out was due to a tight supply allowance.

There was little trouble with the group after the initial episodes with Matson. If anybody had any rebellious thoughts they had only to look at the poor fellow trying to get the stew down his mule's throat to think the better of it.

Once she'd gotten over the initial shock of the magical transformation, however, Cassie could see some hope in it as well. "Look," she pointed out to Nadya and Suzl, "if he can just wave his hands and make somebody half-mule, then nothing is permanent here. Nothing. That means we might have hair again, for example, and those poor girls with the body tattoos might one day look as good as they ever did. Maybe better."

"Or worse," the gloomier Nadya responded. "All we've seen coming out of this Flux are monsters of one kind or another. These duggers, the mule head, that sort of thing. Maybe our new masters, who-ever and whatever they are, just want us as raw material for animals or something. Matson, re-member, said some of his mules were once human."

"Maybe," Cassie admitted, "but I think it can work both ways. All we can do is hope right now."

"I just wish we'd get somewhere," Suzl put in. "I'm sick and tired of this march, march, march. Good or bad, I want to just get it over with. A day or two more of this and I might turn into one of those drooling slobberers myself."

They all pretty much felt that way, but the train's progress was slow and steady, the sleep periods seemingly dictated by Matson's feeling of how tired the marchers were and Jomo's feel of when the horses and mules needed rest. Time seemed to have lost its meaning for them all, although Matson, who carried an elaborate pocket watch, seemed to know exactly *when* as well as where they were. For the rest of them, the "days" were measured only by sleep breaks and were broken down by feeding periods. It never seemed to get completely dark or completely light in the Flux, so there was no way at all to guess what it might be in "real" time.

They were five "days" into the Flux when the first break in the monotony came. They were pro-ceeding normally after a meal break when sud-denly a horse and rider appeared ahead of them and closed on Matson. He ordered the train to a halt and waited as the rider neared and stopped. It was the animal-like Kolada.

Kolada rode the "point," which meant she was often well ahead of the train, perhaps half a day ahead, following some sort of route mark that stringers had laid down but which few were given the power to see or read. Whatever the news it wasn't good, for there were sudden bugle signals of a type they had not heard before and the duggers whipped into action with a frenzy. All strings on mules and people were suddenly dropped, and the mules themselves were led into a circular pattern with the wagons at opposite ends closing each circle. Cinches were loosened, so that the packs formed a crude outer barrier around the mules. The duggers took out their weapons and checked them, then set up patrols both inside and outside the circle. The human cargo was loosed inside the circle and told just to sit.

Jomo took charge of the entire party, moving very fast for a huge man and giving orders in a combination of words and gestures to the other duggers. Matson took one of the duggers with him, leaving ten mounted and one afoot to guard the train, and the three of them went off at full gallop in the direction from which Kolada had just come.

None of the duggers would pay any attention to the fifty-four confused and frightened young people unless they got out of line, in which case the offender was rudely struck with fist or rifle butt. In more than one way this frightened them still more, if only because, no matter what Matson's disposition or powers were, he was human and a known quantity. Now they were completely at the mercy of these animalistic creatures.

They spent a nervous hour or more sitting there, talking low and speculating a lot, until there was a sudden shout from one of the duggers ahead and they heard bolts slide into place and the whole crew tense up.

It was Matson, though, and they relaxed. He

rode up to Jomo and talked for some time, and they could see from the look on his face that there was something up ahead that had considerably shaken the iron man. His face looked almost dead white, and, if anything, he looked twenty years older.

He talked in low, clipped sentences to Jomo, who nodded and then gave a series of signals. Rapidly, the train was reassembled in a loose manner, with the duggers spacing themselves out and keeping guns at the ready. Although they ran the strings back along the mules, they only ran one string on each side back from the mules to the wagons, leaving the young people free inside this makeshift boundary. With a few quick bugle blasts, the train began to move.

It was a good hour or more before they reached the spot, but this was a different sort of march, tinged with danger and excitement. Many of the young people actually welcomed the diversion, but Cassie, along with many others, did not. It was like approaching an accident on the main highway from a distance. You wanted to see what was going on but you knew that when you got there you would find nothing good.

The scene was one of almost inconceivable carnage, the most horrible sight any of them had ever seen. Clearly the mess, spread out almost as far as the eye could see, had once been a stringer train not unlike their own, but one that had been hit with a deadly ferocity by some overwhelming force. There was blood all over, human blood mixing with that of animals, and dead bodies strewn all over the landscape. If you looked hard enough, it was possible to see that this had once been a formation similar to the one they'd assumed back a ways, but it had proved totally inadequate for whatever had hit them.

Matson had recovered some of his composure

and came back to the group. He took a deep breath, then said, "All right. Now you see it. I told you this was a rough place, and now you see how rough it can get. I'm telling you this because I'm going to need your cooperation to go through that mess and see what, if anything, can be salvaged and what we can learn about the bastards who did this. You're going to need a strong stomach for two reasons, so anybody who just can't handle it can remain here or come back here when it gets too much for you. One reason is that it's even uglier than you can tell from here. Some of the animals and people have been partly—eaten."

The group stiffened almost collectively at this.

"The second reason is that this was—oh, hell, it was the other train from Anchor Logh that should have been a day or more ahead of us. You will know or recognize some of those bodies."

Some gasps, chokes, and sobs began from various parts of the group at this news. Matson didn't wait for it to subside.

"Now, not everybody is here, that's clear. That's one reason I need your help. If there's anybody you know who was in that train whose remains aren't there now, I want to know about it. We're only another hard day's ride from help, and if we know who to look for we might be able to save them. Also, whoever did this is still around. This happened only a matter of hours ago at best, from the state of the remains. We have to act fairly quickly, because the Flux tends to break down dead organic matter pretty quickly. I need to keep the duggers armed and on guard, so it's up to you. Volunteers?"

A dozen or so hands went up, including Cassie's, and he nodded and told them to come forward. They did, and walked straight into Hell itself.

Assuming the same size train, more than half the mules had been killed, the rest run off with the attackers. All of the remaining packs had been thoroughly ransacked, with the unwanted part of their contents just strewn about haphazardly. Both wagons had caught fire and been rendered useless, but it was clear that some of the contents there had been salvaged and probably loaded on the remaining mules—and, perhaps, on the backs of the survivors.

All of the human bodies were stripped naked if they hadn't been to begin with, but it was easy to tell the duggers from the other group of exiles by their shape if nothing else. It was a stomach-churning chore to gather up all those bodies and lay them out so they could be potentially identified and counted. Several times members of the party suddenly felt sick; a few threw up, a few more finally ran back to the rest, but were quickly replaced by others whose curiosity or consciences now prodded them.

Most of the victims had been shot, some several times, but others were run through with arrows or spears. Some who had obviously been only wounded when the train was overrun had been put to death, most often by beheading but occasionally by slow dismemberment, the horror still on their faces. Many of bodies had been chewed, with huge chunks of flesh just ripped from them, but it was unclear just what had done the chewing. What *was* clear was that whoever had overrun the train had been human, and probably in numbers far larger than the train's defenders.

Still, laid out, the bodies included some that could not be accounted for by duggers or exiles. These, too, had been treated just as harshly as the others, but they were clearly from some different place entirely.

For one thing, they resembled duggers but had some regularity to their dehumanizing aspects. They were mostly very tall, chunky females reminiscent of the kind that became Temple wardens, but all had undergone animalistic metamorphosis that might show madness on the part of the perpetrator but at least showed some conscious planning.

The most obvious thing was that they all had thick heads of hair that apparently hadn't been cut in years. The shortest hair length was below the waist. Their fingers seemed unnaturally long, too, and terminated in very long, thick, sharp claws. Some of the bodies seemed covered from the waist down in very short fur with animalistic patterns and colorations, almost horse-like in texture and appearance, and all of these had tails resembling various animals—rabbit, horse, cat, they were all represented. Perhaps the most striking thing was their faces, though, with bushy, oddly upturned brows, and pink animal-like noses over mouths that seemed abnormally wide and which contained oversized, slightly protruding canines.

Although in a state of shock over the carnage, Cassie couldn't resist questions. "What—what *are* they?" she asked Matson.

"People," he responded dryly. "Members of a cult. Looks like they got a fair number, too." This last was said without any sense of exhilaration or pleasure. Matson had been curiously more cold and withdrawn since they began, but there was no trace of meanness, authoritarianism, or any other emotional mannerism. He was either holding something in very deeply or forced upon himself a remarkable detachment for the scene.

"Cult?" she prompted, treating him less like the slave master than as just someone else to talk to.

He nodded. "Say you get a dugger type with some talent for the Flux who not only gets out here but can survive. He or she goes nuts, of course, but it's a crafty sort of nuts. Eventually these kind of people pick up other lost balls out here, maybe one day stumbling across a stringer train and catching a few escapees, something like that, or getting people trying to flee a Fluxland. This person gets 'em and imposes his particular kind of madness on them. They become his followers, his worshippers, his slaves—his playthings. If there's enough power available in the leader or in the collection they form a pocket in the Flux. A place where they can live and feed themselves. A real tiny little worldlet. They're around, usually near stringer trails, so they can sneak up and collect our garbage. This one is a lot more than that, though. There are few of 'em that can have the power to take on and lick a stringer train, and those few get known, we switch routes, and they wind up isolated. That's what's so weird about this one."

"Huh?"

"Arden was the best stringer I ever knew, bar none. It would take an army to do this much damage to one of her trains, and she had the biggest, meanest duggers you ever saw. That's them over there. Any cult big enough and smart enough to take her is big or smart enough to take a Fluxland. It just couldn't remain hidden this long, then show up here, on a trail with no previous trouble. Something smells here. Smells bad. *I want these bastards!*"

That last was said with such sudden force and emotion that she stepped back from him. Inside him, not too far from that totally businesslike surface, was an explosion she would not like to see directed at her, even unthinkingly.

She went over to where the bodies were being laid out. It was almost complete now, but she had to force herself to look at them. It was a sight that no church vision of Hell could equal. Those dead warriors from this strange cult—how animalistic were they inside? More than they were outside? If so, could *they* or their kind have ripped out those pieces of flesh with their jaws? It was horrible to contemplate, but there seemed no other conclusion. What kind of sickness could breed ones like those?

Jomo, ugly and primitive as he was, was the only dugger she didn't fear. He came over to her and frowned, the effect producing hundreds of ripples in his broad hairless forehead. "Saw you talkin' to Master Matson. Best you not if you know what good for you."

"Why? He didn't seem to mind."

Jomo looked over at the mass of corpses. "You see any you know in this bunch?"

She nodded. "Several."

Jomo pointed a stubby finger at one off by itself, the figure of a woman, head shaved—or what was left of it. Most of the body was a bloody mess. "That one not like you. That one Missy Arden. Great woman."

"Oh, I see. . . ."

"No, you not see at all! *Missy Arden carry Matson child!*"

Suddenly she understood, and felt foolish. Of course, it made sense, only she had not, frankly, thought of stringers as having sex, let alone children. They were like doctors, teachers, priestesses— when you met them in a store in town or maybe saw them in a public bathroom it was, somehow, shocking and unusual, as if they didn't do the sort of things real people did.

If Jomo was right, and he had no reason to lie, then Matson right now was at his most dangerous, and that could be as fearsome as these cult members.

"Coduro!" Matson bellowed, and a dugger on horseback reigned up, turned, and came over to him.

"Yeah, boss?"

"I give you my string," he said flatly. "Can you see it?"

The dugger looked startled. "Yeah! I—*can!*" It

seemed to awe him, although the others had no idea what was going on.

"You take the string to Persellus. We'll have some time because this cult or whatever it has to stash its booty. Maybe enough time for us, maybe not, but if you start now you should be able to avoid them. They might have a sentry or two just up the string, though, so be careful."

The dugger grinned, a sight that was in itself pretty gruesome to behold, and lifted his rifle. "I think maybe I like that."

"Well, don't let 'em bog you down, either. I want you in Persellus even if you have to kill your horse to do it, and you give the first important official you can meet the whole story. Tell 'em we're coming in, but also tell 'em the size and description of these bastards. We need protection to get in, even if I speed it up, and we better get this pest hole and eliminate it before *they* get strong enough and bold enough to make a try on Persellus. You tell 'em it's somebody with real wizard power. Tell 'em anything you want, but *get them here with a big force as soon as you can!*"

"Got'cha, boss. Rolling!" the dugger responded, then reared back on his horse and took off into the void which rapidly swallowed him up.

Matson walked back over to the mass of now neatly laid out bodies, and counted. Eleven of the beast-women, twelve duggers, Arden, of course, and twenty–nine refugees from Anchor Logh who would grow no older. He looked that last group over, then frowned and walked up and down between the bodies, nodding and mumbling to himself, then looked up and saw Cassie. "You!"

She was startled. "Yes, sir?"

"Notice anything funny about this group? Anything particular strike you?"

She frowned, coming over although she really didn't want to come near that terror again. Absently she looked down at one of the bodies and suddenly could not suppress a sob. "*Oh, Holy Angels! It's poor Canty!*" she managed.

Matson grunted, then took out and lit a cigar. "Cut the hysterics. We don't have time for it. I lost somebody close to me here, too. She's dead, and so's he. If you don't want us to be you'll put them behind you until you get a chance to do something about it and concentrate on us. Now, how many boys were in that Paring Rite shit?"

She fought back the tears as best she could. "Fifty," she told him.

He nodded. "And we have twenty-two in our group, so there were twenty-six in Arden's. We've got twenty-nine bodies from the other group here, and only three are female."

She snapped out of it and gasped. "And some of them were executed after they lost!"

He nodded. "Whoever our bastard is, he only likes the girls. All those fighters were women, and he took all the women while killing all the men. That sounds like Rory Montagne, but that son of a bitch doesn't have enough power for all this."

Despite Jomo's warning, and despite her own situation, she could not break away. It was obvious that, no matter what happened to her later, right now Matson needed a relatively sane human to talk to and she had more or less elected herself. "Who is this Rory Montagne?"

"A cult leader from way back, but thousands of kilometers from here. He's a woman-hater, and, therefore, a church-hater as well."

"Seems to me he *likes* women, maybe too much," she pointed out.

"Oh, no. His hatred of the church is so absolute that his mission in life is the capture, submission, and humiliation of women. Every woman represents the church to him, and every time one becomes his slave or plaything he's scored in his own warped mind. But—he never had this kind of strength or power before. They've been hunting him as long as I can remember, but he's always been a nuisance rather than a real threat. I can see why his attack was particularly savage, though. When he saw a woman stringer he just couldn't help himself." He paused for a moment, then seemed suddenly galvanized into action. "Can you ride a mule bareback?"

"I can ride anything with four legs," she assured him. "So can half of us."

Matson turned and called in the duggers. "We're going to fast march," he told them. "All speed. Cut loose all but totally essential cargo, and get the rest into the wagons. Toss what you have to. Spare rations only." They nodded and set to work. He turned back to Cassie. "Pick your best riders. I want two on each mule. Jomo is already cutting them loose and rigging basic bridles. The rest will cram into the two wagons and I don't care about comfort. I don't care how it's done, but everybody rides, understand?"

She nodded, then hesitated. "Uh—what about the bodies? Shouldn't we bury or cremate them or something?"

"No time. Doesn't matter, anyway. In a week the Flux will have absorbed them, and in a month the rest will be gone, too. Anything that doesn't move for any length of time goes back to energy. Don't stand and worry about those things. They're dead. Move it!"

She did. Four of the twenty mules still had to carry supplies, so that left sixteen available. She went back, not really explaining anything, and started making choices. She wanted the largest people on the mules, to make more room in the wagons, so most of the boys were paired up, and that took eleven of the mules. Reserving one for herself and, she decided, Nadya, she assigned the rest to the larger girls with some riding experience. That still left twenty-two people to fit someplace, and some food and hay had to remain in the wagons. She managed to get twelve in the cook's wagon, although very cramped and uncomfortably, but because of the bulk she only could get eight in the hay wagon. When she could get no volunteers among the girls to sit next to the driving duggers, who were the worst sort of the lot, she pulled Ivon and the poor fellow with the mule's head off their mounts, replaced them with girls, and stuck them on the wagon seats.

Ivon didn't seem too thrilled, but he had too much self-image to refuse to do it. The driver, a hulking, hunched creature with bulging, mismatched eyes and a tongue hanging out of its mouth, giggled and snorted at him and seemed to be having a good time sensing his discomfort.

Matson placed one wagon, the hay wagon, at the head of this new train, and the other in the rear. It looked very strange, but it was a much shorter train now and easier to guard. Jomo had improvised a four-across bridle and rein combination for the four remaining pack mules, and managed them while somehow perched in front of the pack on one of them. Cassie, in the first row of mules with riders, admired the troll-like man's tremendous skill.

They were underway before Nadya, hanging on to her for dear life, asked, "What suddenly made you an honorary dugger?"

Cassie smiled. "I don't know. I guess I've been a professional shoulder to cry on all my life. I never could figure it out but I'm not asking questions."

They did make better speed, but the combination of mules and mostly inexperienced mule riders did not make for a really good pace, and mules tended to set their new pace and come to a halt when they wanted a drink from the canisters under the hay wagon or when they were just too tired. Matson's powers could give them more energy and will, but even he could only do so much with a mule, and it was almost fifty kilometers to this land of Persellus.

They made very good time, but there came a time when the mules and even the horses really couldn't be pushed much further. They needed a rest, and the riders, although still haunted by visions of the slaughter they'd just left behind, particularly the visions of the dead faces of people they'd known and shared a lot with over the past weeks, could take only so much on mule back, bare as their own bottoms were.

Finally Matson called a halt, and they got down, many feeling terrible pain from muscles they had seldom used. They were not allowed to rest just yet, though. The mules had to be tended first, and this time individually, and the stringer and his duggers arranged a security line, or as much of one as they could with most of the packs and hay left behind. The mules would be their primary fortress, although the remaining hay bales were hauled out and spaced around the encampment as firing positions. Only then were they allowed to eat the hard bread and cold beans that was all that was saved, and get drinks of water themselves.

When they were finished, Matson walked over to the group. "Any of you know how to shoot a rifle or shotgun?" he asked them.

There was no response. All save the border guards and the police were forbidden any access to firearms in Anchor Logh.

"I was afraid of that," Matson sighed. "All right, we're still going to sleep in shifts. I want at least two of you up with each dugger at each gun position, and I want a few more on watch in the gaps. It may bore the hell out of you but you just remember your friends back there and what happened to them. If you'd rather live, then you try and not be bored. If you see *anything*, and I mean *anything* out there, or even if you just imagine you do, you sing out. The first one that goes to sleep on duty gets to be another of my mules. The first one who misses something and doesn't give a warning will wish he or she *was* a mule!" He looked over at Cassie. "You! What's your name?"

"They call me Cassie, sir."

He snorted. "Too long. You're Cass. Anybody ever call you that?"

"A lot of people."

"Better to have a strong, one-syllable name that can be yelled in a pinch anyway. You're strong and you have a knack with people. I'm putting you in charge and that means the rest of you take orders from her like you would from me or my people. Cass, you pick your guards for each period, then get some sleep."

She was amazed. "Yes, *sir*!" she responded, shaking her head a bit. She was no more amazed and awe-struck by the sudden promotion than the rest of them, some of whom looked a little resentful. Well, so what? she told herself. Maybe she'd become a dugger herself or something. It sure beat some of the alternatives.

The attack began slowly, with a cautious sounding out. Two duggers, looking battered and bleeding, reeled into view and began half walking, half crawling towards the circle. The alarm was sounded almost immediately, and in an instant everyone was awake and tensely at what positions they could take.

"Don't shoot! Don't shoot! We're from the Arden train!" one of them called out weakly.

"You stop now or this scattergun's gonna end things for you in the next three seconds," Matson shouted back. "How the hell do I know who or what you are?"

"We're from the train, the Arden train," gasped the talkative one, but both stopped where they were. "Happened hours ago. They were all around us. . . ."

"What was her whip's name?" he shouted back, unmoved. "You have three more seconds!"

"Whip—what?" the wounded dugger gasped, looking confused.

"If you don't even know the name of Cuso, then there's no reason to let you live," the stringer said icily, raising his shotgun.

"Oh, *Cuso!* Sure, sure. I thought you meant—"

"Her name was Herot, you scum!" Matson snarled at them and opened fire.

The air was suddenly alive with shapes; terrible, nameless, gibbering monsters who were all hating eyes and gaping, tooth-filled mouths, the dark monsters of nightmare and madness, dripping blood and screaming foully at them.

Matson and his duggers opened up on them, ignoring the flying things and at all times shooting low. From the mass of the monstrous attackers came occasional screams of agony as bullets and shot found their mark in the sea of terrible illusion.

But there was one hell of a lot of them. Matson took a moment to concentrate, and his head snapped back, then forward again with his eyes suddenly burning with power and concentration. "Armies of the void, attend me!" he commanded loudly over the din of battle, and suddenly, around the outer perimeter of the train appeared hundreds of huge, dark apelike shapes with eyes of red fire. The monsters, so huge and thick that they completely shielded the train, started roaring back at the attacking shapes and then slowly advanced outward.

It was a clever maneuver, Matson's best trick.

The attacking cult had only limited power on its own, and that concentrated in its leader, but it used illusion with great skill and cunning, creating for their prey what they themselves feared most and sending it forth in the hopes that those nightmares might equally terrify others.

But there were wizards in the Flux as well as illusionists; wizards who had the power to create out of the void a true and living demon army. Matson and his duggers knew that everything sent against them now was illusion, but the attackers could have no such assurance that the reverse was also true.

And so the stringer, himself a master of illusion, cast upon them a hundred demonic beasts at least as horrible as those being hurled at him, but Matson's beasts all had the same name and it was Doubt, and it had an immediate effect.

The mad shapes attacking the train shimmered, winked in and out, and seemed to lose much of their steam as their creator hesitated in the face of the counterattack. And because of their creator's diverted attention, when the monsters winked out it revealed the ones behind them.

Automatic rifles on wide spray had a devastating effect, even in the void; in the midst of a fading scenario of Hell, bullets found mark after mark, causing odd shapes to cry out and fall back, some dropping in their tracks and laying there in pools of their own blood.

Matson halted his own shooting routine and concentrated once more. "Armies of the void, back to guard this train!" he shouted.

The huge demonic shapes paused, then did a backwards step in perfect unison, then another and another. Matson only hoped he'd been in time. No matter how crazy or frenzied some of these culties were, they'd notice, if given a chance, that for the past few seconds the train had been shooting *through* their allegedly real phantom army. Although the Anchor people could just crouch down and wonder, the duggers understood immediately what the problem was and ceased firing, taking the time to shift positions and thus not be where they would be expected.

Matson stuck the stump of an unlit cigar in his mouth and peered out at the void, which was suddenly deathly quiet and still once more. Jomo, Cass, and several others helped reload new clips into rifles as the break lengthened. "How many did you make, Jomo?" the stringer asked.

"We shoot twelve, maybe more," the big mule driver responded. "They was at least as many left."

Matson nodded agreement. "Yeah, I figure we still got another dozen, maybe fifteen out there. Bastards. I wonder if any of 'em noticed our more than natural shooting?"

At that moment explosions went off all around them, the concussions knocking several of them back, and from all sides huge, lizard-shaped creatures reared up and hissed defiance.

"I think maybe somebody notice!" Jomo called back, and began shooting again into the now crowded void.

"Well, we'll just see how *they* like their eardrums broken!" Matson called back. He made a series of sweeping gestures with his hand and went around in a nearly three hundred and sixty degree circle as the duggers continued their shooting.

Cass continued to supervise the reloading, so that all of the ones who could shoot had an almost continuous supply of firepower. She saw Dar come up to her operation, near Matson, and look at the rifles and then Matson. She frowned. "What are you thinking?"

"Lani—she has to be with *them*. It don't look so hard. One shot . . ."

"One shot and you'll kill yourself and maybe all

of us!" she screamed back at him. "He's the only chance we got. Dar! They killed all the boys last time!"

He looked at her strangely. "You've gone completely over to him, ain't you? You forgot what he is, and you don't give a damn any more about the rest of us."

Before she could reply he launched himself at her. At that moment all of Matson's mentally placed charges went off in a great circle of fireworks so effective that it pushed over not only the attackers but half the train as well.

Dar recovered first, and, in his crazed mental state, struck Cass hard on the jaw with his fist, knocking her cold. In the recovery and follow-up shooting to the concussions, nobody really noticed him pick up her limp body and sprint for a weak spot in the line to the rear of Matson. The giant lizard-things, frozen for a moment in the shock of the explosions, did not deter him one bit, for he did not believe in them. A dugger saw him running with her, but as his rifle was on spray he didn't dare shoot for fear of hitting the unconscious captive on his shoulder. By the time an alarm was shouted and his rifle readjusted, Dar, carrying the unconscious Cass like a sack of potatoes, was behind the monsters and out of sight of the train.

9

POCKET

Cass awoke to a scene out of nightmare. All around her was the void, yet she was not in it any more. She tried to turn and see just how far it was, but couldn't manage, and it was only then that she realized that she was bound to a flat slab of some kind, arms and legs out in spreadeagle fashion, while something also held her through the neck and waist rings, making much movement impossible.

After the first few fuzzy moments she remembered what had happened, remembered Dar's crazy lunge—and then what?

The slab was angled slightly upward, so she had a view of what was in front of her. It was in fact an eerie and impossible scene, an outcrop of reddish rock rising up perhaps fifty meters over which spilled a small waterfall whose effluent landed in a pool below but did not seem to either drain to a creek or flood. There was a cave in back of the waterfall, but it was impossible to tell who or what might be inside. Around the pool were a number of palm trees and small bushes, and there seemed to be a few trees and bushes growing here and there all around the place. The void was just in back of the large rock, and she couldn't imagine where the water was coming from.

She was not alone. It seemed that there were an endless number of slabs set back from the pool area in an eerie sort of amphitheater, and while it was difficult to see much at that level she was certain that each slab held someone, similarly bound as she was.

Around the pool and waterfall there were—shapes. She was far enough away and at a bad angle so that at first she could not identify them, but suddenly she knew what they were. They were women, very much like those bodies at the massacre site. Primitive, part animal, some scampering about with animal-like motions, others crouched down and eating or gnawing on something. They looked like the visions of Hell painted by the church in sermon after sermon. In fact, except for the eerie warm light the whole scene resembled a painting of Hell that hung in the temple at Anchor Logh.

For a moment her upbringing broke through her skepticism. *Have I died?* she wondered. *Did Dar's blow or the attackers of the train kill me?* But no, she decided at last. She might have believed it if she hadn't seen those bodies, but she knew better. Those were real savages who attacked, and so were these. She wondered, though, if Dar had gone on to kill Matson and thus allow the second train to be overrun as well. She could hear, but not see, the noises of mules off to her right.

Suddenly the savage women near the pool stopped what they were doing and scattered, making agitated noises. From the cave behind the small waterfall emerged a group of four of the women carrying on their shoulders a body seemingly strapped to a cross-like structure made of wood. They walked through the waterfall and down a small path to the right side of it, then around the pool, finally approaching Cass and the others on the slabs. There was a neatly drilled hole in the rock at the base of the grisly amphitheater, and the structure and its occupant were hoisted into place so that the base of the cross was securely in the hole. It swayed a moment, but then settled and held firm. Cass gasped as she finally recognized the figure on the cross.

It was Dar.

He looked dazed and only semi-conscious, but in some pain. He seemed to be bound with tight metal clamps around his wrists and by strong rope through the neck and waist rings. It held him secure and helpless, but hardly comfortably.

A large figure now emerged from the cave and walked slowly down the path, around the pool, and up to the hapless man on the cross. This newcomer was dressed entirely in black robes without adornment of any kind, although he wore a large golden medal on a chain around his neck. It was impossible to tell what was stamped on the round medallion from Cass's vantage point.

The primitive women seemed to treat this dark one with reverence and awe, and gathered silently to watch. It was hard to do much counting, but there seemed to be no more than seven or eight of them.

The dark one threw back his hood to reveal a round, distinguished looking face with a carefully cropped goatee and short hair, black once but now tinged with gray. He looked over at the savage women and made a gesture, and they prostrated themselves and virtually grovelled at him. He smiled and turned to the ones on the slabs.

"Why, hello!" he said cheerfully, in a cultured if highly accented voice, almost as if he hadn't really noticed them before. "You are all doubtlessly wondering why I've brought you here today, not to mention where this is, who I am, and what will happen now. I shall be most happy to explain it all to you."

He gave a benign smile and then continued. "I

am Roaring Mountain, high priest of the powers of darkness, anointed so by the Seven Who Come Before, which you might know as the Seven Who Wait.''

There were a few sounds at this, but no great outcry. Most of them had expected as much, if nothing else, from the familiar scenario.

"This is my holy place," he went on, "my *temple*, if you will, a place of life in the midst of the void established for my own and Hell's convenience. No, you are not dead, nor are you dreaming. You have instead received a signal honor. You have gone to Hell while still alive.''

He sighed, but it was clear that he was quite a ham actor and enjoying every moment of this.

"Now, then, that takes care of two of the questions. As to what I, and my followers, and this place are doing here—we are, quite simply, guarding one of the seven gates to Hell. It is not far from here, and while it is guarded by a different sort we can take it, given sufficient personnel, at the time and convenience of our own choosing. And *that*, of course, is what *you* are doing here.''

Cass could already see, with some horror, where he was going with this, but like the rest she could do nothing but watch.

"When we struck our first blow not long ago, we had thirty-five soldiers in the cause, but many of them were outcasts in the void and thus did not have the reason or discipline to be more than, shall we say, rifle fodder. Only ten now remain, alas, but there is cheer, for now we have an additional twenty-six of *you*.''

Cass began doing some mental arithmetic. Arden's train had twenty-four survivors, plus her, plus Dar, there. She felt at least a tingle of excitement and relief that Matson had obviously beaten off the attack. Roaring Mountain had obviously lost too many in the first attack, which must have been nearly suicidal, to have a chance of taking theirs. So she'd been abducted by Dar, who'd escaped the train and been taken prisoner by these people. She had to wonder if Dar had enough sense left in his head to have some second thoughts about that. There was no doubt that this strange man was the same one Matson had guessed was behind it all. Roaring Mountain. Rory Montagne.

"Now, what we will require to eventually *liberate* this gate I estimate at about one hundred smart, dedicated troops. The attack on the first train brought us a tremendous quantity of arms and ammunition which we are still cataloging, not to mention explosives and other useful devices. It also brought us twenty-five fresh, sharp young people to be the vanguard of that new army."

Cass frowned. Twenty-five? That couldn't be right.

"Oh, I know what you're thinking," the dark man went on. "Me? Work for Hell? Never! But consider—it was your own church that cast you out. It was your own kind who branded you, tortured you, then sold you as slaves. It is they who deserve the punishment, not you! See! With your own group rode one of the harlots of the church!" He snapped his fingers, and two of his savages went out of view and came back with a small figure dressed in a white robe, hands bound. But it couldn't be a novice—this woman had a fair amount of hair.

Cass gaped, recognizing Lani instantly. So that was how they'd gotten her out of the Anchor. She looked uncertain and frightened, but she looked up at the man on the cross and gave a short cry as she recognized Dar. The demonic priest's eyebrows went up. "Ah, then you know this fellow. Very good. Darkness provides symmetry, always. *Now look only at me!*" He reached out and pulled her face around until he was staring down into her eyes. She stiffened, then seemed to relax so well that the two savages had to help support her.

"Just like all the others," the dark man sneered, an expression of madness creeping over his face. "Just like all those harlots in robes who are the chief whores, selling out their people and themselves. It is an abomination for women to so rule and control men!" He reached down and ripped off the white robe, revealing her voluptuous naked body. She had, Cass had to admit to herself, one hell of a body.

This, too, did not escape the attention of Roaring Mountain. His madness faded into a broad grin, and he made a few signs with his hand in front of her face. She stiffened, almost like a statue, and the dark man motioned the support away. At that moment Dar seemed to come to. He groaned and looked down at the little scene in front of him in confusion. "Lani?" he managed.

Roaring Mountain turned and looked at the man on the cross. "Well, this is unexpected timing. You, sir, present me with a problem. A moral dilemma, if you will. On the one hand, you defected, bringing with you a much-appreciated offering. On the other hand, Hell's minions in this holy cause must be female, for it is fitting that the just cause of Hell be carried out by those very types who oppose us so desperately. Nor, of course, could I allow the distraction of you to be around while we get about our work. Tell me—this girl here. Sister, perhaps? Or lover?"

Dar still seemed completely confused by the situation. "Lover," he responded.

"Ah! So they start their whoring younger than even I believed." He thought for a moment, then nodded to himself. From his robe he produced a large, sharp knife similar to the one Matson had. "To kill you would be an injustice. Therefore, we must be delivered from temptation and all will work out." He turned to Lani. "Girl? Open your eyes and look upon the man up there."

She did, although still in a trance-like state.

"Do you know him?"

"It is Dar," she responded woodenly.

He nodded. "And you want Dar, don't you?"

"Yes."

"You know what you want from him. You can see it hanging there, can't you?"

Lani seemed to tremble slightly. "Yes. Oh, yes."

"But who do you belong to now? Who must have your total devotion?"

"You, Master."

"Then you must prove your devotion. You must give me what you want most." He handed her the knife, and she took it. "Now go to that which you want most and bring it to me."

They all held their collective breaths, but the savages seemed amused as well as fascinated by the grisly sadism of their master.

Lani walked over to Dar, the knife outstretched. At last he understood at least this much and screamed, "Lani! In the name of all that's holy, no! *Please!*" he sobbed.

The knife moved. Dar screamed, and suddenly there was blood all over. The girl knelt down and picked up the severed genitals and brought them back to Roaring Mountain, laying both the grisly object and the knife at his feet, kneeling in front of them.

Sparks flashed from the dark man's hand, and Dar stopped screaming and was still. The blood and wound on him vanished, and in the pubic region there was a very natural-looking female vaginal cavity, complete with pubic hair.

"He is otherwise unchanged," Roaring Mountain told his captive audience. "I took the model from his own lady love, so in this sense they are one." He chuckled over his gruesome humor. "Dar! Awaken free of pain!"

Dar's body moved, then his eyes opened and again he looked confused. Two of the savages released his bonds and he fell limply to the rocky floor but soon shook his head and got up. All of the onlookers who could still either bear to watch or hadn't passed out just from the shock and horror of the scene waited to see what would happen now.

"Arise, Lani," the priest of Hell commanded, and she did. "Girl, you have been punished for your sins and purged of them. Boy, you have also received justice. Do you both understand that?"

Both just nodded.

"Very well. Then the two of you are the vanguard of our new army. You, Dar, will be my general, and you, Lani, will be his aide. Both of you will lead, together, the mighty crusade. Do you agree?"

Lani, still mostly under his spell, breathed, "Yes, Master." Dar, who still hadn't sorted it all out, asked, "Then we'll be together?"

"Yes, of course. You have paid a high price for it, why not?"

Dar nodded and squeezed Lani's hand. The sight was bizarre. "Then we'll fight for you."

Roaring Mountain sighed. "Ah, true love conquers all. Both of you can go back in the cave and get to know each other better if you wish. We have more business here."

Cass had watched the whole thing and felt sick at it, but she found her emotions mixed. Those two certainly deserved each other, that was for sure, and she felt little pity about their enduring fate, either, for Roaring Mountain had obviously greatly enhanced their lust for one another while rendering that lust impossible to consummate the way they wanted it. The true sickness in the scene was the dark one below, and his powers, which were obviously real—or were they? Matson's had certainly looked real, and they were but illusions.

Roaring Mountain approached the slabs and looked down at his first helpless captive. For a while he caressed, cajoled, and stroked her helpless figure in a scene of particular horror considering that the onlookers could only witness their own fate. It looked like rape was inevitable, but suddenly the dark one stopped, that look of mad fury coming back into his face. "All the same! All the same!" he snapped, sounding both insane and violent. Suddenly Cass realized the source of that madness and that insane hatred. It was the only thing that made sense.

Roaring Mountain was himself full of lust, but he was also impotent. The man with the power to make women worship him and to change the sex of another couldn't get it up himself. How he must be filled with hate! No wonder he could abide no normal male around. Dar, in fact, would have to be his favorite, for the mad wizard had bestowed on the boy the ultimate impotence.

"Nonetheless, you are mine!" he roared, and made a pass over the girl with his right hand. Two of the savages then ran up and undid the bonds, and the dark one held out his hand and pulled the hapless girl to her feet.

She was transformed. She was in fact extremely well built herself, although it was impossible to know how much had been exaggerated by Roaring Mountain's frustrations. From her extremely narrow waist down her body was now covered in a fine brown hair terminating in two very large cloven hooves which the legs had been reconfigured to support, and from the end of her spinal column now grew a short, stubby, goat-like tail. She had a rich head of hair once more, too, of the same brownish color, but her face below her eyes had elongated a good five centimeters, giving her what could only be described as a pug-like snout. Finally, through her hair, rose two short, blunt goat-like horns.

"Behold the first of a new race," Roaring Mountain thundered. "This shall be the model for the future of all harlots of World!" He sounded coldly furious now, and stretched out both hands at the captive multitude. At the end he issued some commands, and the first row was released. All were helped to their feet, and all looked exactly like the first creature he had made.

Cass, in the third row, could only wait for it with mounting horror. Far worse than the transformation, for there was nothing permanent in the Flux and anything done could be undone, was the totally silent submissiveness of the newly made creatures who but moments before had been captive girls just like she. The dark priest did the second row, and they became as the first. It was only when the first group came up to unbind the second that they were close enough for Cass to see the depth of the transformation. In one way, Roaring Mountain was right—this was a whole new race, and she was next to join it!

Well, at least I'll finally have some tits, she thought inanely, her grip on sanity very, very thin.

"Hold!" commanded a deep, booming, authoritarian voice behind them, and Roaring Mountain stopped, then turned and himself dropped to his knees, as did all the savages and transformees, following his lead.

The speaker and object of this worship walked into view. He was *enormous*, standing fully three meters high and fully proportioned with muscles to match. He also had a goat-like head with huge ram's horns, deep purple skin covering his human-looking body, and he wore a loose-fitting robe of crimson satin open at the chest but tied off with a belt at the waist.

"Oh, great Prince of Hell, we welcome thee," Roaring Mountain intoned.

"Oh, get up from there," the giant goat-man muttered disgustedly. "We have business to discuss."

"I was just in the holy process of—" the dark priest began, getting up hastily.

"Of turning excellent raw material into mindless savages. Yes, I know. I'm beginning to wonder about you, I really am. I fear the hangups that attracted us to one another may be too much for you to do a decent job. Well, we'll see." The creature looked up at the dozen or so girls still tied down. "You couldn't be satisfied with the one train. No, you had to go after another one without replacing your losses from the first attack." He sighed. "Sometimes, oh Roaring Mountain, I think I should transform you into a giant asshole."

The priest looked stricken. "Please, Master! I can explain!"

"Bullshit! I went and carved this homey pocket in a very convenient location and handed you the nucleus of an army. If you had any sense you'd have struck at the first train, forgotten the second, and now be well on your way to training that expanded force. Instead, here you are creating a new wild animal species with barely more than you had before! Worse, yet, you didn't take that second train. They'll be back in force, hunting for this pocket now."

The priest looked suddenly concerned. "Then hadn't we better do something?"

The goat-man cleared his throat impatiently. "Yes, I think we better. Any captives from that second train? I mean, any you haven't already transformed into mindless idiots?"

"One, Master—no, two!" He looked up at Cass and pointed. "That one there, for example."

The mysterious giant nodded his goat's head and walked up the rocky surface between the slabs and looked down at her. After what she had just witnessed and now expected to go through, she was anything but taken aback by this great apparition.

"What's your name, girl?" the goat-man demanded to know.

"Cass," she told him. There was no use in being coy, particularly when she knew she was facing the power behind this little throne.

"Now, then, Cass—you were with the second train?"

"Yes, sir."

"Whose train was it? What was the name of the stringer?"

"Matson, sir."

"Um. Damn. And I suppose he sent a dugger ahead to Persellus when he saw the remains of the first train?"

"Yes, sir. Straightaway."

He turned to Roaring Mountain. "Another stupid mistake. I don't suppose you left anybody to take care of that little detail?"

The priest shrugged. "How was I to know there'd be a second train by so soon? Besides, I lost a lot of troops there."

"Idiot." He turned back to Cass. "You don't seem particularly frightened by me."

"In the past few days I've been sold to a stringer, forced marched in the void, cleaned up after a massacre, been in a fight, and just now I witnessed a castration and the turning of a lot of good people into animals, and I was about to join them myself when you showed up. I'm sorry, sir master wizard or whatever you are. I just don't think I have any more fright left."

The giant was impressed. "Now *this* is something special, priest. A hundred like this and we could rule World. And you were about to turn her into a slavish goat-woman!" He paused a moment, controlling his temper. "Do you know who and what I am?"

"A wizard. Isn't that what they call people like you?"

The goat man crouched down, and she could see that the goat head was not some sort of mask. Either it was all illusion or else the man had literally changed himself into this whatever it was. She decided on the latter, noticing that he wore a ring with a serpent design on his right ring finger. She also noticed that he was most certainly left-handed.

"I'm one of the Seven Who Wait," the creature told her. "Does that bother you?"

"Not particularly," she answered honestly. "The church hadn't exactly impressed me for honesty and sincerity. I see no reason why your side should be much different."

He looked at her for a moment. "There is great power in you," he told her. "I can feel it. Tremendous latent power that even now makes tentative probes at my defenses. Your very calmness, your intelligence, and your almost magnetic ability to get into the worst of situations makes me suspicious. I have seen this combination before, in many bodies, with many faces." He sighed and got up and turned to Roaring Mountain. "Come. Your fun here can wait. We must talk and soon, for I must be quickly gone from here. I warn you though not to try your tricks with that one. What she has within her is stronger than you. For your own sake, kill her."

Cass suddenly felt some fear return, particularly when the priest grinned and said, "I'll do it right now."

"No! Not until I am gone." Was that a worried tone in the master wizard's voice? What sort of power, she wondered, did *she* have that even one of the Seven, if that was who he was, would not like to take on?"

The two men of evil walked away, and Roaring Mountain went to the cave. Dar met him at the entrance just inside the waterfall and they exchanged a few words. Then Dar nodded, and the evil priest rejoined his master and they went off out of view. Dar hesitated a moment, then walked out and over to the slabs, then up to Cass herself. None of the savages or goat-women made any attempt to stop him.

Roaring Mountain had given Dar practically everything, she saw. His build, already considerable, was now totally filled and so muscular that you could see every flex or movement in them, and his already strong, lean, handsome face was somehow altered into near total perfection, set off by a crop of thick, black hair. If there *were* male gods, then he was the absolute perfection of them—with one detail importantly missing. He was Roaring Mountain's pet joke.

"Come to gloat?" she asked him sourly. "Or cry on my shoulder, which isn't very good for that sort of thing right now."

"He ordered me to kill you," he told her. "As soon as goat-face was gone."

She sighed. "Well, go ahead. Get it over with."

"I'm not going to do it, Cass." He reached down and freed the restraints binding her to the slab. She sat up uneasily, a little suspicious but feeling that she had nothing to lose.

"Now what am I supposed to do? Run and be eaten alive by those *things* over there?"

He shook his head slowly. "No. They won't hurt you. Look, I did a dumb thing. I did a *lot* of dumb things. I just kept thinking of Lani, and that she was out here, and then I saw you start acting like that stringer's partner and it all just sort of snapped. I kind of deserve this, I guess, but you don't."

She suddenly felt a little uneasy. "Where's Lani now, Dar?"

"Dead," he said softly. "I killed her. I—" his voice choked a bit—"I put her out of her misery, really. That bastard made me a woman who looks like a man, thinks like a man, wants like a man. He made her all sex, frenzied like, and only for me—and I couldn't do a damned thing. She was in torture from his games, Cass—I gave her peace."

She was silent a moment, not wanting to desert him but fearful that Roaring Mountain, who couldn't be far off, might return at any second. "What do you want me to do?"

"Look, they have to have a war party heading this way. I say we take our chances, get into the void, and wait. The odds ain't great, but even if we did it's better than staying here."

She was surprised. "We? You're coming, too?"

He nodded. "Oh, I thought about killing myself, but I got this real urge inside me to pay 'em back. Pay 'em *all* back, like you said back in the gym at the start. I want to get these bastards, and particularly I want to get the ones that caused this back in Anchor Logh. Will you come?"

She thought a moment. "What about the others here?"

"No time, and too big a risk. Either they'll be rescued or they won't, but if we take the whole mob they'll catch us sure."

"All right, then. Let's move."

They walked in back of the slabs and she found it a level area above the encampment, mostly more of the sheet rock with little growing. She could see the whole thing from up there and was shocked to see how tiny the place really was. They had less than twenty meters to reach the void, and they made it before any alarms were sounded, holding hands so they would not get separated.

As soon as they were in the void itself she stopped him. "What's the matter?" he asked nervously.

"We don't want to get too far from the pocket or we'll just wind up lost and alone," she told him. "I say let's walk just a hundred paces in a straight line, counting from now. If we can't see the pocket from there, then we stop and wait there."

"Fair enough for a start," he agreed, and began the counting process. At a hundred paces they stopped and looked back. There was a very slight, almost imperceptible lightening of the void in the direction from which they'd come, but otherwise there was no way to know that anything was there. It provided the only orientation they had, so they decided to settle for it. There was nothing to do now but sit down on the soft, spongy, invisible ground and wait until they had to return or strike out blindly in search of food and water.

"I wanted to bring a canteen, at least," Dar told her, "but all that stuff was over by the mules and so were they." They sat in silence for a while, and Cass lay back and tried to relax as much as she could. Although they were most probably dead people at this point, the immediate terrors were out of the way and she found herself suddenly unable to stop shaking and crying a bit. She just didn't fight it any more, and let it come, and it was a long time flowing from her. Dar held her and tried to comfort her, and it was some time before she realized that he was crying, too.

Coduro had brought half the armed might of Persellus, from the looks of it, including two officers of high rank that were real wizards, albeit of lesser powers.

"One of mine went nuts and defected, carrying off a girl," he told them. "We beat them off and cost them some lives, but with all the captives he's got this bastard has another army at his command. How many troops you got with you?"

The colonel, a bearded man in his fifties but in prime condition and looking ready for a fight, responded, "Fifty experienced soldiers, a chief noncom, and the captain and myself. But how are you going to find a tiny pocket in all this space? They could be *anywhere* by now. We came as an escort, not a raiding party."

"Well, I'll lead you to his pocket," the stringer told him. "I don't know why except I kind of took a liking to her, but I put my string on the girl he carried off. It'll lead us right to them."

"Well! That's different! Tremendous stroke of luck, though."

Matson suddenly hesitated. It *was* an odd thing, him putting that string on the only one that was captured. He'd never done anything like that before in his life, and he didn't know why he'd done it this time. He shrugged, went about his business, and didn't think much more on it as he recreated the strong defensive position. He didn't think the cult could possibly have turned all those captives into troops that could be used effectively in so short a time, but he didn't want to return here and find out he was wrong, either. Finally he remounted his horse and went over to the soldiers. "Let's go get 'em," he said enthusiastically.

Rory Montagne, he thought as he rode. A minor real wizard, able to make changes in individual human and animal bodies but that was all. He certainly wouldn't have the power to create a pocket on his own. The one he'd used for years down near Anchor Dowt had been an old one created by some wizard traveling the void long ago, or so the story went. He remembered when Montagne was still leading a double life out of Haratus, a Fluxland near there, acting as a scenic designer for the local wizard while kidnapping a number of local women, one by one, and hauling them off to this pocket of his for who knew what purpose? Finally the bastard had picked on a woman who happened to be a drill instructor at the local military school and he'd damn near had his balls kicked off and was lucky to escape with his life.

What was he doing here?

The tiny, thin energy trail left by Cass was ragged but not hard for him to follow, since it had his personal frequency. They did not have a long ride before he suddenly raised his hand and brought the troop to a halt.

"What's the matter?" the colonel asked him, hand going to his pistol.

"See that slightly lighter area over there? That's got to be it. The trail goes right to it. I'd like to take a few troopers and scout it first. Best to know what we're getting into."

The colonel nodded and turned. "Fiver! Mihles! Godort! Fall in over here and dismount!"

The three soldiers, two men and a woman, looked tough and smart enough. Matson loaded his shotgun and dismounted with them. "Stay ready," he warned the officer. "Montagne's range is pretty limited—he has to be looking at you to do anything—but he's too much for me to handle." With that he and the soldiers started cautiously forward.

"Sir!" one of the troopers hissed when they were almost to the pocket's border.

"Huh? What's the matter?"

"Over there to the left. One, maybe two shapes. Guards, perhaps."

He looked in the indicated direction and was impressed by the senses of the trooper. These were good soldiers. The figures were barely blobs at this distance, but they fanned out and moved slowly to close the net. At the point where they could finally make out the figures, though, Matson stopped, held up his hand again, and stood up, then pointed his shotgun at the pair. He knew one of them, but the other was a stranger, and he didn't know what they might have done to the one he *did* know by this time.

"All right—both of you! Stand with hands raised, facing me!" he commanded sharply.

They both jumped at the voice, then did as instructed. Cass suddenly recognized the lean figure in black. "Matson! Thank heaven!"

"Or somebody. You understand I don't know who's been messing with your mind, so I have to be cautious. There's three more guns on you two, so come forward and don't make any sudden moves."

They did as instructed, and soon were facing him across less than two meters. Matson reclipped his shotgun and walked up to them, staring at the larger of the two. "I'll be damned! I thought you were a man!"

"I used to be," Dar responded glumly.

Matson stared at him. "Don't I know you?"

Quickly Cass stepped in, telling the story as completely as she could, while trying to spare Dar some of the most painful memories. Matson just nodded and waited for her to run out of words.

Finally he said, "All right. So you say he's changed about twenty of the girls into his playthings, and he's got ten of the others. That's pretty fair, considering that the new ones won't know how to fight. I don't like this goat-headed fellow, though. Handling him will be rough."

"Oh, it's been *hours*," she assured him. "He was going quickly, or so he said. I'm sure he's gone now."

"We'll have to take the chance," the stringer decided. "All right—you two stay here for now. We're still going to keep you covered, so don't move until we tell you. Okay?"

"We won't," Cass assured them. "I just wish you'd brought a drink of water with you."

"All in good time," he assured her, and was off.

They pretty much were able to confirm the pocket's layout and general dimensions that Cass gave them from cautious observation, and a trooper was sent back to bring up the rest. Matson returned to the pair and lit a cigar. "Okay. You sure that cave's got no outlet?"

"I'm sure," Dar told him. "It doesn't even go back very deep, but it's kind of squared off, arranged like a one–bedroom cubicle."

He nodded, and the rest of the troops came up. Matson and the troopers quickly sketched in the layout and the stringer and the colonel mapped out a plan of attack. They had four submachine guns with them, and those were placed at the most likely points of breakout. Matson eyed the guns greedily, thinking of what he could have done to the cult if he'd had even one with enough ammunition. Twenty-five of the other troopers were stationed in between, so there was almost a continuous zone of fire. The others would ride right in, guns blazing, and secure positions inside as quickly as possible, with the hope of driving those inside out to the waiting firepower. If they could not within ten minutes, then the outer circle would move in with two of the machine guns taking the heights above the slabs.

Both Dar and Cass, after getting some water and a food bar each from the troopers, volunteered to go in with the party. Both Matson and the colonel were dubious. "We can't totally trust you yet, but I *would* like somebody there who knows the layout, just in case," the stringer said. "How about they come in with us in the middle of the party, undressed and unarmed as they are?"

The colonel nodded. "If they're crazy enough to do it, why not? Take the two gunners' horses there."

Both Cass and Dar mounted expertly and brought their horses into the formation. Dar gave a dry chuckle.

"What's so funny?" Cass wanted to know.

"I just realized how much easier and more comfortable it is to ride a saddle naked if you're a girl, that's all."

"Maybe you'll get to like it," she returned, feeling better than she had since entering the Temple, despite the imminent battle. "Hell, with those muscles you got bigger tits than I do by far." And, with that, they were off.

10

PERSELLUS

The attack was simple, direct, and quite effective because it was a total surprise. Half the riders came in from one side of the pool, the other half, almost perfectly synchronized, rode in from the other way. The inhabitants of the pocket, as hoped, were first totally frozen in confusion at the noise of the attack, then pulled in several directions, not certain what to do or who to fight first.

Several of the savages, undone by this, simply stood there uncomprehending and allowed themselves to be shot down. One, up in a tree, took the first target of opportunity and pounced down on a trooper, dismounting him. Seeing it, Dar leaped from his horse as the savage raised a bone club to deliver the fatal blow and knocked the wild animal-like woman away. Another trooper then shot her down.

It was over almost before it started, in a carefully planned hail of bullets. Part of the reason was that the newly transformed captives did nothing to fight back the attack. Some died simply because it was not immediately obvious that they were no threat, but the bulk of them simply huddled back in a large mass against the rocks and cowered in terror.

As soon as Cass hit the small grove of trees she

bounded off her horse and looked for signs of Roaring Mountain and his savage creatures, but aside from the pitiful ones huddling in the rocks there were none. The riders made two passes before they seemed to realize this as well, and they met in the center of the amphitheater and stopped, several dismounting and taking up guard positions.

A rider left to gather in the encircling troops, and soon the machine gunners had set up a defensive post on the rocky flat above the slabs from which they could hit almost anything in the pocket.

Matson, still atop his horse, reclipped his shotgun and looked around. "Where the hell is Montagne?"

The colonel frowned. "It was too quick for him to duck out through some escape hatch. He's got to be in the cave." The mounted troops split up into two detachments and rode to the paths on either side of the waterfall. The captain, who was the other wizard in the troop, now satisfied that his people were in control, took the right path, while the colonel, with Matson, covered the left.

"Rory Montagne!" the stringer shouted, his deep voice struggling to be heard over the waterfall. "It's all over. Come on out now. In ten seconds we're going to start pouring lead into that cave of yours, and if a shot doesn't get you one of the ricochets will. Live or die, it makes no difference to us. Your choice."

Suddenly great fire-breathing dragon lizards, each ten meters tall, roared out of the cave and startled the horses. As this diversion was taking place, and drawing shots, a dark figure leaped through the waterfall and into the pool and began swimming straight for the other side. The great dragons were hard for the troopers to ignore, but the colonel wheeled around on his horse and made for the far end of the pool, Matson following.

Roaring Mountain, looking quite soaked, reached

the edge of the pool, pulled himself up quickly, then stopped, seeing the two figures in front of him. He shrugged and smiled at them. Wearing nothing but his medallion, he looked more foolish than dangerous. The dragons vanished.

"You didn't answer Mr. Matson," the colonel remarked calmly. "Or were those hissing illusions your answer? Would you like to take *me* on now?"

The priest of Hell's smile faded and he studied the colonel intently. "Answer me this first, sir, if you will," he said smoothly. "If I were to not take you on, what will happen to me?"

"You will be rendered unconscious, then taken to Persellus to stand trial," the colonel told him. "Beyond it being a fair trial by magicians of your rank I can promise nothing further." It was clear by his tone, though, that he really hoped that the evil one would choose to fight him here and now.

The colonel's confident manner rattled Montagne. He was not, after all, a very powerful wizard, and quite limited in real, rather than illusory, magic. Nor, for all his insanity, was he stupid. One did not take on a wizard who knew your own powers and limitations while you knew none of his. "To Persellus, you say? I understand it is a delightful place, Colonel. I shall be delighted to accompany you."

"First things first," Matson put in. "Montagne, we go back a ways as you might remember, and I know you're not the big man in all this. Now who the hell is the joker hiding behind the goat's mask?"

"Jok—I don't know what you mean, dear boy. The authorities made it a bit hot, shall we say, back home when my dear little pocket was stumbled upon by a military patrol while I was away. I have scouted these obscure pockets for years, so I moved. That's all."

Matson reached down on his saddle and unclipped his bullwhip. The dark man saw it, frowned, then looked over at the colonel. "My dear sir, I have *surrendered* to you! I am under your protection and the merciful laws of Persellus."

"We're not in Persellus now," Matson said coldly. "You killed a very good friend of mine. Worse, you stole stringer property. In the void a stringer is the law in matters concerning his train. You can answer to me, and answer straight, or take on the colonel. Your choice, I don't care which." The bullwhip was unfurled to its full length.

"Colonel!" Montagne implored, but the colonel filled his pipe, started humming an old tune, and looked around at the scenery.

Rory Montagne sighed. "Oh, very well. Yes, I was contacted back home one day by the one you refer to, but aside from the fact that he is one of the Seven I have no more idea than you as to who or what he is. I have seen and heard him only as you describe, in deep disguise. He made this pocket, and he sent some of his minions to bring me here with all that I had. I was to build up weapons and personnel until we were strong enough to attack and secure one of the seven gates to Hell which is not that far from here, that time to be in the rather distant future, I believe."

Matson looked over at the colonel. "That true? One of those things is around here?"

"So I've heard, but I've heard that since I was a kid and I never knew anybody who really knew if it was, or where it was. I been thirty years in and out of the void in these parts and I never ran into it, but I could have been right next to it a hundred times and never known it. You know how the void is."

The stringer nodded. "Well, it's no concern of mine if it's true or not, but I *do* want the bastard behind all this. Montagne, you seem mighty casual about going to Persellus. Any special reason?"

The madman shrugged. "Why not? As I said, it's supposed to be a delightful place."

"And the place where your mystery man is?"

The colonel seemed shocked by Matson's suggestion. "In *Persellus*? One of the Nine? Without the Goddess knowing? Impossible!"

"It would be the ideal place for such a one to hide," Matson pointed out, "and for the very reason you just showed. All I can do is state the obvious. Whether or not you follow it up is up to you. I'm not going to be around these parts very long."

The colonel seemed deeply disturbed by the idea, but simply said, "It will be looked into, I promise you. At least I will bring it up in my report, and higher authority can do what it wishes."

"Fair enough," the stranger agreed. "Now, then, Montagne, one more piece of unfinished business and I'll let the colonel have you. You stole a lot of merchandise from a stringer. As the recovering stringer, I am entitled to it, but I don't like damaged goods."

Rory Montagne frowned. "The mules are in excellent shape, and what packs we rummaged through can, I'm sure, be restored in short order."

"Them," Matson said, pointing to the cowering goat-women. "Put them back the way they were." The whip hand twitched slightly.

"Now how in hell am I supposed to remember what they looked like?" the captive retorted in a helpless tone. "They're *women!*"

"Can you bring back their senses? Memory? Personality?"

"Oh, sure. It was a quick mass job. All I did was push them back from the control centers of the brain. What's the point unless they know exactly what's going on but are helpless to do anything about it?"

Matson and the colonel exchanged sharp glances

at that. Finally the stringer said, "Okay. It doesn't matter to me what they used to look like anyway, so long as they're people again. Just pick somebody in your head at random and make them all look like that, and bring back their minds. If they don't think and talk they're no good to me."

Although some of the troopers were busy surveying the pocket and also repacking and readying the mules for transport, most of the others, including Cass and Dar, stood back watching the show. The latter two were enjoying every bit of it.

Montagne sighed. "I do wish you would send someone to fetch my robe. A prisoner should be allowed some dignity."

The colonel shrugged and gestured to a trooper, who went up, into the cave, and returned with it. It was then carefully searched but there were no pockets or concealed compartments within it and so they gave it to him and he put it on, looking quite pleased, then looked up at the colonel. "With your permission, sir?"

They cleared a path for him and he walked towards the goat-women, who seemed to relax and greet his coming with joy.

"He won't try any tricks, will he?" Matson asked worriedly.

"It would take months to find out his particular frequencies and patterns by deduction, but once he starts I'll know if he's doing it right. You can't alter a spell, only impose a different one. If he undoes it, it has to be all the way, or the math just won't add up."

The stringer nodded, understanding at least the basics as a false wizard.

Montagne was still a ham, and he still put on a nice show of mumbo-jumbo, chanting, and gestures, but finally he made a few basic gestures and the figures of the hapless women shimmered and changed.

"Bastard! I'll kill him!" Dar screamed, and two troopers had to restrain him.

All nineteen of the surviving members of Arden's train now looked exactly like Lani. The black magician turned, grinned, then shrugged. "Well, after all, you *did* leave her dead in my bed. Who else did you think I'd have in mind?" He turned to the colonel. "I'm ready to go now, sir. Take me away!"

Cass shouted at Matson, "You *can't* make him go back with the train! You just *can't!* It'd be like you traveling with nineteen women who looked just like Arden!"

That stung the stringer, and he softened slightly. "All right. Colonel, can we find or make some clothes for those two and let them go in with you? All in all, they've done us a pretty good service, and these will more than make up for my loss on them."

The colonel was surprised. "You mean you're giving them their freedom? A stringer gives something for nothing? Now I *know* the gates will be opened and the end of World is nigh!"

"Cut the sarcasm. The big one will have to face a hearing when you get home to judge his actions, both good and bad. I'll leave that judgment up to your court. Cass I'm not so sure about, but she's done me enough service to buy her way out. That's as far as I'll go."

"Fair enough," the colonel agreed. "Let's see what we can do about some clothing for the two of them, then we'll commandeer two of the mules there to let them ride. You'll get them back when you reach Persellus."

"Agreed. I need a couple of troopers to help me go back and get some packs I ditched back on the route, then we'll be headed in. I have some business in Persellus."

"We'll see you there, then!" And, with that, the

colonel went off to reorganize his troops, Montagne walking before him.

Dar was finally calm enough to be freed of restraint, but he turned his back on the now milling, chattering throng of Lanis and refused to look at them any more.

Matson came over to them, dismounted, and said, "Well, Cass. You heard me there, although I'll never live the story down. Don't disappoint me, now."

"I just wish I could buy my friends out," she told him honestly. "In a way I feel kind of guilty about this."

"Well, you're free, but you're broke, so forget it. However, I want to warn both of you about Persellus. You've never been in a Fluxland before."

Even Dar suddenly grew interested. "What are they like?"

"Well, each one is so different there's no telling, but *this* one happens to be a pretty nice place filled with pretty nice folks, overall. The first thing you have to remember," he said, his voice dropping to a whisper, "is that every Fluxland is the creation of a very powerful wizard, one so powerful that they're like gods. Well, this one's wizard thinks she *is* a goddess. Lives up in a high tower, but really does the part. She can hear and see everything and everyone if she wants to, and she loves to. If you pray to her, your prayers might be answered if she's in the mood. If you say anything she doesn't like, or question her godhood, you'll wish you didn't. The best way to act is to steer clear of even any questions about her and for your own sakes make no even slightly nasty comments. The only way people there can get along is if they *believe* in her godhood, so they do. Even these troops and the colonel. Never mind what you know is true. Act in every way like she's a real deity, because, in real life, she is one. And do not ever

accept an offer to see her, because you'll come out
of it a raving religious fanatic about her. Okay?''

They both nodded, although neither was quite
sure just what it all meant.

Matson left shortly afterwards to return to his
train, taking a half a dozen troopers with him and
his newly acquired mules, packs, and people. That
last made things a little more tolerable for Dar,
anyway.

The colonel proved to be a man of many abilities.
When they came up with two basic trooper uni-
forms, one far too small for Dar and the smallest
far too large for Cass, he made a small gesture and
both fit as if they were tailored for the two. A
second pass turned the water and the waterfall
from clear water to a brown, foul-smelling substance that bubbled and hissed. Nobody was going
to use *this* pocket for a refuge again, that was for
sure. He did not otherwise destroy it, though, since
he fully intended to send back a team of experts on
void magic to study it for clues as to its origin—
and originator.

Finally, they were ready. The clothes felt odd
after so long without any, but they had no trouble
riding as they had before. A third commandeered
mule held the now comatose Rory Montagne, rendered so by a spell from the colonel that made it
highly unlikely that the evil one would awaken
before they were ready for him.

Finally everything was packed, inventoried, and
they were off into the void once more, but with a
difference. Cass was now a free woman, but in a
hostile and unknown place and without resources.
Dar, because of his earlier actions in the train and
against Cass, was technically under arrest.

The colonel was advanced enough in the magic
of Flux to find his own way in the void, although
he *did* have to return via Matson's train route

before he could tie in to the main trail that only a few could see or sense.

It was a slow, relaxed, deliberately paced ride, but it was still far faster than any stringer train could go, even in the speedup configuration Matson had used.

"What will you do now, Cass?" Dar wanted to know.

She shrugged. "I'm not sure. Take each thing one at a time, I guess. Maybe I'll like this place up ahead and just settle down there. Probably not, though. If I could just find some way to earn a stake, I might like to see a little more of World now that I'm out here."

"What we've seen so far isn't very encouraging," Dar noted. "It's all been pretty ugly."

"But there *must* be nice places, maybe even wonderful places, too," she replied. "I mean, these wizards have the powers of gods. They can't *all* be corrupted by it, not completely. Look at the colonel and these troops here. They're pretty nice, and as human as anybody in Anchor Logh. We've seen the worst the Flux has, now it's time to see the best."

They reached the borders of Persellus after a lengthy ride. It was not an abrupt transition, like the pocket, but a very gradual one, as the void slowly gave way to actual forms. First there was the feeling of solid ground beneath them, and the clattering of hooves on rock that seemed so odd here that it startled them. Then there were misty, indistinct shapes here and there, like landforms of one kind or another, and here and there a trace of grass or bushes. The sky lightened, until it turned increasingly transparent, although it was now an odd and unfamiliar pale blue above the fleecy white clouds, with no sign of the ever-present Mother of Universes in sight. The clear blue sky unnerved both Dar and Cass, but they soon got used to it, particularly when they didn't look up.

And, suddenly, they were completely in the land of Persellus. It was, even the gloomy Dar had to admit, a very pretty place indeed.

In effect it was a huge, wide valley with a small meandering river cutting through it. The valley itself was, perhaps, twenty or twenty-five kilometers across, and flanked by low mountains with gentle green slopes that were forested all the way to their tops.

At first there seemed little sign of people or indeed any signs of life, but after traveling a while, the road, now paved and well-maintained, took them through farms quite different from those of Anchor Logh, with broad fields of grazing cows or horses and large houses and barns of an unfamiliar design sitting back from the main road. Clearly such farms were independently managed, probably by single families. They were smaller than Anchor communes, and the buildings could not possibly handle a collective. Just the idea of independently owned and operated farms was as hard for them to grasp as was the blue sky and wizards who did magic.

"Actually," a friendly trooper told them, "Persellus is slightly smaller than Anchor Logh and yet it produces a good deal more. We're totally self-sufficient in food here."

They marveled at this, but could not figure it out. It seemed so—*inefficient* somehow.

They went through one small town, strictly two streets wide and a block long, that seemed to cater to the farming community, and nowhere did they see anything or anyone who looked odd, abnormal, or out of the ordinary. About the only complaint they both had was that the light was so bright and constant here that their eyes hurt.

Still, Cass liked what she saw. "It's peaceful and

pretty here," she remarked to Dar. "And they're farmers, too, which is what I know best. Maybe I can get me a farm job."

Finally they reached the outskirts of the city—the one and only city in the Fluxland. It spread out on both sides of the river valley and up onto the hillsides themselves. Here was the governmental and transportation center of the land, along with the places where light manufacturing went on, from harnesses to farm machinery to lumber and building supplies. It was far smaller than the capital of Anchor Logh, but it was the right size to serve the place. It even had its own version of the Temple, although not right in town.

Ahead, beyond the town, they could see it—a great white tower stretching up into the sky, its top hidden in clouds, its base not seeming to touch the ground. The home of the goddess of Persellus.

The houses, with their red roofs and stucco walls, seemed quite different from Anchor Logh, yet hauntingly reassuring. This place may have problems, as Matson indicated, but it was certainly no chamber of horrors.

Government House was a flat, two-story building made out of the same weathered white building material as most of the structures in the land, but it was a good block long and certainly just as deep. They said their farewells to the troopers with thanks, and followed the colonel into the building to report.

The place looked like any administrative seat, except that there seemed to be equal numbers of men and women working there and that was something of a shock as well to two coming from a culture where only men were in government and administration. The Hearing Room, however, to which they were directed, was not what they expected at all.

It was a large room, somewhat resembling a

courtroom, but the entire far wall was taken up with a breathtaking and somehow three dimensional floor-to-ceiling portrait of a stunningly beautiful woman wearing white flowing robes, a small gold crown, and with an unnerving solid-looking halo over her head and an equally unnatural aura surrounding her body. Her face was looking down and smiling, her hands outstretched, and the more you looked at the thing the more you swore that the entire figure was somehow alive.

The colonel regarded it as such, entering, hat removed, then kneeling and bowing to the figure and remaining that way. Cass and Dar had already decided to follow the lead of the natives, so they did the same, wondering what happened next.

"Arise, my colonel," said a deep, musical woman's voice that seemed somehow distant and echo-like, and which filled the chamber. "All of you may stand."

They did so, and faced the huge portrait. "Holy Divine One, to whom we owe everything, this humble servant begs you to hear his report," said the colonel reverently, all trace of the pragmatic, tough soldier-wizard gone. Clearly this man was in the presence of his god.

"Proceed, my faithful servant." Both of the newcomers kept looking around to find the source of the voice that seemed all around them, but it was impossible to discover—if, indeed, it was there. Cass remembered Matson's description of Fluxlands. If this woman was indeed a wizard of enormous power, then she was in fact a goddess—as far as her mind could control and stabilize an area of the Flux in the image she desired. And she could make all the rules, and change or disobey them, on a mere whim.

The colonel immediately launched into his report, suddenly becoming the crisp military man once more. He obviously had enjoyed the action, and its result, and couldn't resist reliving it with relish. Cass noticed, though, that while he told about the goat-headed giant who claimed to be one of the Seven, he did not pass on Matson's suspicion that he was a resident of Persellus. Apparently the colonel had simply rejected it as too fantastic, for it was clear he would neither lie nor hold back from his goddess deliberately. The goddess let him talk, and waited until the account was complete. Then, she thanked, blessed, and dismissed the colonel, but ordered Cass and Dar to remain. The colonel kneeled again, then backed out of the room and closed the doors behind him. The two of them waited.

Finally she said, "The evil wizard must be tried and punished according to our holy laws, and the two of you will be required as witnesses. However, in light of the colonel's account, we are inclined to dismiss the charges against you, Dar. The madness and evil you both willingly joined and aided is counterbalanced, it seems, by your later actions in unmasking and undoing that evil. However, the fact remains that you *did* take a life, and changed or jeopardized others, and that cannot be totally wiped clean. Therefore, we give you a choice, for some judgment must be rendered against you. First, are the facts that the colonel stated true and complete?"

Dar seemed nervous and a bit startled to be directly addressed by a disembodied voice and a painting, but he nodded. "Yes, Ma'am."

"Is there anything you wish to add to that account before our choice of judgments is offered you?"

He thought a moment. "No, Ma'am."

"If you please, merciful goddess," Cass put in, trying not to stub her tongue. She was learning fast about the Flux. "May I intercede?"

"Continue."

"I have known him all my life. He was one of my few good friends, and I can assure you that he is a good man deep down. Any mere human could be driven mad after the sights we'd seen and the things we had done to us, and, being both fallible and human, he finally cracked under this pressure. Even then, what he did he did out of ignorance, not an intent to aid evil, and when he was given the chance to lead evil he refused and acted for the good. He will live with the terrible torture this evil priest put him through, and its consequences, all his life. Please be merciful with him."

"We are not unmindful of this," the goddess responded. "Nevertheless, wrongs were done and judgment must be made. You must understand that unless these factors were present he would stand trial with the evil priest and share his fate. Still, the fact remains that *you*, for instance, and the rest of your party, did *not* fall victim to madness. A judgment must be made that will serve to remind this poor one of his own inner failings so that, if ever he reaches that point again, he will know and do the right thing.

"Dar, these are your choices. You may request a trial, which in your case would be presided over by the stringer Matson and would include random citizens, both military and civilian. We must warn you that such trials, when they occur, are held under rigid rules of law, and that the best you might expect is to be remanded to a permanent slave status with the appropriate alteration in your outlook to make you a perfect one. You *do* understand that, don't you?"

He thought a minute, and thought of the goat-women and savages of the pocket. "Yes, Ma'am."

"Your other choice is to throw yourself right now on my mercy, and accept as final our decision, no matter what that might be."

He thought a moment. "Your worship," he said,

using the form of address used for high Temple priestesses in Anchor Logh, "I'd just like to get it over with. I feel guilty as hell—beg pardon, your worship—and I'll be mad at myself forever for being so dumb. I'll take what you dish out here and now."

The goddess seemed pleased. "Very well, then. What you did, you did for love of a woman. It is a very old story among humans, and the history of the human race is full of things, both wonderful and terrible, done for that reason, and for the opposite. For the love of that woman you defected to the enemy, knowing she was there. After suffering the most terrible of torments for a man, you then killed that woman, not out of anger or self-pity or revenge, but out of mercy for her own tragic state. The fact remains, though, that had you not run from the train under fire she might not have died. You will have to live with that."

She paused for a moment, and Dar stood motionless, frozen, staring at the eerie picture. Cass felt sorry for him, but was helpless.

"It seems to us," the goddess continued, "that through a very strange chance, the evil one has rendered an appropriate judgment on you. We therefore, by divine spell of a sort that has never been broken by any of the gods and goddesses of World, perfect and make irrevocable your present state, as constant reminder of your own deeds and as a warning if needed to you and to others. Beyond this, no other thing will be done to you for any deeds in the past, and we declare you free and independent. We further stipulate that each of you will receive our total hospitality while you are in Persellus, for so long as you both choose to be here. Dar, you may go now and wait outside, while we talk with Cass." It was not a request.

He bowed his head slightly. "Ma'am, it's only justice, I guess." He did not feel happy, but he had enough sense to remember and back out of the room. Cass was now alone with the goddess.

"You are troubled by our judgment?"

"It's pretty hard on him, I think," she admitted. "He's neither one thing nor the other, and he can't be happy either way."

"That was the idea. However, we decided to explain to you our reasoning, for he will need you at least for a while. Inside him burns tremendous guilt, and with it a self-hatred. We would willingly have restored him for all the reasons you gave, but to do so without also totally remaking his mind and memories would have increased that guilt and self-hatred quickly to the point where he would kill himself. The reasons for everything he did are buried deep in his mind and his experiences, much from long before he was cast out of Anchor Logh, so to remake his mind would have been to, essentially, kill him anyway. We do not do such work for people. By making of him a hermaphrodite, oddly enough, Montagne saved his life, for then he felt punished for his own failings. He, not we, consider this appropriate punishment, and so he remains, perhaps to be useful and productive in some way. He is not without courage, only self-confidence."

She considered it. "I don't know much about psychology, divine one, and it seems a little mixed up to me, but I'll take your word for it. You're saying that only because he's not whole can he be sane."

"That *is* about it," the goddess admitted. "Unless there is something else, you may go now."

She thought a moment. "Except that both of us need jobs, there's nothing, your worship."

"You will find what you need, for you have within you a Soul Rider who guards."

That startled her. "A what?"

"A Soul Rider. Do not fear it, for there is precious little power it cannot command if need be, and it fights the forces of darkness on World. You must only be warned that it uses you in its fight, and so you can expect more danger and adventure. Making a living will be no problem. This is enough for now. You may go."

She wanted to ask a lot more questions, particularly about this Soul Rider, but there was no way she was going to press somebody like this, particularly not now. She gave the bow and backed out the door, closing it behind her.

11

HALDAYNE

An officious-looking woman was waiting with Dar when Cass emerged from the room. Dar looked at her and said, "Well?"

She shrugged. "Tell you later, maybe. How are *you* doing?"

"I'm feeling a little off and my muscles ache, but I'm okay." He turned to the woman. "This lady says she'll see to our needs."

"I am Gratia," the woman introduced herself. "Please accompany me and I will show you to your hotel and give you a brief orientation."

They followed her out of Government House and down a central street filled with small shops and cafes, most with merchandise on racks outside or a few streetfront tables. A small hotel was two blocks down on the corner, and it was clearly a hotel and nothing else. Cass delighted at some of the displayed merchandise but couldn't help comparing what she was seeing to Anchor Logh. There was, it seemed, no equivalent of Main Street, no bars or entertainment area of any kind. The people seemed normal enough, but there was not the gaiety or spontaneity that she expected of people in a city setting. A cautious remark on the lack of some expected services brought a response from their guide.

"Our lives are lived according to the Divine Plan," Gratia told them. "Such things as you describe are the products of evil and are not needed nor permitted here."

They were given vouchers of some sort, pieces of paper with numbers printed on them and another unnaturally lifelike head portrait of the goddess on them, and told that this was the money of Persellus. It was difficult to accept something as flimsy and destructible as paper as money, but this was not Anchor Logh.

They were left in a small hotel room with a map of the central city, the money stake, and recommendations for some of the better cafes and shops in the area. "You may as well relax and enjoy your stay here," Gratia said. "It is unlikely that the stringer train will be able to be here in under three days, and we have scheduled the trial for four days from now. If you have any questions about anything here or have any needs in the meantime, do not hesitate to come by my office in Government House and discuss these with me." And, with that, she left.

Dar eyed one of the two single beds in the room and shook his head. "You know how long it's been since I've slept on a real bed? I wonder if I can do it?"

Cass laughed. "Well, if you want to be homesick for the stringer train, then you can always strip and lie on the floor."

A room both had originally taken for a closet turned out to be a bathroom, something both had never seen individually connected to a hotel room before. There was no power except wind, water, and muscle outside the capital of Anchor Logh, and when in that city both had stayed in communal quarters. It was some time before they even fully figured out how all the things worked, and marveled at hot water coming from taps without any pumping or pre-heating, and they spent some time flushing and re-flushing the toilet and trying to figure out just how it worked.

"As for me, that's the tiniest shower I've ever seen but I'm going to use it," Cass decided, stripping off her makeshift uniform. "How about you?"

Dar nodded. "I think it's strictly one at a time in there, though. I don't think I'd fit with anybody else. I still wish it was a tub, though. My legs are killing me and I'd like to soak them."

He undressed, and at least part of the reason for his distress was painfully evident. There was some blood on his legs, large and hairy as they were, and it disturbed him.

Cass still found it hard to get used to the sight of him like that—a true god, huge and musclebound, looking and sounding like a man who lifted weights casually and bent steel to relax, except in that one area. And that, of course, was his problem. The big, strong he-man was going to have to have periods explained to him. It was rather clear now what the goddess meant when she said she would "perfect" what Rory Montagne had done to him.

Later, a bit cleaner, they went shopping, both picking plain, practical clothes, such as tough denim pants and simple work shirts. They also picked up toiletries and various portable packing kits for their stuff. Neither overdid it, wanting to be able to travel light if they had to. Both also picked high boots that gave good protection and support, but only Cass picked fairly high heels which gave her a little extra height. She still did not come up to his broad shoulders, but it made her feel a little more even with the world. She also selected a dark brown flat-brimmed hat with a string tie to secure it while riding, and a hand-tooled leather belt with a plain silvery oval buckle, just because she liked the look of it.

Afterward they ate at one of the recommended cafes and found the food quite good although rather plain and unvaried, except for a seeming national passion with fancy pastries. Obviously, the goddess loved fancy pastries.

After sundown, however, the whole city just plain died. There was no nightlife at all, and no real diversions. It was clear from their shopping expeditions that the people of Persellus lived for their jobs and families and did very little else recreationally. Not that they weren't an apparently happy lot, but they seemed content with everything as it was and doing what they were doing and had no real curiosity, ambition, or even much of a competitive spirit. When looking for her belt, a leather shop had directed her to another down the street, for example.

Reading matter seemed to consist mostly of book after book of the goddess's musings, aphorisms, ramblings, and the like, most of which was tough going and made very little sense. There appeared to be little education beyond basic skilled trades and reading and writing for business reasons. They didn't need doctors because when they got sick or injured they just prayed to the goddess and she healed them. They didn't need scientists or engineers, because everything worked through the goddess's magic, even the water and electricity. Smoking, drinking, dancing, gambling, even basic entertainment like plays was forbidden, and foul language was strongly discouraged, which made Dar realize what a gaffe he'd pulled in using the very mild "hell" in the "presence" of the goddess herself.

It was, in fact, so deadly dull a town filled with such incredibly dull people that it almost drove both of them nuts. Even the humdrum farm life of Anchor Logh was a thrill a minute compared to this place. By the end of the second day they were

both so bored that they decided on the third day
to rent horses and see a little of the countryside.

But the countryside, too, had the same dull sameness as the town. The only problem they had was
occasional small bouts of vertigo now and then,
after which something would be slightly changed.
Mountains seemed a bit taller one time than
another, houses seemed to grow and shrink now
and then, and when they got back to town there
were minor, subtle differences in the look of the
buildings and even the people.

"The best guess I can make," Cass said when
they were back in their hotel room, where the
furniture and fixture designs seemed very slightly
different, "is that since this land is entirely the
product of the goddess's imagination, she sometimes makes little changes now and then, like re-
decorating a room. Or maybe it's just that, like us,
she remembers things a little differently than they
really were, and, unlike us, how she remembers
them is how they become."

"Still thinking of staying here and finding a job?"
Dar asked her. They had not really discussed the
future.

She shook her head. "Nope. I think when Matson
gets here I'll ask for some suggestions and, if I can
afford it, travel along with him for a little while
until I find a place I can really settle. You?"

"Oh, I'll come along, I guess. I sure can't see
somebody like me fitting in around here, that's for
sure. Oh, maybe if I joined the army or something
like that, I might make do, but I could never call
this home or fit into their family pattern. I don't
think *she* had me staying around in mind." He
sighed. "I wonder if there *is* a place where I'd fit
in?"

She shrugged. "I'm not sure. I'd like to know
what a Soul Rider is, though. Nobody around here
seems to know anything about it."

"Maybe Matson will. He's been around and seen everything, and he'll be in tomorrow."

She nodded. "None too soon, either." She thought a moment. "You sure about coming with Matson, though? I mean, there'll be all those Lanis, and they sure aren't the kind of people Persellus would want."

"I've licked that, I think. Look, I'm part Lani and part me. If I can't take people who look like her, then I may as well pack it in, right?"

She couldn't argue with it, but she hoped it was true.

They saw Matson first when they were summoned for Rory Montagne's trial. He looked clean and relaxed, although irritated that his cigars could not legally be brought into the Fluxland proper. He looked and felt naked without one stuck in his mouth.

All of them were seated in a comfortably appointed "witness room" well stocked with cold drink and pastries while waiting to testify. They greeted Matson warmly, and he reciprocated in his usually reserved stringer fashion, but when he asked how they liked Persellus and both silently spelled out "D-U-L-L" he had to chuckle. Finally Cass got around to business. "How much for a ride with your train?"

Matson grinned. "A week ago you'd have paid your arms and legs *not* to be anywhere near my train, now you're offering money to get back in?"

"As passengers, not cargo," she was quick to point out. "There's a big difference."

He thought a moment. "Well, Persellus money's not much use to me, although I could credit it to an open account here in the name of Anchor Logh and get something more transportable in return. Tell you what—if you supply your own horses and packs, and buy what supplies you'll need for at least a week's travel, I'll take you along as duggers—without pay, of course. You're both pretty good with animals and Jomo's got more than his hands full with the nearly double–sized train, even though we're going to pare it down a bit here. We'll try and give you a few shooting and close fighting lessons, too. How's that?" He paused a moment. "But no hysterics over the human cargo, no going nuts seeing people who look like other people, things like that."

"I'll be good," Dar responded, knowing who that was directed towards. "I've done some real thinking in the past few days, and I'm not the same person inside that I was."

That settled, Cass asked, "How come they're going through all this formal trial business for that scum? Why not just let the goddess deal with him and be done with it?"

"Well, now, that's kind of hard to explain," Matson replied. "First of all, he's a wizard. A real puny one, I admit, but a real one nevertheless. There's a sort of a fraternity that all real wizards belong to, mostly to protect them from each other. They've got their own rules, and their conduct has to be judged by other wizards of equal or greater rank before they can be disciplined. It sounds stupid, I know, but every one of them does things all the time that might be considered criminal to others, so they insist on being judged by their own standards. Next time one of the judges might be in the dock, so he or she wants to make sure that *they* followed the rules when *they* were judges. See?"

The door to the courtroom opened and a tall, distinguished-looking man entered. He looked to be in his late forties or early fifties but in excellent condition for that age. In fact, age had been very kind to him, and he was lean and handsome, his silvery gray hair complementing his dark complexion.

"I am First Minister Haldayne," he told them. "I am, in effect, the prosecutor in this case." He picked up one of the gooier pastries and ate it. "In a few moments we'll be calling direct witnesses. Just tell everything exactly as it happened, adding or subtracting nothing, and don't volunteer anything. Just answer what questions are asked, and let me be your guardian against defense questions. Above all, don't get emotional if you can help it, making moral judgments on the defendant or calling him names. The standards here are a bit different than in a normal court of law." They all nodded, and he left, then returned a few moments later. "Mr. Matson, if you please."

Matson went in and the door closed, and both Cass and Dar regretted not being able to see or hear anything. They were used to open, public courtrooms.

Matson's testimony apparently didn't last long, and Cass was called next. Haldayne offered his left hand to her to help her up from her overstuffed chair, and as she stood she noticed on his right hand a small but distinctive gold ring. Suddenly she remembered that he'd eaten the pastry with his left hand as well.

She had little time to reflect on it, though, as she was ushered into what appeared to be a traditional courtroom, although with a board of three women and two men acting as judges, and no jury. Haldayne examined her on the facts, and she told her story, almost absently, trying not to be fixated on the man himself but unable to totally betray her preoccupation. The more he talked, the more he moved, the more she was sure.

Rory Montagne looked relaxed in the dock, acting as if this somehow did not concern him at all. He had given a slight smile and wave when she'd entered, and listened to her testimony while absently gnawing on an apple. If she was right, she thought nervously, he had every reason to be unconcerned.

The defense put only a few clarifying questions to her, then she was dismissed, and Haldayne led her back to the jury room and called Dar. When the door closed again, she turned to Matson and whispered, "That man Haldayne—he's the goat-headed boss! I'm sure of it!"

Matson frowned. "Haldayne? But he's the big-wig around here, the most powerful wizard in the land, second only to the goddess herself."

None the less, she outlined her reasons and her instincts, and he did not dismiss them. "It both fits and it smells," he told her. "The trouble is, we'll need a lot more proof than you can give for it, and I'm not sure how to get it. Do you think he knows you suspect him?"

"He could hardly ignore it. I wasn't being very subtle, I'm afraid."

"Hmmm. . . . Well, even if he *is* our man, he's unassailable as he is, but if he's as good and as careful as he has to be he won't want to leave any loose ends."

She looked at him nervously. "You mean he might try and come after me?"

Matson nodded. "I think you better buy what you need this afternoon and get down to my train. Just follow the road the way you came in. I'll try and clear my business this afternoon and get back there. If he's really one of the Seven in this kind of control this close to a Hell Gate somebody will have to be notified. Damn! I wasn't headed that way, but after Globbus I think we'll have to take a detour to Pericles. Well, maybe it won't be a total loss. Pericles always likes fresh young women."

She looked up at him sharply. "Watch it!"

He shrugged. "No moral judgments, remember? Besides, there's a lot worse places to wind up than Pericles. But you watch it from now on. He may try anything at any time, and if he *is* our man and if he's also what he claims to be, he's one of the most powerful wizards on all World. He'd have to be just to reach First Minister in Persellus." He thought it over. "Still, if I were him, I *wouldn't* touch you at all. It'd give him away, where all we have now are strong and unsupported suspicions."

She suddenly remembered the goddess's comments on her. "Matson? What exactly is a Soul Rider?"

The question took him by surprise. "Huh? Where'd you hear about *them*?"

"The goddess said I had one inside me."

His mouth dropped and a light seemed to dawn in his head. "So *that* explains it! I was wondering if I was too long in this job or what. Uh huh. A Soul Rider. Well I'll be. . . ."

"You *do* know, then!"

He nodded. "More or less. They are—creatures. Not much is known about them, except that they're parasites of some kind and they hate the Seven so much they get their hosts in a whole lot of trouble. One picked you, probably back in the Anchor, and most of what happened after that was at least partly its doing."

She grew nervous. "Parasite. Will it—hurt me?"

He chuckled. "Well, depends on how you look at it. Supposedly they pick people, ordinary people, and get inside them, and all of a sudden those people get into a whole lot of trouble. Things happen to them that wouldn't happen to most folks in a lifetime. Now I *know* you're on to something here with this Haldayne fellow."

She felt very uncomfortable. "Then, it might have been this Soul Rider that caused me to find the Sister General fixing the lottery in the first place? And the reason Dar took me and only me when he ran?"

Matson nodded. "Probably. But, remember, it's

also responsible for somehow getting me to put my string on you so we could follow your trail and find the pocket. And I don't think it was coincidence that Montagne was stopped just before he changed you into one of his—creatures, or, maybe, that Dar had an attack of conscience and freed you. In fact, the odds of us finding you first were pretty slim, but we did. And now you've drawn the attention of somebody who at least thinks he's one of the Seven."

She thought it over. "I'm not sure I like being a puppet of a—thing." She shivered slightly.

"Well, they're not human, whatever they are, but they're on our side. You can't expect them to act like people would, but they're not all bad. In a pinch, they're supposedly stronger than the strongest wizard, which is why, I think, the goddess won't shed any tears when you leave."

"Still, this makes what happened to Dar even less excusable. I mean, if this *thing* caused him to do what he did. . . ."

"Nope. You miss the point there. He did that himself. Taking you along might have been the Soul Rider's idea, but not him running out or anything else he did. In fact, he was completely on their side until it was either kill you or let you escape, in which case he had to go, too, or his neck would have been chopped. You see, it's the goddess's opinion that he only saved you because he was forced by your protector to do so."

"Oh. I see. I'm not sure I agree with it, but I at least can understand it a little better now. I—"

She was about to continue when Dar returned, and all conversation in that direction ceased.

"Thank you for your help," Haldayne told them, sounding sincere. "The judgment will be rendered some time this afternoon or evening. I think he's far too insane for any appropriate punishment, but we'll see. You may all go now."

They got up and left quickly, Matson following them down to the street. "Remember—move quickly," he cautioned Cass. "If he's as good as I think he is, you can't even depend on the goddess for help in a pinch."

"I'll remember," she assured him. Dar looked bewildered, and she added, to him, "I'll explain later. Let's get back to the hotel—we're getting out of here as quickly as possible."

By the time they'd packed their meager belongings, bargained for horses, saddles, and riding gear, picked up what supplies they thought they would need, and checked out with Government House, it was close to dark. Matson had been right on one thing, though—everybody concerned seemed unnaturally glad to see both of them leave.

Although he had taken her word for the urgency and gone along, it wasn't until they were on the road out of Persellus that she felt safe enough to explain to Dar what was going on. He thought about his own brief contact with the goat-man, and admitted there were some similarities, although he was by no means as certain as she about it.

It was well into night when they passed through the small farming village, and they were grateful for the paved road as the stars gave very little light. They stopped to rest the horses, though, in a grass field near a small creek, and while just sitting there, silently, they heard sounds from the direction they'd just come, the sounds of several horses riding steadily towards them.

Cass frowned. "This is too dead a place to have that kind of traffic."

Dar nodded. "Maybe it's Matson with some others."

"I doubt it. He said he had just a little business and he said nothing about horses or passengers." She thought a minute. "Get the horses and let's keep very quiet and still off the road here. We can't outrun them, but they don't have to see us, either."

He nodded and did as instructed. There was nothing particular to hide behind, but it was a very dark night and they couldn't make out the road from where they were, which was down in a slight indentation made by the creek. A small wooden bridge over the creek was not far.

The riders reached the area but did not hesitate, and they could hear the hollow sounds of hooves hitting the wood, echoing hollowly across the landscape, and then they were gone.

Dar breathed. "Could you make out anything about them?"

"Not a thing. Just a blur. There were at least four of them, though." She sighed. "I wish we knew more about weapons and had some around."

"If they reach the train and we're not there, they'll be back," Dar pointed out.

"Maybe. But they'll have to have some excuse when they get to the train, and that should bog them down. No, I think they'll get close to the train, then lay ambush for us just up from it. It would make sense, and if any of them's a wizard they won't attract the duggers, either."

"We could stay here until daylight. That might make it a little easier. There may be people around, and Matson'll be on his way back."

She considered it. "I don't think it'll work. For one thing, down this far there weren't many people. I don't remember *any*, do you? And they're not going to stay all night. When we don't show after a while they're going to come back slow and sneaky."

"Well, what then? If we get off the road we're lost good and proper and you know it."

"It's mostly unfenced this far along, and I guess it's not more than another seven or eight kilometers to the border and the train. The river's over there, maybe a few hundred meters. Let's follow it down. It's going pretty much the same place but it's less likely to be covered, particularly by only four people."

Having no other suggestion, Dar agreed. They followed the creek down to the river, then nervously waded the small creek just up from its joining with the larger body of water. It was fairly deep, but not deep enough to be a problem to two riders used to horses.

The ground, however, was pretty wet, and the depth of the creek told them that the river would be an obstacle in case of any sort of attack, almost certainly too deep to cross. Fortunately, this far down there were few tributaries to worry about, and each one seemed to be shallower than the one before, telling them they were getting close to the border. They thought they were going to make it easily when the river suddenly curved away into the dark hills after making a bend bringing them close enough to actually make out the road.

They stopped to consider what to do next, and there was an ominous rumbling from off to their right. Dar looked over in that direction and saw the hills suddenly light up as clouds rolled in impossibly fast. "Thunderstorm," he remarked.

"Looks pretty odd for a real one," Cass responded uneasily. "A good wizard could whip one up, though, and light up the whole landscape and us with it. I'd say we'd better make for the road and just make a run for it as fast as we can."

"I'm with you," Dar told her, and they kicked their horses into action. Suddenly a great roaring wall of fire rose up in front of them, spooking the horses and causing them to stop and rear. Less experienced riders would have been thrown, but both Dar and Cass managed to stay in the saddle, if barely. The wall of fire spread, until it encircled them on three sides. With the horses already near panic, they had no choice but to take the one exit, even though they knew they were being forced into a trap.

They cleared the fire, then halted as they saw four riders on horseback ahead, spread out to receive them, guns in the hands of all four. The wall of fire vanished abruptly, and Cass cursed herself for not betting that it was an illusion and urging her horse to jump through it, but the four riders were still somehow illuminated, as were Cass and Dar.

"Just stay where you are and make no sudden moves," one of them, a man, said. "The fire may have been a trick but the bullets are real. You two, get down slowly and walk towards us, real slow now."

They did as instructed, until they were right in front of the four riders, all men of middle age, all bearded and wearing farm work clothes. Cass couldn't help but remember that the goat-man, according to Montagne, had had his "minions" move the dark priest from his old pocket to the new one. These, then, must be minions of the mad priest's boss.

"What do we do now?" Cass asked them.

The leader chuckled. "Now, ain't that something! Look at 'em, Eck! Two pieces of ass pretending they's men. Neither of 'em look like they'd be any fun a'tall. I sure don't want 'em. Any of you?"

There were a few sniggers from the other three, but no takers.

"Then I guess the answer to your question about what to do next is to pray," the leader said coldly, steadying his rifle.

Yeah, sure—pray, Cass thought sourly, then hope soared for a moment. Yeah! Sure! Pray! She only hoped that Dar had enough sense to roll when she did, for there was no way to tip him off. And pray she did.

"Oh, great and divine goddess, deliver us from evil!" she practically shouted, then dropped and rolled at the same time. The leader, caught off guard, fired, but neither target was there any more.

Cass had just made for the grass, but Dar had other plans. While Cass just kept praying in a low tone, he leaped up from the side and pulled one of the men off his horse. The man fell, dropping his rifle, and Dar picked it up as the others were turning to meet the threat, then dropped and rolled once more, coming up in front of them, rifle pointed at them. The fact that he had only a vague idea of how it worked or how to hit anything with it was something *he* knew, but they did not.

"Drop your weapons!" he commanded sharply.

The leader turned and grinned at him. "Why?" Suddenly the whole area was brightly lit as if from a suspended floodlight, although no source was visible. Dar looked down and was startled to see that he was now pointing a stick at the men.

While a second helped the fallen comrade to his feet, a third dismounted and walked over to where Cass was still lying, now fully exposed, and gestured with his rifle. She got up, but did not stop praying until ordered to shut up.

"Who sent you?" she demanded to know.

"What's it to you?" the leader asked. He thought a moment. "You know, boys, we could use a simple spell on 'em to make 'em easier to take, if you know what I mean."

"Now you're talking, Crow," the one called Eck responded. "I always did hanker to screw that little milkmaid up at Gorner's. You know who I mean."

Crow made a pass at each of them with his hand. Cass looked over and was startled to see not Dar but the vision of a very pretty and much smaller dark-haired girl. She knew it was just Dar, and that it was all illusion, but it was still startling. She wondered what she looked like to them.

"Get them clothes off now, and don't be too gentle about 'em. You won't be needing them afterwards," Crow said ominously.

Suddenly there was a great flash of lightning, striking very near them and spooking the gunmen's horses a bit. Crow looked puzzled. "Now what the hell is that? I didn't do nothin'!"

"Sinners! Blasphemers! Agents of Hell! You dare this in our domain!" came a familiar woman's voice, angry as they had not heard it before. "For this you shall pay beyond your imaginings!"

"It's the goddess!" one of them cried, and Crow said, "But Haldayne promised she wouldn't—"

"Haldayne!" thundered the goddess, and there was lightning all over the place. "So it *is* true! Well, first we will deal with you, and then we will deal with First Minister Haldayne, formerly of Persellus, soon of Hell." A lightning bolt came out of the sky, then split into four finger-like segments much like a ghostly hand, then struck all four riders simultaneously. All four, including the one newly remounted, toppled out of their saddles to the ground, screaming in agony as they continued to be enveloped by the electrical field. There was another flash at each of the four points, then silence.

"You were right to call upon us," the goddess's disembodied voice told them. "We heard you accuse Haldayne in the witness room but could not believe it. We elected to go along with you and discover the truth and now we have."

"Those four men—what happened to them?" Dar asked her.

"Transformed. Take them along as presents for your stringer. Use them to pay for what you need. I must now attend to their master. Do not fear the four, for they are imprisoned in their own minds, unable to act or do anything at all. They are property, and they are yours, and they will now see what the other side is like." And, with that, they sensed that the presence was gone.

Cass and Dar approached the four figures nervously, and were struck by what they found. Both she and he looked themselves again now, and there was very little light but enough to see close up.

"Well, she certainly has a single mind when it comes to punishing men," Dar remarked.

All four men were now vacant-eyed and not very attractive but quite nude women with shaved heads and tattooed behinds. They seemed to be waiting for Cass to do something, so she finally said, "All right, you four—mount those horses and follow us." All four got up and obeyed their instructions exactly.

"I think we'd better get moving," she told Dar. "There's going to be all Hell breaking loose, literally, around this land soon and I want to be in the void when it does."

Dar nodded, and said, bitterly, "You know, this is the first time I really regret not being a man down below."

"Huh? What do you mean?"

"I'd love to show *them* exactly how it feels to be on the other end of things."

Cass had to laugh. "Welcome to the world *I* live in all the time!" she said.

12

MATURITY

Even on the periphery of Persellus they could feel the giant struggle going on inside. In one sense, Cass, Dar, and the duggers had to fight back urges to return, at least for a small distance, to the reality of the land proper to see it for themselves, but they did not. They had their responsibilities to themselves and to the train, for one thing, and, for another, they did not want to be caught up in such a fight between two supremely powerful wizards. When the land changed just because of a lapse in the goddess's memory, what might be the changes when she was directing all her energies to fighting a powerful foe with neither combatant having either much thought or much regard for the people caught in the middle?

Still, there was the sound of thunder and the ground beneath them shook like all of World had suddenly come alive and revolted. The animals grew panicky and hard to control, and Jomo and his two new assistants struggled to keep them calm.

"Maybe we'd better move completely into the void," Cass shouted over the roar.

"Too late," Jomo yelled back. "We not be able to get them formed. Best just hold on!"

And hold on they did, sometimes with the help of the Anchor Logh exiles, for what seemed like an eternity. Suddenly, though, *very* suddenly, it all stopped dead, and everyting became quiet and still. After so long fighting scared animals and being in the midst of what felt like a great storm, it seemed almost unnatural to go back to the normal lifelessness they had so taken for granted.

After sorting the mess out and settling down, Dar wiped his brow, sat down on a pack, and said, "Well, I guess somebody won. Wonder who?"

That suddenly was uppermost on all their minds. For Cass, it was particularly unnerving, since if Haldayne was the victor he would waste no time coming after her, and perhaps the whole train, to keep the news secret as long as possible, and they were up against a wall. Without Matson, none of them could navigate the void, and even Kolada, the train's "point" or scout, could only take them back as far as the massacre or, perhaps, to Anchor Logh. That route would be pretty easy for Haldayne's people to trace.

The duggers were particularly distressed that Matson had been in the midst of all the pyrotechnics. Some doubted that he was still alive at all, but others, particularly Jomo, held that he would come. Clearly, if anyone *could* have gotten through that stuff, Matson was the one.

No matter how any of them thought, the decision to wait was easy. There simply wasn't anything else to do. Cass talked Jomo into finally reorganizing the train enough to move it completely into the void and beyond the reach of any ruler of Persellus. It was a difficult and time consuming procedure even though the total move was only a little more than a kilometer, but they agreed and, at least, it took their minds off anything else for a few hours.

It struck not only Dar but their erstwhile comrades how very easily Cass was taking over, giving more orders than suggestions now—and being obeyed by the duggers. She set up the new camp in a defensive position, then posted riflemen both front and rear. This done, she ordered a general inventory of supplies and ammunition be taken, for they didn't know how long they would be stuck there.

Jomo paid her a high compliment. "Too bad you not know how to string. You seem sometime to be ghost of Missy Arden."

Finally, though, all that could be done had been done. The supplies were quite promising—with the recovered material from the Arden train taken from the pocket and the subsequent recovery of the supplies dropped by Matson before coming in, they had sufficient food for people and animals for a long stay, perhaps two to three weeks if they conserved carefully. Water, however, was in shorter supply and could pose a problem. Because it was so heavy, stringers rarely took along more water than they had to, depending on their knowledge of small stringer-created water pockets to replenish their casks. There was probably one or more of these on the Anchor Logh route, but as the trip had been short enough Matson hadn't bothered to stop and so they did not know where any might be. Still, if they didn't stay too long, it was possible that they had enough water to return to the Anchor.

"What's the use, though?" Cass asked Dar and Jomo. "We'd get back, maybe, but only as far as the clear spot—the Anchor apron. That's assuming we all didn't go nuts in the void without Matson's powers to protect us."

Dar thought it over. "Well, the goddess was nice enough to take our damned tattoos off, so we wouldn't be marked. The duggers would have the train to deal with in signing on with the next stringer who came along. I think you and me could talk our way back in. I don't look much like I did, and I bet they don't remember what Arden looked like all that much. You could say it was Matson who was ambushed and you, that is Arden, survived. Or you could stay with the duggers and make your own deal with another stringer."

She looked at him quizzically. "You want back in Anchor Logh? What on World for? What is there for you back there now?"

He grinned. "I could always join the priesthood. *That* would drive 'em nuts, wouldn't it? At least I'd have a shot at those bastards in that bar back there, and maybe at the Sister General."

She shook her head. "No. As much as I'd love to see her get what's coming to her, and as much as I'd *really* love to see what they'd do if you *did* apply for the priesthood, I don't think it'll go. Somehow we've got to warn somebody of Haldayne and the threat to the gate."

"Yeah? Who, for instance? And where? And how? And are we so sure that the bad guys won?"

"You want to go back there and find out? As to the who, well, if the gates to Hell are real, and Haldayne really is one of the Seven, then it follows that the Nine Who Watch must exist someplace, too."

Dar chuckled dryly. "Gates, Hell, the Seven and the Nine. Just stories. Who do we have to say they aren't? Roaring Mountain? Even his friends agree he's living in a different world. Haldayne? It's a good gag to get those that believe in the stuff but don't like it to come over to his side, but that's all. You don't need demons from Hell to be bad, but maybe the bad need the demons as much as the church does."

That was a pretty good point, but she just wasn't ready to change her entire life view that easily, not yet. Roaring Mountain had been sought out and transported a tremendous distance to do his dirty work here. Men with power such as Haldayne's didn't grow overnight, either—clearly he had a long history and knew much of World, and such a one, whether one of the Seven or not, would have a host of enemies, probably other powerful wizards, and few friends or allies.

"Jomo?"

"Yes, Missy?"

"How long might it be before another stringer train came this way? Best case and worst case?"

Jomo was not dumb, but his mind worked in a very literal fashion. "Best—now. Worst—never."

She sighed. "No, I mean, what would be your best guess?"

"Mr. Matson not go back to Anchor Logh for long time. Has lot of orders for Anchor Logh. That mean train must be coming soon, yes?" He hesitated a moment. "Unless Missy Arden plan to go back."

And that was part of the problem. With Arden gone and her plans unknown, it might have been she who would carry the wanted materials back to the Anchor. Or it might be another stringer on his or her way here now—but how far off? Just when on his long route did Matson expect to meet this possibly imaginary train going the other way?

She sighed. "We'll give him one day. Three meals. Then I think we have no choice but to go back to Anchor Logh and wait for another stringer, trading what we have for what we need until then. It's either that or sneak back into Persellus and get water from the river. Any volunteers?"

Jomo was unprepared to give up Matson so easily. "I go in. Take two, maybe three slaves."

Dar sighed and stood up. "Oh, all right, *I'll* go. No, not you, Cass—if Haldayne's in charge you won't last ten minutes. Me he couldn't care less about. At the most it'll take a couple of hours."

She started to protest, and realized that part of her protest was based on her still uncertain feelings about Dar deep down. He had gone over once to Haldayne's side—would he take the chance to join up again? He had quite a present to deliver Haldayne if he did—not only her, but the whole train and detailed knowledge of its defenselessness and predicament. Finally she relented, though. If he were bad, he would eventually find a way to betray them anyway. Best to find out now. "Who will you take?"

He walked over and examined the hay wagon and its casks. "Two should be enough, I think. It's a simple crank siphon system." He walked back and sought out Suzl and Nadya, who had not up to this point recognized him. He brought them forward and Cass greeted them warmly. "Look," she told them, "we'll try and buy your way out of this if we can, I promise. And I won't order you to do this. It might be very dangerous in there right now."

"We'll go," Nadya told her. "It is far better than sitting here." Suzl nodded agreement, and looked up at Dar. "Might even be fun."

They pulled out towards the edge of Persellus, Dar with the reins holding the four mules, the girls sitting on either side of him.

"It's hard to believe that you're Dar," Suzl remarked, "although once you told us you can see it. Wow! If you'd looked this good back in Anchor Logh you'd have had every girl begging for you, even the priestesses!"

He laughed. "It's the magic out here. Wish I had some to use! I'd give both of you long, brown hair and get rid of those purple numbers."

The edge region of Persellus looked the same, but as they proceeded into the land proper there was a devastating alteration. While the area nearest the border was untouched, the distant skyline showed a terrible change in the now early morning light. Across green fields to the horizon, the land turned suddenly dark and brown, and in the distance there seemed to be dark new mountains growing up and split near their summits with cracks belching fire and smoke. Everything up ahead seemed bathed in that smoke and flame.

Dar sighed. "Well, I guess we know who won. One thing's for sure—ain't nobody coming through *that* back this way any time soon."

"It's pretty nice down in here, though. I guess I can sort of feel what it was like before," Suzl commented. "So this is a Fluxland. Even with that stuff over there, it's not as bad as I thought."

Nadya looked up at him. "You're the boss now. At least, some of the boss."

They turned off the road as soon as the river was visible to them. It looked reasonably clean and unsullied at this point, since it flowed towards the capital and not away from it. They had no trouble backing the wagon down near the bank, uncoiling the sipons, and quickly filling all the casks. After, Suzl and Nadya just wanted to lie in the grass for a bit, luxuriating in the feel and smell of something real for a change. Dar came and relaxed beside them.

As he stretched out, relaxing for a moment for the first time in quite a while, the two girls snuggled up close to him. Their intent, and movements, were pretty obvious, and he felt for them. For the first time, and for this little time, they were free, unwatched, unchained or roped, in a setting that was peaceful and nearly idyllic after all that they'd experienced. He liked the situation, and he liked and sympathized with them which made it all the better. He thought briefly of Lani, and found it not painful but really more, well, nostalgic. He'd seen that group of Lani look-alikes back at the train and found that they no longer affected him much at all. That was the past, and all the terrors that had happened to him were because he had refused to let go of the past but chased it instead. No more. The future was unknown and probably bad, but living in the present was more than acceptable.

He felt himself getting turned on, and it was an odd sensation, both physically and emotionally. He very much wanted to get inside these two, but, almost at the same time, he wanted *them* in *him*. He understood what it was, and sighed. His head wanted what it always had, while his working part was sending the opposite messages. The two didn't cancel out, they coexisted, making the tension inside almost unbearable. When Suzl's hand headed for the obvious place, he suddenly forced himself. "No!"

They both stopped. "Why not?" Suzl asked. "Who will ever know? Or are you still hung up with—"

"Lani? No, that's gone."

"It's Cass, isn't it?" Nadya guessed.

He chuckled. "No, not that, either. You remember what I said about magic? Well, I got rewarded with this body for doing the right thing, but I also got punished for doing the wrong ones. Go ahead, reach in and grab what you can find."

Curious and a little fearful, Suzl did, and when she hit the area she felt around, disbelieving. "Oh, by the Heavens!" she breathed, and Nadya looked puzzled. Now it was Nadya's turn. She gasped and exclaimed, "He's a girl!"

"That part of me is, yeah. The rest is what you see." In a way he was glad it was out in the open, particularly with them. He knew he'd faced this for a long, long time.

Suzl thought a moment and chuckled. "Dar— were you a virgin? I mean, did you ever get the chance . . . ?"

He grinned. "No, I wasn't a virgin. I had a couple of times early with some older women, and Lani and me, we figured it wouldn't matter. In fact, them older women taught me a whole lot of stuff I'd never have thought of otherwise."

"Show me," Suzl said.

"Huh?"

"Show me."

"But I can't—"

Both girls laughed. "You'd be surprised. We never did it with a guy, because we just *knew* we'd wind up pregnant, but we still had the urges. So after we'd see a couple of boys we really wanted, and couldn't have, we'd sneak off and sort of, well, pretend on each other."

And, while volcanos belched in the distance as a land was being torn asunder, they showed him, and he showed them, and what he did to them they did to him. And it felt real good and lasted quite a while.

They were still at it—it seemed impossible to stop—when, during a silent period, Dar's hearing picked up a distant sound coming closer. He froze, then rolled over and hurriedly got dressed again. "Wagon coming!" he warned them. "We better move it!"

"Let 'em come," Suzl said dreamily. "It can only get worse than this, it can't get any better."

Dar, however, had experienced far too much to take such an attitude. In fact, his interlude with the two girls had the curious effect of energizing him, and his mind was clearer and more at peace with itself than he could ever remember. Still, Suzl was right about one thing—any wagon close enough to be heard couldn't be outrun at this stage. He went to the wagon and got the rifle, which had a clip in it. He still couldn't hit the broad side of a barn, but with its spray control, he was assured, if he just aimed in the general direction and pulled the trigger anything within range would get struck by at least one of the sixty small but powerful bullets it would spew in less than a second and a half.

The wagon approached, behind a sweaty team of horses being driven hard. It was of the canvas covered type, similar to the one they were using, and looked fairly empty from the way it rocked. The lone driver looked over, spotted them, and with some difficulty slowed his four horse team and pulled off to the side of the road, a weapon in one hand and the reins in the other.

"What the hell are *you* all doing here?" Matson wanted to know. Then he spotted the water casks and understood. "All right—you get all my property back right now. Let's move! That mess back there is expanding and I've barely been able to keep ahead of it."

There was a cry of joy from the duggers at Matson's arrival, and several fired shots of celebration in the air. Cass was overjoyed as well, not only by Matson's sudden arrival but also by the return of Dar and the two girls. Matson, however, was having none of it, and quickly snapped orders to get the train in line and prepare to move out. To Cass's attempt to welcome him he just snapped, "Why are you just standing around? You're working for me, now! And where the hell are my cigars?"

It wasn't until the train was formed and well on its way, with Kolada given the string lead and dispatched ahead, that Matson relaxed at all and became approachable. Cass dropped back from her point opposite Jomo at the head of the mule train until she, on her black purchased horse, rode parallel with Matson. He acknowledged her with a nod and said, "Jomo tells me you did the whole defensive setup and even thought about the water. That right?"

She nodded. "I didn't know if you were coming back or not, but I had to act like you weren't."

"It was good thinking. I got out of there barely one step ahead of the new matrix and had to outrun it for four solid hours. If I'd stayed overnight like I originally intended I wouldn't be here now. Something just told me that Haldayne couldn't resist a stab at you, and that would flush him out, force him into a revolt."

"I hear from Dar that he won."

"Pretty sure he did, anyway. Bubbling, boiling, smoking—that place is turning into a real old-time view of Hell. Too bad, although it's got to be livelier than it was under the old bag."

She really couldn't argue with the sentiment, although, unlike him, she also couldn't forget the poor people whose lives, if not snuffed out, would be radically and permanently changed—and certainly not for the better.

"I brought some trade goods with me," she told him. "Four more girls and four good horses." At his raised eyebrows she told him the story of the encounter the night before that had saved her but precipitated the destruction of Persellus as they had known it.

"Fair enough," he responded. "They'll help make up for some of the ones Arden lost in the attack."

"Not so fast! They're not gifts, you know."

He assumed his stoic pose, trying hard to suppress a smile and not quite succeeding. "All right. What do you think they're worth?"

"Come on!" she chided. "You know that I'm ignorant enough of the way the system works out here that you'll skin me in the deal no matter what. I deserve at least a little consideration."

"Why? We're even as far as I'm concerned. More than even, in fact, considering that you've gone from slave to woman of property in record time."

"That may be, but the fact is that we—Dar and I—aren't free just because of *your* kind generosity. Even if you hadn't freed me before, you wouldn't want anybody with a Soul Rider in your stock. I'd be a time bomb waiting to go off with any customer, and in the end you'd regret it. And, as I understand it, most of these people are not going to stay the way they are when they get delivered. They'll be subject to the magic of the land or wizard that gets them. That makes Dar a lousy property, since he's locked in that way until a stronger wizard than the goddess comes along, untangles her spells, and writes new ones. That reduces his value a lot, I'd say, so it was no big thing to free him, either, particularly since you get nineteen more than you bargained for. And, as you pointed out not long ago, we're working—for free—for our ride and using our own supplies. So what *do* we owe you?"

The smile could no longer be suppressed. "All right. Granting that, this is still business, but don't give me any more of that poor little innocent shit. I have this feeling that even without your damned Soul Rider you'd wind up running this train anyway if I looked away for a moment or didn't read every little contract clause. Now, understanding that, you tell me what you want and I'll tell you what your four slaves and four horses will buy of it."

She thought a moment. What *did* she want, exactly? She had the feeling she should consult with Dar, but she decided against it. Matson would just use him to rob them both blind.

"I want freedom for as many of my friends as I can buy," she told him. "I also want some kind of stake and passage to a place where I—we—can enjoy and earn our own livings."

He laughed. "You want a lot for four horses and four slaves! Now, the stake needed would depend on the place, wouldn't it? And I don't think you really *have* a particular place now, so long as you have that Soul Rider inside, anyway, and that could be for life."

"I think I wouldn't mind being a stringer," she told him seriously.

"I doubt it. For one thing, you're too soft-hearted. You start thinking of that cargo as *people* back there instead of just more trade goods, like horses and mules and hard goods, and you start bleeding for them. You couldn't help it, even though none of 'em can ever go back to Anchor and they'd all go nuts or die quickly in the Flux without a wizard looking over 'em. Anyway, it's a closed guild. If you aren't born a stringer, you can't be one. And if you tried to set up in competition, other stringers would get together and do you in. Part of the code, and good business. And we don't have partners, just employees. Still, I agree that you're doomed to wander. Want a job with a stringer train, then?"

She grinned. "That might be the next best thing. But I wouldn't want a job where I had to stay out of the Fluxlands and Anchors with the mules and wagons, or where I just stayed a few hours."

"That's not a problem," he responded, understanding that they were in fact negotiating. "Most duggers don't go into Fluxlands because they don't want to or they're afraid they might get kidnapped or used by the powers that be. Some of 'em are just sensitive about their looks and don't feel comfortable outside the void. As for Anchors, I've had a problem the last couple of years because I didn't have any total humans to help me with the packs going in. Had to depend on the locals, and they *charge*. The average layover is three days, and would have been back there if things didn't feel funny and if I didn't have this big human cargo to deliver down the line, eating me broke the longer I have that many on my hands."

She nodded. "Fine. So the Anchors allow only people they consider as human as they are inside, and you need humans. I'm human. I don't know whether Dar would pass their inspection, though."

"Probably. They're not as fussy so long as you look normal. They have the mental image of duggers as you know them. He, or she, or whatever it is, would have to be careful that nobody found out that secret, though. Anchorfolk are so damned scared of anything different that a mob would tear him to bits and get a medal for it. You should know that."

She nodded. "I think he'd take that risk. I assume we work for expenses in the various places."

"Expenses, hell! You get a salary on account. Anything you spend anyplace you get deducted. Anything left over at the end of each circuit, which is most of a year, you get credited to a stringer account. If you live long enough, don't get fired, and keep your costs down you can retire to the Fluxland of your choice someday. Or sucker some friendly wizard into making the pocket of your dreams, which is what most of 'em do."

"So there are some friendly wizards. I'd begun to wonder. Seriously, though—how many duggers that you know of ever lived long enough to retire?"

He shrugged. "Well, none *personally* . . ."

"Uh huh. It's a deal."

He laughed. "Impulsive, aren't you? You decided on this first thing, didn't you?"

"Well, I admit I had it in mind. I wasn't sure whether you wanted to travel with a Soul Rider, though."

"That's more serious than you think. But there are pluses with the minuses on that. Potentially you're stronger than any wizard, although it's useful only in defense, I hear. That's fine. What protects you protects the train. Of course, you're a magnet for trouble, but out here I'm not sure I could tell the difference anyway. At least your Rider's concern is also mine now, so maybe we'll work together to get rid of that and it'll be done with you."

She looked at him with interest. "Then you're going to report this?"

"Honey, I'm going to do at least that. Haldayne's bad for business right where he is, at the intersection of three good routes. He ordered an attack on, and was responsible for, a massacre of a stringer train, so nobody's safe until he's eliminated. As soon as we unload as much as we can in Globbus, not to mention alerting them there só the route from this side can be closed, we're heading for Pericles. Not the whole train—I'll just have to eat expenses on what I can't unload, although I'm going to take some merchandise with me to Pericles because I think there might be a market for it."

"What's this Pericles?"

"The home of one of the oldest, battiest, most degenerate and powerful wizards on all of World— and, incidentally, the dean of the current Nine Who Guard."

She gasped. "So there *is* a Nine! But—what do you mean by 'current'?"

"Nobody lives forever, even out here. I think the old boy told me once that his grandmother was one of the originals. He's barely, he says, six hundred years old."

"Six hun—oh, my! Do you think he's really that old?"

"Could be. But he's the strongest of the Nine, and therefore the only one publicly known. If he's been around that long, and known for at least a hundred years, then he must be one hell of a wizard because that makes him automatically one hell of a target." He sighed. "Well, I guess that concludes our business. See if your friend wants to go along or what, but the job's open either way."

"We haven't settled anything," she responded. "I just got hired, that's all. I still want some of my friends free."

He sighed. "You need an advance, so the four

horses will take care of that for two of you. But what if I freed four of your friends in an even trade? They'd have no jobs, no defenses, no place to go, and I'm not about to hire on *six* new hands, none of whom can even shoot. All you'd do is kill 'em for sure, or give them to Globbus or someplace else for free. In the Fluxlands, everybody's either owned, if they have no Flux power, or employed if they do. If any of that lot had much power we'd have seen it by now."

She hated to admit it to herself, but she had to agree that he was right. It was very easy to say "You are free!" and feel good about it, but they would be free in a land where they would be at the mercy of just about everyone and powerless to prevent slavery at no gain to themselves or anyone else, and no input by anyone into how and where they would be used. If she could free them to return to Anchor that would be one thing, but even she would only be a visitor in that realm now, there at the sufferance of authorities and on a limited permit. "Well, there are three I'd like to free, anyway."

"Nope. Two is tops. I can't handle any more. After that the cost becomes counter-productive. The only reason I can handle four of you is that I'm sure one or two of you will screw up and never return from one place or another, at least in any usable form. And those two will work strictly for the value of the other two slaves we sell until they exhaust their accounts. Then we'll see if they are worth keeping or if they're fired. No other guarantees, no other deals than that."

"Mister generosity."

"I'm not generous. I'm your boss. And I'll fire your ass and that of our musclebound friend if I'm the least bit unhappy. No more lip, take it or leave it."

"I'll talk to Dar when we stop and then let you know," she told him. "How far to Globbus?"

"Oh, it's about sixty kilometers from here. We average a little better than twenty kilometers a day, so that's three days. Closer than Persellus is to Anchor Logh by a fair amount. In fact, it's about the same distance to Anchor Logh from Globbus or Persellus—I had to go out of my way to do some business that, damn it, will probably never get done now."

That "night," as train time was measured in the void, Cass put the proposition to Dar, who seemed interested although unhappy that they didn't get more. "You really want to be a dugger," he told her, "and I can't see any other place I'd fit in. Hell, anyplace else I'm a freak, but out here I'm *normal* compared to most of 'em."

She nodded. "That's what I figured. Now comes the hard part, though. Which two?"

He didn't even have to think. "Suzl and Nadya, of course."

"Not Ivon?"

He chuckled dryly. "That bigmouth was hiding behind a wagon while you girls were reloading rifles in the fight. He's also still scared to death of the duggers. I like him, but for all his muscles he'd never fit in around here. I think the two girls will."

She had to agree, but found it surprising they agreed so readily on both choices. "You three spent an awfully long time getting the water. We just about gave you up for dead. Something I should know about now?"

He sighed. "Aw, hell. We took a three-way roll in the grass, Cass, if you must know."

"But—"

"Hey! If the Sister General can do it, why not us? Besides, I can't help it. I still like girls. And what man is going to give *me* a tumble even if I was willing to do it? Jomo?"

She didn't argue that point, although she suspected that there were some men who'd be delighted with him the way he was. Considering the people she'd already seen in Anchor as well as Flux, that would be a minor oddity hardly worth noting. "What I mean is, I didn't really think that those two were that way."

He chuckled. "They never tried the other way, but they were willing. Then they—found out."

She was fascinated. "What about—you? How do you feel about it?"

He grew very serious. "It was really kind of funny. Until now I been real tight about the first time it would happen, but I knew it had to happen. Now, hell, it's like I'm free, a whole new person. I got lucky, that's all. Most folks would have turned away, or treated me like I had some deathly disease, or something, but they didn't. Funny, too—those shots must have worn off, 'cause they got real turned on, if you know what I mean." He paused and looked suddenly concerned. "This doesn't poison them for you, does it?"

She shook her head. "Of course not. In fact, it says something about them that they accepted you as you were. It means they'll fit in this crazy setup. Let's call them over."

The two girls were delighted at the news, but distressed that they were to be the only ones. "It makes us feel so *guilty*," Suzl told them.

"I told Cass about back at the river," Dar told them.

Both looked slightly embarrassed. "Is that what it is, then? Because we . . ." Nadya said finally, her voice dropping off. "But we didn't intend to. It just sort of built up in me the longer we were in that place."

"Me, too," Suzl agreed. "Stronger than I ever

felt before, and it didn't matter who or what. I'm just glad Dar was there. If I was alone and feeling like that I'd have screwed a horse if one came up. Nothing personal, Dar."

He nodded. "That's funny, though. I felt it, too. Still do. I just put it down to the shots wearing off."

Nadya shook her head. "Nope. None of the others have it. It was something in the air, I guess."

Cass thought it over. "Something in the air. . . . Maybe part of Haldayne's new world that was strong enough to seep through. Who knows what urges somebody like that has, or what sort of thing he likes? If the goddess could absent-mindedly rearrange a couple of mountains because it slipped her mind how they were and she liked them better that way, then his own ideas might change things as well, even without him consciously willing it. Maybe emotions run stronger than will, or at least ahead. It would make sense."

"A whole land run like Roaring Mountain's pocket," Dar said, and shivered a bit.

Cass got back to business. "Don't feel that was the reason. At least, not the only one in either of our cases. I picked you two before I knew. You're both farmgirls, you know how to ride, and you're adaptable. Look at most of them back there. Still mostly dead inside, just waiting for the ax to fall. That's what sets the four of us apart—we accepted what was and went from there. They are probably better off where they're going if they can't go home. We're going to beat this system, and maybe have some fun doing it."

She went forward and told Matson of their decision and their choices. He was surprised only at one thing. "No men, huh? Didn't pick out anyone for yourself?"

She shook her head. "No. I gather by that comment, though, that you knew about them."

He grinned. "I could hardly avoid noticing. For the record, those two are the best of a mediocre lot, I think, from past judgments. They may work out, although they'll have to watch themselves in the Fluxlands—and Anchors, too, if they get into any. Attractive humans, male and female, have a habit of disappearing there. In either case I'm dealing with a wizard who has more power in his little finger than I have in my whole body or with a church with absolute control of a large population of ignorant idiots, which means it would cost me too damned much to get help and I have no real pressure. There are other stringers if I become a problem. No, I'm satisfied. Dress up the train a bit. We'll get them presentable in Globbus." He paused. "But what about you? If you want to blow the account, you could get some hair and maybe remake yourself if you wanted to."

She thought about it. "No. I've been this way and I think I'll stay this way, at least for a while."

He stared into her eyes. "You ever had sex? With anybody, I mean, of either sex?"

She was startled by the directness of the question, but felt comfortable enough with him to answer it. In fact, around Matson her feelings were oddly different, although she couldn't really put her finger on it. "No," she said softly. "Never."

"Never wanted to?"

"Oh, sure. I had the urges, yes. But I'm just not the sort that boys want, that's all."

"Maybe. Maybe for *some* boys, or men, that'd be true. Most of 'em only look at the outsides in Anchor, which is why I call 'em all dumb and ignorant. If I only looked at outsides in the Flux, I'd never have the best dugger team on World and I couldn't stand ninety percent of the Fluxlands. Arden, now, wasn't pretty by some standards, although she sure knew how to make herself so when it counted. She was as bald as you, you know.

Kept it that way because she said she didn't have time in the void to mess with her hair."

The only view Cass had had of Arden was pretty ugly and not conducive to knowing anything about what she had looked like in life. "I didn't know that," she told him.

"You sure you're not running from sex? I've seen it before. Women who get to where they try and make themselves as unattractive as possible. Confess, now. You got rid of those shots back in Persellus."

"Maybe you're right," she responded, her mind a little mixed up at what he was saying, wondering if in fact it was true. "But maybe it's just that I don't want somebody attracted to me just because I faked it all with fashions or even magic spells. This is crazy, but I really do *like* being me, and, right now, I've never been happier in my whole life. Does that sound like I've gone mad with the void or what?"

"No," he said gently. "No, it sounds like you did something most folks never really do, in Anchor or Flux. You grew up. Most folks never do. Most of *them* never will, never would in any case. That's the bottom line in why I took you on. Now you have to grow up one little bit more or else you're going to lose something. Either you can hide behind that boy's face and voice and keep forcing those feelings down or you can say the hell with it and let it out. If you hold it in and hide, then you'll still make a hell of a good dugger but you'll never be a complete human being." He pointed to the regular duggers, all misshapen, most deformed inside and out. "The Flux will just reinforce it, like it reinforces their own problems. Ever think that any of them has enough on account to get themselves done back to any human form they want?"

No, she hadn't thought of it. "You mean they're that way because they *want* to be like that?"

He nodded. "They're all hiding, just like you. Oh, they're not all hiding from the same things, but they're hiding all the same. We'll never know what turned them into those forms, so we'll never know what keeps them that way. But's that's *you* over there, Cass. Now."

She didn't like that idea, but she was in a minor state of shock from his talk, and she didn't want to admit that he might be right. "So what would you suggest? I shoot the profit making myself into a glamorous sexpot? *Who* wouldn't last long in Flux or Anchor?"

He shook his head negatively. "No. If you like it that way, be that way. But be that way because it's practical, or comfortable, or it's just *you*, not because you're hiding behind it."

She thought back to that time in Anchor, about all the rejection and her own attitudes and feelings. Was Matson right? Could it be true? "So what do I do if it *is* true, which I don't think it is."

"If it isn't, prove it. Take the plunge."

She smiled grimly. "Yeah, that's an easy dare. Take the plunge with who? Jomo? Nagada? One of the fake Lanis? Seems like everybody around here is either female or not exactly human."

"There's one," he said casually, blowing a smoke ring. "Me."

She stared at him as if he were suddenly some strange and terrible creature, the man she'd imagined when she first was scared stiff of the sight of him that day back in Anchor Logh. Her emotions were so jumbled up inside her she could neither understand nor sort them out. "You?" She paused a moment. "It's just Haldayne's influence. You got a jolt along with them, and coming on top of Arden's death. . . ."

"Could be," he agreed. "Probably at least a little. But that doesn't mean that anything I said was wrong. Look, I'm not asking you to marry me, just take a tumble up in the hay wagon. The only chance you'll have to screw your boss and get away with it. Yes, or no? It may be your only chance—I'm going to work the tail off the four of you from now on, and you've got to learn how to fight and how to shoot to be any good to me in the long run."

"You aren't just teasing me? I mean, this is for real?" She felt oddly distant, her mind and body a confused mess and somehow out of control.

"Nope. Serious. I'll even pour us each a shot of good brandy so you won't have the cigar smoke."

"Yes, all right," she heard herself saying, as if in a trance.

He got up, and she followed him. They walked forward after he took a small bottle out of his own pack, and he cleared away a couple of dugger guards, repositioning them well away from the wagon. He jumped up, turned, then helped her up, and then put the tarps down front and rear, lighting a small lantern inside with a match so that there was a small amount of light.

They were in there the better part of two hours, and there was little doubt to anyone who noticed what was going on in there, but the only conversation heard was his sudden exclamation, "I'll be damned! You really *are* a virgin!" and her soft, nearly unintelligible reply in a tone of voice she had frankly never used before and never knew was there.

"Was," she responded dreamily.

13

GLOBBUS

The next two days were extremely busy ones, offering little time for the newcomers to have their minds on anything other than business, but it was obvious to those who knew her that Cass had changed. She seemed more relaxed, more at peace with herself, and, if anything even more determined to learn what could be learned and make the most of every opportunity.

As for Cass, while she felt different she couldn't quite explain what that difference was. It was less in the experience itself than in the sense that some enormous load had been lifted from her mind. It was an odd sensation, but out here, in the void, she felt completely and totally free for the first time in her memory.

Matson had been marvelous that night, even cautioning her that the blood and mess would not happen again, but she hadn't cared about that. After, though, he hadn't really referred to it nor treated her any differently than before. He was the boss, and a pretty fair but tough one, and that was all right with her, too.

Equally gratifying to them all was the way the duggers had accepted them, although there was still some strong, underlying suspicion of Dar for his actions in the fight and they bore down on him far harder than on the others. It was clear that he would win their confidence and respect only by superior conduct in the next fight and not before.

It was also clear that the additions, two of them, anyway, made the train dugger-heavy in the sense that there really wasn't enough extra work for four of them. To everyone's surprise it was Nadya who proved the most worth, after Cass of course, helping equally with the animals, supplies and repacking, and even cooking. Although Matson had agreed that they would not have to have anything to do with their former fellow captives on this trip, since they knew them, Nadya also proved adept at the literal stringing technique and didn't mind the nasty comments and envy from the others. Suzl, on the other hand, did the minimum necessary and seemed to spend most of her time with Dar.

Still, they got some arms training, and some other fighting techniques as well, but clearly it would take far longer than the two nights and few breaks they had for the starter lessons. Although Dar proved to be the best natural shooter, it was Cass and Nadya who were presented, their last night out, with their own guns by Matson on recommendation of their dugger trainers.

The final day in would be a short one, and Cass rode up to Matson as they approached the Fluxland. "Just wanted to know something about the place before we got there," she told him.

"Well, it's like its name. Exactly," the stringer replied casually.

"It's like a globbus? What's a globbus?"

"It isn't anything. It's a nonsense word. And that pretty well describes the place. It was set up by the guild the wizards have as one of three places where young wizards could study and practice and perfect what powers they have."

"You mean it's like a school?"

He nodded. "In a way. But no school you've ever

seen before. Think of the mess a hundred or so practicing—and mostly not very good—young wizards might make, then multiply that by the number of students who went through it, and you have an idea of what real insanity is."

"It's dangerous, then?"

He shrugged. "If you mean in the sense of kidnap and kill, no, it's not at all dangerous. But if you think of it as a playground for a bunch of children of gods, then you get an idea of what it really is. Just remember to stay on the road, trust nobody and believe even less of it, and stick to the central district which is fairly safe and sane by comparison. Don't let one of the locals sucker or seduce you into something, no matter how innocent. They have what is known as an implied consent rule."

"What's that mean?"

"It means that nothing you see can hurt or affect you no matter how it seems otherwise unless you give your implied consent to it. It's a game with them to get that implied consent, and you don't have to say 'yes' to something to give it, which is why it's implied. Just think everything through and use all your common sense and you'll find it is something of an experience."

She went back and briefed the others on what he'd said, but she couldn't answer their questions because Matson either couldn't or wouldn't. The only way she got the implied consent idea across to herself, as well as the other three, was to remind Dar of his experience in trust in the bar at Anchor Logh that had cost so much.

Globbus began in the manner of all Fluxlands, with things becoming a bit more solid, normal senses returning, and, finally, it opened up into a real place in every sense of the word. Or was it? It was very easy from the start to see why Globbus was nonsense.

Grass grew in multicolored striped and checked patterns. Cows and horses in the fields had any number of legs and even heads, and looked like creatures put together by a bunch of drunks and then painted in outlandish patterns. Trees in places looked like nothing they'd ever seen, and some grew upside down, roots high in the air, while others had weird looking fruit. Dogwood would occasionally bark at them, and pussywillow purred or hissed, and at one part tiny crabapples scuttled back to their branches, pincers closing. Hills and bushes were sculpted into fantastic shapes, and even the sky often changed colors and at one point was half a dull pink and half dark as night, with stars shining, some of which had the disconcerting habit of occasionally racing to new positions and patterns as you watched.

Water flowed in no particular direction, and some waterfalls flowed up. Large clouds floated by overhead and suddenly decided to make obscene gestures at the travelers below. Few people were seen, and none close up, until they approached the center of the Fluxland and its university proper.

There were buildings now, large and small, no two even remotely alike. One very normal-looking stone house was atop a high and very fragile-looking tree with no sign of a way up or down; another was a traditional cottage with peaked red slate roof, sitting upside down on its roof point. As they watched, two rather ordinary looking young men approached the house, stood there, flipped upside down in the air, then walked in the upside down door, their heads about three meters off the ground.

It was a bit much for any of them, but it was particularly stunning to the captives, for this was the first Fluxland they had ever seen. Most just gawked in disbelief or tried not to look, particularly at some of the people, who were only theoretically people. It was easy to see, looking at them, why *this* Fluxland was no inhibitor to duggers. The entire train moved into the center of what could be loosely called "town".

The street was not crowded, but was nonetheless a mob scene. In front of them, a small horse was riding a man, while on a porch two ugly-looking old dogs were arguing in perfect human speech about the proper solution to an abstract mathematical problem. People with two heads argued with each other, while others looked lizard-like or were part animal, part human, part something else. It was, nevertheless, less a chamber of horrors than a lunatic's view of World—no, *every* lunatic's view of World, all at once.

There was, however, an area in the center that looked normal. It was really four huge two story square buildings around a central open plaza, but that plaza had a large circular stage in the center and cordoned off areas of turf all around it. It was empty now, but it was clear that it was used often.

"That's the Market Block," Matson told them. "That's where we're going to unload most of our surplus merchandise in three days."

"Three days! You mean we have to spend three days in this place?" Dar exclaimed nervously. "I mean, two blocks over there is a square rainstorm—and it's raining *up* into the clouds!"

The stringer grinned. "Yep. I hadn't expected to be here so early, but it's not bad so long as you can get used to the people and animals and whatever wandering about. So long as you all stay in this area, within the Market Block and the four big buildings facing it and on the streets between them, you're safe. There's shops and services available in these places that you can't get anywhere else, particularly at decent prices, because they're all practice shops for the best students with specific talents rather than the general type like the goddess or Haldayne."

"You mean the Rory Montagne type," Cass noted sourly.

"Yeah, like that, but service oriented rather than criminal types. It's all magic, of course, but it's all the permanent type. Just about none of this is illusion, remember. There's hotels in that building over there, as well as holding areas for the Market Block. That one next to it has a huge number of eateries of every size and type. The building across from the hotel is the services building. That's where you go if you want numbers removed or hair or a whole new you. The one across from the food pavilion is the merchandise mart. Got it?"

They nodded. "Now, how do we draw on our accounts?" Cass wanted to know.

"First you say you're with the Matson train, then sign for it when they give you the bill. I'll let you know any time you want what your balance is, since they're all posted to the train bill at the hotel center. Most Fluxlands have their own money of some kind, just like the Anchors, but the universal unit, used here as well, is the kil. It's short for kilogram, but nobody knows now what it's a kilogram of. That's long lost in history. It's broken down into a hundred grams, of course, but don't look for it. It's all on paper, and settled on common bills paid out of established accounts."

"Well, that's fine," Nadya put in, "but how do we know how much *we* have to spend of this money?"

He thought a moment. "You don't, since I haven't sold your stakes yet. Cass, you and Dar should figure on no more than two hundred kils each, while Suzl and Nadya might have a little more— but, remember, you two girls, you have to stake yourselves out of that when we pull out, so keep it in the fifty to seventy kil range. That's for everything here except hotel, which the train picks up."

It was clear from the central lobby of the hotel

building that they were far from the only train in Globbus. In fact, there were at least four, and Matson was greeted with shouts and waves from a host of duggers, most of whom looked even worse than his, and at least one tall, dark, exotic-looking female stringer who ran up and gave him a big hug. Cass had to suppress more than a little tinge of jealousy, but she kept control of herself. It was just a reminder of the new enigma, that the unattainable, now attained, was still unattainable.

The rooms were large and comfortable; in fact, more comfortable than those Cass had stayed in in Persellus, with the floors fully carpeted and a small parlor area with two chairs and a sofa. The room had a bathroom, and Cass, who elected to stay with Nadya, had the joy of being the old sophisticate showing the rube the joys of running water and flush toilets.

They weren't needed to check in the team and cargo, so they were free as soon as they were settled in, and the foursome met again in the lobby and went first to the food pavilion to eat. The amount of choices was overwhelming, although some of the prices gave good indication of just how far a kil did, or didn't go. Although they had all dreamed of a real restaurant meal, they decided to settle, for now, on sandwiches and beer from a walk-up. They noticed, though, that the first floor only was devoted to countless eateries—upstairs were all sorts of bars, entertainment joints, and other signs of a wide-open place the likes of which even Main Street had never seen.

After eating, they decided to tend to first things first, going to the "services" building and trying to ignore the six men and women going by who had wheels instead of legs and feet and seemed to just roll along effortlessly, as well as the woman with the body of many men's dreams and the head of some sort of short-beaked bird and other oddities.

Dar did remark, though, that in *this* company he was absolutely ordinary, and there was no denying that.

The building directory listed what seemed to be hundreds of service experts, most of whom were specialists in things they couldn't make head nor tail of. What, for example, was a master of sustentation? Or a storax modifier, for that matter? And did they really want to know?

Fortunately, there was an information kiosk at which to ask for what was needed. In point of fact, the kiosk was asked directly, for it was a human-looking man down to the waist, but below it he had a huge, round mass on which he could apparently swivel. He was surrounded by a rack with all sorts of handouts, particularly accessible because in place of those legs he had four hands. He looked at them as they approached and said, "May I serve you?"

Cass swallowed hard. "Tattoo removal and hair growth?" she tried tentatively.

The information kiosk nodded. "Corridor C, office 202," he responded briskly. "General cosmetic alterations." One of the arms shot out. "Right over there. Anything else?"

"How about breaking transformation curses?" Dar asked.

"General, group, specific, or personal?"

"Ah, personal."

"Corridor F, office 509."

They nodded and walked away. "I'd say let's see about you two first," Cass said to Suzl and Nadya. "After, we'll check on Dar's situation."

"I can meet you," Dar suggested. "I don't need anything where you're going."

It was agreed, and the three young women headed for the designated corridor and office. The sign on the door said to walk in, and they did to a small waiting room. One wall was covered with pictures of all sorts of people and creatures and combinations of same involving women, the other involving all men. Obviously, this one did quite a bit more than they were after.

A small window slid back, revealing a very dark woman's face. "Yes?"

As briefly as they could, they explained what they wanted, and Cass added, "I guess I can stand some minor work myself." She hadn't intended to, but there was something about seeing that lady stringer embracing Matson that just changed her mind. She knew it was silly, but it meant very little one way or the other.

The woman emerged from a rear door into the waiting room. She was stark naked, with dark brown face, hands, and feet, but her body was covered in very fine fur that was alternately black and white striped, in a spiral pattern from neck to legs. Her thick, wiry hair was snow white except for a single wide black streak running from brow all the way back, and she had long, pointed ears and a short, shaved tail with a furry white blob at the end. When she talked, it was noted that the inside of her mouth was black with a snow white tongue.

She took note of their attention and smiled. "Do you like it? It was one of my old teacher's last works for last year's total body collection. It didn't sell, for some reason, but I liked it so much I kept it."

"It's—stunning," Nadya responded truthfully, hoping not to be pressed.

The woman seemed pleased. "Step back into here, all of you, please."

They followed her a bit nervously through the door, Cass starting to rethink the whole proposition of any changes in this way. There were four large chairs in back lined up in front of a single long mirror. The woman indicated that they were to each pick one and sit down, and they did, growing more uncertain.

"Now, then. Most of my designers are off right now, but I think I can handle the three of you. Let's start with you," she said, going first to Suzl. "Nice build. A good foundation. We could do a lot with you."

"Just some hair and get rid of the tattoos," she told the woman.

"About twenty added centimeters and a slight body realignment will do you wonders," the striped woman suggested. "As it is now you'll run to fat and get chunky as you grow older."

She actually considered it, but finally rejected it. There followed a whole series of attempts to get her to accept hair with an unusual color or pattern, but she decided on straight, shoulder-length, and black just the way it had been. The striped woman sighed and you could see she thought that Suzl had no imagination or spirit of adventure whatsoever, but she stood back, made a pass with her hands, and Suzl gasped at her reflection. It was like greeting an old friend you'd thought lost and gone forever.

The tattoo and thumb stain went with the hair. "Now, the hair is low maintenance," the magical cosmetologist assured her. "It will stay at that length and style unless you change it, and if you do just wash it before changing it and it'll remain the new style. If you wish, I can have it grow normally, but right now it can be cut shorter but will always grow back to that length and set."

"That's fine. Wonderful, in fact," Suzl assured her. "Now all I need are some clothes."

"I could give you a treatment similar to mine—no design if you prefer, color of your choice—that would make clothing unnecessary up to forty degrees or down to ten below."

Suzl passed.

Nadya got much the same spiel from the woman, who was obviously aching to be "creative" and not finding any takers. Nadya chose a permanent dark brown pageboy and declined even the modest offer to do something about her slight overbite. By the time the striped body wizard got to Cass she was resigned. "Just hair and tattoo, right?"

"I don't have any tattoos. They were taken care of before," she replied. "Actually, I'm not really sure what I want."

The magical cosmetologist brightened. "Tell you what. Let me try a few things out on you. No charge if you don't like them, and I'll change anything back at any time."

It was tempting. She looked over at the other two. "Suppose you go check with Dar? I'll meet you there or back at the hotel."

They agreed, signed the required small papers they were handed, and were gone, although Nadya remained a moment and said, "Don't get carried away. You may hate yourself tomorrow."

She grinned. "I'll remember. Nothing radical."

But, the fact is, what was done was a lot of fun. Rejecting the exotic or freakish, the cosmetologist tried a variety of hair styles and colors, subtle facial adjustments, and body adjustments. She found out exactly what it was like to have large breasts and a sexy figure and decided that it wasn't her style. At least now she *knew*, she told herself.

But is was finally a matter of small changes that she settled on, mostly after telling Miss Rona, as the cosmetologist was known, that she was, after all, a mule whip on a stringer train who had to remain both practical for the job and human for entry to Anchor. She had an odd impulse for long hair, and finally Miss Rona suggested a reddish brown, thick and straight, coming just below the shoulders, and showed her how to tie it up or into a pony tail, the last her preferred style. Her face was softened a bit, losing a little of its boyish look while not changing all that much, and her complexion was darkened to a light olive to complement the changes. On her body, she wanted strong, hard muscles that would not have to be maintained but would not give her a mannish look, and this proved amazingly easy.

To balance, her shape was slightly recontoured, her hips slightly widened so now her work pants would hang on them at the waist, and her breasts were slightly redone so that they were still small and required no support but were clearly there and perfectly formed. In the end, most of the changes were so subtle that, except for the hair, it was difficult to really point to them, but the overall effect of the changes was to make her unmistakably female.

Miss Rona, in fact, was delighted. "This sort of very small detail work is the most challenging," she told her. And so was the forty kil bill, which couldn't really be disputed since the whole thing could be withdrawn with a few waves of the striped woman's hand. She sighed, decided that it was worth it but that this was *it*, no matter what, and signed the slip.

No one was at the kiosk except the kiosk, but he told her that the others had gone back to the hotel. Nadya was in the room, just relaxing, and she was enthusiastic over the change in Cass. "Perfect! Just perfect! It's more you than you, if you know what I mean."

She appreciated the compliment. "For what it cost, it better be. If I have any money left, I'll buy some spare clothes. I think it's time for you to get some, though."

She sighed. "I suppose. It's been so long they'll feel funny just to wear." The merchandise building, though, changed her mind, and they both spent quite a while just trying on various things. Both finally opted for practical wear, more or less stringer fashion, yet in colors other than the stringer's basic black. Although she bought a pair of boots, Nadya carried them back to the room, finding that the clothes actually made her feel human again but that her feet and lower calves revolted against footwear. For the moment, she decided to remain barefoot.

Dar and Suzl weren't back in their rooms yet, so the two women decided to eat without them.

"I forgot to ask—how did Dar's session go?" Cass wanted to know.

"Not good. They said it was powerful and complicated and would take real experts to work out. They wanted over a thousand kils up front to do it, too, with no guarantees."

Cass whistled. "How'd he take it?"

"Pretty well. A lot better than Suzl, I think."

The handsome young man approached them in the bar and stood there for a second. He was young, perhaps only a couple of years older than they, and extremely human, although his hair was white save for a small reddish spot near the peak. "Ah, you are the man with the problem?" he asked tentatively.

Dar looked up at him. "Yeah. Are you the budding god the guy near the kiosk talked about?"

The young man chuckled and sat down. "I suppose so, although I have no ambitions to carve out any little worldlets and preside. I am entirely interested in research, in learning everything there is to learn about these powers. Until I can get a position here, though, I have to support my researches on my own, hence my friends over at services. They get a small percentage for sniffing out people like you, pardon my language." He looked over at Suzl. "I can see why you are anxious to be rid of the problem, sir." She smiled at him.

"Can you do it?" he asked.

The young wizard shrugged. "I don't know until I take a good look. But I won't charge unless I can at least help. Is that not fair?"

Dar looked at Suzl, who nodded. "Sounds fair to us."

"Then come with me now, if you can."

"We can. But how much will it cost?"

"Shall we say a hundred?"

He thought a moment. "That's almost all I got. I have to eat for the next couple of days, you know."

"Seventy-five, then, but no less."

"I'll make it up," Suzl told him. "I'll take it back in trade."

They left and followed the young man outside, then down a side street and out of the Market area. Dar started getting a little nervous.

"Just in here," the young wizard told them, and they stopped by a small pyramidal building, then went inside after him. It was a small pyramid on the outside but a large rectangle on the inside, crowded with all sorts of junk as well as the remains of half-eaten meals and lots of dust. There was, however, a carpeted clear area in the back near a bed that obviously had last been made when the boy arrived in Globbus. "Now, take off your clothes."

Dar did, and was subjected to a minute and somewhat embarrassing physical examination. "Fascinating," the wizard muttered. "Just fascinating." He stepped back and looked at Dar again.

"It's superior work," he told them. "Among the best. I've seen many variants of this—there are lots in Globbus—but the math here is simply brilliant. Who did it, did you say?"

"The former goddess of Persellus."

Brows went up. "Former?"

"She was overthrown and, I assume, killed a few days ago."

"Too bad. A great loss to the science. Still, I can follow the basic formulae." He closed his eyes and appeared to be in deep thought. Finally he said, "I think I have the spell's complement. If I understood what she did correctly, that is. There is, however, some risk."

"To his life?" Suzl asked apprehensively.

"Oh, no, nothing like that. The application of the complement could, conceivably, go more than one way, since it's not an undoing of the spell—we don't have the weeks necessary for that and you don't have the money to shorten that period—but an effort at applying an equal and opposite spell superimposed over this one. I *think* it will work, but there is a slight percentage that it could push him all the way to the female matrix, physically and psychologically, or it might split him—twelve hours totally and completely female, twelve hours totally and completely male. There is always a risk in this sort of thing, you must understand. That's why the specialists demand their money up front."

Dar looked over at Suzl. "You really want it?"

She nodded. "I do. If you're willing."

He shrugged. "What have I got to lose? Go ahead."

The young man closed his eyes once more, and his head snapped back, then forward once again. He staggered but did not fall. Suddenly he came fully erect, his eyes opening, and he seemed to struggle with his right hand. A single gesture was made with the trembling hand, and Dar felt a slight tingling. "Now!" the young wizard shouted, and Suzl screamed.

Dar turned towards her, concerned, and the young man looked slightly upset. "Now that's a *curse*! Damn!" Suzl fainted, and both rushed over to her, picked her up, and put her on the bed.

"What's wrong with her?" Dar demanded to know. "She wasn't even in this, damn it."

"I'm afraid she was, and I didn't notice it," the wizard replied. "That is one tricky curse you have. It took the complement and deflected it to the nearest receptor. Here—let's get these pants off her."

They did, and Dar gasped. "She said she wanted it, and that was all the curse needed for implied consent," the wizard explained. "Now she's got it, as solidly as you got yours."

"But I still got a woman's crotch!"

"And in my judgment you always will have. And, unfortunately, she will now always have what you lost, the complement being as strong as the original."

"But—it's so *big*! And she's so short!"

"Well, it *is* a scaled-down version of yours," the wizard told him. "I did what I could to keep it proportional, but it *is* the complement to your curse, and so basically your pattern. Uh—of course there will be no charge. I admit I *have* learned a great deal from this curse."

Dar shook his head. "And what I learn about guys in bars is of no value. Damn!"

Suzl stirred and came to, having fainted mostly from the shock. She looked puzzled, then felt gingerly in the crotch area. "Oh, by the Heavens! It's real!" She groaned, then sat up on the side of the bed, then got to her feet. "How do men *walk* with these things?"

"The same way women walk with breasts like yours," Dar responded. "You just are used to it."

"But it's—*huge*! On you, it'd be okay. On me, it's grotesque." She looked over at the wizard. "Take it away! Take it back!"

The young man looked sheepish. "I can't. It's beyond me. It may be beyond anybody but the best. That goddess wasn't only good with curses, she was devious as Hell."

She stared at him. "You mean I have the same curse *he* does—only backwards?"

The wizard nodded. "That's about it. I'm afraid the curse construed you to ask for it, and since it couldn't give it to your man, here, it gave it to you. You're stuck."

She sat down again on the side of the bed and sighed. "And I never even found out what it was like to be a woman, damn it." She sighed again. "But, then, neither do men." She looked up at the wizard. "Will it work?"

"It's a proportional model of his. It'll work if your mind wants it to."

She stood up and put her pants back on. "Ugh! More shopping to do. Something to support this thing and some pants with real give in the crotch. These *hurt*!" She looked over at Dar. "Well, it isn't exactly the way I wanted it, but I think at least in one way that you and I were made for each other."

14

COUNCIL

"Now let me get this straight," Nadya said, sounding confused and bewildered. She stared at the small, attractive, well-built woman and the huge muscular man in front of her. "You, Suzl, are the man, and you, Dar, are the woman? Holy Mother protect me!"

She and Cass had now heard the complete story but still couldn't quite believe it. Even so, Cass, relaxing in a chair and chewing idly on a stick of hard candy, said, "I have to say, Suzl, you're taking it a lot better than I would."

She shrugged. "I was real upset for a while there, but then the more I thought about it the more I—accepted it. You know, I think I'm the only one ever taken in the Paring Rite who wasn't really sorry to go. I used to sit there and dream of what was beyond dull, stodgy Anchor Logh. Sometimes I'd imagine myself as something different. Part horse, maybe, or cat, or something. I always knew there was something else out here, beyond the Flux wall. I imagined it as something like it is—a world full of freaks."

They, Nadya in particular, started to protest but she silenced them, and, at the moment, she had the floor.

"Uh-huh. Freaks. You know, like in the old

children's stories of fairies and trolls and all that. Well, thanks to Cass and Dar I'm out here and I'm free, and now I'm a freak. Maybe I'm Flux crazy now, but I kind of think that this was like, well, my dues. I'm one of them now, and it's not so bad. I'm still sort of getting used to it, even with the wizard's help. He said something about men and women's centers of gravity being different, whatever that means. All I know is that every time I don't think and cross my legs the old way it *hurts* like hell, and I'm always aware that it's there."

"You'd hardly know it, what with those black denim pants hanging so low on your hips," Nadya said.

Suzl shrugged. "It was either that or get 'em super-baggy in the crotch. Besides, I kind of like it this way. I can still be me and still be a freak, like Dar. And you wouldn't believe how fast and how easy it turns on, with all the sensations concentrated in that one place. I think I understand men a lot better now."

"You better," Nadya murmured. "Uh—have you tried it out yet?"

Suzl giggled. "No, but I plan to. Better shape up, girls—I'm the man around here, pardon the bosoms."

"It doesn't make any difference out here what sex you are," Cass put in, stirring from her chair where she sat. "There doesn't seem to be any men's or women's jobs—just jobs. That's why you two won't have problems, except maybe getting picked up by the wrong people in bars."

"I'm swearing off bars for a while," Dar told her. "So far I've been in two and both haven't been exactly great experiences."

They were about to go further when there was a sharp knocking on the hotel door. It startled them, because they weren't expecting anybody or anything as yet. Cass got up and went to the door, opened it, and found Matson standing there. He looked at her and frowned as if slightly puzzled at her new look, but he recovered quickly. "We won't have to detour to Pericles after all," he told them. "The old boy I wanted to see is here in the hotel right now. He and some friends of his want to see all four of you in one hour, Room 224. Be there and we can settle this as far as we're concerned."

"We'll be there," Cass assured him. She hesitated a moment, then asked, "Like the new look?"

"Hadn't noticed," he responded curtly, turned, and walked down the hall. Crestfallen, she watched him go down the stairs.

"That rat," Nadya commented, and she turned and shook her head.

"No, he's not a rat, just, well, unobtainable in the long term." The ironic thing was, although they didn't seem to know it, she had obtained the unobtainable from him, knowing that he was as out of reach as ever.

"What's that all about?" Suzl asked.

"Probably another thing like the trial we told you about. Give the same information to a bunch of powerful wizards and then they'll decide something or other about Haldayne and Persellus. After today it won't concern us, though."

Dar sighed and looked down at Suzl. "Well," he said hopefully, "we still have an hour to kill."

Room 224 turned out to be a large rectangular end room that was obviously rarely used as a place for anyone to stay but rather for small receptions and gatherings. It had been set up in this case with a head table in the front and a dozen or so folding chairs for an audience. Matson was there, as were two other stringers—the dark woman Cass had seen when they'd arrived and another, a huge, beefy man with a full beard and cold brown eyes.

Also present were two duggers, obviously the chief train drivers for the other two. One was totally reptilian, down to being covered in green, scaly skin and having a snout-like face with fangs, sex indeterminable, while the other was a man whose skin was all blotched and twisted, like a long-dead corpse. The foursome sat with the duggers, nervously eyeing the reptilian one. They didn't care so much any more about the walking corpse—he looked too much like a couple of duggers in their own train.

Soon, three people entered. The first was an elderly man with long, flowing gray beard and hair that looked as if it had not only never been cut, but also never washed, combed, or otherwise cared for. He used a short cane to walk on, and seemed slow and stooped with age and infirmity. It was hard to imagine him as a wizard of power like the handsome Haldayne.

The second was a young looking woman with a rather attractive face, although she was only a meter high, had bright green skin and dark green hair, and shell-like ears, while the third was a very fat man with a nearly bald round head who looked more than slightly drunk. None were the sort of people who inspired confidence and dynamic leadership by their every look and gesture.

They took their seats up front, the old one with difficulty, and for a moment said nothing, just looked out on those whom they had summoned. Finally the fat man and the tiny green woman looked over at the old one and he nodded absently. "The room and its contents are clean, although we have a Soul Rider present," he croaked in a voice that was barely audible to them. Cass jumped a little at that but decided to hold her peace for now. "That is either a very good sign or a very ominous one, depending on how you look at it." The other two nodded slightly in agreement.

"Now, then," the old one continued, "I am Mervyn, the lovely one here is Tatalane, and on the other end is Krupe." He brought up his cane like a rifle, and from it shot a tremendous spray of yellowish white energy. It struck the walls, then coated them as if a living thing, then floor and ceiling as well. When it passed under their feet it gave a very mild numbing sensation that lasted only when you were in direct contact with it. "These proceedings are now sealed," Mervyn told them. "What proceeds is for our ears alone. Although only three of our fellowship of nine are present, it is sufficient for action in this matter. I am going to call upon each of you to tell me the various facts that you know directly in this matter. We will begin with the attack on the Arden train. Mr. Matson first, if you please."

Matson stood and gave a general, brief description of the discovery of the train, its grisly contents, and his conclusions from that evidence. Then Suzl and Nadya were called upon to supplement, then Cass up to the time she'd been knocked out, and, finally, Dar. He was hesitant in telling his part in the story and his feelings at the time, but this was brushed aside by Mervyn. "Just the outline," the old one told him, "no moralizing or excuses. We are aware of what happened. We are reading your reactions when these things are called up in your mind."

Eventually, in this fashion, step by step, the entire story was told to them. The three listened passively, prompting only when necessary, and made no comments or gestures at anything told them or not told them. Ultimately, with the impressions of Persellus gleaned from Dar, Suzl, Nadya, and Matson, the tale was told.

The three then lapsed into deep thought, not apparently conferring or even showing awareness of the others' presence, but finally Mervyn said,

"Stringers Hollus and Brund, what do you think of this?"

"Sounds like Haldayne, all right," the bearded stringer commented. "Cheeky bastard to use his own name like that, though."

"Yes, isn't it? And you, Hollus?"

"I never had a run-in with him, but it's clear to me that he ordered the deliberate murder of a stringer and took control of a valuable crossroads. This cannot be allowed."

The two duggers were also called on for opinions. Both, except for wishing to avenge the duggers more than Arden, echoed Hollus.

"If we were to take on Haldayne, it would require not only the three of us but an army," Mervyn told them. "There are enough raw souls in a land that size to make its retaking very hard. Knowing Haldayne, he would never take us on directly, but he would make his minions, his conquests, and his would-be conquerors pay dearly for each tiny bit of Fluxland. We see only two choices. Either we retake Persellus bloodily, or we act to seal it off completely and totally reconfigure the trade routes. That is, isolate it and write it off."

There was some consternation among all three stringers at that. "You *can't* just reconfigure those routes!" Matson protested. "It would take *years* to reestablish new patterns and get word to everyone. Not to mention the fact that it would take one of you near there permanently just to make sure his buddies didn't break through and unseal the land."

"And yet the object of this exercise seems to be to draw us into a direct confrontation," Tatalane said, speaking for the first time. "He deliberately invites attention by moving this madman and then exhorting him to attack the stringers. He could clearly see the string on Cass and could have easily eliminated it, but instead he allowed it to remain, meaning certain discovery of the pocket. He changed his shape absolutely while in the pocket, yet seemed to go out of his way to display his manner, his ring, and his left-handedness to Cass. Any one of these might be overlooked, but the combination was certain to rouse suspicion. Even so, when he could stay out of her way, he deliberately places himself in close contact with her in Persellus, then, when she could still prove nothing, sends four inept minions to subdue her, thereby proving her story. Clearly, too, Matson was allowed to see and then escape when it would have been child's play for Haldayne to have taken him, his train, and Cass."

"Well said," Mervyn approved. "So he did everything but raise a flag to cover the sky of World saying, 'Here I Am—Come and Get Me!' He *wants* a fight, that is certain. He knows who and what he'd be facing. That, too, leads to two different possibilities. Either he is certain he can win, or he wishes to lose. It is that simple."

Cass frowned. Why would anyone want to lose a battle?

"Good point," Mervyn responded, as if she'd spoken aloud. "Why, indeed would someone want to lose a battle? Perhaps to prove to us that we saw a danger, met it, and vanquished the evil? Then we would all go our merry ways, satisfied in a job well done, and look elsewhere for the next evil. We would overlook what Haldayne really does not wish us to see."

"But what could that be?" Hollus asked him. "I know the crazy man said they were going to attack the gate, if there is one, but I didn't think that was possible."

"Insofar as we know, the Guardians of the Gates of Hell have never been defeated or even tricked," Mervyn assured her. "Nevertheless, the conclusion is inescapable. Remember, however, that we know the location only of four of the seven gates. We do not know how many the Seven might know of—perhaps all—nor what they might have accomplished on one or more. The conclusion is inescapable. There *is* a gate lying between Persellus and Anchor Logh. We must assume that, somehow, Haldayne has access to and perhaps control of that gate no matter what logic says to the contrary. That is what he wishes to hide from us."

"So what do you propose?" Matson asked him directly. He was growing impatient with the long-winded theorizing.

"We must recapture Persellus, if only to do what he expects," the wizard told them. "We must also find out what he knows that we do not."

"But it could also just be a trap for the three of us," Tatalane argued. "What if it is—and he wins?"

Mervyn shrugged. "Then we will know at least that the gate is still secure and our successors on the Nine will know and avenge us. But if he loses, then the gate is open to Hell. Haldayne has six of the seven combinations to open the gates. Hell has most certainly worked out the seventh after all this time. If he has a way in, if he can talk to the horrors of Hell, he will have all seven and need only control of the physical gates to open them. My friends, this is grave. We dare not ignore it."

Mervyn thought a bit more. "Hollus, have you enough duggers able to follow strings to get to Domura, Salapaca, and Modon?"

She looked back at the reptilian dugger, who nodded.

"Brund? Can you take the alarm to Zlydof, Roarkara, and Fideleer?"

The bearded man did not consult his dugger. "No problem."

"Are you all three willing to avenge your slain comrades?"

The three stringers huddled in whispers for a moment. Finally, Matson said, "We are agreed that this thing can't be allowed to go on. Otherwise *everybody* will be doing it."

Cass smiled slightly at that. That, really, was the feared stringer, the terror of Anchor and Flux—one who saw all World as a giant ledger sheet, the battling storekeeper who would leave his lady's body to rot in the void but take strong action when his trade was inconvenienced. How utterly romantic.

"Matson," Mervyn continued, "your train will be the point and guard along the route from here to there. We will supply equipment, explosives, and fifty good fighters to staff your outpost, all at least minor wizards."

"Will they take orders?" he asked sourly.

"They will because we will tell them to. You three also have between you almost two hundred young people from Anchor ready for the block. We will remold them and use them."

That got the stringers upset again. "Who's going to pay for all this?" they all demanded to know.

"Who is going to buy them if we tell them not to?" Mervyn responded with a slight smirk. "However, we guarantee you an equal number for the market out of conquest if we lose them. Further, we will ourselves fill any specific goods orders intended to be picked up in the old Persellus. That should restore a tidy bit."

Mollified, the stringers sat down once more.

"Hollus, Brund, you will work with Tatalane in getting these new troops into line. Hollus knows Haldayne, which should simplify matters a good deal, while you, Brund, are particularly gifted with explosives, their transportation and use. This will have to be done in a newly created pocket between here and Persellus. There should be no traffic in either direction between Haldayne, Matson, and you, so it should be perfect—and private. We also have two Anchors to draw upon and I intend to do so. Since the four of you appear human and will pass muster at the gates, I am detaching you temporarily from Matson's service. I hate to break up a happy couple, but Dar and Nadya must accompany Krupe to Anchor Abehl, as we have no one from there here to assist. Because both Suzl and Cass have direct knowledge not only of the Anchor but the Temple of Anchor Logh, you two will come with me to Anchor Logh. There are things I must know there."

They all four looked at each other in some distress. "I think I know the Temple as good as Suzl," Nadya responded. "Why split up the teams?"

"Please do not waste time second-guessing me. We must move and move quickly. Do you not think that at this very moment Haldayne's spies aren't going mad trying to penetrate the shield on this room? However, just this once, I will explain that the rather unusual aspects of two of you are required for effect in Anchor, and both of you cannot be in the same place when the places you might be needed are three hundred kilometers apart."

Dar looked at Suzl, who shrugged and grinned. "Have fun. I know *I* will!"

He grinned back. "Yeah. I always wanted to see the inner sanctums of a Temple."

"This Council is now adjourned," Mervyn pronounced, "and will convene again in twenty-seven days at the proper points around Persellus. With divine help, perhaps we can convene once again in Persellus. Normal precautions have been taken so that details of this meeting cannot be picked from your minds. However, it is essential that we all get to our work and out of Globbus as soon as possible, for while compromise is inevitable we need not give the demon any advantage."

The energy field retreated, flowing first back into the walls, then along them and back, it seemed, into Mervyn's cane. Cass and Suzl went up and approached the old wizard, as the others approached and talked to their appointed leaders and guardians. The wizard's eyes, an enigma from a distance, seemed surprisingly sharp and full of life and energy up close. "Go, get your packs, sign out at the hotel desk, and wait for me there. We will go together. I rather imagine you are looking forward to this."

"I'm not too thrilled with asking the Sister General for help," Cass responded honestly, "but at least I'll have the chance to get word to my family that I'm all right. It'll be a shock to anyone who knows us to see us again. I don't know anyone who ever met anyone who went out in the Paring Rite and returned."

"I'm just gonna have fun," Suzl told him. "I can sure defile their holy Temple and surprise a whole lot of people."

"It is true that this is an unprecedented event for Anchor Logh, but this whole business is unprecedented. Win or lose, I fear that our dear World is going to come in for some severe changes by the time this is all resolved," the wizard said seriously.

"Damn. And before I saw most of it the way it is now," Cass muttered.

They left him and went immediately back to their rooms. Nadya caught up with Cass as they approached their door. "Tough luck. But we'll get together again. I sure would like to get back home and rub it in their noses, though."

Cass nodded. "I know—but I'd much rather be going back *with* an army than to get one. I still can't believe Anchor would ever send forces into Flux, not even on the request of the Nine Who Guard. We shall see. At least you can tell me what another Anchor is like. I've been curious to see how much they're the same and how they differ."

"Not like Fluxlands, that's for sure. Not with the church in such control—*huh?*"

Suddenly the lights in the room went out, and both felt extreme dizziness and a sense of falling. Nadya recovered in what seemed like only a few moments, and looked around. The lights were back on, the door was closed—and Cass was nowhere to be seen.

Cass drifted in a dreamy, uncaring fog neither asleep nor awake, not dreaming, not thinking, but just so, so relaxed. . . .

After a while there were voices, distant and indistinct at first but growing clearer with time. She heard them, a man's and a woman's voices, but it made no impression on her.

"She is well protected," said the woman clinically.

"She has improved her looks a good deal," the man's voice noted. "I guess she really is in love with that stringer. Ah! Unrequited love! Takes me back to my youth."

"You never had a youth, love. Still, we won't get it by spell. That leaves it in my department. Good thing a drug is a drug."

"So long as we keep it that way and there's nobody around to counteract it. It's simple and direct."

The woman seemed to be fumbling with something, and there was a mild pricking sensation on her arm. They waited a while, just chatting pleasantly. "Lucky for you I was here. Your crude methods would have killed her before she talked."

"Luck had nothing to do with it. I summoned you because I needed your help. Geniuses are few and far between, my love."

The woman snorted. "She's under but good. Let's get that spell off her." There was a sudden tingling, and Cass felt herself being drawn back to reality.

She was aware of everything, of every noise, feeling, sensation, more aware of such things than she had ever been.

"Wake up, Cassie! It's your mom and dad here!" the man's voice called to her, and it *did* sound just like her father. She opened her eyes and saw, with some surprise, that she was under a tree in the pasture just outside her old farm, and her Mom and Dad were there, looking down at her.

"I know you're only seven years old, but you must have had a big, bad dream," her mother told her.

"Oh, yes, Mommy! It was real *scary*, too."

"Did you dream about the old man with the cane that shot sparks again?" her father wanted to know.

"Uh huh."

"What happened this time after he shot sparks all over that room? You have to tell us your dream to make it go away."

And, so, she told them, repeating the entire account verbatim, just as it happened. All about the terrible looking people and the talk of war and strategy, all the way to when she walked back to her room with her imaginary playmate and they woke her up. It was all there, better than she could have remembered it any other way.

"This is bad," her Mommy said. "You've been too clever for your own good, Giff. The old boy's already on to you."

"And what'll he have?" her Daddy responded. "Persellus and a vague suspicion and nothing else. Eventually they'll scratch their heads, maybe put extra guards around the Gate, and that will be that, for all the good it'll do them."

Cass frowned. Her Mommy and Daddy were talking such funny stuff, the kind of stuff in her dreams, but to each other, not to her.

"What about her?" Mommy asked, pointing to

Cassie. "So long as she has a Soul Rider she's a mortal danger to us all."

"But we can't destroy Soul Riders, whatever they are. Kill her and it just takes over somebody else whose identity we *don't* know. No, I prefer my enemy in plain sight."

"You just can't leave her here, though. That thing could come out and attack at any time."

He chuckled. "Not yet. If it acts too soon it might get one of us but it'll be useless later on and it won't know the facts. No, I have a better, more effective idea. An original one." He turned to her. "Cass, you cannot move, but see me now as I am." Her father dissolved into another figure, a man she also knew. Haldayne. And, beside him, the woman, too, was visible, and she knew her as well. She knew, but she couldn't believe. Sister Daji! The sexy but dumb consort to the Sister General!

Still gorgeous, still sexy, but hardly dumb. Not this one. Even the odd, ignorant tone in her voice had vanished, although she still had that very odd accent.

Haldayne grinned, and it was obvious that he liked to have his victim know who was doing it before he did whatever it was. He put out a hand on her forehead, and it was warm and wet. "All memory flies," he intoned, "all that is there is null."

Her mind literally became a complete blank. Cass no longer thought at all.

"So, genius?" Daji taunted. "That isn't going to stop a Soul Rider when it wants to take charge."

He grinned, and made a pass with his hands. Cass seemed to shrink down until she was very small, standing and looking up at giants.

Daji looked down, and saw a magnificent looking falcon. She nodded approvingly.

"What will you call her?" Haldayne asked.

Daji thought a moment. "How about Demon? It seems appropriate. But what good does *this* do?"

"My dear, I said I was a genius. There is your passport back through the Guardians. They will not harm a Soul Rider and its companion. I know—I've done it once before. She is a falcon. She thinks she's a falcon, too, and will respond only to you and only to the name Demon. She is devoted to you, will obey your simple commands, and that is all. Now you just take her back to Anchor Logh, then keep her on a leg chain as a pet. Feed her mice and insects and she'll adore you forever. And, most importantly, there is no power in Anchor."

Daji brightened. "Oho! I see! But what if it breaks away, or betrays me at the Gate?"

"It won't. I have presented our powerful but predictable Soul Rider with a series of moral dilemmas. If it wants to learn the truth, as it must, it must accompany you all the way to Anchor. Otherwise it will never learn it, and it knows it. On the other hand, if it goes to Anchor, it is trapped, at least for the life of the bird. That should be more than enough time, I would think. Do not, however, let her off her chain. It *can* and might fly long distances, over walls and into Flux. That's what it plans on doing, you see, which is why it will cooperate with us. And, so long as you continue to perform that little chore, we are safe."

She kissed him. "Giff, you really *are* a genius!"

15

HELLGATE

They flew from Persellus as great winged creatures of their own imaginations, out from the Fluxland now remade in his image and into the void, following first the stringer trail marks, small bands of energy seen as a criss-crossing network of lines below them, then special marks on a frequency intended for their eyes alone. Held by a small chain to the foot of one of the creatures, the falcon called Demon flew with them, having no trouble keeping up.

Finally the small lines below split and then joined again a ways off, outlining a circular pattern between them. They descended carefully, landing at the point of the first split, and their forms shimmered as they landed and became once more human figures. Now both walked forward, leaving the trail lines, to a bright point ahead that only those trained and gifted as they were could see and understand. They were almost upon it before it took true form.

The Hellgate was actually a saucer-shaped depression in the void, very regular, solid, and smooth, and immune to the void's energies and powers. A long ladder seemingly made out of the same stuff led down from the edge to the floor below, where, in the center, there was a dark circular area that was the true entrance.

Daji calmed the nervous falcon and looked down, wishing she could calm her own nerves so easily. "You're sure this will work?"

"You got here that way, didn't you?" he soothed. "Nothing bothered you emerging from it."

"Yeah, but I had sent a couple of those silly novices through first to make sure. What's to prevent the Guardians from letting *her* through and killing me?"

"The Soul Rider won't allow it, because then it would never know. I do admit this is a one-time thing, my dear, but I feel much better with you not gone so long from Anchor but merely a few hours."

Never before, since she and Haldayne had intercepted the real Daji in Persellus and substituted her as an indistinguishable carbon copy, had she met with him in the Flux. Always it was Haldayne, flying over the walls in the form of a common raven, who had sought her out. He, of course, could not change back from raven shape once in Anchor, but he could talk and discuss things with her virtually within the Temple. Now he had summoned her, through the gate, for this very purpose—to trap the Soul Rider in Anchor as he would be trapped.

"You must do it," he told her, "or the entire plan is lost. No one recruited you as one of the Seven—you volunteered, and you accepted my leadership freely and of your own will, without reservations. Either go back on that now, and lose it all, or trust me and go."

She knew that what he said was true, and that if she refused it would not be merely the plan that died. Still, it was a terrifying thing to be asked to do, to enter a Hellgate from the Flux and survive. She took a deep breath. At this point she was dead either way, and only if Haldayne was correct did she have a chance. He did not risk leaving Persellus at this delicate time, even for a short while, merely to see her off. Without being able to neutralize the Soul Rider, inevitably drawn to such a scheme as this, the plan was nothing but bloody madness. She took a deep breath, let it out, then began climbing down the ladder.

The powers of Flux still operated here in this fixed bowl, but she dared not use them, for they would inevitably attract the unknown Guardians of the Gate—unknown because none had ever seen them and survived. She reached the bottom, her bare feet providing decent traction, and walked slowly and apprehensively towards that dark center spot. The falcon made a sudden fluttering motion with its wings, as if trying to fly away, startling her and almost making her fall, but her nerve held steady and she again pulled the bird back on its chain to her and then held it against her breasts, petting it and somewhat calming both of them.

Up close the dark hole showed a web-like grid of strong cables going completely around it and down into the darkness. She knew what to expect, and gingerly turned and started climbing down, the bird placed down on her shoulder and seeming a very heavy and unbalancing weight. It was not, however, far to the floor, where the webbing stopped and a tubular structure replaced it, going off horizontally in front of her. No horrible Guardians had yet appeared, and she began to relax a bit. She did not doubt, though, that those Guardians existed. Once, at another Hellgate, she watched while sacrificial slaves had been ordered in, saw the flashes of multicolored energies fly out of the dark central hole, and had heard the horrible screams of agony from the slaves as they had been destroyed.

The tunnel was long and sloped slightly downwards, but again was no problem. Although made of apparently seamless material the yellow-orange color of the void itself, it was actually sectioned, and as she reached the first section it glowed for a distance of ten meters in front of her. She walked forward, and near the end of the light, at the gaping darkness, the next section came on. When she entered it, the first section winked out. There were seven such sections, and in this direction it was a long, long walk indeed. Now, though, she reached the end, and before her was illuminated the gate itself, a great swirl that might be solid, might be energy, or might be itself alive. To her right was a large, blocky machine that did not seem to belong to this eerie place, with its hundreds of small squares and its read-out screens. This was the locking mechanism, and the ultimate trap for anyone attempting to open the gate, clearly placed here not by the builders of the gate but by someone, or something, else. To walk into that swirl, without all seven machines being fed their unique combinations within sixty seconds, would trigger instant vaporization.

But she turned away from swirl and machine, to the wall opposite the locking device. There was nothing whatsoever to mark or otherwise distinguish the wall from any other part of it, unless you knew the proper pattern. She pressed it in several spots with the flat of her hand, eventually tracing a pattern that had no meaning to her. A section of the wall glowed bright red, but she did not pay any attention to it, turning around instead to see an intricate pattern now traced on the floor of the tube, almost in front of the machine. It was a duplicate of the pattern she had just traced with her palm on the wall, enclosed in a circle of red. She walked to it, then into the center of it. There was a slight moment of dizziness, and the Hellgate vanished, replaced with the view of a dark and damp sub-basement piled high with the signs of work.

She stepped off the cleared and swept spot and into dust and debris, and as she did she felt all sense of the Flux leave her. It made her feel empty, as it always did when she entered Anchor, as if something wonderful and important had been taken away.

She had left her regular robe here when she'd left, and had reentered naked so that she would be as unencumbered as possible. She groped in the dark and found a small light switch, then pushed on it. A small, naked light bulb hanging from a wire came to life. She saw her robe on the nail, then managed to put it on, although she found she had to remove the bracelet binding the falcon's chain to her to do it properly. She had a few seconds of nervousness at that, but the falcon made no move to escape. Now she reattached it, and slid back the bar that sealed the door to outside entry. She opened it carefully, stepped out into the corridor, then reached back, shut off the light, and closed it again. She fumbled in her robe, found the key, and then locked the door again from the outside. She had spent a lot of time making the door look like nothing more than a bunch of nailed-on boards covering a crack in the foundation, and it was very convincing.

A dozen novices, working secretly at night for more than six months under her direction, had first discovered the old door, then taken up the old concrete flooring inside the room. The sub-basement was a secure area: the wardens and their monitors did not reach this far down, and, in fact, only the Sister General and the chief warden had keys to the area at all, almost never used except during the annual maintenance checks. It had been easy, though, to get the key from the Sister General's safe and give it to the raven Haldayne, who, of course, easily returned two so identical they even had the same old markings under a microscope. Things done in Flux held as they were in Anchor, within, of course, the physical laws of Anchor. No huge flying creature such as she had become from Persellus to Hellgate could fly in Anchor—it was a violation of the fixed laws of physics. But a raven was a raven, in Flux and Anchor, and so was a falcon.

She went swiftly now through back passages and service areas she knew by heart, avoiding the wardens' mechanical security sensors as only one with an intimate knowledge of the building could, then took the small back hidden stairway to the Sister General's luxurious apartment, using combinations even the Sister General had probably not bothered to learn. Explaining the falcon would not be a great problem. She had one of the very few VIP necklaces given out by the Sister General that made her immune to most of the security devices in the temple. The wardens would not necessarily see her go in or out at any time, nor would they bother to note or log it if they did.

After checking and finding, to her relief, that the Temple chief was not home, she checked the time and then the schedule on Diastephanos' desk. She had selected this time because the Sister General was supposed to be out of town visiting some of the local churches for three days, but there was no way to guarantee that the old bitch wouldn't louse her up by coming home early. Clock and calendar said that Sister Daji had cut it close, but still had a margin of several hours, perhaps a whole day, before the play began again. That would be very convenient.

She removed the falcon-restraining bracelet once more and clipped it around the brass air conditioning duct, letting Demon perch on the back of a chair. The bird still seemed very calm and somewhat confused, and that suited her fine.

She went to the intercom and buzzed the wardens' office. "This is Daji," she told them unnecessarily, using the vacant and ignorant intonation she always used. "When is she coming back?" There was no need to say who "she" was.

"We expect her any time after eight this evening," a warden told her. Again she glanced at the clock. Barely three. "Thanks," she said, and switched off. Almost five hours.

She took a long, comfortable bath, then put on only the loose, open informal robe and called services. A novice was sent up immediately, who took her dirty clothes and also received a written notice signed by the Sister General for the special construction to be·sent up. The novice bowed and left. Poor, brainwashed idiots, she couldn't help thinking. She recalled the ones who'd done all the work for her below. All now were Haldayne's creatures, having tested the Hellgate passage before she dared go through.

She got a bite to eat from the small kitchenette while she waited. After twenty minutes or so, the buzzer rang and two novices delivered the solid wood perch she had ordered at Haldayne's instructions days before. She thanked and dismissed them, then took it over and placed it by the Sister General's desk, then moved Demon from her odd perch and attached her to the ready-made one. She fed the bird some raw meat from the small refrigerator, then went to work on the sewing machine in her small and normally unused office area. Soon she had a scarlet hood, which fitted over the bird's head. As she'd hoped, the falcon went to sleep.

She sighed, finally relaxing, and realized that Haldayne had done his homework well. This time he'd thought of all the angles, of that she was now certain. This time, for the first time, a known and guarded gate would be totally in the hands of the Seven, making only three to go. If it worked here, it would work, with variations, elsewhere. The long centuries of frustration would be nearing an end.

Now she redid her hair, applied perfumes and make-up, then went back into her office, lifted the sewing machine off its cabinet, reached in and took out three medium-sized pill bottles. She removed one pill from each, then replaced them in their hiding place and resecured the sewing machine. She went back into the living room area, turned on the small entertainment console and took a tiny clear cube no larger than her thumb nail and put it in the device. Standing there, she dictated a long string of sentences, then programmed the device. It would play until she shut it off, but when she shut it off it would self-erase.

She poured herself a whiskey and soda, then took the three pills, then went over and turned on the recorder to playback and sat back in a large, comfortable chair, feet up.

It took several minutes for the pills to take effect, and she just lay there, relaxed, and let them do their job. The recorder kept going, and, finally, it was the only thing in her mind.

"All memory gone, floating, relaxed, so pleasant, so free of any thought, any worry, anything at all, just feeling so, so good and relaxed. . . . You are Sister Daji, and she alone is you now. Let her come, let her become you, flow into you, so that she alone is in control. . . ." Then came a series of instructions to Daji, an explanation of the falcon and perch, and an account of what she had been doing these past three days. She drifted into a deep, deep hypnotic trance.

Haldayne had created Daji by working in Flux with the real one, before he transformed her into another of his creatures. The Daji persona was then transferred, also in Flux, to her, where it resided, complete but separate from her. No chances could or would be taken of any compromise in her identity, which was totally submerged, inactive, until brought forth again by a special trigger command given by Haldayne or one of his agents or another of the Seven.

And so the woman who awoke with a start in the chair was *not* an agent, nor did she even know what the Seven were. She was, in fact, a carbon copy of the original Daji, a woman with the body of a goddess, the mind of a child, and an insatiable worship of and lust for older women. The agent of Hell had not minded. Otherwise, this sort of life would have been unbearable.

The woman in the chair frowned, annoyed by the prattle of the recorder. She got up, went over to it, and shut it off. The recording on it erased automatically. She popped out the small module, picked another at random and popped it in. A lively tune began playing, which she started humming along with and dancing to. Eventually she tired of the game and went into the Sister General's office and walked up to the sleeping falcon. "Oooo, my pretty birdie! Daji's just gonna *love* you to death."

It was well into the night, and the Sister General had long ago returned. Now both she and Daji were asleep on the bed in the next room, and the entire complex was in darkness save for a small nightlight in the commode.

Deep below the temple, below the sub-basement and foundation itself, below even the glassy-smooth rock base, something triggered on. Now there was a slight hissing noise in the sub-basement itself, and in the area marked in dull chalk in the empty and damp room a form took shape. None in Anchor could see the form, and none in Flux would want to. It was a creature of pure energy, yet so terrible was it to gaze upon that humans would go mad at the sight, could they see it at all. Slowly it looked around, not seeing as things of flesh and blood saw but sensing energy and receiving direction. Slowly, it stepped off the chalk-marked area in the floor and up to the door. Although the light was still switched off, the lone hanging bulb suddenly glowed.

It paused only a moment at the door, then seemed to flow under it and out the other side. Once in the corridor, which itself became lit as the bulbs received the energy from the creature, it moved slowly and deliberately down to the far end, where a complex of machinery whined dully. It merged carefully with the power grid, not wanting to overload it, although those still awake not only in the Temple but throughout the capital's electrically powered area frowned and noticed lights seemed to be burning brighter and electrical devices seemed to speed up slightly.

Firmly in the power grid, the creature rode it, searching the entire Temple area until it came upon the one place it was searching for. The tiny nightlight in the Sister General's bathroom glowed, then flared and burnt out, as the creature entered, but other lights came on in their ghostly fashion. In the bedroom, one of the sleeping women gave a muffled cry, turned over, and was soon fast asleep again.

The creature was not heading for the bedroom, but for the Sister General's office. The rear area was again in darkness as the lights in the office came eerily to life.

The Soul Rider inside the sleeping bird read the intense energy field and was confused. It knew the nature of the creature, but could not comprehend how it had gotten here. Still, it understood that the unknown power that directed its destiny had sent an ally, although it was unprecedented in form. The Guardians of the Gates of Hell were in fact creatures of Flux with a specific mission, and to have one detach itself from that mission was almost impossible to believe.

The Soul Rider sensed the Guardian, but had no common language to speak to it, if, indeed, such a creature had speech. Still, when the Rider understood that the Guardian was about to touch its host, it screamed out, "No! Do not destroy the host!"

Energy touched the sleeping bird, and engulfed it, then transformed it. Matter became energy, and the stronger of the three entities now carried the other two in a manner that had no words to describe. Back again they went to the bathroom, and into the electrical system at the nightlight. Again, all electrical devices flared in the capital, and in the wardens' security office the alarm board rang. The startled warden looked up at the board, which showed every single alarm in the Temple triggered all at once, with all the tiny lights flashing on and off. "Damn!" she swore. "A stinking short on *my* shift!"

Below, the Guardian emerged once more from the power grid and walked to the door in the sub-basement, then flowed under it and back to the chalk-marked area. The area glowed for a moment, and then they were in the tunnel at the gate to Hell itself.

The Guardian moved swiftly up the tunnel, which blazed with light, then up through the hole and into the air above the saucer-like depression. The Soul Rider and its companion were flung high into the air and out, away from the gate and into the void.

The Soul Rider was confused and bewildered, but lost no time in acting. Having been present at the casting of the spell on its host it knew the counter, and rushed it into form, with modifications to suit the occasion. It did not understand what had just occurred, but it certainly knew why.

The energy that had been transformed from matter became matter again, reconstituted. Cass burst into sudden consciousness, remembering everything, including the details of what had happened while she was in bird form, although it all seemed distant, unreal, almost like it had happened to someone else. Her last clear personal memory had been going into the hotel room in Globbus.

Instinctively she stretched out, and was startled to find that she did indeed have wings. So she was still a bird, and it had been no dream, but she was now in Flux, thinking, remembering, and free. She wondered how she had gotten here, since the last bird memory was the Sister General and Daji playing with her, then hooding her to sleep, but here she was, suddenly whole in mind and flying through the void.

Only it wasn't a void.

Below she saw the void as wizards and stringers saw it, a criss-crossing network of complex lines of differing colors and intensities. They had an insubstantial look to them, much the same as the afterimage of a swinging light, but they were fixed in place and could be followed.

She banked and circled a moment, staring at the patterns, flying as if it was the most normal and natural thing in the world to her, but she felt some concern. She knew she had to get back, to warn Matson and the others, but which of those strings led to Globbus? Which to Persellus? Which to other places, perhaps Anchor Logh itself?

Although there were countless secondary strings, there were only three main ones, so she picked one at random and followed it, hoping it would lead eventually to someplace that would orient her. Although there were no real landmarks except the occasional patterns in some of the secondary strings, she knew that she was flying abnormally fast and realized that she was feeling neither hunger nor thirst. The Flux was supplying all the energy she required.

She was upon it almost before she realized it, breaking through into Anchor. At that moment she felt herself start to drop like a stone, and with great difficulty she turned herself back into the void, thankful that she had had enough altitude to make it in time. Strength and that curious sense of weightlessness returned. Now, at least, she knew where she was, for below her as she'd started to fall had been the apron and gate to Anchor Logh.

Now two main trails led from Anchor, and she pikd the right-hand one, remembering Matson's comment that Globbus and Persellus were almost the same distance from the Anchor. She realized after a bit that she still wasn't certain if this was the route to Persellus or to Globbus, but she had no choice now but to follow it and pray that there were no other forks. Suddenly she passed over two figures, odd enough to see along any route in the void. She was going too fast to tell much about them, but banked, slowed, and approached them again, flying high enough, she hoped, to avoid their detection but just low enough that when she banked and came around again she could see more about them.

Both were mounted on horses with just saddlebags for their gear. One was a young, handsome man dressed in riding clothes who had a full, light beard. The other was a small, well-built woman, bare from the waist up but wearing a broad-brimmed hat and blue denim work pants. She recognized the figure. *Suzl!* But who was the other man? An agent of Haldayne's, or one of Mervyn's men? After all this, she decided she had to risk an appearance. At least these two, alone, would be easier to deal with if the man were an enemy than an armed and wizard-filled camp suspicious of everything and likely to shoot first and ask questions afterwards. She came around again and this time dipped low in front of them, so both could see her. She saw their faces look forward and up, and their mouths droop, but they made no hostile moves. Both riders, however, stopped, and she circled once more as they watched and landed right in front of them.

With a shock she saw that she was as large as they were, if not even larger. They stared at each other for a moment, and she wondered if she could speak. Finally she said, "Suzl?" It sounded right.

Suzl frowned. "Cass? Is that *really* you? Holy Mother of Universes! What in hell happened to you?"

Feeling a little relieved, she responded, "First, who's that with you?"

The young man chuckled. "Why, my dear, I am Mervyn." His voice changed, taking on the old man's low, broken cackle. "We are what we choose to be in Flux."

She looked back at Suzl. "Is that right?"

She nodded. "Yeah. Second biggest shock I ever had. You're the third. What happened to you at the hotel? Who changed you into—that?"

"I'm not sure what 'that' is," she told them honestly. "Some sort of bird, I guess."

"Some sort, yes," Mervyn agreed, and made a gesture. Between them appeared a huge mirrored surface, and she could see herself.

Her body was that of a giant falcon, and her arms were wings, but her underside, raised up and facing them, was human all the way, and she had her own face, although feathers replaced hair on her head. She stared at the reflection for a moment more in wonder than in shock or horror.

"The only reason I didn't bring you down was

because I sensed the Soul Rider still inside you," the wizard told her. "It has certainly delivered you from evil." The mirror vanished, and both riders dismounted and sat down, relaxing. "Now, then, tell me all that you have been through. Spare nothing."

She went into extreme detail, although it still seemed like a dream to her. When she finished the wizard just nodded and sat thoughtfully for a moment. Finally he said, "It is very clever. It is, in fact, diabolical. It should have worked completely, for I know that while a Soul Rider can exist in Anchor its powers there are minimal and mostly involved in influencing specific actions of others. I would love to know how you escaped, how *it* escaped."

"I'm not sure *I* do," Cass replied. "I don't have any real memories between the time they stuck that hood over me until I was suddenly flying in the void, but there's a sense there of something— terrible. I really can't describe it."

"I can read it inside you, but aside from verifying your sensations there is nothing more I can make of them. It is certainly not anything I've ever experienced from a Soul Rider before, nor are they particularly—terrible, as you call it." He sighed. "No matter for now. It is a question now of what to do next."

Cass looked at them. "If you're such a powerful wizard, how come you two are riding to Anchor Logh? Couldn't you just transform the both of you into flying things like me and make it quicker?"

"I could," the wizard agreed, "but, for one thing, we would arrive without bags or horses, and that would terrify the guards. There were also other factors, not the least of which was timing. I needed some time to think, and it would not do to arrive too early. If we got the aid we are seeking they would be hot to ride out immediately and on their own, and that would be disastrous. And, finally, I wanted to check this route in detail, for it forms the third arm of the triangle with Globbus, Persellus, and Anchor Logh, with the Hellgate in the center of that triangle. I wanted no surprises, and could trust none but a wizard of my rank to do the survey. I suspected that Haldayne was not acting alone. Otherwise he would not be so bold in his actions."

"Well, you'll clearly get no help from Anchor Logh, not with dear Daji as the power behind the throne."

"On the contrary, I think we *will* get it. This dual personality trick is a favorite of Haldayne's in Anchor, because it is impossible to detect there. By the same token, a command from a third party must be made in order to summon up the original personality."

"But surely Haldayne and she have agents in the Temple, ones that will find out I escaped and trigger it."

"Perhaps," Mervyn replied, "but perhaps not. All the Daji personality knows is that her pet escaped and is gone. This will upset her for a while, but the Sister General will console her and give her a new toy or something and she may forget all about it. The agents might never know, or never know the importance. Even if they *do* find out, they must trigger the other personality, and one or more must be taken through this intriguing gate access and then get to Haldayne, who must respond. This will take time, particularly since those agents are unlikely to be wizards of any significance. By that time we will have had our audience."

"Maybe," Cass said dubiously, "but what good will that do us? I mean, if this woman is this highly placed, then she's probably got agents or corrupt innocents all over the place. That army might wind up fighting on the wrong side if at all."

"But I don't *care* about its loyalty," Mervyn told her. "Don't you see? Haldayne has rigged things to lose. They will contribute and they will fight well with us because of that alone. After—well, think of this. Isn't it obvious to you by now that we must not only conquer Persellus but Anchor Logh as well?"

Both of the others looked shocked. It really hadn't occurred to either of them until now.

"And, if we do, I certainly would prefer a good share of their army out under *our* control in Flux. It'll make things a lot less bloody, I suspect." He laughed. "No, now that we know it all, I think we are about to give a truly bitter pill to Mister Haldayne." He sighed and got up. "And now we must let the others know of our plans. That will mean a slight inconvenience."

"I could fly back with it," Cass suggested. "I kind of like this."

"No, unless you were lucky enough to come across a first class wizard they would at least try to kill you, certainly not listen to what you have to say, or believe a word of it if they do. I'm afraid I must go, but this time I will take the express. You two are still half a day's ride from Anchor Logh. You go on, and I will catch up to you."

It was Suzl who looked distressed at that. "But how will we find our way in the void?"

Mervyn chuckled. "That should present no problem at all. You see, as she is just discovering, Cass is a wizard herself and a fairly strong one, although limited right now to her own self."

"What!" they both cried in unison.

He nodded. "It took this stress and trauma to bring it out, although it has been latent all along. That is why the Soul Rider chose you. I knew it the moment I sensed the Rider, for Riders are limited to using the powers and abilities of their hosts. That is why your escape is so puzzling—Flux has no power in Anchor, as you well know. Now that you know, and now that crisis has brought it out, you can use it. You could not have found us unless you were following a main trail—correct?"

Cass nodded soberly. "Yes, that's true. I found I could see them. But I thought it was the Soul Rider or the transformation."

"No. It merely brought them out in you. Now, understand, you have power but no knowledge. That means that this power as regards specific things will affect only you or that which you need or which threatens you. Without much study and much mathematical training you cannot know how powerful you really are or use it practically. But you can follow this trail, and if you need water you can find or even create it. Besides, I still want a good look at this whole route by a wizard I can trust. You fill that bill."

"But—what about this form?" she asked lamely.

"If you concentrate hard enough, you can be anyone or anything you wish to be, with any attributes you need," he told her. "It will take much experimentation to get it right all the time, but you should at least have no problem whatsoever in becoming yourself, for you know your true form better than anyone. Try it now. Just close your eyes and concentrate on your old self. Picture it, and want to be that way again. Go ahead."

She did as instructed. She remembered herself, not as she was, but as she remembered that slightly redone Cass in the mirror at Miss Rona's. She pictured it, remembered it, and called up the same amazed satisfaction.

She opened her eyes. "See? Nothing?"

"Oh no?" Suzl responded. "Don't you feel a little—shorter? And maybe a little hairier?"

She looked down at herself, and gasped. She

was, in fact, human once again. That body looked very familiar, although it was stark naked. She brought her arms up and looked at her hands. Her *hands*! She felt her head, and there was hair there, although not tied, just streaming down. "I did it," she said wonderingly.

"That you did. And if you need to be a bird woman again, just think of that image you saw. That's the way it works on a personal basis."

She grinned. "I'll be damned! Wow!" She hesitated a moment. "But—wait a minute. I can't go into Anchor dressed like *this*."

"Why not?" Suzl asked. "That's the way you left it."

The wizard shrugged. "We'll have to teach you a few simple tricks when we can. For now—" he snapped his fingers—"that should do it." And, suddenly, she had on a short-sleeve red pull-over shirt, brown work pants, and boots. "Yeah, you will. . . ." she breathed.

"Well, I'm off. If I'm not back before you get to Anchor, wait on the apron for me. Under no account go in there alone. Particularly not you, Cass. If word is out, Haldayne will have you marked for instant death this time, Soul Rider or not."

16

HOMECOMING

They rode along for a while, just getting up to date.

"After you disappeared, and Nadya came screaming out of the room, there was holy Hell to pay all over Globbus, I'll tell you," Suzl said. "It was pretty clear after the initial search failed to find you, though, that you'd been snatched and carried off, and there was no problem guessing by who and where to. They met again after that and switched some things around, particularly the training and stakeout stuff, but otherwise they just accepted it. There wasn't anything they could do short of attacking Persellus then and there, and they weren't ready to do *that* yet, no matter how much we screamed at them."

She thought for a moment. "How did Matson take it?"

"He was pissed. Took it as a personal insult. Wanted to ride in with a rescue right away. I think he really likes you, Cass."

She smiled. "I wonder what he'll think when he finds out I'm a wizard? Me—that's still pretty hard to accept."

Suzl shrugged. "I don't know. There was always something funny about you, ever since we got caught up in that Paring Rite. Even when bad things happened to you they turned out O.K."

"Does it change anything between us—as friends?"

"Not on my account, uh uh. Might be good to have a friend with some power around here. What about you, though? Everybody says when you get that kind of power you go nuts."

"Maybe I always *was* nuts, so it doesn't matter. I don't know, Suzl. I guess I don't really believe it yet. Back in the gym, when we all got together and swore we were coming back and take our revenge on Anchor Logh—I didn't believe that, either. Not for a minute. And yet, here we are, heading back in, with you and me knowing that they plan to do just that. I'm really off balance, and have been all this time. I mean, just think of the others."

"Huh?"

"The others taken in the Paring Rite, not just in Anchor Logh but all over World. Almost nobody escapes becoming somebody's slave or somebody's thing. And yet, here we are, right in the thick of great events like World's never seen before. Maybe *causing* a lot of it. I never thought of myself as any great mover and shaker. I mean, I'm still me, Cass, off the farm at Anchor Logh."

Suzl shrugged. "Maybe it's because we think of those big movers and shakers all wrong. Maybe we build 'em up after they're dead and gone or something into saints and angels and all that. I think maybe that all those greats really went to the bathroom same as we, and maybe got stomach aches and thought of themselves as folks just off some farm. And they probably were."

"Yeah, but why us? Why not a couple of the others? Ivon or Kral or Jodee, for example? And why now?"

"I think it's just gotta be somebody, sometime, and we just happen to be it. I don't think it's planned. Look, the way I see it, this bastard

Haldayne came up with this plot and put it into operation. This brought forth your Soul Rider or whatever it is, who picked you because you were the first one it ran into who had this power or whatever. Now, whether or not it was that thing or you that went nuts and violated the Temple we'll never know, but maybe it picked you because it knew you were the type to do just that. Who knows? This Mervyn reads minds pretty good, I think, and if *he* can, why not a creature of some kind? Once you were stuck with it, it used you and your power to unmask the plot. All because it was just floating along or something and you just happened to be the first one in the way. See?"

She sighed. "Maybe you're right. Uh—this Mervyn and you have been riding along for some time. Did he do anything about your—problem?"

She laughed. "I don't have a problem. Other people might, but I don't. Oh, he looked at it, decided it was too complicated, and offered to turn me one hundred percent male. *That* he could do."

"And you refused?"

She nodded. "I like it this way. Because you got snatched we had extra time, and I went over to one of the bars. Had a ball with it. Nope, I like it. No more periods, no more afraid of getting pregnant, none of that. But I *like* the way I look, and I *like* my tits and ass. I got the best of both worlds. There's lots of guys who only like other guys, you know. I'm the only one you know that can have it both ways and not be a pervert." She giggled at that.

"And Dar, of course."

"Yeah, well, maybe. But he's still pretty hung up on his maleness, and I don't think he'll ever have the kind of freedom I feel."

"Speaking of freedom, how come the shirtless look? It's sexy with your equipment, but hardly usual."

"Men don't have to wear shirts if they're comfortable without them. Oh, don't worry, I have a couple packed for dear old Anchor Logh. This is just kind of a turn-on. Makes me feel really free, that's all."

They rode along, laughing and joking like two schoolgirls. When the horses seemed thirsty, Cass found it easy to identify which of the off-trail strings led to water pockets. It was all becoming very familiar very fast now. She was beginning to enjoy this newfound sense and the power it brought, and she only hoped she had enough self-control to keep from going wild with it. That, of course, was the madness of the wizard.

Mervyn still hadn't returned by the time they reached the border of Anchor Logh. Because traffic was being stopped in Globbus and was not likely to come via Persellus, they felt reasonably safe in remaining there, just inside the Flux. Cass did not take Mervyn's warning lightly—Haldayne now would kill her on sight, since time was so crucial at this point that he would bet the Soul Rider would not find another suitable host in time to stop him.

"He seems so confident," Cass said worriedly. "But Haldayne's good, real good, and he knows more about his enemies than they do about him."

"Sure, but if he's on to the fact that we know about his lady love there in the Temple, he might just give it up as not worth it," Suzl responded hopefully. "What's the use of fighting it out if you can't gain anything?"

Cass shrugged. "Who knows what he thinks? I wish I knew more about what this was *really* about."

"Huh? Sleep through your religion classes? It's all checking out in that department."

"Well, maybe. But I've been through that gate to Hell, and I've seen the so-called sacred seal. The gate's supernatural enough, but that seal is a

machine, Suzl. Real strange looking all right, but
a machine all the same, a very fancy kind of machine but still a relative to the ones in the capital
and the Temple. It sure wasn't put there by the
ones who built that Hellgate—it just looks too
different, that's all. More like something *we* would
build if we knew how. Now, if the Holy Mother
and Her Blessed Angels forced the demons into
that hole and then sealed it with the seven seals,
why did they use a machine? Why not just use the
Flux power, or godly powers? And don't give me
that crap about the ways of gods and demons
being unknowable to humankind. *Somebody* knows.
Haldayne, for example, knows, and maybe Mervyn
does, too.''

"Yeah, but the old boy didn't know the gate
connected to the Temple until you told him. Boy! I
never saw him so shook!''

Cass nodded. "The big thing is, if you can use
this gate to get to the temple in Anchor Logh, then
the odds are you can get to other Temples through
other gates. That says to me that, for some reason,
it's the Anchors that are important in this, not
really the Flux, and I'm sure old Merv's wondering
now just how many Anchors Haldayne's side already controls. He sure knows more about those
gates than Mervyn and the others.''

Conversation drifted to other things as they
waited.Time hung heavy in the void if only because
there was no sense of it. Finally, though, a huge,
dark shape came from the direction of the trail.
They watched, ready to dart into Anchor if need be,
but the enormous flying shape landed, shimmered,
and changed into Mervyn's old man form, and
they relaxed. Cass saw that there was a certain,
indefinable *something* radiating from the man that
marked Mervyn as Mervyn and no one else to her.
Suzl, however, needed her nerves calmed, for she
had none of these senses.

The wizard walked up to them carrying a small satchel. "I've notified everyone I could find of your information—those that needed to know it, anyway," he told them. "We want to keep your escape secret, and I'm afraid I didn't tell them the source, so you are still officially missing, even to my fellow sorcerers. We are going to move up the attack, even though we might not have everybody, just to keep Haldayne off balance." He put down the satchel, fumbled with the catch, then opened it and reached inside, first bringing out a cube, almost a meter square, of some undefined grayish substance. He put it in front of him, stepped back and made a gesture with his wrist. The cube shimmered, grew, and seemed to inflate as if it were some sort of balloon, until, standing there, was a full-sized living mule. "It's so convenient when you have to to be able to compress them down to maximum survivable density," he said, ignoring their total lack of understanding.

He reached down into the bag once more and pulled out clothing. "We are going to have to be convincing," he told them, "and have easy access. Both of you get undressed here and now. We're going in undercover, you might say."

After she undressed, the wizard handed her a robe. It was the scarlet and gray robe of a parish priestess. She put it on, and it was a bit too large for her. "Well, grow into it. You're going to have to change your appearance totally here and now anyway. We want as many basic differences between you and your original looks as possible, and height is important because it's the first thing noticed. I want you *very* tall in bare feet—call it a hundred seventy-five, even a hundred and eighty centimeters. *Very* tall. And looking like nobody you know."

She frowned. "That's tough. Aside from my friends, the only women I can think of enough to concentrate on are my mother, my sisters, and those two priestesses."

He sighed. "Oh, very well. Stand still." He made a flinging gesture with his hand, and suddenly the robe fit very well indeed. She towered over the very short Suzl, who stood back and nodded. "Not bad. Maybe you ought to keep that."

She desperately wanted a mirror—so desperately that the reflective surface Mervyn had used before materialized in front of her. She was stunning, very tall and perfectly proportioned to the height. Even her figure was absolutely perfect, and, unlike the experiments at Miss Rona's, it felt very comfortable. Her face, a near-perfect oval set off by very large, dark brown eyes and short hair of the same color, and her light brown skin made her almost the living model of religious pictures of the Holy Mother.

She wished the mirror away and was startled to see not Mervyn but another woman there, this one about halfway between Suzl's height and her own, also dark and attractive but dressed in a skin-tight outfit of what looked like red leather, with high red boots and even a cape. The strange woman was helping Suzl into a black outfit—a stringer's outfit.

"Don't be so shocked," said the strange woman in a deep, melodious voice. "We have to see a high priestess in a Temple. You didn't expect them to let me just walk in the way I was, did you?"

She laughed, feeling that sense of recognition she could not define. This was the third guise for Mervyn, and the most confusing of all. Since Suzl refused to permit a disguise by sorcery, she was instead going in slightly different clothing. She was soon dressed as the shortest, cutest stringer in anybody's memory. Mervyn then went over their cover names and stories and rehearsed them until they got it right. Suzl would be Sati, the name of a real female stringer that would be on the guard lists, but a stringer who had not been to Anchor Logh, being relatively new in the business. Cass would be Sister Kasdi, of Anchor Bakha, an Anchor far to the southwest of Anchor Logh but still closest in that direction, and an Anchor in many ways similar to Anchor Logh. She was given a spell-reinforced history and geography lesson that made her feel like she really had lived there. Mervyn would be Mera, a professional woman.

"Matson told me that they were anxiously looking for an electrical engineer," he told them. "I have some knowledge in that field and I think I can pass as a possible applicant for the job."

Satisfied, they mounted, Cass taking the mule as was appropriate for priestesses, although she hated the side-saddle riding method that tradition dictated a priestess adopt exclusively. All set, they rode into Anchor.

Suzl had taken, apparently in Globbus, to smoking and slightly chewing on thin, crooked little cigars. While it was all part of the self-image she now had, she stuck one in the side of her mouth as they rode in and it gave a very good added effect to her stringer act. She led the mule with Cass aboard by a small rope, with Mervyn bringing up the rear. Suzl's whole expression and body took on a look of arrogant tolerance of the surroundings, like a government minister forced to tour a garbage dump, and she was obviously enjoying herself to the limit. She rode right past the shantytown of tents and dugout buildings and the small semipermanent population of duggers there and right up to the gate. A guard watched them, and when she stopped in front of the opening he called out, "Who are you and what is your business and intent?"

"My name is Sati, stringer," she responded boldly. "I am still apprenticed, and was delegated to take these two from the Hollus train at Globbus, which is not heading here, up to Anchor Logh and the Temple."

The guard vanished for a moment, then the outer gates closed with a dramatic rumbling. They waited there a couple of minutes, and then they opened again. There were now three soldiers, well armed and looking spiffy, on horseback in the gate, and they rode towards the waiting trio. Cass recognized the officer who led them as one of the men at the gate that terrible night they'd left Anchor Logh.

Suzl barely glanced at them, but reached down into her saddlebag and pulled out a small book, handing it to the officer. He looked it over, then looked at the three of them, and frowned. There was nothing unusual about such detached deliveries—they happened all the time—but his job was to ensure that these were legitimate. He rode out a bit further so he could see the guard atop the tower. "What do you say?" he called up.

"Checks out, sir," the guard responded. "She's on the last list given to us by the guild, and she's apprenticed to Hollus."

He nodded to himself and turned back to her. "And what is your cargo?"

"Two passengers, that's all," Suzl told him. "Sister Kasdi was sent over here from Anchor Bakha for some specialized training in the Temple, and Miss Mera was traveling with another train when Matson came through with the word that you were looking for engineers. She decided to come on up and look your charming land over to see if she can save herself a longer trip to another job." Cass admired how Suzl made the words "charming land" seem like the nastiest of insults with sheer intonation.

The officer looked at the other two. Cass looked back at him, smiled sweetly, and gave him a blessing with her hand. It unnerved him for a moment. Finally he said, "All right, will you two ladies please dismount?" They did, Cass with slight difficulty she hoped wasn't obvious. "Stringer, you come in first and file the papers for the passes. Ladies, these two troopers will remain with you until we have passed through, then take you through with them."

Suzl, the animals trailing, rode confidently into the gate and the officer followed. It closed, there was a pause, and then it opened once more. Suzl, at least, was back in the land of her birth.

They followed behind the troopers and into the gate, which closed behind them. One of the troopers turned and said, "Our apologies, Sister, Lady, but we must arrange for a search. Please remain in here and do not move until someone comes for you."

Cass looked over at Mervyn, but just got a shrug. For him it was just routine, but to her this was a new experience. She wondered, though, what all the fearful and prejudiced folk of Anchor Logh would feel if they knew how silly and useless their dreaded gate and defenses really were? It was pretty obvious that people went from Flux to Anchor and back all the time, no matter what the official line was—or even if the officials quoting that line knew it.

They waited there a few minutes, and then a priestess came into the gate. She was quite young, her robe of light yellow very plain and unadorned, saying that she was not long out of the novitiate. Clearly this was a bottom-rung job.

She approached Cass first, who outranked her by her robe's indication, then kneeled. Cass had seen this done enough to have no problems with it. "The blessing of the Holy Mother be upon thee for eternity," she pronounced. "Be free and do your duty."

The young priestess rose, bowed slightly, and responded, "We thank thee, Sister, for thy understanding and blessing. Humble apologies to you both, but it is required that you both disrobe completely for physical examination. You have seen out there what lurks in Flux, and while we realize that it is most unnecessary on your part we can make no exceptions."

Cass smiled, undid, and removed her robe, letting it drop to the ground. Mervyn, dressed more complexly, had more of a problem, and was assisted by Cass in reaching the same state.

For a groveling priestess not yet even allowed to have a name of her own or use the personal pronoun, she was most thorough in her inspection. Clearly she did not want to be here forever, or worse, and just one slip and worse it would be.

Finally she nodded and said, "Please put your clothing back on, and again our humblest apologies."

"That's all right," Mervyn soothed. "If you had seen what we have seen in Flux you would know just how important your job really is."

She smiled, not realizing how totally irrelevant that job was.

The priestess in yellow led them to the other side, where Suzl waited, looking impatient and bored. Both of the newcomers were given a form to sign, and then issued passes good for one week maximum. Of course, should they be allowed by the Temple to stay, then they would be granted citizenship.

The officer and a trooper assisted Cass in remounting her mule, then they were off along the main highway to the capital. They were well along and far out of sight of the guards when Suzl finally laughed. "So much for their security. Checked you two over with a microscope, and you both phony as can be, while they just kept shoving papers at me and never even looked me in the eye."

"I counted on that," Mervyn told her. "Remember, a bureaucrat does not believe in Heaven or Hell, Church or Government. A bureaucrat only believes in paper."

They rode on, stopping overnight in Lawder, a small town about halfway to the capital. Cass found her disguise both annoying and fun at one and the same time. Annoying, because as a priestess she had no money and had to more or less beg for food, drink, and lodging from the locals and was really prevented from going to the bar and other public rooms. It was fun, though, in that she was treated deferentially by almost everyone, and it was funny to watch them try and control their language and behavior around her. She found some diversion, though, in the fact that, as an outside priestess, everybody wanted to confess to her and this became the main agent of barter. It was obvious that many sought absolution from sin but did not relish confessing to their local priestess, who would be living in the same town with them.

Since she had been through the ritual on the supplicant end most of her life, she knew all the proper things to do and say, and it occurred to her more than once that this, more than anything else, was the most effective way in which the church had the pulse of, and control of, the entire community. They barely needed the spies and agents she had imagined when she'd seen the dossiers on that screen. All they needed was weekly updated reports from each and every parish priestess on the confessions of the faithful.

She soon had quite an earful from the locals, too. Clearly Anchor Logh was not the calm, straight-laced community she had always imagined it being. It was one thing in Flux, but here, in a place she thought she new, she began to feel a stranger.

*   *   *

They set out again the next morning, Suzl feeling a little grumpy because Mervyn had stopped her fun in the bar short of the payoff. She knew, of course, that this was not the time, and that there was much danger in exposure, but it still irritated her.

By early afternoon they were approaching the capital, and as they passed a large farm Suzl and Cass halted and looked suddenly serious.

"What's the problem?" the wizard asked them.

"Over there is where both of us were born and raised," Cass told him. "Our families are still there. I'd hoped to be able to see them, tell them I was all right." She sighed. "I guess I can't, looking and sounding like this."

He thought a moment. "If you can pull it off, not blow your cover or break down, it might be all right if you just, say, carried the news as a third party," Mervyn said. "Do you think you can act the part in front of people you know? They won't know you, remember, for you are someone else."

"I'd like to try—for their sakes," she responded honestly. "I think, after all, this is something I *have* to do."

"All right then," he agreed. "Go and do it. We will go ahead and register at the hotel. Don't take more than one hour, then follow us in. That will give us a chance to settle and get the lay of the land, as it were. Meet us there, and we'll discuss what to do next. And if anything goes wrong here, *anything*, break off and come to us immediately. I want no surprises here that we don't generate."

She nodded. "I will. The Holy Reverend Sister Kasdi will behave." She turned to Suzl. "Want me to pass on any word about you?"

She thought a moment. "Just tell 'em I'm free and I'm happy." She had a sudden thought. "I hope nobody who knows me is in town now." She alone appeared, at least, the way she had been.

"There is very little chance of that," Mervyn told her. "It is midweek, after all. Let's cross that bridge when we come to it."

They left Cass there, and for a while she hesitated. Here it was—the large box she had come to check that day that now seemed so long ago, the day she had seen Matson riding in. The difference between that child and her now, although separated not really all that long in time, was an unbridgeable chasm.

She decided, though, to walk down the road, and tied up the mule at the post box. How many times had she walked down this same road to those buildings? She looked over at the pastures and could still identify and name just about every horse and cow she could see.

Finally she reached the familiar complex, and made the almost automatic turn that took her to the blacksmith's shop. The old sounds of iron being pounded and reshaped caused her heart to skip a beat, and she began perspiring despite the slight chill. Could she do it—or not? She sighed, and took several deep breaths to get hold of herself. As she had told Mervyn, she *had* to.

She walked in the barn-like open doors of the smithy and saw her father there, dunking a horseshoe in water, as two other smiths and three apprentices worked elsewhere. She approached her father, the tension rising within her. He looked up, frowned, stared a moment, then put down his work and came to her. "Yes, Sister? What can I do for you?"

She repressed the urge to fling her arms around him and hug and kiss him as she so desperately wanted to do. Instead she said, "You are the father of the girl called Cass who was taken in the Paring Rite?"

He suddenly went a bit tense and white. "Yes. What's this all about?"

"I have news of her."

He looked suddenly very concerned and she could see the emotions within him rising, despite his efforts to contain them. "Speak," he said hoarsely.

"I have just come through the Flux from Anchor Bakha. During that journey I met many from this Anchor. Most are suffering as expected, but your Cass is doing well."

He looked very interested and slightly relieved, but he wanted to know more.

"I cannot tell you of the Flux, except that it is very strange," she continued, struggling with the words. "However, there is some opportunity there for those with special talents. Your Cass and three others from this riding have broken their bonds and now work as paid employees for a stringer, mostly tending to animals. They were healthy and seemed happy, but were anxious that I carry news back to their families."

She could hardly believe it. Were those truly *tears* in her father's eyes? Never, ever, had she known her father to cry, not under any conditions, and she was so touched by it that she had to fight back tears herself.

"Cass also wanted me to inform others that the ones called Suzl, Dar, and Nadya are also safe, well, and have jobs and careers. Alas, for the others—there is the purging. Will you see, though, that their families also get word?"

Her father broke down at that point, dropped to his knees and took and firmly clasped her hand. It was at once both touching and embarrassing, but she knew she had done the right thing. She also knew that she'd better get out of there before she broke down completely herself.

"I must go," she managed, voice breaking, "but I am glad I could bring you some joy. Cass said to t-tell you s-she loved you, and missed you, but that she was probably happier now than she would have been back here."

He didn't want to let go of her, but she managed to break free and walked out, leaving him sobbing in his shop. She walked briskly back down the road, the light wind stinging the copious tears that now flowed unchecked and unstoppable.

It was dark and she was once again in the city before she had completely cried it out.

She went immediately to the hotel, tying up her mule, and went inside. Suzl was sitting there smoking one of her little cigars and looking through the paper, while Mervyn was checking the hotel directory. They saw her, and came over to her. Suzl saw at once what sort of experience it had been for her. Her eyes were puffy and red.

"How'd it go?" she asked gently.

"It went fine. The job got done with nobody the wiser, but I'm afraid it was pretty hard on me."

"Poor kid. It must have been tough."

She nodded. "Real tough, but worth it. I'll never regret it no matter what happens from here on in."

Mervyn came up to her and whispered, "Let's step outside for a moment, Sister." They followed him out into the darkened street. "All right," he went on when he was sure they were not being overheard, "we're in too late to do anything tonight. Sister, you will have to stay at the Temple, of course. Just relax, act the part, and get a good night's sleep. In the morning, go out and wait for us in the Temple Square." He paused for a moment. "I'm afraid you're going to have to go through their whole rigamarole."

She shrugged. "I think my lessons will hold up. Don't worry about me—I've been more places in that Temple than anybody not working there, and if your spell holds they're not going to be able to make much use of hypnotic drugs to get any information."

"It'll hold," he assured her. "Go. We have a busy, and risky, day tomorrow."

She nodded, and led her mule down streets she knew so well towards the great, lighted Temple spires.

"Any problems?" Mervyn asked her in the crisp, clean morning air when they met in Temple Square.

"None that I know of," she told him. "I had to do some explaining, and a lot of praying and chanting, but that's about it. It's not bad when you've got rank. Novices to wait on you hand and foot, private rooms with all the amenities, soft feather beds. They know your covers, though—I had to tell them that."

He nodded. "Don't worry about it. We won't need them long. Come."

Together all three of them went up the Temple steps to those forbidding bronze doors, opened them, and stepped inside. Cass saw that Suzl was playing the memory game from her glances. *In there is the chapel, down there is the gym where they marched us, over there are the Temple boarding rooms for young girls in town, over there is the library stairs....* She had done much the same the night before.

Mervyn seemed to know his way around pretty well. "They're all built pretty much the same," he told them. Standardization. They went down the library stairway but did not make the turn to go down the next flight to the library itself. Instead they stopped, and Mervyn knocked on an unmarked door opening onto the landing. It opened to reveal a puzzled warden. "Yes?" she asked.

"I am here to deliver a message to the Sister General. Can you take one to her from me?"

The warden looked hesitant. "I can't just disturb

her for any old thing. You can take it up with the proper channels."

"I have no time to be put off by bureaucrats whose job it is to put me off," he responded curtly. "If you get this message to her, she will see me. If you do not, I will raise something of a stink that will be as unpleasant for you as for me. At the end of that time I will probably be hauled off to jail, but the Sister General will get my message in the report and then we will change places, or worse."

The warden did not seem moved by this, and made as if to close the door. Mervyn stuck his foot in it, then pushed the warden backwards with a shove. Clearly that woman's body he'd tailor-made for himself had a lot of nasty surprises, for the larger, tougher-looking warden flew back as if struck by a sledgehammer. Aghast, Suzl and Cass followed him into the wardens' room.

Three other wardens were in there and came on the run when they saw the problem. Mervyn reached behind to his long cape and brought out an automatic rifle. They stopped, unable to believe that anyone would commit such sacrilege.

"Sati, shut that door. You on the floor—get up and get over with your sisters. *Now!* And all of you just stand there and stay away from any nice little buttons or consoles. I am a creature of Flux and I will not hesitate to shoot. If I do, the spray this thing makes in stopping one of you will kill all four of you."

Suzl reached under her shirt in the back and pulled out a small automatic pistol, reinforcing Mervyn and freeing him to move. "You four—come into the outer room here with us. Don't touch anything or try anything funny."

They obeyed, hands high, but they glared at her. "You'll fry in Hell for a thousand lives for this," one hissed.

"I already been there, honey, and it don't scare

me a bit," she snapped back. "Ca—Kasdi, you watch 'em and if you see one of 'em pull anything funny, you yell and they're gone."

"You'll never get out of here alive," one of the wardens said smugly. "You know that, don't you?"

"If I don't, neither will you," came the equally tough reply. Suzl, Cass noted, was loving every minute of this, and there was genuine hatred and contempt in her expression and manner. This was no act. She ached for revenge.

Mervyn studied the control panel for a moment, checked out its switches and relays, then found the master manual and thumbed quickly through it. He found what he was looking for immediately, and tapped four numbers on the intercom pad. There was a buzzing sound, then an unfamiliar voice answered. "Sister General. What is the problem?"

"There is an urgent message here for the Sister General's ears alone," he said into the speaker. "It is urgent. Put her on at once."

There was a sigh at the other end, and the connection was muted for a moment. Finally a far more familiar voice said, "This is Sister General Diastephanos. What is the nature of this emergency?"

Mervyn looked over at Cass, who nodded. That was her, all right.

"The Seven Who Come Before have gathered at the gates of Anchor to release the spawn of Hell," he said carefully. "The Nine Who Guard call upon the holy church for aid."

There was a long pause, and then the Sister General asked, "Who is this?"

"Pericles," he responded.

Again there was silence. Finally she asked, "Are my wardens all right? I assume it wasn't easy to get in to use the intercom."

"They are mad and angry and vengeful," he told

her truthfully, "but aside from a slight bruise on one of them they are in fine shape."

"Who's watch officer?"

He looked over at the four. One of them said, sourly, "Daran."

"Put her on."

Mervyn gestured with the gun and the chief warden came over to the intercom. "She's here," he told her.

"Daran, this would not have been necessary if you had not refused to carry the message. These people are not criminals, nor are they committing sacrilege. How many are there?"

"Three, Your Worship," the warden said glumly. "Two have guns, and the third's pretending to be a priestess."

"She may very well be one," the Sister General snapped back. "Now, listen carefully. You are to escort these three to my office without delay of any kind. Understand? I want no trouble and no revenge. If there is any trouble or any action of any kind taken against them you will all be exiled to Flux immediately. I mean that."

"But Your Worship—"

"No buts! Deliver them immediately, healthy, and with no problems and I will forgive all. Do anything else—*anything*—and you will all curse the day of your birth and the parents who bore you. That is all."

The watch officer sighed. Mervyn smiled at her and handed her his rifle. She seemed startled, then undecided, suppressing an urge to fire anyway. Instead they walked into the other room, where Suzl handed over her pistol as well. There ensued a great debate among the four in which the watch officer had to exercise abnormal control just to keep them from tearing the three limb from limb or at least working them over with rubber hoses. Once the officer had made her decision, though, she stuck to it. When the warden who had been shoved back tried to attack Mervyn anyway, the watch officer struck her in the mouth with the rifle butt. She looked mad, but finally calmed down, as blood from a small cut trickled from the side of her mouth.

"Now, then," sighed the watch officer, "let's *all* go see Her Holiness, shall we?"

Leaving the guns in the security office and then locking up, they all walked back upstairs, into the chapel, then back into the sacristy. Cass had a feeling of having been here before, but now she was with someone who knew the way.

Ultimately they reached the first of three security doors. Obviously the Sister General's own area had been reinforced since Cass had blundered in. Each of the doors could be opened only from the inside, by someone who first could look at whoever was out there and take action if necessary. The wardens generally expected their way to be barred at this point, and action taken, and seemed extremely surprised when each door opened for them with no hesitation.

Finally they reached the office of the Sister General. It looked much the same as Cass remembered it, although she'd had a very different view the last time. Sister Daji was nowhere in sight, but to the left of the Sister General's huge desk the falcon perch still stood, and why not? On it was a falcon.

The Sister General looked at the mob, then said, "That will be all, wardens. Retire to your posts and await my instructions." They bowed, bewildered, and exited.

She looked at the three of them in turn, settling on Mervyn. "I don't have to guess which one of you is Pericles."

"It's been a long time, hasn't it, Des?" he responded lightly.

The tone and question startled both Cass and Suzl. It was obvious now that, somehow, these two actually *knew* each other!

She came over and hugged the wizard. "You wore that guise just for me, didn't you?"

He laughed. "I figured if nothing else you'd get a photo from the police with a report on my doings."

She laughed. "You always *were* the one for direct actions. But, enough of this for now. I'm going to have problems with my security staff for a long time over you three. What is this really all about?"

Mervyn looked around. "Is it just us in here?"

"Yes. I cleared the rest out. Please, all of you, have a seat and we'll talk."

"Not everybody was cleared," Mervyn remarked casually. "I see we have a spy over there."

She laughed. "Oh, Demon. Yes, my secretary went roaming in the marketplace while I was away on business and bought her as a surprise for me. Unfortunately, she seems to like the secretary far more than me. She's safe, though."

Mervyn nodded, and Cass began to wonder if she in fact *had* dreamed the whole thing. Was it instead some odd story planted in her mind by Haldayne? Was she, in fact, loosed with false information in her mind to confuse and disrupt the Nine? She felt suddenly very confused.

"Haldayne has taken Persellus and means to move on the gate," the wizard said simply. "We are mounting a massive force to retake it, supported by myself and two others of the Nine." Quickly, and in a businesslike fashion, he outlined the entire plot, leaving Cass out of it completely, though, as well as Daji and the part Anchor Logh played in it. She listened attentively, her face grim. When he had finished she asked, "What do you want me to do?"

"How large is your troop force?"

She thought a minute. "I don't have the exact

figures, but not counting the new recruits in training after Census, about a thousand."

"Let's count the recruits."

"Then, perhaps a hundred more plus training instructors. But we need a minimum of three hundred to man and guard the borders."

He nodded. "That's fine. Give me five hundred under your best officers and noncoms. Get them in Flux and I'll see they don't crack. Once we break Haldayne's shield we'll need warm bodies to overrun and root out what's left of Persellus. He's very strong and has had time to prepare."

"Do you think you'll catch him this time?" she asked, apparently getting caught up in the adventure of it.

"We're going to try. That's all we can do, no more. There is nothing I would like more, as you well know. Half a dozen times I've had him in my nets and he's managed to slip away. But, with your gracious help, we'll beat him this time, at least."

"You shall have it and welcome," she responded. "And what will you do with it—after?"

He shrugged. "Sister Kasdi has a great deal of talent and is now training under me. A church-controlled Fluxland in such a strategic position would consolidate quite a bit and secure the gate for some time."

She thought about it, and liked the idea. "A church-controlled Fluxland. It was the dream of the Founding Mothers, but somehow it's never come to pass. It would create a church-held domain over a hundred and fifty kilometers southwest." She turned to Cass. "You must do it! You have the best teacher in the world for it. Why, it could be the old dream—the training and university ground for the Church, as Globbus is for wizards."

"I will consider it, Your Eminence," Cass responded carefully, trying to make sense of all this.

The idea of her becoming a Sister General wizard to a Fluxland church indoctrination center was ludicrous at best. She wondered what the Sister General would think if she knew who *really* sat before her in the guise of a tall priestess. Again she felt frustrated that she had no idea what games were being played here, only that everybody seemed to know and understand more than she did.

It was, in fact, as simple as that insofar as getting the troops was concerned. The Sister General herself would give them the commands and see them off, and they would be ready at the western gate in three days. They were ready now to leave, with a total pass from Her Eminence herself, when Mervyn asked, "Where's that secretary of yours? I've heard some stories about her."

She laughed. "Daji? Around someplace, I suspect. Absolutely *gorgeous* body, but rather empty in the head, I fear. I have to keep it that way, if only for security."

He nodded. "I understand. But if you could spare her for these next three days she'll be most helpful, as your secretary, in clearing away bureaucratic barriers just by her presence. I can use her, so don't worry about what she doesn't know."

The Sister General laughed. "You're just trying to get her away from me so you can have some fun. But, all right. Take her. I'm going to be too busy for her anyway, it appears, and she only has one thing on her mind all the time, bless her." She pressed a buzzer and there was a muffled response. "Is Daji about?"

Again a muffled response. She nodded. "Send her up. She's going on a little trip with some friends of mine."

17

SORCERERS

Sister Daji had seemed quite confused when ordered by the Sister General to go with the three nice ladies and do what she was told, but after a little heart-to-heart talk in the other room she went along with it, at least grudgingly. Cass could not get over the contrast between the woman she saw now and the one she had seen with Haldayne. It seemed almost inconceivable that this bubble-brained airhead could possibly be a mistress of Hell and conniving plotter.

They went out the door and down the Temple steps, Daji clutching a small overnight bag. Some birds scattered into the air as they descended the stair, but one bird, a particularly large raven, did not. Instead, he circled and then settled atop one of the lampposts along the sides of the square itself and watched the four figures come forward. There were few people about, although there was some traffic on the streets and a couple of people were sitting on one of the benches in the square, and two yellow-robed Sisters were walking towards the Temple as the quartet walked away.

Still, Cass had an uneasy feeling she couldn't shake off. Something seemed very wrong, although things had been going well from Mervyn's point of view. It had started with the falcon still in the

Sister General's office, grown worse at meeting Daji, and was now building to the breaking point. She looked around nervously, studying everyone in the square, her eyes finally reaching the two approaching Sisters. There was just something about them, something very odd. . . .

"Everybody watch it!" she cried suddenly. "*Those Sisters are wearing boots!*"

"Caw!" screamed the raven almost immediately. "Caw! Caw! Caw!"

The two "Sisters" split from one another, reaching in and drawing guns at the same instant. Mervyn dropped where he was and pulled an automatic pistol, firing at the closest attacker first. The "Sister" fell back with the force of the shots, blood soaking the front of the robe while her gun clattered as it fell. The other, however, dropped and rolled, and had time to open fire before Mervyn could bring his pistol around. Suzl had dropped at Cass's warning and now rolled towards the first assailant's fallen weapon, while Cass managed to make it behind a post that afforded some protection. Birds and people were screaming and panicking everywhere.

Daji, however, had just stopped and stood there, looking very confused. As a result, she took the full blast of the second assailant's shots and staggered back, then collapsed on the paving stones, writhing and groaning. Mervyn fired at the assassin but scored only a grazing blow. Then his gun went dead, empty. The woman in yellow, realizing this, stopped, raised her own gun, and pointed it directly at the wizard, who had nowhere to run. A volley of shots rang out, echoing across the square and against the Temple walls, and the killer spun and fell dead.

Suzl looked a little surprised that she'd shot so well from such a distance, and smugly blew the smoke away from the barrel. Mervyn, however, was in no mood for gratitude or theatrics. "Shoot the raven!" he cried. "The raven!" He pointed to the large bird atop the lamp, but before Suzl realized what he was saying and could make sense of it the bird launched itself into the air and was soon lost from sight to the southwest.

Cass ran over and helped Mervyn up. "Damn!" he swore. "It was Haldayne and we almost had him!"

Suzl walked cockily over to them. "He almost had *you*, you mean. Where the hell did you get that pistol?"

"Trick compartment in the cape," he told her. "They took the rifle, left the holder, and it was still there. Damn you, though! Why didn't you shoot the raven while you had the chance? I had a spell on you that made you a great marksman. You could have had him!"

"And lost you," she responded, getting a little irritated.

"What do I matter?" he growled. "That raven was Haldayne. If we had gotten him we could have taken Persellus without any real losses."

She shrugged. "Sorry. Next time I'll let you die and shoot every damned bird in sight." She looked around. "Where's Cass?" They both looked, and found her kneeling beside the fallen Daji. A crowd was gathering fast, and police could be heard on their way. Mervyn elbowed his way through and knelt down beside Cass.

Daji was mortally wounded, but still alive. Gasping, blood running from her mouth, she looked for all the world a hurt and confused child. She choked once, and then something seemed to grow within her, filling her face and particularly her eyes. Her whole appearance took on a different look, and she coughed and gulped down air. "Damn you!" she screamed, in a far different, more self-assured voice filled with hatred and fear. "Damn that bastard Haldayne! Always the genius! Always the double-dealing genius! I should have known, you. . . ." She shuddered and went limp, and her eyes now held a vacancy that even Daji had never known.

Police and Temple wardens came through, pulling them away. Cass stepped back and shook her head sadly. "It's crazy," she said, not particularly to Suzl although that was who was there. "I actually feel sorry for her. I don't know how I can pity her, but I do."

Suzl shrugged. "Well, she certainly was what you said, that's for sure. Man! That was weird, seeing her change like that."

Cass nodded. At least she was vindicated in her own mind about it all. Daji had certainly been with Haldayne, and that meant the rest of it was almost certainly true as well. She looked up for Mervyn, and saw him with the authorities inspecting the body of the first killer. Both assassins were dead, and when the robes were opened they all saw that under those robes were two hard-looking women dressed in farm clothes.

They spent the next several hours with the police, giving statements of the events. The pass from the Sister General was absolute, and avoided many embarrassing questions about why they were there, but there were still the statements, which had to be checked, typed, and signed, and the individual interrogation of each as to the exact sequence of events. The administrative chief of the Temple showed up to clear the way for them not to have to reveal any more than they chose, and to carry back copies of everything for the Sister General, but it was still a mess. Neither killer was on the registry, nor had they any record of entering Anchor Logh. This bothered them all more than the killings themselves, as unprecedented as they were, because it meant that either there was a leak in the wall guard or else these two had come from the only place where the unregistered could possibly come from—the Temple itself.

That was not the problem of the trio from the Flux, however. "You know this Anchor pretty well. Can we take different indirect routes back to the gate?" Mervyn asked them.

They thought about it. "There are lots of back roads, so long as you don't mind camping out in fields," Cass told him. "But there's really no place to hide from somebody who knows them as well as you and also knows what you look like."

He nodded. "I thought as much. I'm going to pull rank with the church, then, and get us a full police guard all the way back. I want no more lopsided ambushes."

They returned inside the police station and Mervyn composed a long note to the Sister General, sending it back with the admin chief. They waited a good hour or more, until a lower ranking priestess in admin gray returned with instructions for the police, and they had their escort and more.

There were no further attempts on them, and Mervyn wasn't surprised. "The object of the exercise was to kill Daji first, then me if they could. You two were totally optional."

"Thanks a lot," Suzl grumped. "But—why Daji? Because we had her number and maybe could have learned a lot from her?"

"That, of course," the wizard agreed. "I knew we were in trouble when I saw that falcon there. It was meant to confuse, but all it did was signal that they knew something was wrong."

"It sure confused *me*," Cass told him. "I thought for a while that the whole thing had been a Haldayne-inspired hallucination."

"Which was exactly the intent. But when it failed, and we arranged to have Daji come with us, they knew their subtlety had not paid off and took direct action. They could not afford one of their chiefs in my hands. She would know vital things far beyond this immediate crisis."

"Then the plot is really foiled, huh?" Suzl put in. "I mean, their agent's dead."

"One agent. Someone saw us taking Daji out, and someone received orders to kill her. Haldayne might have started the killers, but he couldn't possibly have been inside the Temple. I'm afraid that all this shows is that Anchor Logh is already as conquered as Persellus, and woefully ignorant of the fact. We shall not know it all until we have dealt with all our problems, and perhaps not even then." He turned to Cass. "First things first. We must go into Flux and prepare you."

"Huh? Prepare me for what?"

"Your ordination and conference, of course. It will be done by the Sister General herself in front of the troops at the west gate just before we march."

"My *what* and my *what*? Hey! Wait a minute!"

"It is necessary for a priestess to lead the forces of Anchor into Flux. They are terrified enough now, as you would have been not so long ago. They need what is called in scripture an Adjutant to lead and protect them—a high-ranking priestess who is able to stand and use the Flux and protect herself and them. Don't worry—it's the required part of the Holy Books for all in Anchor Logh to read right now, although it's so obscure and in one of the codices that is rarely paid attention to. In short, we need a wizard-priestess. The Adjutant, when created, is second in rank only to the Sister General herself."

"But, wait a minute! Don't *I* have any say in this? I mean, I'm not even sure I *believe* in that stuff any more, at least not the way it's taught, and I sure don't want to give up sex and the Flux power now that I've found them."

Suzl gave a raised eyebrow at that but said nothing.

"Obviously it's too obscure for you, as well," Mervyn responded patiently. "The Adjutant is considered a somewhat supernatural figure. She comes from Flux and returns to it, although she is, of course, able to travel to Anchor. It exists for the very reason that a lot of the rest exists—it is convenient when the rules have to be bent. In this case, men raised to be terrified of the Flux are being asked to go into it and do battle. Think of how *you* felt when *you* first went in. It's not so bad. You'll be a High Priestess in Anchor and a wizard in Flux, and you'll need more training as a wizard than *this* job requires."

She thought it over. "How long has it been since the last—Adjutant—was appointed?"

He thought it over. "Three, maybe four hundred years, I think. They all run together after a while. But now there will be two, each accompanied by a Flux warrior."

"Huh?"

"A Flux warrior, it is said, is the reincarnation of one of the greatest warrior angels corrupted and exiled to World after the Rebellion. Because they were of the highest rank then, they are cursed to live their lives in Flux, and to be known because they differ from humans only in one specific attribute. That attribute is not defined, but that only makes it convenient for our candidates."

Suzl grinned. "Like me, you mean?"

He nodded. "Like you. And like Dar."

Cass gasped. "So *that's* why you split them up! You had this in mind all along!"

He nodded. "But your vanishing act nearly spoiled it. I was determined to take a dugger or whatever, but, fortunately, I didn't have to."

Suzl giggled. "Just think—only weeks ago we four were stripped of it all and cast out of Anchor.

Now two of us are gonna be High Priestesses and the other two are angels! This is crazy but I love it!"

Cass nodded, not sharing the mirth. "Yes, lucky— if we survive all this. Not like the rest of them marched out with us. Not like the ones in Arden's train."

"Oh, let the dead be cremated and their ashes returned to the life of the soil," Suzl quoted from the holy books. "Now is now and I am me, and I'm having a ball."

The void, which had been so terrifying before, now seemed like a welcome friend to them, offering peace and quiet and relative security. Mervyn wasted no time becoming his favorite old man's character once again, but after a short session with Suzl to brief her on just what her part in this was, he sent her back to Anchor, to the apron area, with an eye to getting as much information and rumor from the resident duggers as possible. Mervyn wanted to know how the wall leaked so easily, and it was also a way to have Cass alone for a while.

"I know you're wondering about all this," he began, "and that will never stop, I'm afraid, for none of us knows the answers. We, and our forebears, however, do know much more of the history and geography of World than the church permits to be taught, simply because part of our mission was to save the books and records of the past. Not all survived, alas, particularly from the earliest days, but much did."

Humanity, he told her, had once been far greater and more numerous than now. There was once, as near as they could understand it, a great empire of humankind, which included but was not restricted to World. "This is only one world of men, perhaps the only one left now. Once, however, there was the concept of empire."

In this great time in the far past—fully thousands of years before—man had had a great civilization, an ideal community where all were free and had—if not directly then through machines—the powers and wonders of wizards. The forces of Hell rose up to attempt to destroy this civilization, and there was a great war, such as none today could even imagine. In the end, humans defeated the forces of Hell and pushed them back into a place outside our very universe. But the battle had not been without great cost, and the empire was shattered and destroyed and with it most of the race and most of its worlds.

"It was here on World that the final battle took place," he said, "and it was here, at last, that Hell was pushed out of all we know and the gates to Hell were sealed."

"Then the machines I saw at the gate were those of that lost empire," she responded, understanding it better. "They were the means by which all was sealed."

He nodded. "However, all did not go well here, either. The church, originally set up to guard against those gates being opened or tampered with, as well as to guard all the old knowledge, became corrupted, as new generations saw it as an avenue of power. Still, the system, even with what we have lost, has held for all this time. There *were* those who disagreed with the system, however, and sought to preserve what could be preserved. Nine people, all great men and women of their time and all great wizards, copied, begged, borrowed, or stole all that they could and moved into Flux. They did not desert the church, but rather felt the church had deserted them, become too large, political, and bureaucratic. These Nine hand-picked their successors, so that when it finally came their time there was always someone ready to step in."

"And those are the Nine Who Guard?"

He nodded. "We guard not only against the forces

of Hell but against the follies of humanity as well. None of us are saints, but we have somehow managed to do our jobs and keep the faith. Besides, it's not bad being a wizard of such tremendous power here in Flux. We also keep our hands in with the church, as it were. No one can become a Sister General or higher without spending time with us in Flux, if only to totally understand the nature and threat that Flux presents, and, of course, to read and learn the literature forbidden or destroyed in Anchor."

"So that explains why you knew Sister General Diastephanos!"

Again he nodded. "Yes, she trained with me long ago. Twenty years or more, I'd say."

"She sure didn't take all the moral lessons."

Mervyn grinned. "Oh, it's not that terrible. The fact is, the holy books are quite a bit less strict than the rules the church now imposes. That particular section, which you'll not read in the Temple libraries, actually specifies that none will engage in sins of the flesh with any man after ordination. In the early days, for example, it was rare but not unheard of for priestesses to be widows with children, and in the early days many a 'scarlet woman' or one with family problems or pregnant with a child born out of wedlock joined to regain status and respectability. The church had such a potential to be a unifying force for World. Instead, it became the dictator of it."

This was a far different picture than the one she'd had growing up, and, indeed, the one she'd formed since leaving Anchor. She began to realize both the potential and the loss to World of its corruption, and it made her feel more than slightly angry. In a sense, the church had become to Anchor what each ruling wizard was to a Fluxland. Corrupted by power, each had inevitably exercised that power to the fullest. It was a strong vision it presented, of a church keeping knowledge alive, and providing a moral and cultural unity to World, while government, as a separate entity elected by Anchor, would rule subject to the voters, not the church.

"And Haldayne, Daji, and the rest? What are they?"

"Wizards, just like the Nine and the other powers of Flux. Their organization is, in a sense, a mirror image of the Nine. In their own minds they have a noble purpose in which the ends justify any means. They believe that humanity can never regain its former greatness but will remain in primitive stagnancy until, believe it or not, an accommodation with Hell is reached."

She was shocked. "An accommodation with *Hell*?"

"That's right. You see, even though the gates are sealed and guarded, some slight leakage gets through. It was designed that way. It may seem strange, but our basic power source seems to be those machines in the gates, which generate excess energy from the seal as they maintain it and then transfer this excess to the generators in the Temples. Without them we would have no electricity at all, since we really don't know how to generate it on a massive scale. We keep everything working by removing parts that go bad and giving them to wizards in Flux who are good at making exact copies of things. Since the art of being a good wizard is mathematical, they can look at a part that they have never seen before and have no idea what it is or how it works, and make a copy that *does* work. They don't know how they do it, but the only explanation is that the math is wrong on the broken one, and they can figure out where it's wrong and make the equation balance."

"So we depend on these Hellgates for a lot, and Anchors really depend on Flux."

"Interdependence. Flux is a cruel place, subject

to the whims of the powerful and power-mad. It is by its very nature impossible for more than a handful of people to be free or independent in Flux, or even remain human. It is nice if you're a wizard, but no great discoveries arise in Flux. It simply devours a larger number of people than it can possibly replace. Hence, the trade of people for what Anchors need. Ideally, Anchors should be the seats of learning, where great things are produced by a free and unified people, while Flux produces what is needed. Unfortunately, deep down, it is difficult to tell them apart."

"And the Seven believe that Hell is the only way out?"

"That's about it," he agreed. "You see, in some of the gates, because of that leakage I mentioned, it is possible for Hell to communicate with one in the tunnel. The demons of Hell are cut off from our world, but are immortal, and know how the machines work and the nature of Flux and Anchor. To early wizards frustrated by having godlike powers that were very limited over a finite piece of ground, the lure of ruling all World, as one great Fluxland under their total domination, is irresistible. And if it means selling one's soul to Hell, it seems to thcm a small price to pay. They are the ultimate corruption power brings, and they delude themselves that they will be partners with Hell and not make us all its last victims so that Hell will finally attain its goal to rule the universe—alone."

They went on like this for more than two days, and in that time Cass believed she gained a true picture of what was going on. Much, as Mervyn had warned, was unknown—the nature of the Soul Riders, for example. To her, there *did* seem to be a divine plan for the rescue of humanity and its restoration to greatness, a plan subverted by the weaknesses humans had. Those who now ruled the church had all been shown this path, but all, in the end, had been corrupted by their own power or deluded themselves that they were making small changes or reforms and that any major changes would take generations. The forces of Hell were real, and on the march, but it only reinforced the church's resolve to keep things the way they were, thereby substituting the total evil of Hell with a more banal evil done by humans.

Finally, Cass was briefed and prompted on the ceremony to come, and felt she was finally ready, although it still seemed like a lot of foolishness to her. She felt a little guilty, being used as a lucky icon for a lot of scared and possibly doomed troopers.

The ceremony itself was quite impressive and flashy. A platform had been set up just inside the gate, and Cass, her horse changed to snow white for the occasion, was led in by Suzl on her black mount. Cass had made several decisions herself on this, one of which was to use her own normal form and make no more pretenses about her identity. She felt any threat to her individually was over as much as it ever would be. The reasons were no longer there.

She entered dressed only in a plain robe of white, as a novice. It was important that she be ordained in front of them, even though the Sister General already assumed it. And the troops were all lined up, as well as a great mass of common people, to see the show.

Diastephanos, who had understood Cass's role in this from the start, made it a long service, with lots of ceremony, all of the sacraments, and lots of scripture reading. It was all necessary not for its own sake, but to show the people of Anchor Logh, long taught to fear the Flux and have no truck with it, that in this case only it was the right thing to do.

Cass participated fully, finding the whole thing

oddly moving to her. And, once all vows were exchanged and she was fully ordained, it was then time to accept the job, exchanging her whites for robes of lavender satin trimmed with ancient designs in gold thread, and to accept a septre only slightly smaller and less ornate than the Sister General's own. It was then concluded, and she turned and looked out at the crowd for the first time. All eyes were on her, and, for the first time, she realized that they had accepted all of it. In every sense of the word, even legally, she was to them and in fact a high priestess of the church.

She stepped down from the platform and went to the troops who would go with them, standing at attention next to their horses. As she passed each, she could see in their eyes the absolute confidence they placed in her. It shook her a bit, to realize the full responsibility she had been forced to take on. And when she stood before them, they all knelt and bowed their heads, and she gave them the blessing they expected, meaning it more than she intended.

"Soldiers of Anchor Logh," she said at last, hoping her voice would carry and not tremble. "We set out now on the most important mission in our long history. Hell is out there, almost at our gates, invading our land at will, killing our citizens and threatening us all. Do not fear the wizardry of the Flux, only respect it, for we have the strongest wizardry, the righteousness of our cause, and the support of the Nine Who Guard. The divine will is not known, except that victory is assured if we prove worthy of it. The creatures you will fight will be of flesh and blood. Some of you may die, but you will do so in a cause so noble that you will be reborn with greatness. Others will live, to enjoy the great honor that awaits. We cannot know our fate, for only Heaven knows that, but we can know and fulfill our destiny. Will you ride with us now?"

"We will!" came a chorus of responses that moved her even more.

She walked to her horse and mounted it, then held the septre high. "Then mount and follow me!"

In groups, they passed through the west gate and out onto the apron. A way had been cleared from the dugger shantytown to the Flux, and they again formed up. Suzl and Mervyn, still in his old man's role, rode out of Flux to meet her, then turned to form a threesome leading the way. Suzl leaned over and whispered, "Wow! You really look great!" Cass smiled and winked, although she was aware of the enormous weight she was now carrying, and held the septre up, then angled it forward. The troopers, she'd been assured, had been briefed by Suzl and Mervyn as to how to ride the void. She hoped so, for they were off.

Mervyn dropped back to the rear as the entire column entered the Flux, just to make sure there were no stragglers or unexpected surprises. Cass did not need him to lead. She felt the power of the Flux instantly, and the glowing strings of energy came crystal clear. She decided to ride as far non-stop as prudence said the horses could take, so that there could be no last-minute defections. Suzl, still dressed in stringer fashion, checked out the formation and felt every bit a stringer with a very strange train. She wished, however, she had a dozen or so duggers to help out.

They finally stopped at a water pocket, a small area undistinguished from the rest of the void except for a wizard-created pool of clear water large enough for people and horses. Mervyn, who was well practiced in elaborate magic, created the spartan food for them all. They were quite impressed, but many of them had already lost a good deal of their fear in the boredom of the void. The terrible Flux was proving only a wasteland, and the only wizardry so far was entirely on their side. By the end of the second day, Cass guessed, they would be getting both cocky and itchy from too little threat and too much boredom.

Sentries were posted and they bedded down for the night, with Mervyn agreeing to sleep first and then take over from Cass. She readily agreed, and just sat there by the pool for quite a while, looking at her reflection in the water and absorbed in thought. Suzl, acting the old hand, checked out the rest and then came over to her. "You seem pretty quiet," she noted. "Problems, or does it come magically from putting on the robe?"

Cass smiled. "Thanks. I need you, Suzl, to remind me just who I am and where I've come from. Any problems?"

"Nope. Not really. A couple of 'em made passes at me and I had a good deal of fun letting them discover why I was along and what was so different. Now they're scared silly of me. It's fun giving orders to guys the smallest of whom are a head taller than me."

She looked at Suzl. "You know, when that curse backfired I figured you were out of luck, but the more I look at the way this whole thing is turning out I think you got the best of the deal in many ways."

Suzl suddenly looked at her seriously. "What's wrong with you? Only weeks ago we were two naive farm girls scared of getting sold as slaves, who knew that if we didn't we'd be pressured into marrying some ignorant farm boy, stuck having a mess of kids and stuck in a boring job for life to boot—or joining the priesthood and having our brains mashed and everything worthwhile a no-no. You know deep down that you would never have accepted it. It would've killed you. Me, too, which is why they decided my number would come up. 'Psychologically unfit for normal socialization' they once called me. I snuck in and read the teacher's report. I'm eighteen and a half and I've already lived more than I would have in ninety years of Anchor Logh.''

Cass nodded. "What you say is true, and I don't deny it. I'm not longing for what was. I simply said that you have the best of the deal. You're free, independent, and tough. You'll roam all over World and see everything and have a ball. I envy that."

"Well, why can't you? Hell, you're a *wizard*. You don't even need a stringer."

"Partly because I *am* a wizard," she replied, then added, "and partly because I am a priestess."

Suzl looked at her oddly. "Now aren't you taking the show just a little bit too seriously? Me, I'm stuck as I am. Lucky for me I don't mind a bit. But you—you can be anything, do anything you want to do."

Cass sighed, knowing that she could not explain it, particularly to one such as Suzl. Still, she said, "No, Suzl, I'm trapped just like these poor soldiers and all the rest who got thrown out of Anchor. I'm just beginning to realize how trapped I am. You remember us talking about little people becoming important by accident? Well, I'm discovering that when you become important you get trapped as well. That's okay for now, let's drop it. I'm being forced by Mervyn and the rest to make a decision, a big one, and I'm not ready to make it. I'll have to settle it within myself."

Suzl just shrugged and shook her head. Finally she said, "I wonder what a battle in Flux is like?"

18

BATTLE

It was understood by the officers and men that the Adjutant would not lead them into battle, but would direct it instead from a command post. They didn't mind, since harm to her was the worst thing they feared. She did visit with them, though, informally. She really felt like they were her people, after getting to know some on the trail. It was now a major duty of hers to hear their confessions, because, as battle neared, they began once again thinking of this less as a new game. Unconsciously, perhaps, she wove a spell, finding that she could remember all the details of each of them.

This was far different than playing priestess back in Anchor Logh. For her, too, this was no game, and they needed her desperately. She left the strategy and tactics to others, leaving her troops only when she had to consult Mervyn on a particular spell to ease a young boy's problems. She found no trouble on an individual basis; they seemed to believe and accept everything she told them, including cautions against prejudice towards those not quite human and of Flux.

And many of them were strange indeed. The Flux wizards had strange tastes and bizarre imaginations, it appeared. And they kept coming down the road from Globbus and from the direction of Anchor

Bakha, and from trails that came to the far side of Persellus as well. A mighty army had been assembled, the mightiest, perhaps, ever seen on World since Hell was sealed. A mighty army to meet an unprecedented challenge to the future of World, the one thing all of the forces, no matter how strange or inhuman, had in common.

Suzl went off for a while to see if Nadya and Dar had returned yet. Cass didn't know how long she was away, for time had lost all meaning to her in her single-minded devotion to what she saw as her duty, but one day, as Cass was walking back from another full round of counseling and confessionals, she spotted the familiar figure on the hill near the local command post.

Suzl waved and ran to her, and they hugged. "Did you find them?" Cass asked.

"Oh, yeah. You ought to see Nadya—decked out just like you and acting just as crazy. Dar's even crazier—says he's gonna lead the attack from his side. He's going to get his fool head blown off." She paused a moment. "Guess who I came up with? Matson!"

Matson! The name was like a cold bucket of water in Cass's face. Suddenly that became the most important thing in the world to her. "Where is he?"

Suzl jerked a thumb towards the tent. "Up there. He and some of his duggers who volunteered are leading in a Fluxland crew." She shivered slightly. "One that's really weird. The people are the animals there, I think."

She brushed by Suzl and walked over to the tent, then paused as she saw him, sitting on a folding chair, cigar clenched in his teeth. He was apparently waiting for someone, and glanced up at her, then away, not recognizing her at first. He looked back again, frowned, and got up. "That you, Cass, in that church getup?"

She laughed. "Yes, I'm afraid it is. Mervyn stuck me good."

"We heard how you got snatched and then escaped, more or less," he told her, not referring to Suzl's comment that he went nearly crazy at the abduction. "I'm trying to decide whether or not to dock your pay for the period."

"You *would*, too, wouldn't you? You stringers are a tight lot."

He got up and walked up to her. "Is it allowed to kiss a priestess?"

"My feet and my hand," she responded jokingly.

"Yeah, and my ass, too," he came back in the same vein. He grabbed her and kissed her, very long and very hard. Finally he broke away and said, "I want you back with the company when this is through. Look, I've got to talk some things over with the old boy and the midget, but we'll meet in Persellus, you hear?"

She nodded, her head spinning. "Yes. In Persellus."

After she left him, she still felt in some kind of a daze. She had been, she knew, at war with herself these past few days, and she now knew which side had won. She was a wizard, and, therefore, she *could* have him, and he was everything that mattered most.

Before Persellus could be invaded, the three top wizards had to first break what they called Haldayne's shield. This was not a barrier in the physical sense, but more a mental zone of control. Each Fluxland was the product of the unrestrained mind of the controlling wizard, and it was as large and as stable as that wizard's will. To invade before that control was broken would only mean that the attackers would come under the will and control of the defender. There was not much profit in that.

However, breaking the shield was not the end of

it. Haldayne had first broken the goddess's shield, then faced her down physically, and only then was he able to impose himself on the land. With his shield broken, the land would still remain his and in his vision. To remake the land, and make it stick, the wizards would have to progress to a point within the Fluxland where their own powers and wills could reach the farthest corners of Persellus. That ground, which might be all the way to the capital, would have to be won the hard way.

Watches had been synchronized, and the three top wizards positioned at the three decided-upon points of entry. Like most Fluxlands, Persellus was basically circular, although with jagged edges. At the appointed time, with only a small company of carefully selected junior wizards for any direct protection, all three of the chief wizards stepped into the land of Persellus, and began walking forward until they met resistance. Haldayne had to keep them out, or surrender control. Haldayne was not the type to surrender anything easily.

Behind the wizards, a good three hundred meters behind, came the leading edge of the troops. Cass had been ordered to remain behind, but as time wore on and things seemed stalled, she impatiently saddled her horse and rode toward Persellus, passing backed up troops, light artillery, and supply wagons. After all this, she decided she was not going to miss at least seeing what was going on.

What was going on was awesome and spectacular.

The countryside had changed so much she would not have recognized it as Persellus. Dark, rumbling mountains spitting smoke and fire were all around, and the countryside was covered with a fine gray ash. She finally determined where the river was, but it was mud and ash-swollen and choked with debris. Although the landscape was lit with an eerie glow that made it possible to see great distances, the sky was black as pitch, with no stars, no Heaven, nothing to break it.

Ahead, far in the distance but so enormous that it dominated all else, was a tremendous figure illuminated in lines of energy. It had the rough shape of a man, rising up from the ground, but its head was horribly demonic. It was no projection, despite the fact that it was seen only by the outline of the blazing energy, for it moved and roared a terrible, hateful sound that went through the very ground and made it tremble. It was battling something—three strong, solid, straight lines of force directed at it from the ground. One struck it from behind, one from its left side, and one came from the small, wizened figure of a man seated in a folding chair in the middle of what passed for the road directly ahead of them.

The great energy beast was strong, and it would occasionally reach out and grasp one of the energy beams as if it were a rope, fight with it, then force it away, but it could not deal effectively with three such attacks from three different directions. Each time it concentrated on one, the other two took advantage to attempt to coil themselves around its ghostly body. Still, it had been fighting this way for hours.

Cass was enthralled with the display, and at a loss to understand why most of the soldiers in back acted bored and uncomfortable and were not watching at all. She suddenly realized that what she was watching and hearing was on a different frequency than normal, like the stringer's strings. The soldiers were not interested because they could neither see nor hear it.

The great beast was clearly tiring, and the energy beams were having more and more success. One from the side finally reached the creature's neck and began coiling itself around that hideous face. The demon reached up to tear the beam away, but now Mervyn shot out at the thing's legs, while the one behind—that would be Tatalane—grasped at its arms and tried to pull them away from the neck.

Mervyn pulled, and the beast roared and rocked, then bent over, barely keeping on its "feet." A second beam now went for its neck, and then a third. The creature screamed in agony, and there was a sudden great, blinding flare of light in the distance and, a bit later, a tremendous thunderclap rolled down the valley that all could hear. When Cass could see again, the far horizon was clear.

Two junior wizards helped the old wizard to walk back to a wagon. They lifted him in, gently, then took the reins. There was the sound of horns all about, echoed in the distance. The shield was down. Haldayne retained his control over what he'd had, but could no longer exercise control beyond it. If he tried, he'd send the land back to Flux, and have nothing to defend.

The troops advanced perhaps a kilometer when they met resistance. Well dug-in defenders of Persellus opened up on them with massive machine gun fire, and the air all around them went chill and was filled with terrible shapes from Hell itself.

The initial advance was cut to shreds by the fire, and frustrated by its inability to see the enemy positions past the illusory phantoms. The defender's task now was simple. They far outnumbered the attackers, and while they had few decent wizards, neither did the attacking forces for a while. The effort of breaking the shield was great, and it would be hours, perhaps more, before any of the three chief sorcerers could be in any condition to help. Haldayne, too, was in much the same shape, but he would also regain strength the more time went on, perhaps enough to reestablish and extend his shield. Because of their inferior numbers, the attackers had to advance well into the country before this could happen, or the scenario just played out would happen again, with Haldayne able to redeploy and even by spell resupply and reform his defenders so that the next round would be just as costly. If the attackers stalled for any great length of time, each and every time, they would be wiped out.

Cass watched from her original position, well back of the fighting, but she could see everything clearly. More and more troops were filing past her and marching towards those deadly gun emplacements, then dropping and trying to dig in. Artillery was set up near her, and soon the boom of cannon fire was added to the din, as the gunners attempted to line up on the machine guns. She watched the carnage with mounting horror, saw the field littered with the dead, and was revolted as she had never been in her life. Never in her most terrible nightmares could she imagine the reality of this massacre.

She glanced over and was startled to see Matson, cigar and all, sitting high on his horse and directing some—creatures—who were hauling up some very odd-looking things. They appeared to be a large number of parallel metal pipes all lashed together. When they were in range, he gave a series of signals and smaller shapes moved up behind the tubes. In less than a minute a hundred tubes, almost at the same time, erupted with a roar and flashing smoke and fire, and ahead the gunnery positions were pounded with an entire line, perhaps three hundred meters across, of massive explosions. The roar was deafening.

The small creatures behind the tubes, whatever they were, were fast and professional and moved to Matson's barked orders. A second salvo went off, and, after the last explosion had discharged, there was a roar and cheer from troops up ahead. They moved forward. Matson's guns had pushed back or wiped out the machine gun nests, and the columns moved forward once more.

Another kilometer, and suddenly the ground opened up ahead of the advancing troops, like a giant mouth. They fell in, and it swallowed them and closed again. From behind came more withering machine gun and rifle fire, pushing the attackers back.

Less than a hundred meters from Cass's new position, Matson frowned, barked more orders to the creatures hauling the tubes forward, and rode up to the forward command group where the junior wizards were conferring with the field commanders on how to overcome this obstacle.

The stringer shouted something at them, and they nodded, and two of the junior wizards went back with him to his launchers. She waited, as they all did, to see what was up.

To her surprise, the troops were now ordered forward, and they went slowly, nervously, to the area of the trap. All defending fire stopped suddenly. When enough soldiers were on the area of the trap, it opened again, swallowing them, but at the same time Matson's tubes opened up, concentrating their rounds on the opening. This time there were no explosions, for the tubes shot not explosive rounds but huge balls of some gooey substance. The mass filled in the mouth before it could close, and as it tried it just compacted the new material, which seemed to quickly harden. Cannons opened up on the gun emplacements beyond the "mouth" at almost the same time, and again troops moved forward. The "mouth" shimmered and shook and tried to free itself, but it was hopeless. Matson had effectively filled it and paved it over.

It went like that for some time, although time became blurred into the sameness of death. Haldayne had a huge population to call upon, but he couldn't use them. His own volcanos had filled in enough of the valley to make any massive deployment of forces from behind very slow and difficult. The geographic strategy he had laid out to keep the attackers on a single, predictable line of march worked against him as well, and he had three sides to defend.

Mervyn, however, was still unconscious, and bird messengers brought news that Krupe, too, was still out, while tiny Tatalane was conscious but very, very weak. Still, there was no sign at all of any attempt to raise another shield, which told them that Haldayne was in at least as bad shape himself.

In what turned out to be more than nine hours of continuous fighting, Mervyn's force had gained almost fifteen kilometers, Krupe's twelve, and Tatalane's sixteen, but that last was the most important. She was coming in from the side, which had a couple of nasty volcanos in the way but was also the least defended, there being no natural road in from that point. Terrain had been her biggest enemy, but now that she had somehow cleared the mountains she was on a plain heading directly for the capital.

Cass rode back to a field kitchen and got a canteen filled not with water but with beer, then headed for Matson. He was surprised to see her, but he looked very, very tired and suddenly very old, and his shirt was soaked with perspiration. Still, he managed a smile. "I thought you weren't supposed to be up here with the common folk," he managed to joke.

She threw him the canteen. "Here. Drink your damned religion."

He caught it, opened it, and swallowed, then looked surprised and pleased. "I'll be damned! It's *beer!*" He said that last like it was the most wonderous and beautiful word in the language.

He put it down and sighed, then looked out at the fighting not far away. They were bogged down again, this time by a very large number of well dug-in troops. "Sure is a bitch, ain't it?" he said wearily. "You better get back a little, though, Sister Cass. Stray bullets are carrying back farther than this."

"I'm a whole lot more bullet proof than you," she told him, "and you don't look too worried."

He turned and looked out at the battle. "Well, I—" he began, then he was apparently hit by an invisible fist that knocked him off his horse, the canteen flying out of his hand.

"*Matson!*" she screamed, and jumped off her horse and ran to him. The entire front of his shirt had been ripped away by whatever it was that had hit him, and it seemed as if his chest were one huge bloody wound. He was still, his mouth open, blood trickling from it. She took his hand, squeezed it, and screamed at him, "*Matson! Come on, you good-for-nothing stringer! You beat the odds! You always beat the odds! You can't do this to me! Not now!*"

But there was no response. She felt a presence near her and whirled, seeing Jomo. "Jomo!" she cried desperately. "Get a healing wizard here! Hurry! He's been hit!"

The enormous tears in the huge blob of a man looked very strange, but the dugger shook his head, then knelt down and checked out Matson's body. "No use, Missy Cass," he said, voice trembling. "He gone to see Missy Arden."

"*No! Oh, Holy Mother above, please! Not now! Not him! Not yet!*" she sobbed. Jomo got up and tried to pry her gently away from the body. For a while he could not budge her, nor could she do anything but sob and stare at Matson's lifeless body. Suddenly she shook off the giant dugger, got up, and turned facing the battle, a strange expression on her face. She seemed to radiate power, the kind only powerful wizards do, and the dugger stepped back nervously and just watched.

She looked out at the bodies. Everywhere there were bodies, everywhere there was blood and terror and death. In that moment something snapped within her, snapped for good. Now she understood, at last, that what she had been telling Suzl was only part of the truth. She was not any victim of chance, but the one chosen. Everything that had happened said that she was the agent of divine will. She had wavered and fallen, as the church had fallen, because of human frailty and weakness, and because of this Matson had to be taken from her. She knew that now, understood that it had to be this way. Every step she had taken, every new experience, from the point at which she'd first entered the forbidden sacristy, had been directed to this one destiny.

"No more," she muttered under her breath, looking at the fallen bodies stretched out as far as the eye could see. "No more," she said again, louder now, the tremendous power rising within her. It was will that brought it up, but emotion that triggered it. She stuck out her arms, palms out, as if to stop something coming down on her, but it was something different she wanted to stop. All sounds of battle, of people yelling and guns firing, vanished in a roar in her ears. There was only a single will now, and it was directed forward. She felt the power as she had never felt it.

And the Soul Rider provided the required mathematics.

Far off, in the capital, a weak Gifford Haldayne was taking a drink and waiting it out, trying to regain what strength he could. He felt it at once, and knew it for what it was, and cursed himself for it. Damn their eyes! They had a fourth World class wizard in reserve!

He frowned, then staggered, suddenly, from the

force of a psychic blow. "What the hell is *this*?" he asked aloud, amazed. Never in his entire life had he felt such power, such force, such single-minded direction of will. This was something totally new, and totally frightening. This was no doing of the Nine, or Seven, or any combination of Fluxlords. This was something new, and terrible, and beyond even his ancient comprehension. He had a sudden, queer thought. *What have I unleashed?* he wondered, but he did not dwell on it now. He knew what he had to do, and he knew he had only seconds to do it.

He released control to the new force, changed to a raven, and was out of there like a shot. He was fifty kilometers into the void before he even allowed himself enough time to realize just how close it had been.

On the battlefield, Mervyn awoke with a strange sensation inside him. He got up weakly and made it forward to the seat so that he could see out and ahead of him. The sight that he saw was as unprecedented to him as it had been to Haldayne.

Cass, in lavender robes stained with Matson's blood, walked forward towards the battle. As she did, the firing stopped on both sides, and the face of the land and sky trembled and changed. All around her the darkened and blood-stained volcanic ash changed into life itself, into fresh, green grass and flowers. It spread continuously out, touching the front lines and causing soldiers on both sides to stop, turn, and stare. The sky above lightened until it attained the dark blue of Anchor, and the landscape rippled as in Anchor as the great orb of Heaven filled the sky, sending its multicolored light down on the scene.

The wizard was awed by the power coming from her, and the total mastery of the Flux and its complex mathematics and physics despite her almost complete lack of training. He had, indeed, set the conditions up and put it all in motion, but he had never expected anything like this. In fact, he had to admit, he hadn't in the end expected anything at all.

The zone of Fluxland influence now extended from horizon to horizon, the volcanos becoming green rolling hills, the river crystal clear and running its normal course.

The soldiers of Flux and Anchor on both sides of the battle could not, in the main, sense any of the magic, yet it radiated from her frail form and touched them all. They threw down their weapons as she passed, and fell in behind her as she continued her walk.

She drew strength from the Flux, not only for herself but for them, and she walked without stop all the way to the capital, with those of both sides following silently. From the rear and from the side others streamed in from the other two attacking forces, and their enemies.

The town itself had been transformed. No longer was there a goddess's tower or Haldayne's great black castle, but in the center was a huge Temple, the largest ever seen, radiating from its perfect surface the colors of Heaven. As she entered the city limits, the townspeople lined the routes ten deep, throwing flowers at her and at all the soldiers. All fell in as the parade passed, and moved to the central Temple area, where they filed in before the great steps and back as far as the eye could see. All stopped at the base of the Temple steps, but Cass kept walking until she was at the top. Only then did she turn and face the crowd, which was suddenly silent.

"People of Flux and Anchor, hear me," she said, and her voice somehow carried clearly throughout the boundaries of the land. "I am the Adjutant not of Anchor but of Heaven itself. Corruption has strangled humanity long enough. There is the corruption of the church in Anchor, and the corruption of wizardry in Flux. Both have held humanity too long in their grip. You have just endured a great battle, but to what end? Hell is but the ultimate corruption of the human soul, and it flourishes and grows and feeds upon that corruption. Thousands of brave, good people have just died, mixed their blood with this land, and for what? To make things better? *No!* To keep things the same." She paused for a moment, took a deep breath, and continued.

"To keep things the same," she repeated, saying it bitterly. "So what choice did we have? *We were offered only our choice of Hells!* To this I say, no more. No more. It is *evil!* I renounce such evil. I rebel at such a choice. The Holy Mother cries out to me, 'No more! No more!' I reclaim this land in Her name, and with Her power, and I rename it Hope. I do not bind you to my will, for then I would be as guilty as those who now run World. Instead I offer you a partnership, and hope, and no more. It will be no easy road, to reform our ways, to rebuild our corrupted church, to make for ourselves a world of free men and women who will not fear Hell because it will have no way to gain a foothold inside us. You, all of you here, can be the vanguard that will revolutionize World. We may be weak at times, we may stumble occasionally, we might even suffer failures and disappointments, but we will *try*."

Again she paused, allowing the message to sink in. "Now go," she told them. "Go free of mind and free of entanglements so long as you are in Hope. Let all who live in this land open up their hearts and homes to those who do not. Those who wish to join in the mission, whether wizard, soldier, slave, dugger, half-human or inhuman, may meet me in this square tomorrow, either physically or in your hearts. I will know, and reach you. I was ordained by the church as Sister Kasdi, so that will be my name henceforth. Hell cannot stand against me. Only you can." And she blessed them, turned, and walked into the Temple.

She walked straight back to the chapel and then to the altar, and knelt and prayed and performed the sacraments that only a priestess could, and reaffirmed her vows. Only then did she turn and see that there were others in the chapel. They were people that she knew. There was Mervyn, looking very spry and pleased with himself, and Suzl, and Nadya, too, in robes just like her own.

Nadya smiled and came forward, then took and kissed her hand. "They ordained me as Sister Tamara. I, too, will keep that name and proudly." They embraced and kissed, and there were tears in both their eyes. Finally Nadya said, "I knew, somehow, from that very start, that we were destined for something different, something new. I would never, however, have guessed *this*."

Cass smiled. "I know." She sighed. "I guess we'll have to postpone our adventurous tour of World."

"Only until the next life," Nadya replied.

Cass smiled and turned to Suzl next. "And what about you?"

"I think you're a powerful wizard and a stark raving lunatic," she told them. "However, this sounds interesting. As long as you can stand somebody who's psychologically unfit for society hanging around, and a cynic at that, I might just stick until I see how it all comes out. If nothing else, you're gonna need somebody around with the guts to tell you what lunatics you are, just to keep from vanishing into your own little worlds. I may not be one of the faithful, but revolution kind of appeals to my nature. Besides that, I'm unemployed. I have to sponge off *somebody* and it might as well be somebody important."

Cass and Nadya both laughed, and Cass stepped forward and took her hands. "All right, 'psychologically unfit.' As much as I think you might be dangerous to have around, considering the *real* wording of that chastity clause, I'm glad to do it." She paused a moment. "Have you seen Dar?"

Suzl's face grew serious. "He's dead, Cass. He died bravely, from what I hear, saving a couple of people's lives in the process."

She had no more tears to give to grief, but she felt it anyway. She let go of Suzl's hands and turned to Mervyn. "Now, don't tell me you planned all this or I'll make an exception of my love rule in your case."

"I primed the pump," he admitted, "but I was still surprised to find water at all, and least of all a fountain." He sighed. "What will you do with it all now?"

"What I said, if anybody returns, that is. Even if *nobody* returns."

"And what of the unfinished business?"

"I haven't forgotten it, but it must wait until we're organized here. I don't think anything will be tried right away. They will be far too interested in me to think about anything else."

"I agree," he responded. "I'll talk it over with Tatalane and Krupe, but I'm sure we'll all help. It *must* be done. It is long overdue. Otherwise we'll be stuck here like this forever and eventually Haldayne's bunch will win."

She hesitated a moment. "You know who is behind this, don't you?"

"I think I do, and my joy at this outcome cannot quite balance my grief. Still, humanity lives again. Empire is reborn as a concept, and, perhaps, as a reality. The Empire of Flux and Anchor. The concept itself is staggering."

"Come," said Sister Kasdi. "We have much to plan and work out between now and tomorrow."

19

ANSWERS

Five hundred and fourteen border troopers had ridden out from Anchor Logh, and only two hundred and twenty-seven had returned, although, thanks to Flux magic, their wounds were healed and they felt pretty tough and proud of themselves. They were also the objects of awe among the local population and their fellow troopers, and told their battle stories time and again to enthralled audiences. Ultimately, though, even heroes have to go back to work, and they were all returned to duty.

Because they were more than a quarter of all the remaining guards, it was inevitable that, in many cases, long stretches of the border wall and the drains through it were guarded by these returning soldiers. Because of this, the invading army had little problem in breaching the wall along a more than two kilometer stretch halfway up, without, in fact, the rest of the guard force even knowing that such an invasion had taken place. They continued to guard the wall against attack from outside long after the enemy had a fully established force and was marching in strength on the capital.

There was little resistance because it was so obviously futile, and while whole families wept as the conquerors marched by they could not resist these battle-hardened veterans with anything but insults and more tears. Without guns, which were outlawed in Anchor, there was no chance of even inflicting a minor blow. Most of the population seemed dazed by it all, in fact, for this sort of thing simply did not and never had happened as far as they knew. The compact between Flux and Anchor upon which the church and its people depended was suddenly in ruins, and it was a simply inconceivable event. Anchor's own children, cast into Flux as a part of that compact, now returned to it.

The Temple was the one trouble spot, and not easy to take. It was built like a fortress of materials so hard that diamonds could not scratch it, and it was guarded from within by a force of armed wardens with electronic traps and devices. Bronze doors, however, needed far less than diamonds to blow apart; they needed only a good, solid shot from a single cannon.

Inside, confused, frightened, and dazed, the Temple staff prepared for the inevitable rapid fall. Behind still-locked doors piles of papers and other documents were burned, and the administrative section worked feverishly as the invaders conquered level after level to rid the Temple of hard evidence of its activities and files. They did as best they could, but they could not destroy it all.

One figure slipped through a little-known rear passage and went down a long series of old and dusty metal stairs and through doors that creaked and groaned from disuse to the sub-basement. For a moment it stood there, looking at the small power transformer network buzzing away, then walked over to the grid, reached down into a large bag, and picked out a small rectangular cube with two small buttons on it. The figure then pressed both buttons simultaneously and tossed the brick into the metal cage hiding the wires and transformers.

Quickly now she went up to the section of wall

that seemed boarded, pressed on two spots, and the boards swung away on hinges to reveal a door. She did not wait for a key, but took a pistol and shot out the lock, then kicked the door in, then flipped on the light switch, climbed over the rubble of crumbled concrete and masonry to a spot in the rear of the room with chalk marks on the floor. She looked down at them, pistol still in hand, and mentally traced the strange and incomprehensible design. In an instant she was standing not in the room, but in front of the great machine that guarded the gate to Hell.

She paused to stare at it all for a while, now feeling no great hurry. She had never been here before, and the sight was awesome. There was something almost suicidally hypnotic about that swirling mass at the tunnel's end, giving one the same feeling as she might get standing on an incredibly tall spot. She turned, though, and walked up the tunnel, each section lighting as she passed, until she reached the wire grid to climb up and out. She realized how badly out of condition she'd become in climbing up and out, but she made it to the bottom of the saucer-shaped depression, then walked up the slope to the metal ladder there.

"There is no way out for you," said a voice from above, at the top of the ladder, echoing across the depression and sounding ghostly and almost inhuman. She stopped, and instead of trying the ladder stepped back from it, pistol still in hand, and looked up.

"Who's there?" she called. "Show yourself!"

A somewhat familiar figure moved to the edge of the ladder and looked down at her sadly. "You have been in Anchor too long. That pistol cannot harm me here."

She fired anyway, emptying the entire clip. The figure at the top of the ladder just stood there, unmarked and unmoved. In disgust, she tossed the pistol away, and it fell with a clatter and rolled back down the depression.

"I *know* you!" she shouted, frustration building within her. "Who are you?"

"You ordained me Sister Kasdi," came the reply.

"What do you want with me now?" called back Sister General Diastephanos.

"I want to know why. You weren't like Sister Daji, a professional undercover agent. Nobody shot you full of drugs and gave you orders to turn. You're the same woman who left Pericles full of commitment and dreams."

The Sister General looked up at her in disgust. "You're barely nineteen, I think. What can you possibly know? Your ordination was a political show for the benefit of the masses. You have no background in theology, let alone management. What gives you the *right* to judge *me?*"

Cass sighed. "The same right Haldayne had to murder and rape and destroy. The same right you, in the end, used to pervert the scripture and rule Anchor Logh. *I have the power, and that gives me the right.*"

That stopped the Sister General cold for a moment. Finally she said, "You ask me why. Why are you doing *this?* Because you see a church corrupted and a people forever stuck in one place. You can't change it. They make you so accountable, send wardens from Holy Anchor to keep tabs on you, to eliminate you if need be. You play the Queen of Heaven's game, and send her her dues, or you don't play at all. So you settle back and enjoy being dictator of your own little world, becoming fat and corrupt like the whole rotten church, or you do something. Anyone who is for the overthrow of the church is on the side of the frustrated. There is less difference between the Seven and the Nine than you realize."

"There is less difference between the Seven and

the church than *you* seem to realize," Cass came back.

"You are so young," the Sister General sighed. "You may win your little revolution. It's happened before—oh, yes. But each time a better wizard comes along, or age and all those people you depend on to keep your revolution going begin to enjoy their own power, and become corrupted by it. You can't keep tabs on it all, nor can you live forever. The church, however, has had two thousand years of practice. It will entice and corrupt those it can, ultimately conquer the rest with its power to unify, and, if it cannot conquer you, it can wait you out. You can't win, but Haldayne can. When you are finally old enough and frustrated enough to realize this, you will see that the Seven is the only hope humanity has."

"You might be right," Cass admitted, "but I have seen the Seven at their worst, and there is no hope at all if you are. I choose to believe that you are not right, not so much because I deny your view of human nature, which is so well proved out in both Anchor and Flux, but because the alternatives are too terrible to bear. If, in fact, we cannot win, then maybe the human race deserves what it gets, whether it's the church, or Haldayne, or Hell itself. But if we don't *try* to win, then we most certainly deserve it all."

"You speak the beautiful dreams of youth, but, in the end, you will become me."

"Perhaps *you* need to have some of those beautiful dreams of youth restored yourself. Come up to me, and surrender yourself to my visions. We can use your vast knowledge and experience to avoid the same mistakes." She put out her hand over the top of the ladder.

Sister Diastephanos shook her head sadly. "I am too old, and it is too late, for me to join a fool's parade. But, tell me, please—how did you know?

Even poor Daji had no idea she was doing my work."

"She knew, I think, as she died. She understood the depths and layers of Haldayne's tricky mind, although the full plot only came to her when he so coldly allowed her to be sacrificed on his orders. There are no windows in the Temple. The order had to be given by intercom from inside by someone who knew exactly who and what Daji really was, fast enough for a messenger to signal out the front doors before we got there. But, clearly, nothing on the scope or scale of the excavations in the basement, the vanishing of novices, the addition of new personnel smuggled in through the drainage pipes in the wall, could have remained hidden from the wardens and the Temple at large without your knowledge. Your own spies, and the spies of the Queen of Heaven, would have betrayed it."

She sighed. "When I saw Pericles I knew that she would eventually figure it out. That was why I gave the order to hit her first, *then* Daji. But Haldayne was outside, and he reversed the orders. I knew there would be only one chance to get Pericles, but Daji was far more of a threat to Haldayne." She paused a moment, took a deep breath, then said, "I believe my time is past now. I could not bear to witness your childlike innocence destroyed." With that she turned and walked back to the black, gaping hole.

Cass gasped and cried, "No! Come with us! We will forgive all! This need not happen!"

The Sister General paused a moment, then shook her head sadly, and descended the mesh to the floor of the tunnel. Cass scrambled down the ladder, but had barely reached the bottom when there was a sudden flare of bright energy from the hole, and a single, agonized scream, and then silence and darkness once more.

She resisted the impulse to run to the tunnel,

knowing that the Guardians would not harm her, but she decided not to. There would be nothing there. Instead she turned and started back up the ladder, but as she did she began to do something that Sister General Diastephanos would never have understood.

She wept, and repeated prayers for the newly dead.

20

QUESTIONS

We are the spirits of Flux and Anchor . . . .

"You'll have to excuse the candlelight," Cass apologized. "We're trying to get a whole network of oil lamps set up so we can at least function."

The wizard Mervyn nodded and took a chair. "Perfectly all right. Still, it's times like these when one appreciates the ease of Flux. Just snap a finger and, *poof*, all the light you need. I often think that our ancestors must have taken electric power for granted. Otherwise, why have such a building with no windows and no manual air ducts?" It *did* smell stale and musty, but maintenance personnel assured them that enough air was moving due to pressure differentials to pose no major health hazards, although they had closed down the least ventilated parts of the Temple.

"We'll have it again some day," she told him. "Already we are scouring the land for experts who can rebuild the system, and there are enough Flux wizards to duplicate the damaged parts once we have them sorted out. Some of your people have already taken a look at it and told me that it is theoretically possible to have far larger storage of this energy and even transfer it by wire to smaller storage and distribution points. If possible, I would like to one day see the whole of Anchor Logh wired up."

"I told you that energy physics was one of my hobbies. I'll take a good look at everything before I leave and then research it in Pericles. We can copy the books well enough, if only we can find a few good trained technicians to translate them into fact. In the meantime, how's it going on your front?"

"I've never seen so many people so eager to change sides. It's amazing the level of cooperation we're getting."

"Human nature, that's all. Already the sermons are going out telling how Haldayne and the Seven had corrupted the Sister General herself, and how you are here to restore normalcy. They know you are an ordained high priestess, and things have been getting back to normal, so they'll buy it. No, I'm talking about the long run."

"Well, Sister Tamara will be installed as the new Sister General. It will be a popular choice, since she's from the Anchor, and we can count on everyone to minimize the age factor. The first thing we'll start doing is short transfers of Temple personnel in small groups from here to the Temple in Hope, where we'll sort the bad, the good, and the reclaimable. Once we do the Temple, we'll do the parishes one by one."

"They won't all be easy to convert. Not deep down. Not voluntarily, anyway."

"I know that. But I and a number of others have been reading every single bit of scripture bit by bit, and there is a scholarly team compiling information. Although the whole project will take years, I've already directed them to specific areas and found some very fine and useful things. Vows, for example. In order to come back to Anchor as a priestess, all will be required to undergo the sacraments of ordination and conference once again in Hope, but this time with the knowledge that a binding spell will be cast at the same time. This spell will simply render them incapable of violating their vows for any reason, nor any added vow they may be required to take in the future. I don't think it will be long before we have a purified church here, no matter what their intent."

He chuckled. "Clever, and effective. And you?"

"I am going to be quite busy working with others on the restructuring of this society. Barbarities like the Paring Rite must be replaced by more humane practices, and we must remove this deep prejudice against Flux and its people on the part of Anchorfolk. The worst offenders we can help in Flux itself; for the rest, it will be slow, but I am leaning towards a required trip by all schoolchildren of certain ages from here through the void to Hope. Rooting it out in the young is the best hope for a true breakdown of fear and prejudice. We're just beginning to set up our own training system in Hope, and we will need far more instructors of wizard caliber. Of course, any priestesses who show talent in that direction will be redirected there. I'm going to be very, very busy."

"That may be true, but the Holy Anchor isn't going to be too pleased about all this. You will get inquisitors first, then demands, and finally the whole region will be excommunicated and a holy war against it declared."

"They have to come through Flux and through areas of our control to do anything, and then they will have to break my shield. Militarily and magically I believe we are well defended. The next trick will be to spread it out, bit by bit, until we are too much of a movement to stop by any thought of direct action. It will be busy, but exciting."

He nodded and grew very serious. "Cass, much of this will depend on you for a long, long time. You realize that. The rest of us can help, but you will have to carry the load or it will fall apart."

She nodded. "I understand that."

"What I must know is if you are really ready for this type of lifelong commitment. You're human, and you have all the weaknesses that brings with it. Heaven knows, *I* understand that. And you're a powerful wizard. Later on, when I spend much time with you in Hope, I will show you how to perfect that power, possibly the strongest on World, although that's by no means certain. It has been my experience that no matter how strong you are, eventually you find someone stronger."

"You mean, will I turn into the goddess or worse? I'm going to try hard not to. I'm no puritan, and power for its own sake doesn't interest me. I do not want to be worshipped."

"No, it's more than that. Look, let me hypothesize something. It's just for the sake of argument, no more, but it serves its purpose."

"Go ahead."

"Suppose, right now, a live and healthy Matson should walk through that door. What would you do?"

She thought of his battered and torn body there on the battlefield. "It is a meaningless question."

He paused a moment. "Suppose I were to tell you that Matson was in fact still alive?"

Her heart leaped into her throat. "Are you serious?"

He nodded. "I'm serious."

She seemed to shrink back into her chair and become, all at once, very small and very young once more. Her emotions grew jumbled again, and she faced the problem square for a while. Finally she remembered that Mervyn still sat there, and that he expected an answer.

"I will always love him," she said sincerely. "I won't disguise or mask that. But I realize that it's too late now to do anything else but what I am doing. I feel that I was *chosen* for this. I have already resolved to apply all vows, without exception, to myself. In fact, if there was a way to bind myself to my own spells I would do it. I must be an example in all things."

The wizard nodded approvingly. "There *is* such a spell, or at least a method. We of the Nine must use it to fully become one of the trust. But it is a terrible spell, and not one to ever take lightly, for it cannot be reversed by anyone, including yourself, under any circumstances, but it will do nothing to ease the mental pain and anguish it might cause."

"Then you must show me how to do it. I cannot possibly ask anyone to obey what I myself am above, and it will provide the example and also prevent my abusing this power."

He sighed. "That is its primary purpose when we apply it to ourselves—that we may never become our enemy. But you propose a far more complex one, one that you may often regret."

"No, you don't understand. I regret *this* situation I find myself in. I regret the responsibility. I regret the lack of freedom. I most of all regret the self-sacrifices I must make. But I understood, finally, out there on the battlefield, that I really have no choice in the matter. It was cemented by my confrontation with the late Sister General. We are losing our best to the enemy, and we are murdering our future and our hopes. What I said to her I was really saying to myself. Only once in many generations, I think, does somebody come along with the right combination of luck and will to get into a spot where they can revolutionize things, change things for the better. When it does come about, you can turn your back on it, in which case you are guilty of the most terrible of sins, putting yourself before the future not of others but of the race. Or, you can try without total commitment, without any willingness to sacrifice yourself and what you love, and wind up like Diastephanos or

Haldayne. Or you can accept it and devote your all to it. Those were my choices, and I know which one I now have to make."

She paused a moment, and then added, "You know, the more I have thought about this, the more I'm convinced that I'm not unique. In fact, I suspect that somebody has this sort of opportunity fall into their hands in some way quite often. Maybe it's just somebody on a local level who says, 'this is stupid, or cruel—let's find another way' or something like that. They just don't have the nerve to make a total commitment, and so evil prevails as usual."

"You're probably right," he agreed, "but you *are* unusual, you know. Very few make such a total commitment." He sighed. "Would it help if I told you that I have no idea if Matson is dead or alive?"

She gasped. "But you said—"

"I said, 'Suppose I were to tell you'."

"That's—cruel."

"I had to know. And, I think, you did, too."

She sighed. "You're right, of course."

"The stringers attempted to recover all of their own. Matson's body was not among those logged with us. It's barely possible, but not likely, that he lives. I just thought you should face that fact, not only for the obvious reason but for the other."

"I know, and I thank you for it. Uh—what other reason?"

"Cass—you're pregnant."

That hit her with more of a shock than the idea that Matson somehow survived. "That's impossible!"

"You're still a virgin?"

She coughed. "Uh, no, but it was only once, with Matson, out on the trail. My first and only time. I thought the odds were against you getting pregnant anyway, and certainly not on the first try!"

He shrugged. "That's a young girl's self-delusion,

common as long as there has been a first time. Yes, the odds are way against it, but so long as there *are* odds they hit somebody. I suspect that your own power, which has a mind of its own, might have been operating there as well. Subconsciously, at least, you wanted his baby, and in Flux, for a few of us, wishes can come true."

"But—after all this? The transformations, everything . . . It isn't possible!"

"It is and you are and that's that. There's nothing improper about it. It was before any vows were taken."

She nodded. "But—it's impossible! How can I manage it? And how do I explain it? The new Sister General of the Reformed Church has a child."

"You should learn by now that heads of churches can sell any rationalization they want to the devout, particularly when it doesn't violate true scripture. It *would* be a tough thing to explain to the old church, whose general practices forbade any but virgins becoming priestesses, but we are returning to basics here."

She sank back in the chair once again. "Damn!"

"High priestesses don't curse in front of others," he cracked. "But, seriously, you will be in Flux most of the time. It is not necessary to have it."

"But it *is*! Don't you see—it's the only thing left of him. He wanted one, and it was supposed to be Arden's, but she was killed. No, somehow I will manage." She sighed. "I need to be alone for a little while with this. Then I have to start getting things ready for Sister Tamara's installation."

"I understand," he told her. "Don't worry. I'll be around if you need me."

The candles blew out when he closed the door on his way out, but she did not get up and relight them. For quite a while she just sat there, being, for a moment, little Cassie, alone in the peace of the darkness.

We are the spirits of Flux and Anchor, and some call us demons. . . .

She had the spell memorized. It was incredibly complex, and she did not understand it, but she understood its meaning. Now she knelt at the altar in the Temple at Hope, completely alone, and performed the full sacramental service. In the midst of it, she paused, and without hesitation executed the spell.

"I am a priestess of the Holy Mother of Universes and an instrument of Her Holy Church and will," she said softly. "I vow that I shall always be a priestess in all things and in all ways, and that I shall never violate my sacred trust nor deviate from my cause.

"I vow that I shall devote my life and my power to the uplifting of humanity and the reformation of the Holy Church. I vow that I will never use that great power for selfish gain, but only to further the sacred causes and the divine will.

"I reaffirm my vows before thee, that I shall in all things obey scripture as regards myself and others; that I shall live as the humblest of my priestesses, owning nothing; that I shall keep and never violate the sacraments; that I shall go beyond thy vows and be in all ways forever after chaste.

"I further vow that I shall never ask of another anything which I myself am not willing to do, nor be false to myself, my flock, or my faith in any way. To these things I bind myself, willingly, now and forever."

She continued with the service, but there was a new, strange light in her eyes, for she could see the future in her mind's eye.

We are the spirits of Flux and Anchor and some call us demons. It is possible that we are such, for certainly we know not our nature or our origins. . . .

In the great golden palace at Holy Anchor, Her Perfect Highness, The Queen of Heaven, was looking over the account books and scowling. There was a sudden fluttering in the window nearby, and she looked up, irritated, to see a large, fat raven perched there. She stared at it and frowned. "Be off, bird!" she snapped. "Shoo! I have too many headaches right now to fool with the likes of you!"

"You haven't begun to know what a headache really is," the raven squawked back. "We, my dear sister, are in deep, deep shit. . . ."

Slowly, sparing no details, he explained the new situation. She listened attentively, nodding now and then and asking an occasional question, but otherwise letting him tell it. Finally, he was finished, and she sighed wearily.

"I suppose you have a grand new design for dealing with this?"

"Of course. But I'm willing to hear alternatives."

She thought a moment, then said, "With much patience, and a great deal of pressure, this might be yet turned to our advantage. An uprising will panic the Fluxwizards and Anchorfolk alike all over World. A holy crusade could cement our control."

"You mean to contain it, then? I thought of turning it instead."

"We will try containment first. If that doesn't work, then we will try your more devious ways. Do not worry, my brother. I know exactly what to do. . . ."

The Soul Rider saga continues with
Empires of Flux and Anchor
coming soon from Tor Books